Dangerous Methods

The Agency

Volume Two

Dangerous Methods

K.P. Merriweather

Majestik Multimedia · St. Louis

Dangerous Methods
The Agency: Volume 2
Published by Majestik Multimedia
A subsidiary of Create Space Independent Publishing Platform

First Edition

This book is set in Georgia Type Text, with some portions in Imperial BT.

Printed in the United States of America
First Edition: March 2014
First Printing: March 2014
Second Printing: December 2015

ISBN-13: 978-0615986067

ISBN-10: 0615986064

For more awesomeness, visit *Majestik Multimedia*!
www.majestikmultimedia.com

ONE

... After eliminating what was no longer human, it is possible to give a new direction to technological development - a direction that shall lead it back to the real needs of man, and that also means: to the actual size of man...

The next step would be to remove what was not sufficiently human, and finally nothing would be spared except what fitted a certain ideal concept of humanity...

***

Erik Hart sensed movement and his eyes snapped open. He found himself in a moving vehicle, with his body covered by a lightweight flannel blanket. Erik sat up, forcing the blanket falling at his waist and he shuddered slightly from the cool early morning air that blew in from the open side passenger window.

Looking around, Erik noticed he rest in the backseat of a roomy coupe sedan and realized he wore a simple navy jumpsuit and white canvas shoes with no socks.

Two men wearing white lab coats over casual business dress occupied the front driver and passenger seats. The driver, with combed forward mid-length medium brown hair and thick sideburns adjusted the rearview mirror with a trembling hand.

Erik noticed the worried gray eyes staring back at him and he glanced aside at the right-hand side mirror at the passenger who had shoulder-length sandy hair, horseshoe-style mustache and pale violet eyes.

"*It's Hernando and Suber,*" Erik mused and turned his gaze out the window. He saw they were on a lone stretch of two-lane road, entering a wooded area.

Gazing skyward, Erik observed the sun slowly rising in the far eastern horizon, casting the dull gray atmosphere with pale pinks, oranges, and yellows tingeing the edges. At the surface level, the maples, oaks, and pines came closer together as the developments of the city became sparser and turned into vast emptiness, filled with prairie grass and ragweed.

"I really need to get out of here," Hernando grumbled. "It's been three hours since my last cigarette!"

Suber grunted in return and withdrew a steno pad and pen from the glove compartment. "I don't advocate unhealthy habits," he answered and leaned forward in his seat, scribbling his pen across the page.

"Screw you and your damn habits," Hernando spat. "Drive the damn car!"

Suber gave a mischievous grin as his pen continued scratching at the pad. "Haven't you heard that I'm notorious for pulling over during a drive to write whenever inspiration strikes?" he teased and paused momentarily, flipping the page then continued writing.

"Get a tape recorder for fuck's sake!" Hernando protested.

"Please, Suber, take over. If I don't get a smoke in, I'll vomit!"

"So vomit."

Hernando reached into his front pocket with a free hand and Suber swiftly whacked him across the knuckles with his pad. Erik stifled a laugh in response when Hernando shook his fist at Suber.

"What the hell?" Hernando fussed.

"You're better focused when you force your nervous energies into driving," Suber said sternly. "Besides, it's smart and it keeps us all alive!"

"Where are we going?" Erik finally asked once Hernando made a sharp turn, dodging striking another car that came perilously close to the road's striped median.

"Damn drunkard!" Hernando grumbled as he quickly swerved, avoiding the low valley on the side of the road.

"Watch it, Hernando!" Suber yelled when his pad went sailing out the window. "Stop the car!"

"No!" Hernando pressed the accelerator and hunched forward.

"Fine, stop the car and you can have two cigarettes!"

"Make it three!"

"All right!"

Hernando slowed the car, and then pulled over on the curbside after braking. He idled the engine, waiting as Suber wildly unbuckled his seatbelt and yanked open the door. Suber rushed out, running down the shoulder.

"*Se lo merece!*" Hernando muttered and he shut off the engine then rolled down the driver's side window.

"Where are you taking me this early in the morning?" Erik

asked as Hernando leaned forward, tapping the car lighter.

"We're taking you to The Center," Hernando replied and withdrew a pack of cigarettes from his shirt pocket.

"What is that place and why do you have to take me there?" Erik demanded. "Isn't Mister Greenfield worried about me?"

"Right now, he couldn't be worried about anything," Hernando said flatly, tapping the pack gently against the dashboard. Forcing a filtered tip appearing at the package's top, he put it to his lips, pulling the box away then set it back in his pocket.

Erik gripped the edge of the seat. "What are you saying?"

"Number Three, listen, it's all very complicated right now," Hernando replied irritably and tapped his fingers along the steering wheel, waiting for the lighter to turn completely red. "You have to go to that place for a while for treatment and as for what it is, it's like a rehabilitation center."

"What are you trying to restore?" Erik spat, unbelieving. "I'm fine, thank you!"

Hernando shook his head, unable to answer and the lighter clicked, popping out after its underside turned red. Extracting it, he placed the glowing metal to the tip of his cigarette, burning away the paper and expelled harsh smoke. Hernando inhaled deeply, shutting his eyes as he leaned back into the seat. He let out a heavy sigh in relief, blowing smoke through his nose.

"I can't really tell you, Number Three," Hernando said softly and set the lighter aside on the dashboard. "I'm sorry."

"You're not sorry at all," Erik grumbled.

"What else do you want from me?"

Erik grunted and sat back in his seat, glaring at the man

who continued smoking in silence. After Hernando finished one cigarette, he tossed away the lone tip out the window and pulled out another in the same ritualistic fashion.

"Why wouldn't he be worried?" Erik snapped. "Is it because his job's ended and he's no longer needed, like I am?"

Hernando looked back at Erik, stunned. "What are you trying to say?" he yelped. "Nobody's getting rid of you!"

"Then give me a straight answer!"

Hernando grunted and ignored Erik as he resumed smoking. Suber approached moments later with his pad and opened the door.

"Let's get going," Suber said, tossing his pad on the seat.

"After I finish," Hernando grumbled. "You promised me three, remember?"

"How many he's had so far?"

"You're asking me?" Erik spat. "Why should I care?"

"I'll just drive this metal box into a ditch," Hernando muttered, restarting the car. "Let it blow up. Hell, it'll save us both and that nut-job Corbin the expenses!"

"Corbin?" Erik kicked at the seat. "Let me out of here!" he shrilled. "You're trying to kill me!"

"No, wait!"

Erik punched the back of Hernando's head then slugged Suber in the chest when grabbed for. Suber fell back on the ground and Erik cried out when pain erupted behind his eyes. He clutched his head, doubling over.

"¿Qué pasa?" Hernando asked, glancing at Erik through the rearview mirror.

Erik moaned and his vision flashed red. He cringed, hearing

another voice, dark and sinister talking over him.

You're not doing so well, are you?

"I'm not sick!" Erik cried. "I'm not!"

They're waiting for orders...

They're going to destroy you, erase you, bury you...

You can't plead with those monsters; you can't reason with them...

With no witnesses...

"Hey, hey!" Hernando called, turning in his seat. "Why are you freaking out?" Erik screamed and Hernando grabbed Erik by the shoulders, shaking him. "Calm down!"

"Let go of me!" Erik shrieked and pulled away from Hernando's grip. "I'm not letting you kill me!" Erik clamored over the seat and jumped out the car, dropping onto the ground below.

Rolling to his feet, Erik faced Suber who blocked his path, holding a cellular phone.

"What's the matter?" Suber asked. "We're not the bad guys here."

Erik backed away and Hernando immediately got out the car.

"What's your issue?" Hernando shouted.

Erik picked up a rock and hurled it at Suber, striking him across the face. Suber let out a yelp and staggered back, stunned. Erik bolted in the opposite direction, taking off into the forested valley below.

"Shit!" Hernando yowled and gave chase.

Erik crashed through branches and tore through shrubbery, trying to make his escape. He pulled away the overgrown greenery and halted when he approached the edge of a ravine, looking down at rocky canyon below.

Backing away, some of the loosened rocks gave beneath Erik's weight, falling beneath him and he let out a yelp as he slipped. Striking the ground, Erik struggled keeping his footing and scrambled back, only kicking up more dust and stones.

Hernando approached moments later, panting hard for breath. His eyes widened and he made a mad grab for Erik, pulling his sleeve. "Stop moving!" Hernando cried. "Don't move!" Erik froze, gasping weakly as Hernando dug in his heels. "Easy, easy..." Hernando crouched low and took a hesitant step rearward, then tightened his grip around Erik's wrist.

"Let me go," Erik pleaded. "You're trying to kill me anyway, right?"

"No," Hernando snapped. "We're trying to keep you alive!"

"I don't believe you!"

"I'm not letting you go. If you kill yourself, I'm coming with you."

Erik looked up, appalled. "Why?" he wailed.

"Because I promised someone."

"Hey," Suber's voice called from above. "Are you all right?"

"Yeah," Hernando called back. "We're barely hanging on over here!"

"I got a rope! Hold tight!"

"Who did you promise?" Erik demanded.

"Genovera!"

Erik paled and felt his control slipping as he suddenly grew weak.

"Hey!" Hernando shouted. "Hey, hey, don't go out on me

now!" Hernando yanked Erik back from the edge to more stable ground. Suber came down moments later, taking careful steps as he held a rope in his hands.

"Come on," Suber called. "I don't know how long that tree's going to hold!"

"Shit, shit, shit!" Hernando hissed, grabbing the slack end Suber threw to him and pulled against it, while dragging Erik up with him.

Suber also grabbed a hold of Erik's other arm, helping him up. Pulling Erik to a level area, Suber crouched beside him as Hernando plopped on the ground, drained.

"You all right?" Suber asked and waved a hand in front of Erik's face.

Hernando moaned and ran a hand through his messy short brown hair. "Fucking scared the shit outta me, kid," he complained. "Don't do that to me!"

"Wake up!" Suber called and clapped his hands.

Erik stared out into space, unable to hear them.

"What's the matter with him?" Hernando complained.

"Catatonia, you think?" Suber murmured.

Erik shut his eyes, unable to focus. When he opened them again, he faced the pale beige walls of the apartment where he stayed.

Erik groaned and sat up, rubbing at his face. He shook his head, then rubbed at his temples. Planting his feet on the floor, Erik scrutinized his alarm clock with a split-flap display, frowning when he saw all the numbers read zero. He grunted and struck the clock.

"These dreams are going to be the death of me," Erik

murmured and ran his hands through his hair. His telephone rang and he picked up the receiver. "What do you want?" Erik answered.

"What a rude thing to say!" said a familiar female voice over the line.

"I have a raging headache," Erik complained and opened the nightstand drawer, withdrawing a bottle of painkillers.

"We have a new assignment," said the woman. "You won't have a lot of time, so listen carefully." She said a series of numbers and Erik stiffened when the pain increased in his head, spreading behind his eyes. "Do you understand?"

"I think so," Erik replied and popped the cap on the bottle.

"Now be quick about it. Make sure no one sees you."

"Will I see you later?"

"You will."

Erik hung up the line and swallowed several tablets, then chucked the empty bottle aside. Shuffling across the hall to the bathroom, he turned on the tap and ran his hands under the water, gulping down the pills.

Splashing water on his face, Erik looked up at his reflection, staring back at a tired young man with shaggy sandy red hair, sunken violet eyes, and several scars across his crooked nose, his right cheek, and down his left eye.

"Who are you?" Erik muttered. The telephone rang again and Erik ignored it, taking his time showering.

Later dressing in a dark shirt, slacks, loafers and overcoat, Erik headed for the kitchen, filling the percolator. The phone continued ringing off the hook and Erik grunted, picking up the receiver.

"Why do you keep calling?" he yelled.

"You really should get an answering service," said the mysterious woman.

"I'm hanging up."

"Don't take too long. Your target will be out of the state in an hour if you don't hurry!"

"Trust me, I got it."

"He'll be at the meeting downtown. It's the thirteenth floor, the penthouse."

"Anything else?"

"Dress nice. He like his boys pretty."

Erik growled under his breath and threw the receiver at the wall, then stormed out the apartment.

TWO

Walking down the city streets, Erik turned up the collar of his coat as the cold winds increased its intensity and put his hands in his pockets. He felt a sheet of paper and pulled it out, withdrawing a fifty-dollar bill. Noticing a gruff young man pushing a cart of flowers from the street corner, Erik approached, handing him the money. The man stopped, surprised as Erik took a large bouquet of roses and camellias.

"Keep the change," Erik said and headed for the large office building across the street.

Entering through the glass doors, Erik reached the front desk and tapped the bell.

"Deliveries are in the back," the clerk said without looking up from his monitor.

"This goes to the thirteenth floor."

"Elevators are on the side there."

"Thanks." Erik walked briskly for the elevators and spotted a woman with curly reddish-brown hair wearing blue-tinted glasses stepping on the cable car. "Hold it," he called and hurried before the doors hushed closed. The woman held it open and Erik stepped in, smiling warmly at her. The woman blushed slightly when Erik studied her, taking in her form in a navy blazer with matching skirt and dark blue blouse.

The woman cleared her throat and shyly ran a hand through her hair. "Which one?" she asked as she pushed a button.

"Thirteen."

"Oh, you're one of his new playmates, eh?" The woman pressed the other button and the cable car slowly began its ascent.

"I guess you can say that."

"He's dangerous."

"How so?"

"You'll find out."

"Has he always been into men?"

"It doesn't matter who he tries to control."

"And you'd think women would be easier."

"Too willful I suppose." The bell pinged and the doors opened. "This is where I get off," said the woman.

"Here," Erik murmured and withdrew a violet from the bunch. The woman smiled, the flush deepening across her face as he put it in her hair behind her ear.

"Thank you," said the woman, stepping out. She waved at Erik as the doors closed and he grinned.

After reaching the last floor, Erik stepped off into a large room with cream carpeting and canary walls, facing a single oak desk that had a female security guard and a male clerk. Erik approached, smiling brightly at them both.

"Special delivery," Erik chirped.

The officer stood and withdrew her service pistol. "We need to check you first," she snapped and waved her gun at Erik. "Set it down, slowly."

"It's just flowers," Erik protested and dropped what he held, scattering the roses on the floor. Erik held up his hands as the officer approached and pat him down. "Hey, at least buy me dinner if you're going to feel me up," Erik complained and pushed her hand away. "I don't know you like that!"

"Who are you here for?" demanded the sentry as she continued her search.

"Lay off the junk," Erik objected when the officer squeezed his crotch.

"You could be hiding something," the officer said, smirking.

"It's not that package," Erik quipped. "He called me and told me to stop by."

"Who's 'he'?"

Before Erik could come up with an answer, the clerk waved at Erik. "You can go," he said. "He's expecting you."

Erik pushed the woman away and stormed past the desk, stalking into the next room that had panel windows displaying the city skyline. A large glass desk with a silver attaché case and a heavy-duty rugged laptop rest on the edge before a large stuffed leather chair with its back turned to Erik.

"You'd better be alive," Erik snarled as he approached. "Because if you copped out, then my life would've been a whole waste of time!"

"Your life?" a rough voice growled. "What about mine?" Erik came around the chair and paused when he found it empty. "They told me you were coming twenty minutes ago... They're not nice orders."

"I need to make it count." Erik snapped. He peered at the open laptop, noticing it had his data on the screen.

"That's why I started this company." Erik whirled around,

searching for the source of the voice. "I wanted to save lives, not extinguish them."

"That's an outright lie and you know it!" Erik shouted. "You're killing people with those monsters!"

"They lost sight of their original goals - I never did."

"Then come out here and face me and prove me wrong!"

"I can't do that. You're misguided... You think by killing me, you'll save something."

"Yeah, myself!"

"You can't be saved."

"Everyone has that one chance," Erik thundered. "I'm taking mine." He grabbed the attaché case off the desk and headed for the door, only to pause when two men in black uniforms and dark visors barred the exit.

"I know what you came here for," said the man's voice. "Did you think I'd give it up that easily?"

"Sure," Erik said, grinning. "You left it right in the open." He chuckled as the men withdrew their pistols. "So are you going to add more to your body count now?" Erik vaunted. "Have at it."

Erik swung the case as they fired, deflecting bullets. He barreled forward and smashed the case against one gunman, taking him down. Grabbing his arm, Erik turned the man around as his partner shot again, killing him. Erik threw him forward and dashed out into the lobby as the security guard approached. He ducked down when she fired and the other man shot her in return, killing each other.

Erik faced the desk clerk who stood with his hands in the air, shaking.

"Where did he go?" Erik demanded.

"Downstairs!" the clerk yelped.

Erik ran to the elevators and growled when he saw all the lights lit. He hurried for the stairs and kicked in the door, hearing footsteps clamor down the stairwell. Looking over the railing, Erik caught sight of the man in a dark suit.

"You run fast for a dead man!" he shouted down at him.

"Shit!" the man yelped.

Erik climbed on the railing's ledge, waiting until the man was in sight. He then jumped off, smashing into the man below as he rounded another set of stairs and they tumbled the rest of the way.

Crashing into the door marked 'EXIT', Erik groaned as he struck his head against the metal. He sat up, facing the man with short white hair who suffered a broken neck; his body slumped across from him.

Erik reached forward and searched the man's body, taking his wallet and keys from his slacks pocket then felt his blazer pockets, withdrawing a blank white key card and a wireless earpiece transmitter.

Erik pocketed the items he took and staggered to his feet. Opening the door, the emergency alarm buzzed and a rush of cold air entered from the outside. Erik put the case in the door, propping it open. Grabbing for the body, he slung it over his back then picked up the case and pushed the door out.

Hauling the body outside, Erik clenched his teeth when he saw several parked cars and a small garden at the end leading to the outdoor stairwell. Hurrying for the alley outside the garage, Erik spotted a large refuse bin and approached it, hoisting the body into it with a crash. He heard sirens and tensed.

"*I can't go home,*" Erik thought as he took off down the alley. "*I don't know where else to go!*"

Erik came to a stop when a dark sedan blocked the alley's path and backed away when the engine turned. The door came open and Erik cautiously approached. Peering inside, he faced the curly-haired woman with the tinted glasses he met earlier.

"Need a lift?" she asked, smiling. "I'm not dangerous."

"Thanks," Erik said and set the case on the floor as he slipped into the passenger seat. "You don't look dangerous."

"Did your date turn out badly?"

"I guess you can say that," Erik replied and shut the door. He grabbed the seatbelt then turned to lock it in place and froze when he faced a semi-automatic pistol pointed in his direction.

"You know when this goes off," the woman said, still smiling, "it makes a really loud noise."

"I-I know," Erik nervously replied.

"This one has a hell of a kick too; you need to use both hands."

"I'm sure you're right." Erik drew a shallow breath as the color drained from his face. "W-why are you telling me this?" he stammered.

"Do you know how to use one?"

"I'm not a big fan of guns," said Erik weakly.

"In this world, you need to protect yourself."

"With the way The War's going, soon there won't be anyone left to shoot," Erik gibed.

The woman chortled. "Is that so?" She put the gun on the dashboard. "You've got a lot of guts," she said. "I like that."

"Good to know," Erik muttered and blew a relieved sigh.

The woman gasped when he slumped forward and grabbed his shoulder, shaking him.

"Hey," the woman called. "Hey, wake up! I wasn't going to kill you!"

"Hey!" a voice called from afar. "Hey, Justin!" Erik's eyes snapped open, looking up at a young man with tanned skin, dark curly hair and indigo eyes standing over him, hand extended. Erik squinted up at the young man, perplexed.

"Who...?" he started.

"Don't tell me you've got amnesia!" the young man said, frowning.

Erik blinked and a name immediately surfaced to mind. "Kevin...?" he said slowly and the young man grinned, nodding.

"That was one nasty hit you took," he said brightly. "Thanks."

Erik grabbed for Kevin's hand, getting pulled to his feet with a firm grip. "What happened to me?" Erik asked.

"Don't you remember?" Erik shook his head. "That guy they call Tank Shannon hit me up for test answers again. You decided to clean up for me for a change." Kevin put an arm around Erik's shoulders. "I didn't know you could take hits like that!"

"I didn't either," Erik replied and Kevin chortled, tousling his hair.

"Well stop getting sacked if all it's gonna do is brain ya."

"I'll remember that next time."

"Well, I need to stop visiting the detention office anyway." Kevin let go, picking up his backpack at Erik's feet, then walked ahead. "So, are you gonna help me with homework or what?"

"Why do you keep fighting?" Erik asked, hurrying along his

side. "If anything, it's not going to make your dad notice you. He's too much of a drunk to see it!"

Kevin came to a pause and Erik bumped into him. Erik backed away as Kevin looked down at the ground. "Well..." He sighed and shook his head. "Don't worry about it."

"Then what is it?"

"Sometimes I have dreams, of having wings, of flying..." Kevin ran a hand through his hair. "I want to fly far, very far away from this dump. Just getting to be somewhere else and being somebody else, you know?"

Erik shrugged his shoulders. "I don't have dreams like that."

"Don't you feel that you're missing something?" Kevin turned toward Erik and put his hands on his shoulders. "I mean, really think about it!"

"I can't say that I have..."

"Look at me," Kevin said seriously. "I'm being real with you here."

Erik took in a shallow breath, looking into his dark blue eyes. "I–!" Erik's face flushed slightly. "Well, now that you mention it... I always wanted to ask you something."

"Ask me what?"

Erik swallowed hard and pried off Kevin's hands from his shoulders. "I'm sorry," he murmured and pushed past him, walking onward for home. "Never mind it..."

"It's something obviously important!" Kevin called at his back.

"I can't think of the words I want."

Kevin jogged up to him then matched his stride. "Just say it," Kevin pressed, "come on, right off the top of your head."

"If I did," Erik grumbled, "you'd smack me."

"What are you trying to say?"

Erik stopped walking when a large cloud of dust covered the skies, followed by the scent of burnt insulation. They looked skyward, noticing the fiery hues of the late afternoon sky.

"It looks like the sky is burning!" Erik cried as sirens wailed in the distance.

"It seems more like there might be some problems at the mines," Kevin replied. "Wanna check it out?"

"Sure, why not?"

Kevin let the backpack he carried slip off his shoulder and dug through it, withdrawing a pair of clip-on skates and a two-piece skateboard. Kevin tossed the wheeled clips to Erik and he caught them.

"Where'd you get something like that?" Erik asked as he adjusted his shoes.

"Someone sent it to me," Kevin answered as he snapped together the frame. "I never saw it before, anywhere..."

"Do you know who makes it?"

"I asked around if anyone made stuff like this, with the two platforms for the feet and the center bar that snaps in here to make the frame... But nobody heard or saw anything like it."

"It seems cool, but wouldn't the center of gravity be weaker in the middle because of the bar?"

"I thought so too, but there's like a weight in here to keep it balanced."

"Does it come apart easily as it goes together?"

"After I get to where I need to be, I just press this button and the bar comes out. It even has a lever back here for braking."

"Maybe they know you well enough to test new skateboards..."

"I never signed up at the shop," Kevin admitted, setting the board down on the ground. "Whoever made this knew what they're doing... I'm just as clueless about who made it." He picked up the backpack and slung it over his shoulder. "It showed up on the stoop one day. Nobody claimed it."

"Is there any art on it?"

"None at all, not even a name." Kevin shrugged his shoulders. "But I'm not complaining. If it was for me, then that's pretty awesome."

"Let's get down there before we miss out on the action!"

They took off, skating for their intended destination.

THREE

Approaching the scene of a large fire, Erik was taken aback by the strong flames flaring from the large red brick building that had numerous blackened windows. A legion of firefighters in red jackets and black helmets surrounded the factory, carrying hoses fighting to douse the flames.

"The old conversion factory's gone up," Kevin remarked, leaning against Erik. "This whole street's supposed to be cleared but I guess everyone wants to see what's going on."

"How would something like this happen?" Erik murmured. "Didn't the plant just have a commercial about how they had the best safety record in twenty years?"

"Maybe it's an electrical short."

"You're right... who knows with buildings this large or that old...?"

A large explosion erupted from the burning factory, spraying bricks and glass. The firefighters scrambled, seeking safety elsewhere.

"Clear out!" the fire chief called on his bullhorn. "Everyone clear out! This thing's about to go sky high and straight to Hell!"

"Come on!" Kevin yelled, tugging at Erik's sleeve. "Let's get away from here before we're shot straight to Hell too!"

"Who would want to stick around?" Erik yelped.

"Hurry before our asses get toasted!"

Erik skated away and Kevin ran after him. The next explosion blasted everything back, generating a forceful shockwave that threw everyone down. Erik grabbed for Kevin's hand before everything went dark.

A loud clanging brought Erik back to consciousness and he sat up with a start. Taking in his surroundings, Erik noticed he rest against a large willow tree and beneath him were several scattered iridescent stones across overturned clay and granules of shale. The sound of loud whirring machines, metal striking stone and voices shouting directives assaulted his ears.

Standing, Erik stretched and yawned then paused when he saw he wore a dark green jumpsuit. Shrugging his shoulders, he then made his way out of the canopy of low hanging branches. Pushing the leaves aside, Erik felt the earth shift and looked down, standing at the edge of a crater that had a ladder against the shallow earth.

Looking up and around, Erik spotted many other blond-haired blue-eyed young men wearing navy jumpsuits working at various aspects of moving earth, sifting or striking into it, breaking hard rock.

"Yo, Ferdian," called a familiar voice. Erik turned, spotting Raider approaching in tan jumpsuit and heavy boots, hoisting a pickaxe on his shoulder. Around his waist, he wore a heavy leather belt equipped with a chisel and small hammer. "You zonin' out again, man?"

"A quick nap is all," Erik replied wearily.

"You shouldn't be so tired."

"Maybe I'm coming down sick?"

Raider snorted. "If you say so." Raider frowned when Erik reached out; touching Raider's long black hair he wore in a loose braid. "What?" Raider asked, pushing his hand away.

"It's different..." Erik said, bemused.

"Yeah," Raider answered, grinning. "Wonky oven."

"Why...?"

"I was made that way." Raider gently jabbed at Erik's chin. "C'mon man, quit spacin' and help me out!"

"With what?"

"Man, you're really out there today!" Raider handed Erik the pickaxe and he looked down at it, dumbfounded. "You okay?"

"I don't know..."

"Look, it's easy." Raider took it back, demonstrating the actions of hammering. "You bring it up, down, bam! You bust shit, clear it out, do it again."

"Why?"

"That's what we do." Raider hoisted the tool over his shoulder. "You *sure* you okay, man?" Erik nodded. "Come on, let's go." Erik followed numbly after Raider. "Here, we're in sector three-eighty-five."

"Listen up, boys," called the supervisor over the noise. Stomping across the yard, a muscularly built man with silvery-streaked light brown hair tied back in a loose queue, wearing a dark brown jumpsuit wielded a clipboard in one hand and a large two-way radio in the other. "We're having a rotation, so listen up." Sheltering his steel blue eyes as he scanned the field, he pointed ahead once the noise began to die down. "Group two-twenty-seven-Gamma, haul ass to Sector three-forty three klicks east. Group nine-eighty-Delta, shift four klicks north and resume operations in Sector four-eighty..."

"Which group are we?" Erik asked over the overseer's calls once Raider came to a pause at an entranceway leading to darkness below.

"He ain't gonna call for us," Raider replied as he ducked into the mine, "so don't worry."

"Why are you so confident?" Erik followed after, watching the light of the outside quickly diminish. "Shouldn't we have a lantern or something...?"

"Your eyes are gonna adjust in a minute."

"So why are some groups being moved around?"

"They're getting a watch on them. If they ain't good enough, they're little giblets for the machine."

"What machine?"

Raider snorted, shaking his head. "Man, you're so out of it."

"I guess I'm sick."

Raider scoffed. "That's a new one."

"What?"

Hearing the clanging of metal, Erik bypassed others in the same attire, hacking at the dark walls that had metal supports, extracting iridescent stones embedded within. Erik felt warmer the further they descended into the darkness, watching the workers scratching away at the interior or hauling what they pulled out in large containers into a cart resting in the center of the path.

"Here's our spot," Raider said brightly. "You pick up; I cut down, got it?"

"Sure."

Raider smashed the axe into the wall, tearing away at the surface of lime. Erik sifted through the excess, tossing it aside in a large pile on the other side of their area. He clenched his teeth, noticing how his eyes adjusted to the pitch darkness of the place, giving everything within a faint blue outline.

"*I should be blind here,*" Erik thought. "*No one can see in the dark.*" The more he continued throwing out unneeded rock, the clearer his sight became and the blue outlines that covered everything slowly gave way to shape and color. His vision sharpened and Erik gasped, noticing Raider chopping away at the sidewall, concentrating on the task. "*I can see him clearly as if a light's down here! I don't understand...*"

Raider hit another space and the metal gave way to a different sound, releasing a low drone. "Jackpot," Raider said and tossed Erik the pickaxe.

Erik quickly caught it, appalled. "You could've beaned me with that thing!" he fussed.

"You're fast," Raider said as he withdrew the hammer and chisel, "don't worry."

Striking the surface, Raider dislodged the extraneous material then reached in, ripping out the mysterious object with ease. He tossed it to Erik and Erik dropped what he held, catching a small globe of glassy crystal glowing dimly in pale blue light.

"What's this?" Erik demanded and studied the sphere, noticing it had a small crack across its surface.

"Pure Corite," Raider replied, sheathing the chisel and hammer. "That one there's special."

"Why is it?"

"It ain't jagged pieces of shit everyone else finds. The ones that's got air trapped in it makes 'em special." Raider leaned in closer, lowering his voice. "Hide it, okay?"

"Sure..." Erik tucked it into his jumpsuit pocket, flushed by the warmth surging through him. "What can I use this for?"

Raider glanced around then pulled Erik closer. "There's this guy on the hill," Raider said softly. "Take it to him, okay?"

"Why just him?" Erik snapped, incredulous. "Why nobody else?"

"Look, man, he ain't like nobody else, dig? He's gonna help ya remember."

"Remember what?

Raider pulled away and kicked up his pickaxe. He continued hacking, appearing busy.

"How is our progress?" a voice called from behind. Erik turned around, only to get blinded by white light in his face.

Erik felt a firm hand shaking him and he moaned, slowly coming to. His eyes fluttered open and he squinted from the bright morning sunshine as he faced Suber on his haunches looking over him, concerned.

"Good," Suber said gratefully, "we're back to the land of the living."

"I don't know what's wrong with me," Erik muttered, sitting up. Checking his surroundings, he noticed he was outside on the ground and looking over his shoulder, he saw Hernando sitting on the trunk of his car, smoking a cigarette.

"Have you always had these episodes?" Suber asked.

"I've been having headaches for a while," Erik replied.

"Has it anything to do with your memory?"

"I don't see how it should," Hernando interjected. "He's got a superb memory... Hell, it's a lot better than mine!"

Erik moaned and ran his hands through his hair. "I'm not sure if I'm remembering or dreaming," he complained.

"I don't understand..."

"The voices keep telling me to remember."

"Voices...?"

Suber raised an eyebrow and Erik explained the best he could of several occurrences, feeling more unsettled when he heard himself speak and not make any sense.

"So... whenever you try to recall," Hernando said slowly, "all you get is blank space?"

Erik ran his hands through his hair again, blowing a frustrated sigh. "I have some idea," he muttered, "but I don't have anything truly that warrants recollection."

"Such as...?"

"Genovera, for instance."

"Damn!" Hernando yelped and quickly fished for the cigarette he dropped. "What about Genovera that you know?" he asked and pat out his slacks.

"Not much... I just had a picture of her."

"I thought she was dead..." Hernando found the cigarette and continued smoking the rest of it.

"Well..." Erik thought about his first encounter and then decided against telling. "*They're somehow mixed up with Corbin,*" he mused. "*I'm not sure what side they're on...*" Erik cleared his throat. "Yes, she is," he said instead. "I had an old picture, but I forget everything else except for her name."

"She was skilled scientist," Hernando said as he finished the cigarette he had, then threw the stub aside on the ground and started on another. "That woman was the finest among those who worked at The Agency. It was a shame she was let go." Erik shuddered at the mere mention.

"Now with her gone," Suber added, "it takes four assistants with a good head on their shoulders to barely match all that Genovera could do!"

"She sounds very impressive," Erik stated. "Why was she let go if she was so great?"

"She went against Policy."

"And what's that?"

"Something much greater than you can comprehend." Suber rose to his feet and stretched. "We need to get going if we're going to make this meeting."

"*Bueno, multa,*" Hernando muttered and slipped off the car's edge.

"Have a little faith in us, okay?" Suber said to Erik, holding out a hand. "We're trying to help, despite the constraints."

"If you say so..." Erik muttered and frowned as he took Suber's hand, getting pulled to his feet.

Trust no one... They only want to hurt you...

Erik approached the car as Hernando got in and Suber's phone rang. Suber waved Erik away and walked several paces down the road, taking the call. Erik shrugged and reentered the car while Hernando leaned his left arm against the door, tapping the side while he smoked with his free hand, his gray eyes distant in thought.

"People can get so caught in their work that they see the

world as nothing but data and statistics," Hernando murmured. "Is Termination really the price of salvaging humanity?"

"Termination?" Erik parroted.

"Never mind what I said," Hernando grumbled and glimpsed in his rear view, then in his side mirror before withdrawing two cigarettes from his pack. He placed one behind his ear and lit the other after the third he smoked burned out down to the filter. When the cigarette failed to catch, he tossed the smoldering cigarette out the window and used the car lighter to light the current one he had. "I'm just a wreck because of my psychopathic boss; there's nothing really to worry about."

"Is there anything I personally should be worried about?"

"You've got more to worry about than your miserable life."

"What would that be then?"

When Hernando said nothing else, Erik blew a short sigh. Hearing a tap at the window, he looked up at Suber waving. Erik waved back and Hernando glanced to his right, grunting. He started the engine as Suber opened the passenger side and stepped in.

"That was Taeo," Suber commented as Hernando took the cigarette that dangled from his lip and put it out in the nearby ashtray. "He wants us to stop at the truck stop before going in... the one we agreed upon."

Hernando nodded. "Is he buying us lunch?" he cracked and stuck the dead cigarette behind his other ear as Suber shut the door.

"We'll find out."

Pulling away from the side of the road, Erik noticed Hernando's hands gripped the steering wheel tightly, forcing his knuckles white.

FOUR

Hernando eased into the lot of a large gas station with a diner attached to the back. Many freight trucks lined in the station's rear. Only one other small compact car and a mid-sized van idled at the pumps.

While Hernando parked alongside an adjacent pump, Suber exited the car and motioned for Erik to follow. Erik clamored out, walking with him toward the diner. He heard a small ring and Suber pulled out his cellular phone from his pocket. Flipping it open, he paused near the gas station's front doors.

"Yes?" Suber greeted and looked around then nodded. "Yes, I see it." He checked his watch. "Ten minutes." Suber closed the phone and waved at Erik to follow his stride, approaching the gas station's steps. Throwing open the door, Suber entered and walked down a small corridor leading to the rear restrooms. Erik kept his distance behind him and spotted the diner several paces ahead. "Do you need to use the restroom?" Suber inquired.

"Not really," Erik answered.

"Well, I do. Wait here."

Suber stepped inside and Erik walked on into the diner area, overhearing several truckers talking indistinctly and tinny rock music playing from a small transistor radio. He leaned against the wall in the corridor, watching the faint traces of stale cigarette smoke curl in the wash of early morning sun spreading through the easternmost windows, splashing red-orange rays over the wooden tables, the various assembled booths and worn blue carpet. Erik heard footsteps approach from behind and immediately tensed.

"Hey, feel like eating?" Hernando inquired as he placed a hand on Erik's shoulder. Erik looked up and Hernando, who had come out of his lab coat leaving on just his white dress shirt with cuffed sleeves and chinos, smiled brightly down at him. "I'm getting coffee. Anything you want in particular?"

"I'm not feeling all that hungry," Erik demurred.

"Well, I suggest you eat something."

Hernando left Erik's side and made his way for a booth. Erik reluctantly walked after him, slipping into the seat across from him. A server approached moments later, handing the two menus without a word.

Picking up the catalog, Erik studied the choices, then set the booklet aside, blowing a short sigh. "I'll take whatever is the cheapest," he mumbled.

"That's the diner special," the server chirped. "You?"

"Just coffee, thank you," Hernando replied.

"Cup or pot?"

"Just one cup is fine; I really don't need any more than one for right now."

"Gotcha." The server took both menus and left the table.

Hernando grabbed his partially used cigarette and fished for a lighter in his front pocket. "Okay if I smoke?" he queried once he withdrew a small matchbook.

"It's fine," Erik replied.

Hernando thumbed out a match from the book and struck it, quickly lighting his cigarette. He inhaled deeply then let out a relieved sigh as he waved out his match.

"Thanks," Hernando murmured.

"What's going to happen once I arrive at this place?" Erik asked worriedly. "Why should I get treatment for something if I'm not sick?"

"Like I said, Number Three, I can't say much about it."

Erik bristled in annoyance. "Why do you keep calling me Number Three?" he demanded and slapped a hand across the worn table. "My name is Erik!"

"I..." Hernando sighed and leaned back, clutching hard to his cigarette. "Sorry, I forgot," he murmured. "Erik..."

Erik turned away, catching sight of Suber as he entered, wearing a pale yellow dress shirt and jeans. He also had removed his white lab coat and seemed more relaxed as he sat in a booth in front of them, facing Erik. He nodded and Erik nodded back.

The server returned with Erik's plate and Hernando's mug of coffee. Erik picked up his fork, poking at a mountain of corned beef and browned shredded potatoes as his appetite quickly dissipated.

"Corned beef and hash, eh?" Hernando probed and stuck his cigarette to his lips. Opening a small container of creamer, he poured in the contents into his black coffee then tapped the ashes into the now empty cask. "Man, I miss that stuff; I used to eat that and giant buttermilk biscuits that just *drowned* in sausage gravy." Hernando sighed contently. "Oh, that was the thing!"

Erik pushed his plate toward him. "Want some?" he pressed.

Hernando put up a hand. "Oh no, you go on and eat it. Enjoy!"

"There's enough for two people, you know."

"Maybe later. You eat first."

Erik took a bite and frowned when he tasted bland meat and potatoes laden in cooking oil. "I don't think I like greasy foods," he murmured and set down his fork.

Hernando chuckled as he stirred his coffee with his spoon and took Erik's plate. "It's okay... It probably needs some pepper."

Erik heard soft talking nearby and looked back to Suber, watching him converse with a man who sat in the booth on the other side of Hernando. The mysterious man wore a dark cap and coat with an upturned collar, his long shaggy dark red hair pulled into a loose queue hanging down his back.

Turning his attention away, Erik idly looked about his surroundings as Hernando ate the breakfast meal and sipped his coffee. After several moments, Erik heard Hernando's fork tap against the plate.

"Will you hate me after this is over with?" Hernando suddenly asked.

Erik turned to him with a confounded expression. "What do you mean?" he retorted guardedly.

"Where you're going," Hernando said softly, "it won't be a very safe place..." He pushed his plate away and lit his other cigarette then put the stub of the former into his drained coffee cup. "I don't want you to hate me once you arrive there and realize what a terrible place it is."

"I won't hate you," Erik promised.

"Please don't... It is a part of my job. I just *have* to." Hernando blew smoke out of his nose, grunting. "Hell, I *shouldn't* be here in the diner with you. You *shouldn't* be eating anything at all, right now." He clutched tighter to his cigarette and leaned forward, folding his free arm across his body as he inhaled deeply. Hernando rolled his eyes to the ceiling and shut them tightly. "Corbin's going to have my ass if he finds out!" he moaned.

"But why do this *knowing* you might get in trouble?"

"You didn't do anything wrong," Hernando murmured. "*We're* the ones doing wrong, all in the name of this fucked up science!" He blew an angry sigh. "I'm just a fool..."

"For science...?"

Suber approached Hernando's side moments later, touching him on the shoulder and leaned forward, whispering in his ear. Hernando's eyes snapped open and he glared at Suber who stood back and nodded solemnly.

"Son of a bitch!" Hernando yelped and dropped his cigarette.

"What's going on?" Erik cried as Hernando pushed Suber aside and rushed from the table.

"Come on, this way," Suber insisted and grabbed Erik by the arm as he stumbled out the booth. "Let's hustle!" Suber took off for the diner's rear door with Erik at his heels and shoved open the glass entranceway with his body.

Barreling onto the lot where the many eighteen-wheelers parked in neat rows, Erik hurried alongside Suber and glanced back, noticing a dark compact car with tinted windows conspicuously in the center of the exit lane. Suber picked up the

35

pace as an engine turned, rumbling loudly.

Erik let out a yelp when taken by the arm and yanked away from the edge of a haphazardly parked car sticking out on the lot. Whirling around out of Suber's grip, Erik spotted the beige coupe sedan speeding up to them. The car slowed down slightly, continuing at a running pace and the side door swung open.

Suber pushed Erik forward and he quickly jumped into the moving car, crawling over to the rear seat. He looked back, spotting the sleek black compact car following closely behind, its driver and passengers dark shadows against the smoky tinted windows.

Suber gestured ahead and Hernando floored the accelerator as Suber finally grabbed the door to swing in and slammed it shut.

"You'd better not get us killed!" Hernando yelled as he raced out the lot.

"Shut up and keep going!" Suber shouted back.

"Who are those guys?" Erik interjected and turned around, looking out the rear window. The dark car fell back, following several paces behind.

"Agents," Suber said simply and quickly took over the wheel as Hernando dug around for his cigarettes.

"How did they find us for fuck's sake?" Hernando grumbled and tapped the car's lighter.

"Just keep your eyes on the road!"

"Shut up!"

The dark car pulled up alongside them and Hernando stomped on the brakes, screeching to a stop. Suber fell forward and Erik struck the seats directly in front of him, then fell to the floor. The dark car continued onward before coming to a stop.

"What are you, nuts?" Suber yelled as Hernando pushed Suber back, hunching down.

"Get the fuck down!"

"Holy shit!" Suber cried when a shot rang out and a bullet pierced the windshield, cracking the glass.

"They're serious!" Erik yelped.

"I know what I'm doing!" Hernando growled and sat up, turning the car around then sped in the opposite direction. Erik looked up, catching sight of the dark car barrel after them in reverse.

"Why are they trying to kill us?" Erik mewed, watching the dark compact screech as it circled around and gunned after them.

"If they meant it," Suber answered, "Hernando would be a dead man now!"

"How can you say they missed *on purpose?*" Erik squawked.

"Get over," Suber snapped. "You're too much of a mess to even think right now!"

Hernando threw the gears into neutral and climbed over Suber as Suber moved over, taking control of the wheel. Hernando took out the car lighter and lit his cigarette, inhaling hard.

"We're going to die, I know it!" Hernando complained as Suber switched gears back into drive. Erik peered out the rear window, spotting the mysterious car keeping pace behind them. Moments later, the coupe's engine knocked loudly. "Oh, fuck!"

"You probably flooded the damn thing with your brainsick driving!" Suber fussed as he pumped the accelerator.

"No, I didn't!" Hernando protested.

The dark car following them began to slow, getting smaller in the distance as they continued ahead. The sedan decelerated and Suber quickly restarted the engine. Turning the key, a high-pitched whine pierced the air as the starter ground.

"The engine's about to go out and the starter's stripped!" Suber snapped.

"I just had it rebuilt," Hernando screeched, "and the starter was brand fucking new since last fucking week!"

"Do you know how hard it is to find parts in this damn city?" Suber shouted. "Get a new car sometime!"

"Until they give me a goddamn raise, that's not happening!"

Suber snorted. "They probably felt vindictive and put sugar in the tank," he said wryly as the engine roared to life, "and ground down the starter just for kicks."

"This isn't the time to joke!" Hernando snarled over the increasing-pitched knocks. "Just keep driving. We've got a full tank anyway."

"I won't be so sure," Suber replied as black smoke belched from the muffler. "If they mucked up your tank, who knows what else they did!"

"Fucking hell!" Hernando moaned as the engine sputtered, then stalled completely.

Suber pulled over on the side of the road once the car lost velocity and threw it in park, forcing the vehicle lurching forward. Hernando slammed open the door and stomped out, pushing up his sleeves as Suber pulled the hood release. Lifting the hood and examining the engine and other parts, Hernando spewed a string of expletives.

"Why are they trying to kill you?" Erik asked timidly.

"What we got was a warning," Suber murmured and sighed heavily, running a hand through his blond hair. "Otherwise, they'd just bomb Hernando's car, not flood his engine, cut his brakes or do whatever else to his precious car."

Moments later, a weather-beaten black sports car with chrome accents pulled up alongside them from the opposite direction of the road. The horn beeped and Suber turned toward the sound up once it backed several paces.

The driver side window came down, revealing a young man with short of raven hair dyed with electric blue streaks, wearing a light pink dress shirt and tinted red aviator sunglasses. He leaned an arm out on the door, grinning.

"Hey," the young man greeted. "Got some car trouble?"

"No shit, Reinswitzer," Suber said irritably. "Now isn't the time!"

"Look, man, I got something for you!"

"If it's something for my migraine, I'll take it!"

"No, much better!"

"What is it?" Reinswitzer leaned over, searching the nearby seat, then turned back, pointing a high-powered semi-automatic pistol at Suber.

Suber warily stared back, never once flinching. Erik sank into his seat, overcome with dread. "What did you come here for," Suber said wearily, "to kill me or warn me?" Reinswitzer calmly pulled back the safety.

"Just trust me." He nodded and Suber quickly dropped back as Reinswitzer fired once.

A soft thump followed in the distance and Erik looked to

his right, seeing only grassy ragweed-filled fields blowing in the wind. Moments later, a dark figure slowly rose to his feet, holding onto a long-range rifle with a scope attachment. Reinswitzer released the safety and fired again, forcing the would-be killer dropping out of sight.

"Done?" Suber groused.

"Yep," Reinswitzer said and set the gun back on the seat as Suber sat up.

"Was that a warning too?" Erik groused.

"I'm not sure anymore," Suber grumbled.

"Hey," interjected Reinswitzer, "just take the hooptie and I'll fix the old jalopy, okay?"

"Thanks."

"Need any fireworks while you're at it?"

"I don't like violence."

"It's okay, I get it."

Suber opened his door and stepped out, then motioned for Erik to exit as well. Erik sighed and clamored out, crossing Reinswitzer's path.

"Looking good," Reinswitzer murmured, grinning. Erik's face flushed in response and he made his way around the car while Reinswitzer followed, opening the door for him. Reinswitzer pulled back the front passenger seat, gesturing toward the interior.

"Thanks," Erik muttered, slipping inside.

"Isn't Rosenthal going to get on your head for helping us out?" Suber asked as he leaned against the car's roof once Reinswitzer let the seat back. "Obviously one of us fucked up if they've got Agents on our ass."

"I don't know which one it could've been," Reinswitzer replied. "Or if it was either one of you at all."

"Someone on the team then?"

"You mean they could be targeting me?" Erik yelped. "I didn't do anything!"

"I'll find out what's up," Reinswitzer replied, shutting the door. "I'm known for taking extended lunch breaks anyway." He grinned, knocking on the car's roof. "Besides, I've got an excuse - I'm still running with the original transmission and the car's thirty-years old!" They both laughed and Reinswitzer left, approaching Hernando offside, greeting him.

Hernando slammed down the hood and stomped for the car as Reinswitzer shut the left open side passenger door. As both Suber and Hernando entered the black sports car, Reinswitzer returned and leaned against the door after Suber shut it and started the engine.

"What is it?" Suber spat.

"There are two under the seat in the case you need them," Reinswitzer pressed. "You never know."

"I don't need them." Suber waved him away. "Really."

"Oh, well," said Reinswitzer simply. "You're right, I can't force you." Hernando picked up the gun on the seat and tucked it into his waistband, then leaned forward, grabbing two more from underneath the seat. He passed them over to Reinswitzer who stuck them both behind him in his waistband. "Listen, ahead are a bunch of them blocking off the road. I don't want you risking getting carved new ones, so I suggest you go back and take the side road on the right. You'll take the long scenic route, but you'll get there in one piece."

"What's the excuse?" Suber inquired as he adjusted his mirrors.

"Simple: your car stalled, you called me up for a lift and I let you borrow mine." Reinswitzer chuckled. "If Corbin blows his stack, just direct him to me."

Suber nodded and Reinswitzer knocked at the window before stepping back. Suber pulled away and Erik looked out the window, spotting the young man waving. Erik returned the gesture and Suber turned the car around before speeding down the road.

FIVE

During the long drive, the ride was silent, with Suber playing the radio softly and Hernando leaning against the door, smoking until he ran out of what he had left in his pack. Hernando's hands started shaking and his left foot tapped as his nervous energies took over.

"Check the glove compartment," Suber said irritably and Hernando did as told. He withdrew a carton of cigarettes with a yellow sticky note posted on the side with his name on it.

"A whole carton!" Hernando said happily and gleefully tore it open. "They're longs too!" Suber shook his head, muttering under his breath. "Hey, we all have ways to cope."

"You should have black teeth by now with all that you're smoking!" Suber grumbled as Hernando extracted a pack and tore it open.

"I do," Hernando replied and chortled. "That's why I wear porcelain fronts."

"Sick, just sick."

The car later entered a one-lane road and the various oaks, pines, and maples gave way to mainly tall pines. Afterwards, they approached a heavy wrought-iron gate patrolled by a pair of guards wielding long-range rifles. The security wore navy jumpsuits with silver buttons, black caps with wide visors and dark glasses hid their eyes. Once Suber pulled up and idled, the guard nearest him made a motion with his hand and Suber cut the engine.

"What's that you got back there?" one guard demanded as they approached Suber's side. Hernando quickly pulled out his tucked shirttails, hiding the gun he had.

"Delivery," Suber snapped.

"What, delivering some kid?" the other guard scoffed offside. "Does he come with batteries?"

"Come on," Hernando grumbled. "I need to take a piss."

"Woods are right there," growled the guard near Suber.

"He's part of the Treatment and Recovery program," Suber said evenly. "I'm already late enough as it is!"

"What part?" asked the guard and gave a facetious grin.

"G-seven forty-five."

"Listen, you stupid fucks," Hernando exploded. "Stop stalling!"

The guard pointed his gun at Suber. "You shut the fuck up," he shouted, "or I blow out his brains!"

"Don't hurt him because of me!" Erik yelled.

"Get out the car." Both sentries stepped back as Hernando and Suber exited the car. Erik also stepped out, clenching his hands at his sides. "Call for Behr, okay?"

"Yeah," said the other guard and made a call on his two-way radio.

An imposing man wearing dark reflective glasses and a dual gun holster with one empty slung low around his hips, dressed in a brown gold-buttoned uniform, came to the gate. He took off his cap with a wide visor and several ranking pins on the side, brushing back his thinning silver hair before resetting it.

"What the hell's going on here?" Behr snapped as he punched at a keypad on the gate's side. His gaze fell on Erik and he bared his teeth. "Oh, I see..." he snarled.

Erik tensed as the heavy iron slowly swung open and the head guardsman stepped out. Hernando raced forward and Behr grabbed for him, twisting his arms behind his back.

"Let him go!" Erik cried. Racing towards Hernando, he froze when a shot rang out, followed by cry in pain. Erik whirled around, catching sight of Suber clutching his shoulder as he sagged against the car. The guard facing Suber grinned as he readied his rifle. "What are you doing?" Erik yelled. "He didn't do anything wrong!"

"We have orders to punish him," the guard replied icily. Erik ground his teeth as the secondary guard approached, pointing his rifle directly at Erik's head. "Don't worry; he's not going to die, kid, unless you make a wrong move."

Erik looked to Suber who clutched his bleeding shoulder, his dark red blood draining from the wound turning almost black. Erik neared him as he staggered to stand and Suber shook his head.

"Don't get too close," he said weakly. "It's too dangerous..." Suber gasped and collapsed against the car as the guard released the bolt and readied the rifle he kept trained on him.

"I'm already involved," Erik spat and glared back at the sentry. "You've got no right punishing him. It's me you want, isn't it?"

"Orders are orders, kid," the guard snapped. "One more step and you're done."

Hernando broke away from Behr, throwing him overhead. Behr scrambled to his feet as Hernando withdrew the pistol and whacked Behr across the jaw with it, forcing him staggering back, stunned.

The sentries turned their attention away and Erik tackled the guard across from Suber, taking him down to the ground. Hernando shot at the second guard in the chest as Behr gathered his composure, correcting his dark shades that almost fell off his face.

Behr threw a sucker punch at Hernando when momentarily distracted, forcing him tripping backwards and drop the gun. He scooped it up as Hernando struck the ground and pointed the pistol down at him.

"Call him off!" Behr thundered as Erik struggled against the guard for his rifle. "Do it now, or he's dead!"

"Erik!" Hernando shouted. "Let it go!"

Erik did as told and grunted when whacked across the face with the gunstock, throwing him rearwards. The guard pointed his rifle at Suber as Hernando scrambled to his feet and ran over to Erik, pulling him upright.

"You bastards," Hernando spat and approached Suber, immediately applying pressure to his shoulder. "You assholes are going to pay for this!"

"Hey, if you didn't play around so much with that piece of shit on wheels," snapped the rifleman, "we won't be pissed at you for making us miss our lunch breaks waiting on your slow ass!"

"Call for a damn medic, will you?" Behr snapped as he tucked the gun he took from Hernando into his empty holster.

"Yeah, on it," replied the guard and relaxed his stance then picked up his two-way radio.

Storming over to Erik, Behr grabbed him roughly by the arm. "You're coming with me, boy," he sneered and dragged Erik ahead down the paved gravel path.

The narrow road lead to three large brick buildings and two tall buildings on the left constructed of red brick. The buildings had five columns of windows lined up in rows of four, a fire escape on the roof, and a large single antenna. The other, built of dark tan brick with many single pane windows all in a row of six with three columns, stood on the right of the tall red one.

"Where am I going?" Erik demanded.

"You're staying in the patient housing complex where it's real nice and comfy," Behr drawled maliciously. "Inhale all this good air you got going for now, 'cause this is the last of the open world you're gonna see for a long, long time!"

"What about school, my teachers, my family, my friends, my life...?"

Behr chuckled. "All that's in the past... That part of you's gonna be excised, boy. All it is, is what's going on right here, right now."

"I have no reason to be here!" Erik protested.

"I knew you wouldn't last long before you needed adjustments," Behr went on. "With the way you like to cut up, I'm gonna enjoy adjusting your face!"

Furthering into the compound, Erik saw high fences enclosed the buildings with barbed wire strung across the top and marked with warning signs signaling they were powered by electricity.

Many guards in silver-buttoned navy jumpsuits, smoky glasses, black caps with wide visors armed with high-powered long-ranged rifles patrolled the grounds and on the rooftops.

A guard approached Behr on the walkway and Behr gave pause, forcing Erik bumping into him. The lower-grade officer saluted Behr and the man gave no acknowledgment. The sentry then dug through his pockets, withdrawing a sheet of paper and handed it over to the senior guard member. Behr snatched it from his hand, quickly scanning the material.

"What the hell is this shit?" Behr growled as he crumpled the sheet of paper. "I'm no goddamn medic!"

"Sir," said the guard nervously, "he was to arrive already unconscious."

"Don't you think I know that?" Behr snapped.

"Then how are we to force him out if we have no chloroform or any other knockout drug?"

Behr laughed darkly in response. "We have other means."

"Sir... I don't understand."

Behr held out a hand and the guard handed over his rifle unquestioningly. Behr then slammed the gunstock into the guard's stomach with his free hand, forcing him doubling over in pain.

"Understand now?" Behr snarled.

"Yes, Sir," the guard moaned as he crumpled to his knees.

Behr let Erik go and Erik clamored on the defensive once the rifle swung at his head. He leaned out the attack and spun around Behr, snatching his pistol. He pointed it at the head guardsman who aimed the longarm at Erik's chest.

"Don't push me," Erik snarled and fired, shattering the

rifle's gunstock. Behr paled, dropping his weapon.

"Damn," Behr hissed as Erik backed away. "You want a fight, you got one." He extracted his secondary gun, a sleek silver and black oversized pistol, and depressed the trigger.

A dull muffled shot rang out and Erik let out a cry when sharp pins dug into his chest and his body seized involuntarily, encased by a hard jolt of electricity.

"Units Five, Twelve, Eighteen: cattle prod in front!" the junior officer called over his radio when Erik collapsed to the ground, gasping for breath. He kicked the gun out of Erik's hand.

Several uniformed men in navy raced across the rolling green, all wielding the same sleek silver and black handguns. Shaking off the initial stun, Erik scrambled to his feet and took off, searching for a way out. Approaching an electrified gate, he turned facing the many guards who closed in around him.

The guards released their electrified barbs and Erik screamed when shocked and collapsed forward onto his knees once his muscles contracted, forcing him unable to move.

"Nice, all very nice," Behr sneered as he sauntered up to Erik. "You belong to us now." He kicked Erik hard in the face with his steel-toed boot, forcing everything into darkness.

The shadows of the dark empty world consisting of the void slowly rescinded and Erik regained consciousness. He found himself in a small white-walled room, sitting in a hard-backed chair with stiff arms behind a low table, wearing a set of clothing consisting of blue scrub shirt and pants with tan socks.

Erik hissed in pain from his aching arms and studied his surroundings, noticing his wrists and ankles strapped to the chair's arms and legs. Looking up, he found an intravenous dripping a clear serum into the veins in the crook of his elbow.

The door to the enclosed room opened, revealing a slender olive-skinned middle-aged man. He had long black hair singly braided down his back and wore a white lab coat over a dark gray suit. The doctor carried in with him a tape recorder and notepad. Setting the objects on the table, he then pulled out of his lab coat, draping it aside on the table's edge.

"Who are you?" Erik asked groggily. "Why am I here?"

"We're going to talk today," answered the doctor, "is that fine by you?"

"You didn't answer my question."

"I am merely a guide to aid you back to a healthy mental state. I'm in charge of your well-being..."

"Some charge!"

"But you can't get well if you don't talk to me!" The doctor hooked the tape recorder to the wall and turned it on, playing a melodious tone Erik instantly recognized.

"That song..."

"What about it?"

Erik searched his mind for the memory attached, unable to come up with anything. He ground his teeth and shook his head.

"*Come on, think!*" Erik yelled at himself. "*Think! Remember!*"

The doctor left the room and returned with a chair moments later. He then shut the door behind him and placed the chair before the table, sitting across from Erik. A small ring erupted in the room and the doctor reached in his pocket, withdrawing a small cellular phone.

"Sorry about that," said the doctor as he pushed the button, shutting off its chime. "I'll turn that off."

"I remember," Erik said quickly. "I heard it before... a phone call."

"What phone call?"

Erik shook his head. "I'm not sure..."

"You can tell me."

"But I don't know who you are."

"Didn't I tell you already?"

"*He's trying to trick me,*" Erik thought, glaring at him. "*I won't tell him anything, not one word...*"

"What won't you tell me?"

Erik sucked in a shallow breath, stunned. "*He couldn't have heard my thoughts...!*"

"You're speaking out loud."

"No, I'm not!" Erik yelled and clenched his hands, shaking. "*It's this man and this medicine they've got,*" he mused, struggling against the restraints. "*It's playing tricks with my head!*"

"There is no use breaking out of there," the doctor said firmly. "You're weighed down by metal harnesses."

Erik glared down at the ties holding him down. "*They're made of leather!*" he realized, staring at the straps weighed down with heavy buckles and locks. "I can break this," Erik hissed. "I've done it before!" His limbs refused to respond and he glowered up at the intravenous administering the clear serum into his system. "It's got to be this - some neutralizing agent..."

"Now, if you would calm," snapped the doctor, "I'd like to

51

talk."

Erik whipped his head forward, sneering. "No," he growled. "I'm not going to talk to you, so forget it!"

"Now, please, don't become agitated," the doctor calmly replied.

"Why am I here?"

"To get well."

"Where am I?"

"In one of the best sanatoriums in the state." Erik let out an anguished cry as his head began to throb. "Is something the matter?" The faint voices returned, speaking to him and he shook his head, trying to drive them out. "Are you all right?"

"Shut up!" Erik screeched. "Stop talking!"

"Who is talking?"

"Them!"

"Who is 'them'?"

Erik screamed, thrashing his head. "Shut up, shut up! All of you!"

"Don't let the voices bother you," the doctor said gently. "Ignore them. Don't listen to them."

Erik suddenly grew warmer and struggled for breath as the ripping ache shot through his left shoulder, traveling down his arm. "You shut up too!" Erik shouted, glaring ahead at the doctor. "You're only trying to make me *think* I'm crazy!"

The doctor rose to his feet, visibly agitated. "I think more medication is in order," he said.

"You'd better not!" Erik froze when he sensed cold steel at his head. He looked up, finding no one there. "If you shoot me dead, then there's no point in asking me questions, now is there?" Erik spat.

"No one has a gun here."

"They're right there!" Erik wailed and sagged against the chair when wooziness took over. Turning, he found the bag of serum another color consisting of orange instead of clear. "Wait..."

"What is it?"

Erik narrowed his eyes at the doctor. "Turn it off," he snarled.

"Turn what off?"

"The damn music!" Erik roared. "Turn it off!"

"There is no music playing."

Erik shut his eyes, counting loudly. *"He can't claim I'm speaking if I'm doing something else,"* he realized. *"Why are they trying to make me crazy?"*

"Do not withdraw," the doctor called over his voice.

"From what everyone's said vaguely about them, they're dangerous..."

"Do not retreat from reality!"

"If someone dies under their control, it's nobody's fault..."

"Open your eyes; look at me."

"The induced lunacy..."

"Open your eyes!"

SIX

Faint ringing brought Erik out of his fog. As he slowly came to, he realized he lay in a comfortable soft bed. Sitting up, he noticed many posters of rock bands and other musical groups donning his walls, along with posters of movie actors and other famous people. The ringing continued and Erik groaned, rubbing at his face.

Stepping out of bed, he shuffled toward the door and opened it, revealing a carpeted corridor. Approaching the top of the staircase, he heard his father speaking in hushed tones to his mother from the master bedroom across the hall. Blowing a heavy sigh, Erik made his way downstairs and picked up the phone in the parlor near the kitchen.

"You got Schumacher," Erik greeted into the receiver. "Name, number, message?"

"Hey, Justin," a friendly voice greeted over the line. "Are you feeling better?"

"Just a bit of a headache," Erik replied. "Thanks for asking."

"I hope your dad didn't chew you out. Mine sure did!"

"He didn't throw stuff at you again, did he?"

"Just rocks this time."

Erik cringed. "Don't say stuff like that!" he complained.

"He was all like 'how can you be such a bloody dumb ass,

Kevin?' and so on and whatever," Kevin went on. "I just laughed at him."

"I wish he wasn't so abusive to you."

"I'm bored," Kevin groused, changing the course of the conversation. "You always have the great ideas, so let's hear one!"

"You're always bored, Kev," Erik answered. "Is your dad out drinking again?"

"Yeah, after that tirade, he got thirsty." Kevin snorted. "So knowing that much, my mom's gotta get him out the drunk tank again."

"How do you do it?"

"I'm just grateful that he doesn't beat me or Mom."

"But he tends to throw stuff."

"That's why you've got to be fast. Or be dumb enough to take a few hits to the chin."

"I don't know," Erik murmured, twirling the phone cord in his fingers.

"So...?" Kevin pressed impatiently.

"I mean, it's hard to keep up with great ideas to keep people confused..."

"Hey, I thought of one really awesome!"

"Let's hear it, Kev." Erik grinned as he listened to the plan, and then hung up the line.

Moments later, a more youthful John Greenfield appeared standing atop the staircase, with his shaggy brown hair loose around his shoulders and a comb-style mustache. He wore sagging-fit denim jeans with a yellow T-shirt hanging out from the rear pocket. Erik noticed the old scars and burns crisscrossing his chest and arms.

"Hey, Ace," John Greenfield greeted, "what's that about?"

"I've got to go see about Kev," Erik replied. "Smiley's in the tank again."

"Keep an eye on him," John Greenfield said gently. "He's a good kid."

"Dad..." Erik started before John Greenfield could leave. "Why does he drink so much?"

"Because he's trying to forget The War, Justin," John Greenfield replied.

"Was it really that bad?" John Greenfield nodded. "But why doesn't it bother you?"

"It does, but I've learned to deal with it the best I can."

"How's that?"

"I figured that if they can develop all sorts of terrible things to hurt people with, why not develop things to save people with?"

"What do you mean?"

John Greenfield smiled slightly as he made his way down the steps. "It's fine, Ace. Just fine..." He approached Erik and tousled his hair. "Now don't keep your buddy Kevin waiting."

Erik nodded and left the parlor, hurrying upstairs. After changing clothes and grabbing his backpack holding his roller skates, he came downstairs and paused at the sight of his father sitting on the couch, staring into a glass of whiskey. Erik said nothing as he walked past him out the door.

Erik found Kevin easily on his favored custom skateboard down the street, working on skate tricks. Kevin wore faded jeans with rips at the knee, a loose tan windbreaker and a bright red helmet that had his curly black hair sticking out from underneath. Erik hooted at Kevin when he tried a jump over a fire hydrant, only to bail and strike the ground flat on his back.

"Hey, Kev!" Erik called and captured the skateboard that rolled away. "I followed the path you gave me and it was difficult! So what's your big idea?"

"That was just a preview," Kevin declared as he stood once Erik returned and dropped the skateboard at his feet. Kevin stepped on the board, watching Erik skate circles around him. "We're playing Extreme Horse. I wanna see how we rate against each other."

Erik smirked. "My tricks are still better than yours," he teased.

"Prove me wrong." Kevin kicked off on his board, coasting down the street and Erik followed beside him. "There's this abandoned house with the perfect setup," Kevin explained. "Pool, benches, low fence, the works..."

"Sounds great!" Erik said brightly.

"We need to hurry before somebody else finds it and trashes the place."

Approaching the large house in question, Erik came to a pause, noticing residents inside. "Hey, Kev," he said worriedly. "I thought you said it was abandoned..."

Kevin also halted and kicked up his board. "I thought so too..." He gave a mischievous grin. "Let's check it out!"

Erik nodded and skated ahead, rolling around the front side. He slowed as he coasted past, noticing a black van in the driveway. Turning around, he spotted Kevin jumping the gate and prowling around the house's side. Erik changed course and headed up the driveway, stopping near the van and crouched down as the front door opened.

"Fuckin' bitch," a male voice grumbled and Erik heard a match being struck, followed by the scent of tobacco. Through the open door, Erik heard voices of others talking and music playing. "What's all this then?" the voice cried, startled. Erik turned around, facing a tall young man with long sandy hair pulled back into a loose queue and green eyes, wearing a denim jacket with matching jeans who held a lit cigarette. "What are you doing here, eh?"

Erik swallowed hard and backed away.

"Can't you talk?"

"What's that, Collin?" another voice called.

Erik skated around the van to escape, only to bump into another person. Taken by the arm, Erik struggled to get free. "Let go of me!" he growled.

"Ain't half the looker, Sidney," said Collin as he came around.

"Keep your mind on business, Collin," Sidney grumbled. "You can play with him later."

"Why are you here?" Erik demanded. "This place was abandoned!"

"Right, *was*," Collin spat, blowing smoke in Erik's face.

Erik coughed, turning his head away. "*Think fast, think fast,*" he thought. "*I need to get out of here before anything else goes wrong...*" Erik spotted Kevin sneaking up behind Sidney, wielding his skateboard in hand. "I, um, yeah," he said weakly. "So, how is the place?"

"Southern Cali ain't too bad," Collin said brightly, leaning in. "Especially with all these hot young things running around..."

"You're so bad, Collin!" Sidney jeered.

"Get your hands off him, you perv!" Kevin yelled. Sidney turned and Kevin slammed the skateboard over his head, forcing him down.

"Hey!" Collin pulled away and Erik quickly tripped backwards, striking the ground.

"Be chill, Justin," Kevin ordered and held the skateboard at ready. "He can't do anything to us."

"Really, yeah?" Collin withdrew a pistol from his back, pointing it in their direction. "I'm not fooling around here. I'll shoot you, I mean it!"

"Come on, Kev!" Erik fussed. "Let's get out of here!"

"No, Kev," Collin drawled. "You'll stay right here with your pretty good-lookin' friend!"

"Justin, make a break for it!"

Collin fired as Erik scrambled to his feet and gasped when the world around him turned hollow, with the only sound consisting of his heartbeat drumming in his ears.

Kevin went down, crumpling as a heap and Collin pushed past Erik, racing indoors. Erik knelt at Kevin's side, growing panicked when a pool of blood began to form beneath him. Turning him over, Erik sucked in a shallow breath, noticing the pierced helmet and Kevin's unblinking eyes.

"Kev, stay with me," he moaned and placed an ear to Kevin's chest, hearing the young man's heart skittering wildly. "Come on, Kev, don't die on me!"

Sidney stirred and slowly sat up, shaking his head. "Damn that firecracker," he groaned. "I knew that pig would muck stuff up!"

Collin came outdoors moments later, hurrying for the van. "Let's go," he called.

Sidney looked up and around, stunned once he realized what he faced. "Glory be!" he yelped and quickly sprang to his feet.

"Yeah," Collin snapped, "glory to the max!" He jerked at the door handle. "Let's split before them coppers come!"

"Fuck you, man!" Sidney scrambled for the van once it started.

Erik snapped to attention after the tires squealed and they pulled out, barreling away. He skated toward the porch and jumped the railing, then flung open the screen door. Hurrying indoors, Erik found various electronic equipment inside consisting of multiple video monitors and audio recording equipment.

"Who were they spying on?" he muttered and came across a telephone resting on a desk. Erik skated over and picked up the receiver. Instead of dial tone, he heard a series of mechanical chirps.

"This building will be obliterated in ten minutes and counting," a female mechanical voice said over the line. Erik dropped the receiver, stunned.

Racing through the door, Erik leapt over the steps and swiftly approached Kevin's downed body on the lawn, grabbing at his sleeve. "Come on, come on," Erik cried. "We need to get you out of here - they wired this place to blow!" Falling back, he struck his rear and tears welled in his eyes.

"Don't leave..." Kevin rasped.

Erik grabbed Kevin and held him close. "I'll stick with you,

I swear," Erik promised. "I know you have nobody else..."

"You're all I got..."

Erik heard a high whine and quickly ducked down over Kevin's body as a large explosion followed, causing everything to go dark.

SEVEN

Erik woke up with a start when he sensed movement and sat up, facing the mysterious woman standing over him.

"See you later," called a male voice and Erik heard the door shut behind him.

"Wait, what–?" Erik started and looked around, realizing he lay on a lumpy blue-upholstered couch in a small apartment with yellowed wallpaper. He looked over his shoulder, facing the white oak door leading to the exit.

"I didn't steal anything if that's what you're worried about," said the woman. Erik turned to her, dumbfounded. "I had one of my friends bring you in." She grinned. "Besides, you're too heavy to carry."

"Why...?"

"You'll prove useful. You got rid of a thorn in my side and I'm glad."

"But...!"

"I really don't care who you are, but if you had that kind of guts, then I assume you're either working for someone pretty nasty or you just don't care anymore."

"I..." Erik ran his hands through his hair, completely at a loss. He furrowed his brow as dull pain throbbed behind his eyes.

"I'm Osphena," replied the woman. Erik nodded, unsure what else to say. "Do you have a name?"

"I really don't remember," Erik murmured. "Do you have something I can take for a headache?"

Osphena frowned and left Erik's side. Erik moaned and lay back, draping an arm over his eyes.

"What did I get myself into?" he wondered. *"What am I doing?"*

"What should I call you then?" Osphena called from the next room.

"Whatever my VitaStat card says, I suppose," Erik called back.

"You don't have any ID on you."

"Don't tell me you had your way with me while I was out."

"Fine, I won't."

Erik's face burned and he blew a distressed sigh. *"I exist,"* he mused. *"I know I have someone out there looking for me. I live somewhere... Yet I don't have a wallet! Who would I ask?"*

Osphena approached Erik with a glass of water and a bottle of pills. She knelt at his side and Erik moved his arm, glancing up.

"Oh, thanks," he murmured and took the medicine from her.

"Did you always have headaches?" Osphena asked as Erik sat up and opened the bottle, then poured out several pills into his palm.

"As long as I could remember," Erik replied. "Only lately they've gotten worse."

"So bad that you can't remember who you are."

Erik nodded. "Right." He took the glass of water and swallowed the tablets.

"Would you mind staying here until you recovered your memory?"

Erik's face flushed. "It's not like I have much of a choice," he murmured.

"You're not imposing on me at all." Osphena stood and smiled gently at Erik. "I'm glad you can stick around for a while. I could really use your help on some things."

"Sure, I think I can help."

"I'm sorry for earlier," Osphena apologized and she took a seat across from Erik. "I was having a really bad day this morning."

"What about earlier...?" Erik looked to Osphena and she continued to smile. "I don't remember..."

"That's okay." She pat Erik's knee. "You know, you're pleasant to talk to and I'm glad you're not crazy."

"What if I was and just forgot that I am?"

Osphena giggled and Erik grinned. "I guess you're right. Anyways, until that time comes, are you hungry at all? What would you like for lunch?"

"Your choice."

Erik left the couch and followed Osphena into the small kitchenette that divided the parlor. He took a seat at a small painted table tucked in the corner on the dividing wall's other side while Osphena went to her refrigerator and pulled out several plastic containers. She withdrew a pitcher of lemonade and set it on the table before Erik then resumed preparing food at the counter.

"Do you ever have bad dreams?" Osphena asked as Erik poured the contents into the glass he still held onto.

"I don't know what to say about them," Erik replied and looked down at the glass he held, staring into pale yellow liquid with small chunks of lemon zest floating among the ice. "Why do you ask?"

"You were moaning and crying in your sleep."

"I guess you can say I've always had bad dreams, ever since I can remember." Erik sat back in his chair and sipped his drink.

"What is it that you dream about?"

"In my dreams I'm someone else... Somewhere else... And in that world, someone's always trying to kill me."

"What a horrible thing to dream! Are you feeling guilty about something?"

"That's the thing - I don't feel guilt." Erik snorted. "I'm afraid a lot of the time..."

"Afraid of what? Death? Dying?"

"I really don't remember."

Erik looked down at the glass he held, cringing when he heard the voices in his head.

Soon they'll find you...

Soon they'll force you to go with them...

It'll be too late then... it'll be the end of you!

Erik glared up at Osphena as she worked at the stove, frying a steak and potato wedges on the gas range. "*What does she want with me?*" he wondered.

"You seem tense," Osphena noted as she passed by the table. "Do you want anything to go with your drink?"

"I, er, vodka if you've got any," Erik answered.

Osphena returned with a half-pint bottle and set it next to the pitcher of lemonade. Erik unscrewed the cap and poured a bit into his glass, then swirled the ice. He tensed when she gripped the table's edge and leaned in. "Do you think I'm going to do something to you?" she asked.

"The thought never crossed my mind," Erik murmured, looking down at his drink.

"Would you rather I did?"

Erik looked up at the woman who smiled warmly. He took off the tinted glasses she wore, revealing wide ocean-blue eyes. Erik studied her face, with soft features and high cheek bones, tanned skin, wavy mahogany hair and full lips. He noticed she had a small mole under her left eye.

"Are you asking me to?" Erik murmured as he put the glasses atop his head.

Before she answered, the smoke alarm shrilled and Osphena turned away, surprised. "Damn it!" she yelped and ran toward the stove, banging pots as she tried dousing the flames.

Erik sipped his drink and shuddered. "A sandwich is fine," he said once Osphena left the stove and grabbed a newspaper. She stood under the smoke alarm and fanned the paper, dispersing the smoke curling around it.

"Yeah, sure, in a minute."

Erik looked briefly at Osphena, then went back to studying his drink. The telephone rang moments later and when Osphena made no motion to retrieve it, Erik left his place at the table and picked up the receiver nestled on the partition behind the refrigerator.

"Hello?" Erik greeted.

"Oh!" said the mysterious female voice, surprised. "What are you doing over there?"

"What?"

"I tried calling you and your line's off the hook. I was afraid something happened."

"Something did, I think..." Erik puffed a short sigh. "Look, don't worry about it. You don't have to go through all this trouble."

"What are you saying? Are you abandoning the mission?"

"What-?"

"Hey?" Osphena called when Erik dropped his glass with a crash. "What's the matter?" She approached and put a gentle hand on Erik's shoulder. "You're shaking... Come, sit down." Osphena pulled away the phone receiver and set it crosswise on the switchhook, then ushered Erik back to the table. She held one hand on his chest and the other lightly on his lower back as she guided him down into the seat. "Your heart's going a mile a minute! Are you okay?"

Erik gasped when he noticed her hand on his chest and took it, holding firmly. "I-I'm sorry," Erik murmured. "My mind was somewhere else and I was surprised when I heard..." He gave a strained smile. "I'm fine really."

Osphena moved her free hand to Erik's forehead and cheek, checking his temperature. Erik closed his eyes and took in a deep breath, inhaling a faint scent of sweet musk perfume.

"You're trembling all over," Osphena murmured. "Are you sure you're okay? You're really starting to scare me a bit."

Erik opened his eyes and flashed a brilliant smile. "Sure,"

he lied, "I'm fine."

"You sure?"

"Please..."

A tinny voice squawked in the background and Osphena abruptly let go of Erik's hand, returning to the phone off the cradle. Erik moaned and put his head down on the table, overwhelmed by uncomfortable feelings coursing through him.

EIGHT

Erik awakened, coughing and gasping for breath, overcome by a faint rotting order in the room. He immediately sat up, finding himself in a hard bed with no pillow in a plain white room with a barred window and an immaculately made bed on the other side.

Pushing off the gray sheets, Erik stepped out and shuffled to the lone closet near the door. Opening it, he found a single stainless steel toilet and sink with one knob on the faucet for cold water.

A plastic mirror bolted on the wall with a marred finish reflected a tired teenager with messy red hair and weary violet eyes who had freckles across the cheeks. He rubbed at his face and looked again, staring back at his usual tow-headed, blue-eyed self.

Hearing a knock on the room door, Erik tensed as it opened before he could answer.

"Is everything okay here?" Reinswitzer's voice called.

Erik turned, facing the young man who entered and stood at the lone washroom's doorway. His light green eyes appeared concerned as he folded his arms across his chest. Reinswitzer also wore a white lab coat over his light pink dress shirt, faded jeans and navy canvas shoes with white dragons on the front.

The red-tinted aviator sunglasses hung in his front pocket.

"I don't know," Erik replied. "Why did they knock me out before bringing me here?"

"My best guess is that in the case you escape," Reinswitzer answered, "you can't figure out where the exits are."

"Why are you being nice to me?" Erik demanded. "I'm nobody special."

"You're just as important as the next one."

"Then go bother with them."

Reinswitzer grinned. "I can't. We're going out to play today." He beckoned to Erik. "Let's go. You've got a test run."

Reinswitzer left his place at the door and Erik followed him down a plain cream-colored walled corridor with ivory floor tiles toward a single elevator. Reinswitzer pressed a button and they waited for the red light above to change color.

"What makes you think I'll be a willing cog to the machine?" Erik muttered.

"You already know the answer to that."

"Then don't be surprised if I try."

Reinswitzer appeared briefly alarmed and before he could open his mouth, the signal turned green and the doors opened, releasing several other men and women wearing lab coats. They entered after the other scientists and technicians stepped off, and Reinswitzer pressed an orange button with three black circles and a bar. The doors hushed close and the cable car began moving slowly downwards.

"It should be a short test," Reinswitzer said gently. "You shouldn't get hurt this time around."

"This time?" Erik spat. "So you *are* expecting a fight out of me?"

"They always fight, especially old dogs like you."

Erik clenched his teeth, looking at his reflection in the elevator door's silver finish. He noticed he stared back at a young man with red hair and violet eyes. Erik grunted and rubbed at his face to look again, only finding his reflection returned to normal.

"Are you all right?" Reinswitzer asked moments later. Erik nodded. "You sure?"

"I'm fine," answered Erik. "My mind's just a little scrambled, that's all."

Reinswitzer nodded. "Well, a bang to the head will do that."

The cable car stopped and the doors opened, revealing a vast empty lot with cool air blowing in from the outside through grated windows. Reinswitzer stepped out, walking with Erik across the lot toward a lone door at the end.

"Let me warn you before you go," Reinswitzer said evenly and opened the door, "I might act a little different for a while, so don't hold it against me."

Erik said nothing, watching Reinswitzer searching the hallway. After finding nothing of importance, they left and started for the abandoned lot's far end. Erik stiffened as the head guardsman Behr approached their general direction.

Behr adjusted his dark glasses tucked into the collar of his open jumpsuit, moving them to the front pocket. Erik grunted and came to a stop, holding his head when pain thundered behind his eyes.

Reinswitzer also halted, alarmed. "What's the matter?" he asked when Erik moaned and doubled over.

71

Behr snorted and approached, narrowing his black eyes at Reinswitzer. "What's the matter, boy?" he sneered, giving him a critical look. "Can't stand the sight of me?"

"Stay away from me!" Erik cried and yanked out of Behr's grasp when grabbed for.

"What do you want?" Reinswitzer demanded.

"I'm going to hunt you, boy," Behr growled. "You've ruined three good men!"

"What are you talking about?" Erik spat. "I don't know you!"

"It's not his fault you suck at your job controlling those ass wipes," Reinswitzer replied, smirking.

Behr glared at Reinswitzer and threw a swift right hook at Erik, flipping him over onto the floor. Erik scrambled to his feet and Reinswitzer held tight to his arm, keeping him from advancing.

"What was that for?" Erik shrieked and spat blood at Behr. "You heartless bastard!"

"I'll have you sucking on my fist before long," Behr snarled and stormed away.

"I'm sorry you took the hit for me," Reinswitzer said apologetically as the door slammed shut behind them. "There isn't much I can do about him taking out his anger on the patients..."

"What kind of place is this would allow him to do that?" Erik complained and yanked out of Reinswitzer's grip. "Don't tell me he outranks you!"

"Technically he does," Reinswitzer went on. "But don't worry about that. Most of us here are generally nice and not all of us are evil, sadistic bastards."

"Whatever!" Erik grumbled. "I don't know why he's acting like we met before... I don't remember ever being in this place!"

Continuing on their way Erik fell back several paces walking behind Reinswitzer, analyzing his surroundings. Above in the open-spaced corridor were fluorescent circular lights buzzing and every several feet, a grated window would break the monotony of the stone wall and painted brick. Erik peered out of one, catching sight of a lot below and vast fields behind it.

"Come on," Reinswitzer called, opening another heavily barricaded door.

Entering a small brightly lit area with one end closed off, the room was surrounded by many windows and one lone door on the other side armed with an automatic lock. Inside the enclosed glass cubicle sat a single middle-aged guardsman with long silver hair at a chair with a pair of headphones on, playing air guitar. Around him were many computer and video monitors and a large switchboard with many buttons of various colors flashing.

Reinswitzer knocked at the glass pane, trying to gain the oblivious warden's attention. "Hey!" Reinswitzer yelled and knocked harder. "Wake up in there!" He withdrew one of the guns he held from his waistband and banged it against the pane.

The guard looked up and fell out of his chair in shock. His hand reached up from the floor and struck a button, releasing steel panels slamming down on all sides of the small glass office, leaving only one side open.

"The hell!" the guard's muffled voice on the other side complained. "What are you tryin' to pull?"

"Damn it," Reinswitzer protested, "it's me, you crackhead!"

"Fuck you, man!" the guard complained. "I could've shot your ass!"

"Right!" Reinswitzer spat and rolled his eyes as he tucked the gun back into his waistband. "Got a G-seven forty-five case for you to run watch on," he said calmly.

The guard appeared at the lone window and squinted at Reinswitzer. He pushed his headphones back, hanging them about his neck and withdrew a pair of large horn-rimmed glasses from his shirt pocket. Putting them on his face, the guard blew a relieved sigh once he recognized Reinswitzer.

"Don't scare me like that, Nathan," the guard grumbled. "Where you gonna be at?"

"Woodlands, Section Forty-B."

"Yeah, got it." The guard struck a button on the switchboard. "Javier's waiting on you. So, what kind of test am I watching?"

"It's the three-S-A test."

Erik grew chilled at the mention as the guard snapped his fingers. "Oh, yeah, that one," said the warden. "Hey, I thought Murray was supposed to do it."

"He got his shoulder messed up."

"Send him some candy, okay?"

"Sure thing!"

A loud buzz resonated in the room and the locked door slowly swung open, revealing an enclosed parking lot. Reinswitzer grabbed Erik by the sleeve and pulled him along. Leaving the lot, they later exited through the driveway then walked toward a little used road. Continuing down the path, Reinswitzer cut across a field with Erik at his heels, heading into a heavily wooded area.

"How long will this test last?" Erik asked when they entered deeper into the woody canopy of maples and pines.

"It depends on you," Reinswitzer answered. A sharp ring penetrated the air and Reinswitzer withdrew a small brick-shaped phone from his slacks pocket. Pressing a button, he put it to his ear. "Hello?" he greeted. "Yeah, I'm about to do the Three-S-A test..." Reinswitzer blew an annoyed sigh. "What do you mean?" he yelled. "He isn't even outfitted yet!"

Reinswitzer motioned Erik to continue ahead as he stepped offside, proceeding with his conversation. Erik walked on, descending onto a narrow dirt path.

After walking for some time, Erik heard an engine roaring, followed by indistinct voices in the air and barking dogs. The sounds later tapered once he approached a clearing. Ahead from the field lay a low valley and a large crater, surrounded by numerous iridescent stones dispersed nearby.

Picking up a small lustrous rock near the edge, Erik felt warmth rapidly consume him and immediate pain shot through his arm. The burning sensation in his hands and arms returned full force and he gasped, dropping the stone as if it were hot.

Erik looked down at the crater's boundary with loose dirt and gravel underneath the leaves and dead vegetation scattered around. Noting the sinkhole had been covered over once before, he kicked at several glittering rocks littering along the crater's sides with his shoe, stirring up dust.

Erik coughed and waved away the cloud of dirt then cried out when pain slowly crept through his joints. He gripped his head, becoming overwhelmed as a memory came to the surface of an abandoned cabin made of redwood that had a plank deck and pane glass windows, surrounded by shifting shadows. He shook his head when the dreadful feelings followed and took off running.

Another set of footsteps followed Erik from behind and he turned, stopping as several men in black jumpsuits with copper buttons exited the shaded canopy, wielding fifteen-gauge shotguns.

Erik stood frozen in place when the apparent group leader, a tall young man with long wavy dark brown hair that had blond highlights feathered on the top and sides, and wavy curls near his shoulders stomped ahead, wielding a decorated saber instead of a gun.

The brown-haired stranger approached, wearing his jumpsuit unbuttoned down to his waist, revealing his broad chest and lean muscular stomach. Around his slender waist, he wore a gun belt with bullets around the circumference and dark wraparound sunglasses covered his eyes.

The stranger stood several yards away and held out his free hand, forcing the other men following him pause in step. He waved back and they retreated several paces, holding their firearms at ready.

The leader then sauntered up to Erik, grinning deviously. Erik noticed the young man was a head taller than he was, and had several tan freckles across his pale face.

The sword fighter said nothing, standing offside and staring at Erik as he nonchalantly twirled his saber. Erik clenched his hands when the painful burning increased, radiating up his arms and throughout his back.

"Hm..." the young man murmured and held his sword at ready. Erik quickly confronted him on the defensive, holding up his hands in guard. The sword fighter switched his stance and Erik switched his, trying to anticipate his attack. Striking out with a thrust, Erik quickly leaned back, watching the blade's point barely touch his nose. "Fast... I like that."

"Don't push me," Erik snarled and turned out as the young man slashed down.

Grabbing his wrist when the fighter stepped forward to reverse his stance, Erik snapped his hold, forcing him dropping the saber.

Erik kicked up the sword when his opponent pulled out and grabbed the cutlass in his free hand, turning around as his sword-wielding opponent reached behind himself. Erik directed the saber at his attacker's throat, facing a high-powered revolver pointed straight at his forehead.

"But I'm faster," Erik's aggressor said, grinning.

"What do you want?" Erik demanded.

"Remember, you must make the first cut."

Erik lowered the sword and let it fall to the ground. "Obviously I'm outmatched," he grumbled. "You want to shoot me, go ahead. It's been done."

"Tough guy, eh?" The young man let out a short laugh. "The killing stroke will come naturally... in time." He depressed the trigger and chortled when Erik flinched once it clicked.

"You pulled an empty gun on me?" Erik yelled and swiftly kicked his shin. The brown-haired fighter laughed, showing no sense of pain and pushed Erik away. "What are you, some raving barbarian?"

The young man tucked his gun back into his rear holster and kicked up his saber, sheathing it across his hips. "I thought it was funny," he complained.

"It's not!" Erik ranted. "I've had enough threats to my life without *you* adding to it!"

"Then teach me a lesson, eh?"

"I ought to knock you out!"

The stranger smiled brightly and beckoned to Erik. "Come on then, knock me out!" Erik's hands shook as he drew his fists and the young man tapped at his chin. "Land a solid on me!" he jeered. "You can do it!" When Erik backed away and lowered his hands at his sides, the brown-haired stranger razzed Erik. "And to think you were so tough!" he protested. "All talk and no action!"

"Your friends are going to shoot me no matter what I do," Erik snapped. "So I'm not going to waste my last minutes on your craziness!"

"Well, that's just too bad!" The young man grinned deviously as he untied the scabbard and raised it in the air. The outfit of armed men standing at ready quickly approached, surrounding them. "So what's your choice?" he asked, tossing the sword to Erik.

"You're not giving me any!" Erik spat as he caught the weapon.

"You do have a choice!" the fighter shouted. "Fight or die!"

Remember who you really are!

Prevail! Fight! Destroy!

"Fight or die, I suppose," Erik growled, glaring at the six men closing in on him with their rifles at ready.

"There's no escape," the leader crowed. "When you're not in your place, I'll put you where you need to be."

"How are you going to do that?" Erik spat.

"You don't know me for now... but once you're through here, you'll fear me!"

"I don't fear anyone!"

"Heh... they all say that." The young man backed away. "Yet if somehow you live through this, I want you to find me." He saluted Erik and ran away.

"I'll find you all right," Erik snarled, clutching hard to the sheath as he withdrew the blade. "I'm tired of all these people trying to kill me!" he hollered. "Just leave me alone!"

"One wrong move," one gunman snapped, "and you're full of lead!"

"That toy knife can't do jack shit on us!" spat another.

"What's it gonna be?"

"You're waiting on me to make a move, is that it?" Erik screamed and tightened his grip. "I just want to be left alone!"

"You will, in Hell!"

"Bring it!" Erik thundered. "You want me dead, then come on!"

"Fire!"

Erik cried out when struck by rubber bullets and staggered back from the barrage, stunned. He glared back and pointed the blade in their direction. "That really hurt," he snarled. "Do you really want to see how sharp this is?"

"Shit!"

Erik's vision flashed red and he attacked, ducking out their punches, kicks and swings from their gunstocks, beating them viciously with the scabbard and slicing into them with tempestuous fury.

Once the last gunfighter struck the ground, Erik heaved for breath, standing over their hacked remains. He swallowed the acrid taste in his throat when he looked at the bloodied saber then back at the mutilated bodies at his feet.

"Who knew you had it in you?" the young man's voice called. "What an incredibly fucking sick job!"

Looking up and around, Erik spotted the brown-haired stranger on the low valley's other side, standing atop a hill. He waved to Erik and continued onward down the other side.

"He knows what's going on," Erik muttered and dropped the sword. "He's got the answers I need!"

Taking off, Erik raced in the direction the brown-haired fighter took and tensed, hearing the barking of dogs following him. His speed increased as he clambered through the narrow path, returning into the deeply wooded interior.

NINE

Erik raced through the forest, tearing through branches and tripping over stones and roots. Breaking through onto a clearing, he happened upon a black van with tinted windows and its rear cab open.

Erik silently approached when he heard keys clattering and found a young man with curly red hair and large-framed tortoiseshell glasses typing onto a notebook computer across his lap as he sat on the van steps. Behind him were several large wire-frame cages and thick iron chains with wrist and ankle manacles.

The young man wore a white lab coat over a black T-shirt, chinos held up with red suspenders, and worn yellow and brown high-top sneakers. Erik coughed and the young man looked up, startled.

"Who are you?" the young man yelped and quickly shut the laptop.

"Who are you?" Erik shot back.

"I've got to get going." The young man stood, clutching his laptop tightly at his side. "Please, don't hurt me," he begged.

"Why would I hurt you?"

"Obviously because you're a bloody mess!"

"They attacked me first," Erik spat. "So unless you hurt me, then I won't hurt you."

"I'm not the one doing all the bad things to you; I'm just a lousy tech and just do as they tell me!"

Erik blocked the technician's path as he tried to hurry past. "First tell me what's going on!" Erik demanded and pushed him back.

The technician let out a yelp and staggered several paces. He tried to push past and Erik immediately grabbed him by the arm. The technician let out a cry and cringed as Erik twisted his arm at his back.

"Please," the technician wailed, "let me go!" Erik let go and the young man stumbled away, wincing in pain. "What strength...!" Erik took a step forward and the technician flinched, his blue-green eyes wide in fear.

Erik put up his hands on the defensive. "What are you talking about?" he demanded, narrowing his eyes. "I just want out of here."

"I-I can't do that."

Erik relaxed slightly and stepped forward to the cringing technician, holding out his hands with palms upward, showing he meant no harm. "Listen, I just need some help," he said gently. "If I tell you my name, will you tell me yours?"

"Yes, yes," the technician moaned.

"I'm Erik."

"Hayden."

Erik blew a frustrated sigh and stepped back. "I just want to know what this place is," he said, placing his hands to his hips, "and why I'm here. What do they want with me?"

"Well, I can't tell you *why* you're here and *what* they do..."

Hayden's hands shook and he shifted on his feet, clutching tighter to his notebook computer. "I really need to get back to my work; I've got a lot to do!"

"What were you doing with it?"

"Getting your test scores done."

"What does the Three-S-A mean in that particular test?"

"Speed, Strength, Stealth, and Activity," Hayden murmured, and then swallowed hard. "May I be left alone please?" he squeaked.

"Whatever," Erik grumbled. Turning away, he heard voices in the distance, accented by Hayden's typing on the laptop.

"*Me importa un comino,*" a familiar voice yelled. "I'm taking a ten-seventy whether or not you stupid fucks like it!" An indistinct shout followed in return. "Oh yeah, so take whatever the hell you want out of my paycheck; I'm working for goddamn peanuts anyway!"

Hernando stormed onto the path, lighting a cigarette with a shaking hand. After taking in a deep drag, he paused in step when he spotted Erik. "Erik!" he yelped, dropping his lighter. "What are you doing here?"

"He just showed up," Hayden replied nonchalantly as Hernando quickly scooped up the lighter off the ground. "His sense of direction needs to be refined."

"Shut up, Hayden," Hernando snapped. "Just tell me the scores and we'll be out of your hair."

"Passed the Strength and Speed portion," Hayden announced. "Unsatisfactory Activity portion and failed Stealth portion."

"Anything else?"

"He might have to get his overall strength increased. Doctor Rosenthal wants to enhance his endurance and stamina, given his prior test results."

"I'm fine the way I am!" Erik protested. "Why are you treating me like some kind of machine?"

"The point is to make you appear weak," Hernando said as he motioned toward Erik. Erik approached and Hernando took him by the shoulders with one arm and pointed ahead at Hayden with his free hand holding his burning cigarette. "It's so that whomever you're fighting will become overconfident and make sloppy mistakes."

"What are you saying?" Erik demanded.

"He's a lot like you, Erik," Hernando said, grinning. "Don't you see it?"

"Not really..."

"Go on, strike him."

"Do you really want me to do this?" Erik asked warily.

"Please don't!" Hayden wailed and stiffened when Erik approached.

"Just try!" Hernando goaded and laughed when Hayden picked up his laptop, trembling.

"I'm not going to hurt you," Erik said evenly as he neared Hayden. The technician immediately raised his computer. "You swing that at me and you destroy your precious data!" he barked. "Then you'll really regret it!"

"Then back off!" Hayden yelped.

"First tell me what place this is!"

"It's a rehabilitation center for violent criminals," Hayden answered. "That's all I can say..."

"I'm no criminal!"

Hernando laughed as he flicked aside his burned-out cigarette and picked up the one tucked on his ear. "Oh, come on, Hayden," he drawled and approached Erik. "I was just fucking around with you!"

"I hate it!" Hayden huffed and glared back. "You bastard!"

"Let's go," Hernando said to Erik, lighting the current cigarette with his lighter. "I'm down to my last two and Reinswitzer's car is an hour's walk from here."

Erik waved Hayden goodbye and walked with Hernando back for the narrow road. "Was he talking for real," Erik wondered aloud, "or just out his butt?"

"I'm not the one to ask," Hernando answered. "Suber might know something about it; I think he's all into it and whatever."

"Why would he say I'm a violent criminal?" Erik asked. "I don't have a record, as far as I know..."

"You were here last year for managing violent tenancies."

Erik came to a dead stop, astounded. "So Hayden might be right?" he cried.

Hernando let out a short laugh. "What do you mean, 'he may be right'?" He beckoned to Erik. "Come on, let's not waste time."

Erik clutched his chest suddenly pounding in pain. "*Is that what Danae meant by having unfinished business with me?*" he thought frantically. "*Did I do something exceptionally violent to her?*"

"*Ay, hombre,*" Hernando said, turning to Erik when he realized he was several paces behind. "What's bothering you?"

"Did I ever kill anybody?"

Hernando snorted. "I doubt it."

"Then why else would I be here?"

"What are you getting at?"

Erik held out his hands. "Look at me!" he shouted. "I just cut into those guys back there! I'm covered in their blood and guts and nobody gives a damn that they're dead!"

"Shit happens."

"They're dead!" The realization hit him hard and fast and Erik clutched his sides when his stomach turned. He turned away, vomiting painfully on the ground.

"Look, what is there to be worried about?" Hernando complained. "Okay, so you tend to snap sometimes, but something sent you there. We're just here to help you figure out why and piece you back together."

Erik spat on the ground, gasping weakly for breath. "So are the other people here that messed up in the head like I am?" he asked weakly.

"In differing degrees, yes." Hernando shrugged his shoulders. "But you just need to worry about getting better so you can go home."

"If you say so..."

Hernando grunted and tossed the smoldering stub on the ground then crushed it with his foot. "We should be about almost forty-five, maybe fifty minutes away or so." He pulled out the remaining cigarette on his ear to light.

"Why do you smoke so much?" Erik inquired as Hernando pocketed the lighter.

"It's because of nerves."

"Really, Doctor Hernando."

"It's a lot of things."

Erik sighed, knowing he was not getting an answer. They continued the rest of the way in silence.

TEN

Once back at the facility, Hernando led Erik to a room marked 'Decontamination' in bold print. Unlocking the door with a key card, they entered a cool room with cement floors and cinder block walls.

Hernando approached a nearby steel locker and opened it, revealing towels and scrub suits in various sizes.

"Medium, is it?" Hernando asked. Erik nodded and Hernando tossed Erik a towel. "I'll be waiting out here. Showers are in the back."

Erik caught the towel and made his way for the rear stalls. Stepping into a cemented room with drains on the floors and lime-encrusted showerheads, he pulled out of his bloodied clothes, throwing them aside on the floor. Turning the knob, Erik grunted when cold water blasted out.

After rinsing off, Erik peered out the doorway and spotted Hernando pacing at the door, turning his pack of cigarettes in his hand. Looking down, Erik saw a shirt and pants with socks folded at the floor. After pulling into them, he approached Hernando's side.

"What's wrong?" Erik asked.

"Oh?" Hernando stopped his pacing and waved at Erik to follow him.

Walking back to the elevators and returning upstairs to the third floor above street level, Erik stepped off, then turned back, facing Hernando as he tapped the pack of cigarettes he took from the carton against his hand. Erik stood in the cable car's middle, keeping the doors open with its sensors as Hernando forced up a filtered tip and put it to his lips.

"You usually smoke when you're extremely nervous," Erik commented. "Also, you chain smoke when you're frightened about something."

"I'm not scared," Hernando muttered, glancing up.

"Then what's wrong?"

"It's going to get worse from here," Hernando said softly. "I can't call you by your name, otherwise, *fallecimiento muerte...*"

"What?"

Hernando held up a clenched hand above his neck and tilted his head back, rolling his eyes to the back of his head while lolling out his tongue.

"I see," Erik murmured and stepped back, forcing the doors close.

"Erik?" a low voice called. Erik turned around, facing a middle-aged man with black hair fashioned into a pompadour style with a white streak down the middle and bushy eyebrows, graying temples and mustache with full beard matching his hair. The middle-aged man, in a tailored dark brown suit, walked stiffly toward Erik with a plain redwood cane that had a pewter handle. "I am Doctor Rosenthal," he greeted as he approached and put out a hand.

Erik stepped away, immediately disgusted. "You're the one who wanted more testing done on me," he spat.

"Well," Rosenthal huffed and lowered his hand. "I'm afraid that's so. I've been assigned to you during your stay here, so if you have any problems, you can come to me."

"Do I really need to be here?" Erik snapped icily.

"You're sick," Rosenthal replied sternly. "You're only here long enough until you get well."

"What am I here for?"

"Sleep disturbances I'm told, and maybe some psychotic episodes?"

"How long am I staying?"

"A minimum of forty-five days."

Erik narrowed his eyes. "Illness has its own course," he said evenly. "So, why should I be mandated to stay here so long if I'm supposedly that ill...?"

"We have medications to speed up the process."

"An answer for everything!" Erik snorted and crossed his arms. "Is it just you?" he demanded.

"No, I have my assistants Misters Fenway and Benedict checking on you. Also, for the times I am unavailable, you may also contact Doctor Schnell."

Erik stiffened when he heard the name. *"Chicago mentioned a man, Johann Schnell,"* he thought. *"So maybe he wasn't really talking crazy!"*

"Do you hear me?" Rosenthal called, breaking into Erik's thoughts. "If you act appropriately, you may be released early."

"What do you mean by acting appropriately?" Erik spat and scoffed. "Why should I care?"

Rosenthal rolled his eyes and puffed out a short sigh. "What else do I mean?" he said in annoyance. "Good behavior, Number

Three. It means obeying all orders given."

"What if the orders given don't make sense?" Erik retorted.

"Did you get a tour yet, Number Three?" Rosenthal snapped in return.

"I really don't want to be here!"

"How unfortunate." Rosenthal motioned for Erik to follow and he limped along with his cane.

"Might as well," Erik grumbled then walked alongside.

"At the end of this corridor is the main lounge," Rosenthal said as he ushered Erik into a large room with a tan leather couch facing a low table and a large-screen television.

Looking around, Erik saw a standing stereo system rest nearby and in the back were table hockey, table soccer, table tennis, and a pocket billiards table. At the far rear, stood a grand piano facing the barred windows. Outside the gated view, one could see the distant trees and hills, closed off by the electric fence and patrolling guards.

"Where is everyone?" Erik asked as Rosenthal led him down the hallway.

"Everyone is at lunch in the dining area."

Approaching another large room of similar layout with plank tables and stiff chairs, except for the couch and parlor games, in the rear were a large stainless steel refrigerator, a double sink, and two microwaves rest on the worn wooden counter. A large screen television played an action film and on the side of the set, rested an identical stereo system.

Erik noticed the eight other young men dressed in fitted beige pants and oversized white T-shirts, assorted at the plank tables and eating their meals in silence. He counted the chairs at the tables and realized they had enough room for fourteen people. Erik swallowed hard when he did the mathematics in his head.

"*I killed six of them,*" he thought in revulsion, stepping back out the room.

"Aren't you eating lunch?" Rosenthal inquired.

"I really don't feel very well," Erik murmured.

"We can give you something for it," Rosenthal said gently. "Go on, take a seat and I'll find some medicines for you."

Erik sighed and reentered the room, taking a seat at the rear table on the far end. He watched the others in front of him talking or watching the film. Erik's gaze then fell on the young man with feathered brown hair with blond highlights who left his meal on his tray untouched with the cover still on. He smiled at Erik, his dark green eyes brightening at the sight of Erik and Erik turned away, averting his gaze.

"Do you drink tea?" another voice said to Erik.

Erik looked up and behind, spotting a tall lanky young man with dark coffee-colored skin, wearing a black yachting cap low on his face, making it hard for Erik to see his eyes. The young man had a thin line mustache and a small square patch of hair on his chin.

"I'm not much of a tea drinker," Erik answered as the mocha-skinned young man held a mug in one hand while tucking a strand of his black shaggy shoulder-length hair from underneath the cap behind his ear. "What kind of tea are you having?" he asked instead.

"We have black, green, and white since they don't allow coffee here." The young man approached the sink and poured some water into the cup, then set it into the microwave and pushed a button, starting the heating process.

"I don't drink coffee, so I'm not missing anything, I suppose."

"Cola drinker then?" Erik snorted and the young man turned to him, also smiling. He pushed up his visor with his hand, revealing wide black eyes with wrinkles around the edges. "I'm Clayton." Erik gave his first name and Clayton nodded in response.

"So, how long have you been here?" Erik wondered aloud.

"Well... that's something I can't really talk about."

"Oh?"

Clayton pushed down his cap and turned away as an orderly in white scrub suit and a nurse in his white uniform who held a syringe filled with a clear serum entered the dining area.

"This medicine's for the sick feeling you have," the nurse said plainly upon approach.

"And why is *she* here?" Erik demanded, gesturing to the orderly.

"In the case you dislike needles," the orderly snapped.

"Are you expecting a fight?" Erik spat.

"You're willing to give me one?"

Erik sighed and held out an arm. He tensed once grabbed for and the nurse tightened his grip, injecting Erik in the crook of his elbow. After draining the syringe's contents, the nurse and the orderly left. Clayton returned to Erik's side with a small plate consisting of an apple pie wedge and a short cup of chocolate milk.

"Is this lunch?" Erik asked as Clayton pushed the meal toward him.

"You came in late, so all you get is leftovers," Clayton answered. "Today was a nice day."

"Are the meals usually bad?"

"It keeps you alive if you want to," Clayton replied dryly.

Erik shrugged his shoulders. "The food doesn't look all that good anyway," he murmured.

"None of it is." Clayton grinned and Erik chuckled.

"Outside time," a voice called. A large bald man with thick dark brown eyebrows and piercing hazel eyes entered the room. He wore a thin black turtleneck straining against his muscular upper body and faded stonewashed jeans with high-cuffed laced leather boots. "Come on, don't make me wait here," he barked. "I've got a lot of shit to do!"

"Take it with you," Clayton said as the microwave beeped. Erik took his meal with him as the other young men assembled into a neat line at the door.

"Mister Fenway," one of the patients asked, "are we playing basketball today?"

"Yeah, it's nice enough." Fenway grumbled. The group cheered and Fenway checked a chart he held, counting how many were going out. "Hey, we're six short, Benedict," he called out in the corridor. "I thought we were supposed to have fifteen once that new shit got in."

"They had an early withdrawal," Benedict's voice called back from the corridor.

Clayton approached Erik's side moments later, holding his steaming mug with a tea bag floating in the dark water. "You look ready to hurl," Clayton murmured. Erik nodded, saying nothing.

Fenway grunted and wrote a note in his clipboard then stomped away. The group followed in step, eventually coming to a door armed with a passkey mechanism, palm reader, and a thumbprint verifier.

Fenway pulled out a card from his pocket and swiped in the reader, then pressed his right thumb onto the small glowing red pad, followed by pressing his left hand onto the larger glowing turquoise pad. A loud buzz resonated in the air and the door opened, revealing a patio and a basketball court. Erik felt disturbed as everyone else ran ahead and he followed Clayton to the patio table and chairs.

"Hey," Clayton called to Erik. "You sure you're altogether?"

"This place is bothering me," Erik murmured as he put his meal aside on the table. "I feel like I've been here before."

"You probably have, but with all the drugs they pump in you, it's really easy to forget."

"You: go play with them," Fenway snapped upon approach and dropped his clipboard in front of Erik. "I don't want to be bothered."

"But...!"

Fenway pushed Erik away. "I need to talk to him," he grumbled.

"Clayton!" Erik protested and Clayton shook his head.

"I'll catch up," Clayton promised. "Your snack will be on the other table close to the game, okay?"

Erik sighed and nodded, then stomped to the court where the others played three-on-three, while the young man with the feathered brown hair stood near the boundary line, keeping score.

Abruptly, loud digital tones screeched in the air and Erik cringed when the thudding pain in his head increased, spreading down his neck and back. Searching around for the source, he spotted the many speakers installed around the premises.

Looking back at Fenway, he saw the director appeared unaffected and Clayton hunched over his tea, shaking slightly in obvious pain. Erik rubbed at his eyes and ran a hand on his neck, sensing the muscles tighten. Moments later, his ears and eyes throbbed and he moaned, shutting his eyes as he rubbed at his temples.

"Let's play Horse!" one of the young men called.

Erik grunted and took a seat at the benches near the sidelines, watching as the game came underway.

ELEVEN

While watching the others trying each player's specific throw to get the basketball into the hoop, Erik felt a tap on his shoulder. Erik turned, finding no one there.

"So, you must be new here," said a familiar voice. "You're cute."

Erik turned around, facing the young man with the feathered dark brown hair and tan freckles on his face. Erik immediately put up his hands. "Sorry," he said, "I don't swing that way."

The stranger's narrow green eyes gave Erik a haughty look as he put a hand to his hip and ran the other through his wavy curls on his shoulders. "Do you hate socializing or something?" he complained.

"It's not that I dislike socializing," Erik snapped. "Why isn't everyone else having a violent reaction to the noise?"

"It's quite pleasant if you don't mind the minor discomfort."

"If you say so." Erik turned away and grew annoyed when the young man blocked his view of the game. "I thought you wanted me to find you," he said sourly, glaring back. "So why are you in my face?"

"I already told you."

Erik blew a heavy sigh and put on a fake smile as he gave

his name, putting out his hand.

"I'm Josef Stein," Josef said nonchalantly. "You can call me Joe if you want... everyone else does."

Erik put his hand back when Josef made no motion to shake it in greeting. "So how long are you going to keep staring at me?" Erik grumbled. "You're creeping me out."

"You're like me, aren't you?" Josef accused.

Erik gave him a blank look in return. "I don't quite follow," he said slowly, growing uncomfortable with the awkwardness between them.

"It's almost like looking in the mirror, you see..."

"We're nothing alike," Erik snapped. "Nothing about us is the same."

"We both bleed, right?"

Erik took a step away. "What does it matter to you?"

Josef took a step forward. "You're a Galkan, right?" he pressed.

"I don't know what that is," Erik muttered and Josef smirked in reply. "Why, is it something important?"

"Don't lie to me." Josef narrowed his eyes. "You're lying," he sneered.

Erik sucked in a shallow breath and took another step away, growing apprehensive. "Then what is it you want from me?" he pleaded.

"Look up at the sky," Josef suddenly said.

Erik looked up, shielding his eyes from the bright afternoon sun shining brilliantly down from behind shifting dark clouds. "It looks like it's going to rain soon," said Erik.

"Oh, apple pie and chocolate milk, huh?" Josef said instead.

"That's my favorite."

"I don't care for apple," Erik muttered, studying the clouds. "I like cherry personally."

"You really should eat something." Erik looked down at Josef who held his plate of pie with the cup of milk resting nearby on the table next to him. "You're starving, aren't you?"

"I'm fine," Erik protested.

"You're too thin!"

"I'm not that skinny!"

"What are your stats then, string bean?"

"Five-eleven and one-forty-five last I've been to the doctor."

"Damn, and they actually think you're worth something?" Josef scooped up a piece of pie in his fingers.

"What's that supposed to mean?"

Josef gave a malicious smile and suddenly thrust the food on his fingers into Erik's mouth. Erik stiffened, staring at Josef in shock and pulled away.

"Chew," Josef ordered and Erik winced from the bitter apples in the dessert. "Tell me," Josef said, grinning craftily, "how does it taste?"

Erik's face distorted in disgust. "It's horrible," he protested and spat it out on the ground.

"You didn't swallow!" Josef retorted and scooped up another piece. Erik slapped his hand away and Josef backhanded Erik, throwing him down on the table. Josef pounced on Erik and Erik grabbed his wrists, struggling to hold him back.

"Get away from me!" Erik shouted.

"I will feed you more!" Josef crowed.

"Somebody get this nutcase off me!" Erik screamed.

"They don't care!" Josef kneed Erik's groin and Erik coughed, seizing in pain. Josef shoved in the pie and Erik gagged as Josef covered his mouth with his hands. "Swallow!" Josef commanded.

Erik threw a punch at Josef, socking his chest. Josef fell back and Erik kicked him away, sending him crashing on the ground. Turning on his side, Erik spat out the food and coughed hard to keep from choking. The urge to vomit came strongly and he moaned as dry heaves wracked his body.

"Oh, you're a bad boy," Josef snarled over Erik. "You're going to need a lot of training." Erik sat up on the table's edge, glaring back at Josef holding the pie in his hand. "Now if you just do what I say, I'll leave you alone."

"Back off!" Erik bellowed.

Josef held the pie several inches from Erik's face. "Now eat it," he snarled.

"You're trying my patience!" Erik thundered and wound up for the hardest punch he could muster.

Josef grabbed Erik's fist, whirled him around, twisting his arm around his back and held him close as he wrapped his free arm across Erik. Erik gasped, stunned at Josef's speed as he leaned in.

"I'm faster than you," Josef sneered in Erik's ear. "Never forget it." He smeared the food and crust on Erik's face as Erik struggled to get out of his hold. "You see, I'm going to destroy you if you ever cross my path." He grabbed Erik by the hair and yanked back his head. "Now tell me, how does it taste?" Erik stiffened when Josef licked his cheek then released his hold, kicking him down to the ground. "Tastes good if you ask me," Josef teased and chortled.

Erik scrambled to his feet, heaving for breath as his rage reached its limits. "What are you talking about?" he hollered. "I don't know you!"

Josef grinned. "You really need to bulk up a bit," he said gaily instead. "Besides, you'll eventually get used to the food here." Josef licked his fingers, smiling brightly at Erik. "It's really not that bad," he chirped.

"That's enough," Fenway called before Erik made a swing. Erik whirled around, facing the orderly standing offside with her arms folded across her chest. The nurse stood next to her with the capped syringe holding an orange serum.

"Do something about that nutcase," Erik exploded, "before I do it!"

"He's not the problem here," Fenway spat. "You're the dangerous one."

Erik glared at Josef who beamed cheerfully in return. "Stay away from me," he roared, "or so help me, you're going to hurt so bad!"

"We'll see about that," Josef retorted and left Erik's side, then returned to the game being played.

Erik grunted and wiped at his face with his sleeve. "*I don't know whether if this is his demented way of showing attraction,*" he mused, "*or he's just screwing with my head!*"

Erik approached the table and picked up the paper cup of milk. Swirling its contents, he downed it, hoping to wash out the bitter taste in his mouth. The liquid burned his throat and Erik dropped the cup, clutching his neck as his throat tightened.

He collapsed to his knees, struggling to breathe.

"Are you lactose intolerant?" Josef called moments later. He approached offside and kicked Erik onto his back, forcing him looking up at the bright overcast sky. Erik blinked slowly as his vision wavered and turned hazy. "Are you dying?" Josef stamped on Erik's chest, jarring him. "You can't sleep out here, you know!" Josef gave another whack and Erik gulped for air when the choking sensation passed. "Let's play twenty-one before it rains."

Erik groaned and sat up, gasping for breath. "Do we have to?" he groused.

"Let's play!"

All noise around Erik abruptly cut off, leaving only the sound of his weak breathing in his ears. Josef grabbed Erik by the wrist, yanking him to his feet and Erik held in a shallow breath when he saw a younger John Greenfield standing before him, patting his back.

"Are you all right?" John Greenfield asked.

Erik shook his head, watching Josef stomping towards the court, basketball tucked under his arm. He turned around, watching the other players who sat on the benches offside, talking amongst themselves.

"Come on," Josef called.

Erik grunted after the ball bounced off his head. He caught the basketball and dribbled back for the court, turning out of Josef's guard then threw it into the basket above him.

"I believe that's one," Erik said as the ball rattled the chained net and fell to the ground behind them.

Josef leaned in close going around him, sneering. "Lucky

shot, is all," he hissed and shoved Erik's side then stalked past, capturing the ball.

"Let's get this over with," Erik grumbled and played against him halfheartedly.

Erik felt out of place as his body at times refused to respond to his mental commands when he moved within a waking dream, with memories of the past colliding to his current present reality.

He froze when he caught glimpses of the younger John Greenfield playing against him in his dress shirt, slacks, and basketball sneakers, sans tie, blazer and oxfords - only to get rudely brought back to the present with a ball check against his head, knocking him down.

"Come on, Erik!" Clayton called to Erik, getting him out of his fog. "Use some smooth moves!"

Erik stopped to watch Josef moving fluidly around on the court, making various spectacular, extraordinary forms. Though he made little effort to score points, if he stood still for too long, Josef threw the ball at him to make him move.

Josef made a head fake and leaned back as he rolled the ball from one hand to the other, tipping it into the basket above Erik. "Thirteen to seven," Josef said, retrieving the ball and threw a chest pass.

Erik caught it and pulled back as Josef approached, dribbling the ball around him. "Two can play your game," Erik snapped.

"Let's see it," Josef spat, slapping the ball out of hand.

Erik raced after him as he whirled around to capture the

loose ball. Josef elbowed Erik back and pulled away, aiming for a jump shot. Erik successfully blocked when he timed his jump and slapped the ball away.

"I believe that's called the Flyswatter," Erik said smugly after Josef caught the ball before it bounced out of bounds.

Josef bared his teeth and threw the ball at Erik's head. Erik caught it and turned serious in his game play, copying the moves Josef used against him.

In return, Josef's forms began to become more exaggerated, his fakes more pronounced, trying to outwit Erik. Erik grew rattled as Josef began using harder checks and he scrambled to keep ahead of one who stayed elusive in a game Erik knew little about, yet somehow, mastered all the mechanics.

Josef shouldered Erik's chest, launching him to the pavement. Erik grunted and looked up at Clayton from his place on the ground. Clayton held his mug of tea in his hands and grinned at Erik.

"Don't let him read you," Clayton said. "Get back up and get your head in there!"

Erik jumped to his feet and stormed over, catching an attempted head shot. "You're sloppy," Erik spat and threw the ball back, then ran after Josef as the young man outmaneuvered around him.

"I'm better!" Josef sneered and rushed towards the basket, dribbling and skipping, hoping Erik would be too unfocused to see what he'd do next while guarding him.

After watching his movements, Erik simply slapped the ball aside once he took on a behind the back shot and caught the basketball before it rolled away. Clayton burst out laughing and whooped for Erik.

"Man, Erik sees them before you make them, Joe!" Clayton called as Erik ran up to the basket, jumped, circled the ball around his body and leaned back before slamming it in. Erik slammed on his feet and slipped to his haunches, wheezing for breath.

"Whoa, he flew!" one of the patients cried out. The chained net rattled as the basketball rushed through.

"That, my friends," Clayton called, "is an alley-oop-'round-the-world-fadeaway slam dunk!"

"You're so crazy," someone from the crowd drawled and everyone else laughed.

Thunder rumbled in the air and Erik rose upright, approaching Josef who glared at him, panting for breath with his hands on his knees.

"You know he's kidding, right?" Erik said.

"Fucking showoff," Josef growled as the ball rolled to him and he stepped on it with his foot to keep it from going past.

"That's twenty-one to twenty," Erik replied simply. "You got what you wanted, now leave me alone."

"Of course," Josef sneered in return and kicked up the ball. He threw it at Erik's head and Erik caught it easily.

"Why are you being such a sore loser?" Erik demanded.

"You never played basketball like that, Brother," Josef snarled and snatched the ball away. "You hated it after street moves were introduced."

"What now?" Erik yelped in shock.

Josef stomped away for the foul line and started throwing the basketball in. The chained net rattled each time the ball swooped in and the ball rolled back to Josef then he repeated his tries. Erik felt a firm hand on his shoulder and he looked up, finding no one there.

"The wind is changing," called Clayton's voice, startling Erik. He flinched and rubbed at his eyes, shaking his head to clear the fogginess. He looked back at Josef who tossed the basketball into the basket with relative ease. Clayton walked up to Erik, nudging him with his elbow. "You okay?"

Erik nodded. "I'm just a little out of it," he murmured. "I'll be all right, though... thanks for asking."

"We'd better hurry on in."

"What about Joe?" Erik asked, following the others who filed inside.

"He'll come around after making twenty-one successful shots."

"What if he misses?"

"He'll start on another line and tries it again."

"He's obsessed."

"That's an understatement."

Erik grew chilled as the sound of the basketball bouncing quickly stopped and the winds around them plummeted to freezing shears. He heard angry steps and turned about, finding Josef charging at him with a raised fist. Erik grabbed his hand before it met his face, shaking as he struggled to break through.

"No one *ever* shows me up!" Josef growled, his dark green eyes turning brown in hatred.

"I'm just a bit better than you when it comes to basketball," Erik said sheepishly. "Honestly, I wasn't trying all that hard!"

"You liar!"

"I'm a natural, admit it."

"Bullshit and you know it!" Josef pulled away and threw another punch.

Erik caught Josef's hand and pushed him away. "Don't start with me!" he snarled.

"How did you get to be so great in basketball, eh?" Josef spat. "You were never interested before!"

"It's called practice," Erik retorted. "I've got magic flowing from my fingertips."

"Shut up!" Josef swung with a swift left, smashing his fist into Erik's side.

Erik crumpled to his knees and doubled over. "Maybe you don't know this, but my memory's screwed up," he groaned from his place on the ground. "I remember some stuff and I don't remember some stuff. Deal with it!"

"I'll take note of that," Josef snapped and stormed indoors.

"Come on," Clayton said gently, extending a hand to Erik.

Erik grabbed his wrist and Clayton pulled him to his feet. "I'm fine," Erik muttered.

"Let's hope."

TWELVE

Returning to the dining area, Erik paused when he saw covered plates on the plank tables and everyone took their assigned seats. An orderly went around with a tray, setting down cups of juice.

"I thought we just had lunch," Erik said, searching the room. "Where's the clock?"

"There are no clocks here," Clayton replied, taking a seat. "There are no calendars either. It's seven if it's breakfast, noon if it's lunch and five if it's dinner and just the same day every day for everyone."

Erik blew a resigned sigh and sat next to Clayton, then uncovered his plate. He recoiled in disgust when he revealed two scoops of seasoned ground beef. "What else will be served here?" Erik asked, pushing his plate away.

"That's it," said the orderly upon approach and handed Erik a cup. "Enjoy."

"Are you mad?" Erik yelled.

The orderly glared at him then his expression quickly changed and he laughed at Erik instead. "You need more meat on your bones," he said with a wide smile. "Besides, you're too damn thin!"

"I want this meat cooked, thank you!" Erik shouted, picking

up the beef patty. "Can't you people see this is completely raw? It's not browned at all, not even for a second!" He chucked it at the wall and it stuck for a moment before sliding down to the floor. "This is uncooked and I don't eat bloody raw food! That mess can kill me!"

"Hey, *steak tartare* is considered a delicacy in some places!"

"Only if it's chopped up with onions or something!" Erik spat. "Let those rich oil barons eat this raw mess, because I'm not!"

"It's not raw," the orderly persisted. "It's just covered in egg, is all!"

"That's still raw!" Erik squawked.

"Protein's good for you!"

"Then *you* eat it!"

"I'm sorry, I'm a strict vegan." The orderly smiled wryly. "That includes eggs and milk!"

"Then what's that?" Erik pointed to the orderly's sandals covering his large bony feet. "That's made of leather, you *strict vegan!*"

The orderly paled for a moment then waved Erik away, chortling. "It's only synthetic leather, silly boy!" he crowed. "It's made of old dinosaurs!"

"Come on, Erik!" Josef chided and the other young men jeered him. "Just eat already! We won't have free time if you hold us up!"

"What is this?" Erik complained. "What madhouse is this?" He struck the table with his fist. "What do you mean?"

"It means," growled Josef as he approached, pushing his tray toward him, "if you don't follow the rules, the rest of us gets punished!"

"It's a stupid rule," Erik snapped. "It's not right for you to be punished if I refuse to eat this horrid food."

"Life isn't always fair, now is it?" Josef grumbled and placed his hands on the edge of the table, leaning forward. "Well?"

Erik glared back, then turned to Clayton who huddled over his tea with his cap hanging low, silent. "No," Erik muttered.

"Listen," Josef said evenly and grabbed Erik's chin in his hand, forcing him looking ahead. Erik straightened his stance and glared at Josef who tightened his grip. "I enjoy my free time here. If I don't get it, I become particularly nasty!"

"I don't care," Erik said icily. "Screw your free time - I refuse."

"You're going to get injected by that nurse that's on my side if you don't eat your meal," Josef growled and returned the cold, hard look. "You really don't want that, now do you?"

Erik clenched his teeth when a nurse offside stepped closer toward him and stiffened when he noticed she held a capped syringe, filled with a dark orange serum. "Fine," Erik said through gritted teeth and Josef let him go.

"Good boy," Josef said brightly and pat him on the head.

"Don't touch me," Erik growled and picked up his plastic fork then jammed the utensil into the pile of beef. He glared at Josef as he bit into it, swallowing hard as he resisted the urge to vomit. Josef watched him intently with an amused expression on his face.

"You really didn't enjoy that," Josef said and tapped at the table. "Come on, eat up." Erik's eyes watered when he took another bite. "Tastes good, huh?"

"I feel ill," Erik moaned.

Josef chuckled and returned to his seat across from Erik. "You'll get used to it," he said brightly.

Erik groaned and held his sides as the sloshing in his guts worsened. Turning away, Erik vomited the meat on the floor and ran his hand over his sweat-drenched face.

"Tasted better going down than up, eh?" Clayton cracked wryly. "Don't worry," he said softly as Erik dropped forward in his seat and hid his face in his arms, groaning in pain. "It's going to be okay. Just avoid Joe for a while... he can get a little intense."

Later after dinner, the other patients were ushered toward the lounge and most of the young men clustered on the floor as Fenway put in a videodisc about teamwork. Josef made a straight line toward the piano and played a soft melody, while ignoring everyone else. Erik walked toward the billiards table with Clayton and waited on him to set the ceramic balls.

Clayton broke the set and the game between him and Erik got underway. As Clayton struck the cue ball with his cue stick, another middle-aged man with short gray hair, comb-style mustache and narrow brown eyes entered the room, wearing a pressed polo shirt and chinos with oxfords.

"I heard there was a problem with dinner today," he said to Fenway who stood near the door, watching the group.

"Yeah," Fenway answered, writing into his clipboard. "Number Three over there wasn't happy with the food served."

"Is he vegan?"

"Chart says he takes a normal diet."

The middle-aged man walked up to Erik and smiled brightly. "Hello, Erik," he said calmly. "I'm Mister Benedict."

Erik cringed when the sounds from the videodisc suddenly turned loud. He gripped the pool cue tightly while Clayton measured his next shot. "How are you?" Erik asked through gritted teeth.

"I'm fine and you?" Benedict replied in return.

"Dizzy."

"I'm sorry to hear that."

"I'm calling it a night," Erik said to Clayton and set his cue stick aside.

"It's fine," Clayton replied and Erik headed for the door.

Benedict followed Erik and Fenway blocked Erik's path, pushing him back into the room. "You have to stay for Group Therapy," Fenway growled.

"My ears are going to bleed if I keep in here!" Erik protested.

"Then let them!"

"That's it," Erik huffed. "I'm out of here, whether you demented people like it or not!" He shouldered past Fenway, only to get grabbed roughly by the arm and yanked back, forcing him against the wall.

"You don't want to do that," Fenway grumbled. "If beating you won't work, we can always have you drugged into submission!"

"Keep trying," Erik spat, "because it won't work!"

"I'm afraid you'll have to be written up for noncompliance," Benedict stated.

"So what of it?" Erik snapped, shaking out of Fenway's grasp. "Give me all the write-ups you like. I'm not staying."

"Get Nelson," Benedict ordered. "It seems we have a Code Black here."

"Which one?" Fenway grumbled.

"Tsenninger. He's the one with Blazejewelski." Erik grew ill at ease as Fenway nodded and left him before Benedict. "You see Number Three," Benedict explained, "we don't do mere 'write-ups' here. They are followed by more *extreme* measures."

"What measures are you talking about?" Erik asked weakly. "Does it have anything to do with Nelson?"

"Oh, have you met him before?"

Fenway returned with another tall thin young man who had tanned freckled skin, long, braided greasy black hair hanging down the middle of his back and a large crooked nose in white scrub shirt, tight button-fly jeans and cuffed leather boots.

Erik took a step back and clenched his hands as the nursing technician glared at him with narrow blue eyes. Nelson approached, reaching for Erik and Erik threw a swing.

"Don't touch me!" Erik shouted as Nelson quickly sidestepped the attack. Nelson countered, slamming his elbow across Erik's chin. Erik's head whipped back and he stumbled rearward, dazed. Nelson then kicked Erik in the chest with a hard front stomp, sending him crashing to the floor on his back.

"I should've known it's the scrappy little fighter," Nelson said cheerfully over Erik and grinned darkly. "What do you want me to do to him?"

"Stabilize him," Benedict commanded.

"I've got just the thing." Nelson stepped on Erik, keeping him down on the floor. Erik grabbed his foot and Nelson jammed his heel into Erik's chest. "Now stay still," Nelson snarled and withdrew a capped syringe containing an orange serum from his shirt pocket.

Erik punched Nelson in the groin and shoved him back, jumping to his feet. Nelson dropped the syringe and staggered rearward. Fenway tackled Erik before he grabbed the syringe and wrestled him down to the floor, pinning his arms behind his back. Erik struggled against Fenway holding him down, vainly trying to throw him off.

"Hurry up!" Fenway barked as Nelson scooped up the needle.

Nelson crouched next to Erik and yanked down his waistband, jamming the needle into his hip. "That ought to do it," he said and injected the serum.

Erik thrashed underneath Fenway's grip and snapped at Nelson when the technician pat his bottom. Fenway slammed his shoulders into Erik's back, forcing him still as Nelson rose upright.

"Stop fighting, punk!" Fenway growled. "Or you're getting more than a beating!"

"Get your hands off me!" Erik screamed.

"Then stop acting up!"

"Fine!" Fenway let go and Erik scrambled to his feet. "Keep that monster away from me," Erik shouted. "He touches me and I swear—!"

Nelson smiled deviously at him, pointing at his eye. "I'm watching you real close, little boy," he sneered. "Don't think you can run from me for long."

"You're dead!" Erik screamed and Nelson backed out of a furious swipe.

"Sit your ass down!" Fenway shouted and punched Erik in the face, throwing him to the floor. Erik groaned when he hit the hardwood, seeing stars.

"I'll get the orders straightened," Benedict said calmly. "It seems the medications aren't working."

"Yeah, do that," Fenway spat. Benedict pushed past him and left the room. "You: sit over there," Fenway ordered, pointing toward the couch.

Josef suddenly stopped playing and left his place at the piano, approaching the edge. He beckoned to Erik and pat the nearby cushion. "Sit next to me," Josef called.

"I'd rather sit with Clayton," Erik grumbled, holding his busted lip.

"He's got other stuff to be bothered with," Fenway snapped irritably as Benedict returned with an armful of charts. Clayton's expression turned blank and he left the pocket billiards table, approaching Benedict's side. Both left the room and Erik rose unsteadily upright, then stomped toward the couch. "Now sit down and shut up!" Fenway growled.

Josef grabbed Erik's hand, pulling him down next to him. Erik froze when Josef stroked his hair. "Feels nice, doesn't it?" Josef murmured.

Erik pushed Josef away. "Stop touching me!" he snapped. "Do you want me to beat you?"

"Do you find pleasure in that sort of thing?" Josef retorted.

"You disgust me."

"Let's enjoy the show." Josef draped an arm around Erik's shoulders and Erik pulled away, then stiffened when pulled into a headlock. Josef leaned in. "You need to stop fighting," he hissed. "Otherwise, you'll be met with much, much worse - something much harsher than a beat down."

Erik punched Josef in the chest and pushed him away once

let go. "Will you stop touching me?" he spat. "How many times do I have to keep telling you that?"

"I can't help it," Josef replied. "You're just too cute!" He reached forward and Erik slapped his hand away, then stood.

"Touch me again," Erik snarled. "Or I will–!"

"Or you will what?" Josef retorted, smirking. "There's nothing you can do to me here."

Erik broke out in cold sweat and doubled over clutching his sides when suddenly overcome by spasms of coughing. He gagged and slipped to his knees, wheezing for pained breath.

"Oh, come now," snapped Josef in annoyance.

"What was in that needle?" Erik wailed.

"A mere tranquilizer, Brother," Josef replied simply. "You seem too much on edge these days."

Erik narrowed his eyes at Josef who smiled brightly down at him. "It's poison and you know it!" he snarled.

"You're right." Josef shrugged. "They're trying to kill us..."

"Why are they trying to get rid of me?"

"You've done something bad, obviously. What did you do?" He perched next to Erik and stroked his sweat-drenched face. "Did you kill someone?"

"Did you?" Erik rasped and shut his eyes as the world around him slowly became tinted in red.

"You most likely got a mix of Star Ruby, Emerald Dust and Fair Jewel," Josef murmured while caressing Erik's hair. "You will get sick, but it won't kill you... well, maybe if the right amount is used."

"What do they do?" Erik asked fearfully. "I already know about Star Ruby unfortunately..."

"Separately, Emerald Dust causes one to fall into an oblivious state and Fair Jewel makes one's senses overloaded by the most minute of stimulation - light, sound, touch even. Since you already know that Star Ruby causes paralysis, I don't need to explain." Josef chuckled. "Anyway, since these little things have different reactions once mixed together, it's known that Emerald Dust and Fair Jewel cause psychotic episodes and with Star Ruby, you suffocate slowly as your body shuts down."

"So they *are* trying to kill me!"

Josef tugged at Erik's hair and Erik's eyes snapped open, glaring up at Josef who looked down at him, smirking. "If they were, that amount would have killed you by now." Josef teased and chortled. "What you got is a warning, Brother."

"How can you put up with this?" Erik hissed and Josef shrugged.

"You get used to it." Josef slapped Erik sharply across the face and he fell back, striking the floor. Josef rose upright, looking down at Erik with a dead expression in his eyes while he rubbed his hand. "Unless you like getting beaten down all the time."

"No one runs me," Erik growled.

"Then they'll run you to the ground until you die!" Josef stepped over him and returned to the piano, banging on the keys striking flats and sharps.

"This will calm your nerves," the nurse's voice said from above.

Erik shut his eyes and gave up fighting when injected again, consumed by pain nearly drowning him in the darkness. He struggled to breathe as it became increasingly difficult and seized when strong hands grabbed him by the arms and legs.

Pulled apart and carried to a new location, Erik felt his body slam down onto a cold metallic surface and his limbs immobilized by thick heavy straps. He struggled against his restraints once he heard a drill whirring.

"This should work this time," Blazejewelski's voice grumbled into the room, his voice echoing throughout. "Nelson, try the scalpel."

Erik stiffened when he felt a slice to his cheek.

"The surgical knife cut cleanly," replied Nelson. "The stone skin property is effectively neutralized from the Fair Jewel serum."

"One of you bolt down his head. We need to get in deep."

Erik felt warm hands hold onto his face, forcing him still. Opening his eyes, he looked up at a familiar face covered by a surgical mask, his worried pale violet eyes staring back.

"I'm sorry," murmured Suber, strapping a thin metal bar across Erik's forehead and chin, securing it into place with leather straps. "I have no control over this..."

"Why are you doing this in the first place?" Erik whispered. "Why are they making you work even though you have a blown shoulder?"

"I have to do it anyway, if I wish to keep my life..."

"The head is into place," Nelson announced.

"Close your eyes," Suber said softly as Nelson pulled up a large-screened monitor attached to a swiveling crane arm showing Erik's head and Suber's latex-covered hands on the screen. "You don't want to see what happens next."

"I'm doing a crosscut," Blazejewelski announced. "Nelson,

prepare the saw."

"I'll have it on standby."

"Here we go, nice and easy."

Erik shut his eyes as Blazejewelski approached with the large two-handed drill. The loud whirring drowned out his scream.

THIRTEEN

Erik felt a firm hand to his shoulder, rousing him from sleep. He looked up, facing the younger John Greenfield.

"Are you all right, Ace?" John Greenfield asked softly.

"I... I think so," Erik murmured.

"You were in quite the shock... You didn't get up for days."

Erik looked up and around, finding he was in a hospital setting, curled on a cushioned bench next to John Greenfield who wore a tan blazer over a pastel T-shirt and chinos with canvas shoes. Erik's sights then lay on the hospital bed across from him, containing his friend Kevin who appeared lifeless, while hooked to various machines that beeped, chirped, and whooshed.

"How did I get here?" Erik asked.

"Both of you were brought in," John Greenfield explained. "You were in another ward, but I decided to check you out against orders and bring you here, hoping you'd come to." He smiled faintly. "And you did."

"Dad, how long will he be like this?" Erik moaned.

"I don't know," John Greenfield murmured.

Erik sighed and hung his head, fighting tears. "I'm sorry," he said softly.

"It isn't your fault."

"He didn't have to protect me..."

"He was your friend, Ace... You'd do the same for him too."

"Why did the guy shoot him? Why?"

"I don't know, Ace..."

Erik bit his fist and John Greenfield draped an arm over his shoulders. Erik broke down in tears, grabbing onto the side of his blazer and John Greenfield ran a gentle hand through Erik's hair as Erik sobbed into his side.

Moments later, a loud crash came abruptly in the corridor and both looked up startled as Mahjin staggered in, leaning against a white wax walking staff. He wore a denim vest and jeans with cowboy boots and his frizzy blond hair hung in his face as a disheveled and oily mess.

"You!" Mahjin shrieked.

"Smiley...!" John Greenfield cried.

"You did this...!"

Mahjin stormed in and Erik jumped out of his seat, quickly leaning out of a grab as Mahjin swiped at him.

"Smiley, calm down!" John Greenfield wailed and grabbed his arm. Mahjin struck him in the chest with the staff and John Greenfield staggered back, stunned. Mahjin then thrust the end forward at Erik's throat.

"You bloody filthy animal!" Mahjin roared. "You and your bunko ideas, always getting him into dirty messes!" Erik winced when jarred in the chest by the staff. "Lad your age shoulda been home abed, 'stead you were out gallivanting about in the flippin' morning where you had no business bein'!"

"Kev called me!" Erik wailed, shrinking back in fear. "It was his idea to go to that house!"

"His ideas, his ideas," Mahjin mocked with enunciation and rammed the stick against Erik's chest, forcing the air out of his lungs. Erik sagged forward and Mahjin held him back, pinning him against the wall. "What's your story, eh?" he bellowed. "He's damned near killed, almost a ghost, eh?" Mahjin whacked Erik upside the head and Erik cried out, cowering. "I ought to strike you down; make you feel what I have to go through!"

"Please!" Erik screamed as Mahjin drew back for another blow.

"Smiley, don't!" John Greenfield cried and grabbed for Mahjin again before he could thrust the staff forward, wrestling his friend by the arm down to the floor. "Let it go, Smiley; it couldn't be helped!"

"Why'd he have to pull a stunt like that?" Mahjin thundered and threw John Greenfield off. He tumbled overhead, striking the floor and groaned as Mahjin turned to him, panting for breath as his rage took over. "Let's see how you feel when your only boy's like this!"

"He thought that much of Justin to protect him," John Greenfield said, slowly rising to his feet. "He's just like you, Smiley!" Mahjin thrust the staff at his throat and forced John Greenfield against the wall. John Greenfield broke out in cold sweat and his face slowly turned pink as his breath thinned when Mahjin pressed hard into his skin.

"He didn't have to sacrifice his life for that fool boy, Jerry!" Mahjin barked.

"You didn't have to sacrifice your leg for my life, Melvin!" John Greenfield wheezed.

Mahjin trembled in rage and tightened his grip. He pushed

forward and Erik ran up to him, only to get struck back by a heavy hand, corkscrewing him to the floor.

"Please, Smiley," John Greenfield moaned, reaching out with a weak hand. He touched Mahjin's face and he gasped, grasping his fingers. John Greenfield clenched his teeth when held in a crushing grip. "Please... Kevin will pull through, trust me!"

"How can I?" Mahjin wailed. "He's dying!"

"He's not dying!"

"The doctors said they can't do any more for him..."

"There's a way, I know it..." Mahjin let go, heaving for breath. "Listen to me..."

A tanned woman with shoulder-length raven hair wearing a violet sundress patterned in white flowers and blue leather sandals entered the room. "Melvin, darling," she cried.

"Genovera!" John Greenfield yelped and Mahjin lowered his staff then leaned heavily against it, staring down at the floor with blank eyes. Genovera approached and took Mahjin by the arm, leading him to the nearby chair.

"Geno, love," Mahjin muttered and dropped into the seat, "I need a stiff drink..."

"I'll get you one, promise," Genovera murmured and kissed the top of his head. She approached John Greenfield and touched his arm.

"Genovera," John Greenfield murmured, smiling sadly. "It's been a while..."

"I've been so busy..."

"He's a handful, I know."

"Come with us, Justin," Genovera said brightly, beckoning

to Erik. "Let's leave Melvin alone for a while." Erik nodded numbly and followed them once they exited the room.

"Let's get a coffee," John Greenfield said, "or what have you..."

"So how's your lady?" Genovera inquired as they walked down the corridor together.

"Why'd you ask a question like that?" John Greenfield replied, smirking. "Shana's fine..."

Erik kept several paces behind, watching them speak about trivial matters. "*I don't understand,*" he thought. "*She's all over him and he's enjoying the attention!*"

They entered the cafeteria and John Greenfield pulled out his wallet from his rear pocket. "Get whatever you like," he said brightly, handing his wallet to Erik.

"Sure, whatever," Erik murmured as he took it and walked near the salad bar, pretending to study the food while trying to overhear their conversation.

Bumping into a middle-aged orderly wearing a white uniform of scrub suit and walking shoes, Erik stiffened when the orderly bared his teeth at him. Erik gulped hard, noticing the smoky glasses he wore and the checkered bandana over his head, hiding his appearance.

"Watch where you're going," snapped the orderly and picked up an empty tray.

"Same," Erik grumbled.

"Are you going to stare at the food or buy something?"

"Stare."

The man tutted Erik, wagging his finger at him. "Cheeky."

Erik stepped aside and the orderly went around, staring at

the choices of pre-made salads in plastic bowls. Erik drifted toward the snack carousel and spun the rack. The orderly approached moments later and grabbed the wire, stopping its spin.

"What do you want?" Erik demanded when the orderly gave Erik a long critical gaze.

"You're Schumacher's boy, ain't ya?" inquired the orderly. Erik said nothing, walking around him. "Here, give him this and tell him he's got the position."

Erik froze when touched on the shoulder and whirled around, facing the stranger who held out a business card. He cautiously took the card and looked down at the paper, reading the name embossed on the front. *"Gateway Protective Services,"* Erik read. *"The best offense is having the greatest defense."* He turned it over, reading the neatly printed inscription on the back. "Wednesday at Ten, Project E." Glancing up, Erik saw the orderly left his side and turned his sights toward the table where his father resided speaking candidly to Genovera. Erik approached them and set the card on the table.

"What's this?" John Greenfield asked, picking it up.

"Somebody gave it to me," Erik explained. "He says you got the position."

"See," Genovera said excitedly and took John Greenfield's hand. "I told you the interview wasn't that tough!"

"Are you sure it'll be safe?" John Greenfield asked nervously. "I don't want my family in danger with the work I'm undertaking…"

"What work, Dad?" Erik asked.

"I'm part of the government's Public Defense Works program," John Greenfield explained, looking up at Erik. "I'll be helping create all sorts of new technologies that will keep everyone safe without having to kill."

"It's a fairly new program," Genovera explained. "Your father here is very gifted."

"So are you, Genovera," John Greenfield replied, grinning as he turned in her direction. She giggled, blushing slightly.

"Well, if you stay at Gateway long enough," she said, "you can pass the rigors of Gen-Tech!" Genovera held her chin in her hand as she blew a dismayed sigh. "I've spent so much time down at the library, getting almost obsessive about passing their quarterlies..."

"I'm just an inspired tinkerer, nothing more."

Genovera smiled. "I'll keep a word in for you, okay? I could use a brilliant assistant."

Erik touched John Greenfield on the shoulder, handing him his wallet. "Can't we go home now?" he complained. "I'm tired and I've got a headache and my stomach hurts."

John Greenfield met his gaze, his cheeks slightly flushed. "All right, Ace. Let's go." He turned to Genovera and gave her hand a squeeze, then let go as he rose to his feet. "We'll talk about work stuff another day."

"See you!" Genovera said brightly.

John Greenfield pocketed his wallet and ushered Erik out into the corridor. "Why do you feel so bad?" he asked softly as they walked down the hall together.

"I don't know..." Erik grumbled.

"Maybe it's the stress from dealing with Kevin and all."

"Could be..."

"I have to talk to Smiley before I go," John Greenfield said. "I want him to know of my new job."

"That's fine."

Erik sat in the chair outside the room Kevin remained as John Greenfield entered and spoke to his friend. Erik nodded off, overcome with sleepiness.

Erik woke up in a cold sweat, hearing a soft tick of a clock. He groaned and sat up, rubbing at his face, then looked around, finding he was in an unfamiliar darkened room.

Planting his feet on the floor, Erik groaned and ran his hands through his drenched hair. He stood and peeled out of his clothes, then felt around in the dark, searching for the bathroom.

Entering the hall, Erik ran his hands along the wall until his fingers came across a doorknob and he opened it, then felt for a switch. Turning on the overhead light, he saw he stood inside a small home office. Against the walls were several low bookshelves and metal filing cabinets, and in the center rest a small oak desk with a desktop computer and few papers and folders.

Erik approached the desk and thumbed through the papers, finding several with the letterhead from Genetic Technologies.

"*We open the door to tomorrow*," Erik murmured, reading the company's motto. Setting the papers aside, he saw paperwork for County Health Control. "*What is she working on?*" Erik wondered, picking up the sheet.

"What are you doing?" Osphena's voice called.

Erik dropped the folder he held and whirled around. His face burned when he noticed she wore a micro-style short black kimono. "W-what do you want?" Erik stammered. "I was looking for the bathroom."

"I hope you didn't pee in the corner behind a chair or something," Osphena complained. "I rent, you know! None of this stuff is mine!"

Erik clenched his hands. "Bathroom, please," he pleaded.

"Down the hall, door at the end."

Erik pushed past her and ran for the door. Finding safety on the other side, he slammed it shut, heaving for breath.

"Are you all right?" Osphena called moments later from the other side.

"I don't know," responded Erik. He slid to the floor on the cool tiles and drew up his knees. "I don't know..."

"You had some kind of bad dream?"

"I don't remember..."

"Is there anything I can do to help?"

"Get me some cigarettes please?"

"Any kind?"

"I don't care."

Erik blew a sigh in relief when Osphena's footsteps padded down the corridor. Erik stood and switched on the light, then stepped into the shower stall. Turning on the hot water, Erik stood under the stream. His left shoulder began to hurt and Erik gripped it, immediately growing afraid.

"Not again," he thought in despair. *"This can't be happening again!"* Erik sank to his knees, overwhelmed.

FOURTEEN

After Erik washed, he wrapped himself in a towel and found a pack of non-menthol cigarettes and a lighter left for him on the edge of the sink. Opening the cigarettes, Erik withdrew one and lit it, inhaling deeply. He leaned against the sink as he smoked in silence, staring at the wall. The door creaked open and Erik faced Osphena peering inside.

"Care to join me for tea?" she queried.

"You don't mind?" Erik asked, holding up his lit cigarette.

"I bought them for you, didn't I?"

Erik grunted and padded after her into the dimly lit kitchen, taking a seat from her at the painted table. Osphena handed Erik a broken teacup with paint stains on the side and Erik noticed the old stains matched the table's colors.

Erik said nothing as he continued smoking in silence and later the kettle whistled. Osphena rose and poured hot water into cups then returned with the pair, setting them on the table.

"I do genetic research for Gen-Tech," Osphena said as she picked up her cup of green tea. "I also work the labs for Health Control part time." Erik grunted. "You know that last virus that killed a lot of people two years ago? I researched and isolated the mutation to create the vaccine." Osphena blew a sigh when Erik stayed silent. "This is really hard for me; please say something!"

"Who are you?" Erik murmured.

"I told you my name is Osphena," Osphena answered. "How could you forget? I told you several hours ago." She gave Erik a wary glance. "What do you remember about yesterday?"

"What about yesterday?" Erik shrugged his shoulders. "I don't know what today is."

"Do you know where you are?"

"Your guess is as good as mine."

Osphena opened her mouth to speak, then closed it and looked down into her tea. After several moments of silence, she finally spoke. "Are you saying that once you get to sleep, you can't remember anymore?"

"I guess you can say that."

"What about who you are?"

"I wouldn't know. Nothing comes to mind."

"Even if you looked at yourself in the mirror?"

"Just another stranger, I suppose."

"Even if you take a nap?"

"Not sure."

Osphena sat back in her seat and stared at Erik while she sipped her tea. Erik crossed his leg at the knee and leaned forward with his elbow on his thigh, dragging on his cigarette.

Looking up, Erik noticed she had an unreadable expression on her face. "Why are you looking at me like that?" he asked, raising an eyebrow.

Osphena gave a wry grin. "I think I found my perfect guy."

Erik's eyes widened and he sat up in his seat. "Wait, hold on!" he cried. "You're not going to use me as some sex slave because I can't remember the day before!"

Osphena suddenly burst out laughing and set down her cup. She gripped the edge of the table, laughing harder. Erik frowned and clutched tighter to his cigarette. "What's with that look?" she crowed. "You can't be serious!"

"Why else would you say something like that then?" Erik spat.

"I need to know how good you really are in handling problems."

"W-what kind of problems?" Erik dropped his cigarette and rose to his feet. "Look, lady, I don't like you like that. I *can't* like you that way." He backed away as Osphena stood. "Please, no, don't do this to me. I can't return the favor."

"Why not?" Osphena asked. "Aren't I pretty?"

"Yes, but...!" Osphena closed in and Erik backed away, trembling.

"Please, don't," begged Erik, "I can't, I won't, I don't want to do this!"

"Any other man would've been jumping on my bones by now." Erik tripped over his steps as he stepped away from Osphena. "They always found me exotic, fascinating... The eyes are like a magnet, they said."

Erik let out a whimper when he found himself cornered between the wall and Osphena. "I can't do this with you!" he cried.

"You prefer men, then?"

"I don't like men."

"Then why aren't you drooling over me?"

"I do find you pretty, I really do," Erik said quickly, "but I can't return those feelings. I don't have them for you."

"Then what feelings do you have?"

Erik moaned when Osphena touched his chest and ran her fingers deftly down his skin. He shut his eyes and shook his head when Osphena then ran her fingers through his damp hair.

"Please, stop," Erik mewed.

"But don't you want to?" Osphena put her hands around Erik's waist and he stiffened then grabbed her wrists.

"I can't, I can't, I can't do this," Erik pleaded.

"Look at me."

Erik fervently shook his head. "No, please, no..." He released his hold when Osphena leaned forward and nuzzled his neck. Erik's eyes snapped open and he grasped Osphena's shoulders, pulling her away. Osphena gasped when Erik shook her violently. "How many times do I have to keep telling you 'no'?" he shouted. "What part of that don't you understand?"

Osphena narrowed her eyes then grabbed Erik by the crotch. Erik immediately stiffened and let go as if she were hot. She released her hold and Erik stood there, dumbfounded. Osphena reached forward, pushing away the towel. When her hand touched skin, Erik's perplexed expression gave way to horror and he shoved her to the floor then took off for the bathroom.

Osphena yowled in pain when she struck the hardwood on her rear then staggered to her feet. Growing concerned when she heard Erik retching, Osphena made her way down the hall and peered in the door, finding Erik's head in the toilet.

"Was that the first time someone touched you?" she murmured.

Erik spat into the water and leaned back on his knees, taking in a shallow breath. "Yes, no..." Erik groaned. "I don't know..."

"Why are you having that reaction?"

"I don't know..."

"What was going through your head then?"

"I don't know..."

"You need to give me something better than 'I don't know'!"

Erik glared back at Osphena. "It felt weird!" he shouted. "It felt wrong! I don't know why it did but it just did!"

"Why?"

"I don't know... It's just creepy."

Osphena stared at Erik, surprised into silence. Erik sat against the wall, facing the toilet.

"I'm creepy, huh?" Osphena murmured after several long moments of silence between them.

"Sure..."

"So you're calling me lecherous?"

"What?" Erik looked up at Osphena, stunned. "No, I-!" Osphena advanced and Erik scrambled to his feet. She grabbed Erik by the face and he shut his eyes as she leaned in.

"Hold old do you think you are?" Osphena inquired.

"I..." Erik took Osphena by the wrists. "I wouldn't know. Without my VitaStat card, I can't tell you."

"It's hard to tell..." Osphena murmured and loosened her grip.

Erik let go and Osphena snatched the towel from around Erik's waist. Erik glared back at Osphena who smirked and held the towel, giving the most severely glacial looks he could muster as he clenched his hands at his sides. "Can you tell now?" he snarled.

"It's still hard to tell." Osphena tossed the towel at Erik and he caught it. She left the room and Erik tucked the terry back around his waist, embarrassed and confused.

When Osphena didn't return, Erik made his way back to the kitchen, finding her at the table. "Promise me something," he murmured.

"How old do I look?" Osphena suddenly asked.

Erik shook his head. "I'm horrible at guessing ages." He waved Osphena away. "Especially since you're tawny, there's no telling."

Osphena scoffed. "What are you saying, that black don't crack and brown don't frown?" Erik appeared momentarily puzzled then he smiled. Taking his seat at the table, Erik lit another cigarette and gulped down his cold tea. Osphena stood and leaned over to Erik's ear. "And to answer your question," she murmured, "the answer is 'no'."

"Why?" Erik mewed.

"I'm going to enjoy my time with you every chance I get once you settle in for the night. You're not going to remember anyway, right?" Erik paled. "Besides, what gal gets a dream like that dropped into her lap like this every day?"

Erik narrowed his eyes and pulled away. "I'll fight you," he snarled.

Osphena grinned. "You can't fight me in your sleep."

Erik stood indignantly to his feet and his world violently spun. He moaned and slipped back into his chair. "You put something...!"

"That's right," Osphena cooed and brushed her hands

through his hair. "I just want to have fun tonight. I promise this is the only time."

"How do I...?" Erik slurred.

"How do you know if I'm not going to do this again?" Osphena chortled and traced a finger around his hairline and down his ear. "You won't know, because you won't remember." She knelt down and blew in Erik's ear. Erik shuddered and his face immediately grew warm.

"Are you...?"

"Going to make you my slave?" Osphena licked Erik's ear and he shut his eyes, moaning. "No, I'm not that cruel of a person."

"Why...?"

"All I'm doing is just satisfying a need." Osphena ran her fingers through Erik's hair. He trembled when he sensed her bare breasts at his back as she leaned against him. "We all have needs, right?"

"I..."

Osphena deftly touched Erik's chest, massaging gently. "Don't you have needs?"

Erik nodded, unable to answer. Osphena's warm breath down the back of his neck and her soft hands caressing his chest were the last things he felt before he fell into the darkness.

Erik cried out, opening his eyes and fought to breathe, quickly coming out of the nightmare. He took in a ragged breath and tried to sit up, finding his arms and legs tied down to a wooden bed inside a darkened room. With his limited view, Erik could only see a wall and a nearby nightstand with a pitcher of water.

"Hey!" he shouted, struggling against his binds. Moments later, the door opened and the lights turned on, washing the white room with harsh florescence.

"Are you feeling better?" the doctor asked as he entered.

Erik groaned and shut his eyes, relishing the darkness behind them. "Why does it have to be so bright in here?" he moaned.

"They say you have not eaten nor slept well these past few days."

"Given the food here," Erik spat, "you wouldn't eat either!"

"They say you lie there, staring into space."

"After all those pills and needles," Erik cracked, "you'd be doing that too."

"Come now, we know you're not merely lying there staring into space, aren't you? You're thinking and remembering, right?"

"What is there to remember?"

"You tell me." Erik glared at the doctor who stood over him, holding a chart in his hands. "Much of it you're remembering is unpleasant, right? Terrible things happened to you in your past, correct?"

"What are you getting at?" Erik snarled. "I never said anything like that!"

"You must allow me to help you get through what troubles you. You must face your fears."

"Then who is Justin?" Erik demanded. "Who is Ferdian?"

"I'm not sure, but I'm sure he's important."

"You liar!" Erik screamed and yanked against the leather restraints. "You know who he is! You know who they are!"

"Why is he so important to you?"

"Don't turn this back on me!"

"I can't tell you why and I'm not certain of how he is related to your problems, but if we talk about it, I'm sure we'll find a solution."

"I don't know who he is!" Erik roared.

"Really? Are you just saying that to appease me?"

"Why would I lie?" Erik hissed. "What do you take me for?"

"There is no need to become hostile. Take it easy and try to relax. I'm sure there's something we have on hand to help..."

"No pills! No shots! I want my head to be clear."

"Whatever you wish."

"I want out of here."

"Don't be in a hurry to leave. You can't force progress."

"Shut your face." Erik stared up at the ceiling. "I'm sick of looking at you. Get out of here!"

"I'll return for you later. Remember, the important thing is that you talk to me so that you can become well."

"Right," Erik grumbled.

"Do you wish to talk about something else?"

"Like what?"

"Genovera, for instance..."

"I've got nothing to say."

"She must mean dearly to you."

"Forget it. I'm not saying another word."

"But...!"

Erik glared at the doctor, narrowing his eyes. "Kick rocks," he snapped.

The doctor frowned in response. "Please, don't fight me."

Erik looked away, returning his gaze back at the ceiling. "Don't push me, then."

"We have ways to get around that."

Erik grunted and shut his eyes, then started counting aloud.

"Don't retreat," the doctor called. "You must not withdraw." He blew a defeated sigh. "You must stay with us," the doctor continued. "You must face your past, otherwise all the progress we've had so far will come to a halt." When Erik continued counting, the doctor grunted. "As you wish. We will suspend for now and try again later. At least take the food we serve you. You will need your strength." The doctor walked out the room. "I'm here for you always, ready and willing to help. Please remember that." The lights turned out and the door shut behind him.

FIFTEEN

Erik slowly came to, sensing warmth against his face. He quickly sat up, finding himself back in the bed with the hard mattress and gray sheets. Erik squinted from the morning sun shining through the barred window, washing harsh oranges against him and the bed.

He frowned, noticing Josef sitting across from him on his berth outfitted only in his issued fitted beige pants and tan canvas shoes, running a boar-bristled brush through his long hair. Noting a used bloodied gauze wrapping rest on the nearby nightstand, Erik grew disgusted.

"What did they do to me?" he demanded.

"You had a very hard night, Brother," Josef replied. "You're in the Treatment and Recovery Program, remember?"

"I don't need to be treated!" Erik shouted. "Why treat me for a problem I don't have? The only thing I'm recovering from is their abuse!"

Josef chuckled and set the brush aside. "You've got a lot to learn, Brother," he said. "You really should feel at home." He stood up and approached, looking down at Erik with a stony blank countenance.

"Why do you keep calling me 'Brother'?" Erik snapped. "I don't know you; I'm not related to you!"

Josef cracked a wide grin. "It's not that you're related to me," he said gently. "It's more than that, you know."

"No, I don't know." Erik narrowed his eyes at Josef. "But what does it really mean?"

"It means..." Josef struck out with a swift punch with his right and Erik caught his hand. Josef slammed him back on the bed using his left and held Erik down by his throat. Erik grabbed Josef's wrist with his free hand once Josef fastened his grip.

"What are you doing?" Erik cried.

"What I'm doing is making sure you never become better than me," Josef sneered. Erik scratched hard at Josef's arm as Josef tightened his grip. "You *will* obey what I say or your miserable life here will become that much tougher!"

"You're lying!"

Josef's grip tightened, putting pressure against Erik's throat. Erik bat Josef upside the head and Josef laughed, unfazed. Erik gagged and began to panic when he felt his windpipe caving in.

"Doctor Schnell is here to see you," Rosenthal called. Josef quickly let go and stepped back as Rosenthal entered the room, holding onto a clipboard. Erik sat up, gasping for air and rubbing at his neck. "Is something the matter?"

"That nutcase tried to strangle me!" Erik shouted. "Do something about it!"

"I don't believe you," Rosenthal retorted.

"You're a notorious troublemaker," Josef teased. "What makes them think I'm the bad guy here?"

"You!" Erik growled and jumped to his feet. Rosenthal slapped the clipboard aside Erik's head before he advanced and

Erik whirled around.

"Stop it," Rosenthal snapped, waving the clipboard at Erik. "Or I'll have to beat you with my cane."

Erik clenched his hands at his sides. "What does Schnell want to see me about?" he grumbled.

"He wants to do an evaluation."

Erik pushed past Rosenthal and stomped out the room, meeting up with a man who had long silver hair pulled into a braid and tired gray eyes. He wore a white dress shirt, black vest, slacks and oxfords, and a navy band with red stripes around his arm. Schnell withdrew a silver pocket watch hooked to his vest.

"I'm here," Erik spat. "What's this evaluation for?"

"It's to check your overall health," Schnell said cordially. "Come along." He put away his watch and smiled gently at Erik.

"I'm not coming with you," Erik snapped.

"Don't you want to get well?" Schnell asked. "Your father is very concerned about your mental health. He told us about the nightmares and the sleepwalking and the angry outbursts."

Erik turned away and paused when pressure pressed against his head, spreading down his face and neck. He cried out, clutching his head as his hearing turned diffused and the voices started again.

Trust no one...

They're destroying your world slowly...

They only want to use you...

"What are you doing?" Erik wailed and clamped his hands over his ears when the voices turned louder.

In our dreams, in our waking hours...

141

They are everywhere and nowhere...

Piece by piece until there's nothing left...

"Stop it!" he screamed. A thunderclap of pain caused Erik to lose balance and he collapsed against the wall. He slumped forward, listless as blood ran from his nose.

Schnell stood over Erik, concerned. "Why are you reacting to me this way?" he asked.

Josef exited the room moments later, pulling into his T-shirt. "What's wrong with him?" he asked derisively.

"Don't worry about him," Schnell said and waved Josef away, dismissing him. "Go on to breakfast; they're waiting for you."

"He can't be that important," Josef muttered and blew an annoyed sigh.

"Please don't pester him. His mental state is fragile."

"Fine, but if he cuts up, I'm on his ass." Josef glared down at Erik and kicked him in the side. "You hear me?" he shouted. "I'm on you!"

Schnell pointed down the hall. "Go!" he snapped.

Josef grunted and stormed down the corridor. Schnell knelt before Erik, withdrawing a silver pen from his slacks pocket. Flipping a switch on its side, he pushed back Erik's head and shone a blue light in his blank glassy eyes. Moments later, Rosenthal's cane tapped down the tiled corridor as he exited the room.

"He seems to be broken," Rosenthal said upon approach.

"Suber mentioned he went into this catatonic stupor before," Schnell replied and put away his pen.

"What caused the malfunction?"

"I'm not sure," answered Schnell. "Possibly memory corruption...?"

"Whatever; just do something about it. Get him up and running." Rosenthal left Schnell's side and Schnell shook Erik gently by the shoulders.

"You need to wake up," Schnell called to Erik. "Come on, now. I really don't want to medicate you." He blew an exasperated sigh and rose to his feet. Withdrawing his cellular phone, he pushed a button and waited for the call to go through. "Hello?" he greeted. "Yes, it's me... I'm going to need some help." He glanced down at Erik. "Number Three is experiencing a Code Four-hundred-nine." Schnell knelt before Erik and put the phone to Erik's ear.

Hearing a series of tones, Erik's eyes refocused and he slowly began to rouse. "What?" he murmured. "What's going on?"

"You need to pull yourself together!" said a woman's voice over the line. "Wake up!"

"I'm up, I think..." Erik looked up at Schnell who seemed relieved.

"Remember; keep yourself alive so that we may meet again."

Erik took in a shallow breath when pain flashed behind his eyes. He pushed Schnell away, holding his head in his hands.

"Not again!" Erik cried when the low drone sounded in his ears. "You're trying to kill me!"

Schnell stood, taking the phone with him. "Go on ahead to breakfast," he said to Erik. "I'll talk to you later."

"My head hurts!" Erik moaned. "I can't concentrate..."

"You need to eat something; maybe you'll feel better."

"Don't make me go in there!"

You need to punish them Ferdian...

Make them hate you, fear you...

"You're stronger than that!" Schnell pressed. "Stop crying and get up!"

Erik groaned and stood unsteadily to his feet. "Why did you want to see me?" he demanded.

"We'll speak later when we have more time."

"Fine, it's your choice."

Erik left down the hall, tense as the noise grew louder in his head and drowned out everything else.

Approaching the dining area, Erik kicked in the door and entered as the heavy wood swung open. He let out a hard sigh in exhaustion and took his spot at the rear table next to Clayton.

Clayton spoke to him and Erik shook his head, unable to understand. Erik ground his teeth in distress when Josef approached, slamming a tray next to him in irritation.

Josef made angry gestures and Erik shrugged his shoulders. Josef bat Erik upside the head and suddenly his hearing returned full force.

"What the hell is wrong with you?" Josef screamed.

Erik winced and rubbed at his ear with the heel of his hand. "I'm fine, thank you," he replied sourly. "Your shouting's not helping either!"

Josef grabbed Erik by the collar and leaned in. "No! You are *not* fine!" He shook Erik violently. "They tested you and you came back 'normal'! You are *not normal*!"

"Normal is just an agreed state of conformity!" Erik retorted and pried off his fingers. "Besides, if being different means being like *you*, I'm *glad* to be normal!"

"I'll make sure you don't speak to anyone else." Josef narrowed his eyes. "They're starting to disobey the rules as well because of your antics!"

"I haven't even been here long enough to be much of an influence and besides, I don't even know what the rules are and I could care less about them." Erik picked up a dinner roll from Josef's plate and bit into it. "No one's ever said anything to me about it!"

Josef narrowed his eyes. "I'm telling you," he said evenly. "You watch yourself around here!"

Erik scoffed. "Why are you so upset with me?" He threw the roll at Josef, bouncing it off his chest. "I didn't do anything to you!"

"Oh, yeah?" Josef crowed. He lurched forward and Erik tackled Josef by the waist, throwing him down to the floor.

"Lay off me!" Erik screamed as he straddled Josef and threw a punch, breaking the young man's nose. "You want me so badly, you got it!"

Josef socked Erik in the throat and Erik fell back, gagging. Josef sprang to his feet and yanked Erik by the collar, immediately wrapping his arm around Erik's neck. Erik grabbed at his arm as Josef squeezed, struggling to pull him off.

"I'm making sure you're not infecting anyone else with your bad behavior," Josef snarled. "Don't think of trying to escape out into fresh air with those weaklings you call friends!" He jerked back and Erik let out a wail as torrential pain ripped through his neck. "I'm making sure you disappear first!"

"Joe, please!" Erik howled and Josef yanked back again, cracking bones. "Stop it!"

"That's enough, Joe," Clayton snapped and punched Josef in the back of the head. Josef cried out in shock and let Erik go, dropping him to the floor. "You want to mess with someone, you mess with me!"

Erik scrambled to his feet and rubbed at his neck, stunned. "What is wrong with you?" he spat.

Josef touched the back of his head, glaring up at Clayton. "I'm dealing with you later," he vowed and backed away. "He can't protect you forever!"

"Don't push me!" Erik retorted. Josef stormed out the room and Erik plopped down at the table, running his hands through his hair. "I can't do this," he moaned.

Clayton approached his side and leaned against the table at his back, gripping the edge with his hands. "What started it?" Clayton asked.

"I don't know," Erik murmured. "I don't know why he's obsessed with me."

"Did he say anything?"

"Other than him telling me he thought I was cute?"

Clayton guffawed. "That's one hell of a way to show affection!"

"Why won't staff do anything about it?"

"They probably find it entertaining, the sick bastards."

"You may be right..." Erik groaned in distress. "Please, don't waste your time trying to protect me. I can handle myself."

"Fine, I won't."

"Why doesn't he ever bother you?"

Clayton gave a malicious grin and tipped his cap. "You'll come to see soon," he said cryptically.

"What's for breakfast then?" Erik turned around in his seat and took off the plate covering on the tray Josef left behind. "This is just terrible," complained Erik when he revealed uncooked stew beef cubes and onion soup. "I'm not touching it."

"You don't have to," Clayton said. "I'm not much of a meat eater myself."

"You can't survive off tea alone!"

"So you'd rather have salty soup and stale bread instead?"

"I don't like either choice, but I need to live."

Clayton chortled. "Right, because you're already skinny enough as it is!"

"So are you!"

Clayton rose to his feet. "So which flavor you want?"

"Surprise me."

SIXTEEN

After the meal, Fenway ordered Erik to stay in the dining area while everyone else went out with Benedict. Fenway stormed up to him with another plate of beef cubes and threw it on the table with a clang.

"Eat it," he ordered.

"No," Erik snapped, glaring at him. "I'm fine with the tea here."

"I will hold you down and shove it in until you choke!"

"Go ahead, try." Erik set aside his mug and held out his hands. "I won't even fight you. Have at it."

Fenway narrowed his eyes. "You know what, I won't force you," he said evenly. "But for each time you refuse to follow the rules here, more privileges are getting withheld."

"Like I care."

"Then you're going to get sent downstairs." Erik paled and Fenway grinned. "That's right, downstairs where they do all those *special* tests."

Erik swallowed hard. "I-I still don't care what you do to me," he stammered. "I'm still going to keep fighting. I don't belong here."

"It's your fault for not complying." Fenway poked Erik hard in his chest. "I've got all sorts of orders written up on you."

Erik cringed when poked again. "You're not serious!" he yelped.

"Oh, no?" Fenway smirked. "We can do all sorts of things to you and there's not a damn thing you can do about it." Erik glared at him and Fenway laughed. "You know I'm right!"

"You're wrong!" Erik thundered, standing indignantly. "You're all mad and so very wrong!"

"Erik, just do what he says," Josef complained as he entered the dining area.

"Forget it!" Erik spat. "I'll break the rest of your face if you keep harassing me!"

Josef grunted and adjusted the tape on his nose. "It'll make things go smoothly," he said and smiled deviously, "for you and for the rest of us."

Erik clenched his hands, growing annoyed. "You make me puke!" he spat. "I don't care about you or them!"

"How selfish!" Josef retorted. "I'll make you do other things if you don't listen!"

"Don't you lay your hands on me!" Erik shouted and shook his fist at Josef. "So help me, I'll strike you down!"

"How outspoken!" Josef rallied. "That's not going to happen."

"Sit yer ass down!" Fenway snapped and punched Erik's chest. Erik dropped back into his seat, coughing painfully. "Now do as I say."

"Forget it," Erik snarled. "Beat me for all I care. I'm not changing my mind."

"So you wanna get drugged into submission then?" Fenway threatened. "All I gotta do is call Nelson and he'll be here faster than you can cry for your momma!"

Erik ground his teeth and picked up the plastic fork with contempt. Shoving down the raw stew beef without much thought of chewing, Erik barely got beyond choking, coughing and clearing his throat to keep it down. After practically inhaling the meat, Erik tensed when Fenway brought another plate to the table.

"Are you serious?" Erik hissed.

"You've got to eat this as well," Fenway said with fake gentleness. "Either do it yourself or get strapped down. Your choice."

"You've honestly lost it!" Erik shrilled.

"Just eat it."

Erik did the same, only to be met with a third plate. His hands started shaking as he took a bite and slammed down the fork when the turning in his stomach sloshed harder.

"That's enough!" Erik screamed and picked up the plate. He threw it at Fenway and the man quickly leaned out the way as the plate crashed against the wall, splattering the bloody beef on the other chairs, table and floor. "I'm sick of it!"

"What's there to understand, you stupid shit?" Fenway demanded. "We aren't against you here."

"Right," Erik snapped back sarcastically. His head whipped back from a hard right hook hitting his jaw and the forceful blow threw him out of his seat.

Fenway stood over him, clutching his hands at his sides. "You do what you're told because it's in your best damn interest," he growled. "If you want your ass outta here sooner, you obey the damn rules so your ass ain't fucked over!"

150

"I'm going outside," Erik declared and rose to his feet. "You want to stop me, try your best!" He turned on his heel and stomped for the dining room exit.

"Where do you think you're going?" Josef snapped and immediately blocked Erik's path. He grabbed Erik by the arm and Erik whirled around, throwing him against the wall. Josef grunted when his head smashed against the partition and the force of the blow left a crater. Josef gasped, clutching his head in agony.

"Don't touch me!" Erik shrieked. Josef glared back and Erik wound up for another blow.

"Let him go," Schnell called. "Let everyone get a little morning air. It can do them some good, okay?"

Erik shoved Josef aside and headed out into the corridor, finding Schnell standing near the door while Clayton stood across the hall. Fenway grumbled curses under his breath as he stormed out the room and stood before Schnell.

"Why are you here?" Fenway demanded.

"I want to talk to them alone," Schnell declared. "I'll be fine. You don't have to protect me." Fenway blew an angry sigh and stomped past him. Josef glared at Erik and followed Fenway.

"Doctor Schnell..." Erik started.

"Listen," pressed Schnell. "You have to bend a bit if you wish to have less harm come to you."

"It's not easy, Doctor Schnell!" Erik protested.

"Just fake their influences if you want them to stop!" Clayton griped.

Erik glared at Clayton, incredulous. "How?" he squawked and waved a hand toward the corridor. "They watch my every move!"

"Eat that shit and throw it up fifteen minutes later! They only check the toilets every thirty minutes anyway." Clayton tapped at his head. "Besides, if you think like they do, you can stay a step ahead!"

"This twisted reality will not be a pleasurable experience," Schnell warned. "Remember enough to get by, but don't forget! Once they find out you're not truly under their control, it will get much, much worse!"

"Why are you two helping me?" Erik demanded. "I don't know either one of you!"

"We know who you are."

You have to be him...

"I don't know you!" Erik cried. "Don't tell me I was here before!" He clutched his suddenly pounding head. "*That can't be right!*" he thought in horror. "*Chicago was making stuff up! He was just spouting off about nothing!*"

Why can't you remember?

"Stop it!" Erik screamed and doubled over as the pain increased. "Shut up!"

Wake up in there! Remember!

"Get away from me!" Erik pushed past Clayton and Schnell, taking off down the corridor. He bumped into Rosenthal who came in from the opposite direction and vomited at his feet, then collapsed to his knees, gasping weakly for breath. Rosenthal frowned and looked up at Schnell who ran down the hall.

"I thought he passed his exams," Rosenthal snapped once Schnell approached.

152

"He's under a lot of stress," Schnell answered simply.

"Maybe more medications are in order."

"Please try therapy first," Schnell appealed. "More medicines might make him sicker than what he already is."

"Fine." Rosenthal prodded Erik's shoulder with his cane. "Get up," he ordered. "You have a session."

"What is it for?" Erik moaned.

"You need to learn about teamwork, a skill you're apparently lacking."

Erik looked up to Schnell and he nodded. "Go on with him," Schnell said gently. Erik sighed and rose unsteadily to his feet.

"Please get this cleaned up," Rosenthal snapped at Schnell, then headed down the hall. Erik followed behind him, led into the lounge area. "Let's sit on the couch," Rosenthal said to Erik.

Erik took a seat on one end of the couch while Rosenthal sat across from him on the other end. "I don't want to be here," Erik complained.

"It's not a matter of what you want," Rosenthal said sternly. "You must realize how sick you are; that's why you're here."

"When will I see my parents?"

"It all depends."

"After forty-five days, then?"

"Maybe."

"When will I be able to leave?" Erik pressed.

"Days, weeks, months... it all depends."

"How long will I stay then?"

"Days, weeks, months... forever maybe. Forever and ever..."

"I can't do that." Erik shook his head. "I can't do that!" He held his head in his hands, overwhelmed. "Don't do that to me!"

"Then do as you're told. Stop fighting and follow orders."

"Whose orders?"

"What does it matter?" Erik turned to Rosenthal and froze when the man withdrew a capped syringe from his blazer pocket. "Once we get what we need from you, you'll be forgotten. No one will miss you here."

"I have my family!"

"They'll get told you died in your sleep from an unknown blood clot." Rosenthal gave a malicious smile. "It's quite easy to fake, you see."

Erik frowned and cold sweat broke out on his forehead and neck. "That needle... It's empty!"

"Right. There won't be anything for the coroner to find if your parents decide to investigate - it's a simple and clean way to die." Rosenthal rose to his feet, pocketing the instrument. "Now that you've been thoroughly warned, I expect better behavior from you. Do we have an understanding?" Erik ground his teeth as he stood, too angry to say anything. "I guess by your silence, you've accepted. Now let's go back." Rosenthal turned away and Erik refused to move.

"No," Erik finally said.

Rosenthal came to a stop and turned around, facing Erik who stood at the couch. He raised an eyebrow, skeptical. "Excuse me?" he jeered.

"You heard me," Erik snapped. "I said 'no'."

"Then you know what I'll have to do to you."

Erik let out a short laugh. "Go ahead, do it!" he shouted. "Have your way; everyone else did!" He beckoned at Rosenthal. "But once you get done, I'll come after you - you push me and

I'll push back because I can only be pushed so far before I snap!"

Rosenthal picked up his cane and Erik immediately stepped under his guard when the man swung, shouldering him back by the chest. Rosenthal staggered back, then swept his cane at Erik's feet, tripping him back on the floor. Erik struck the ground on his back and Rosenthal stepped forward, smashing the pewter end on Erik's head, immediately knocking out his world.

Erik awoke with a start, gasping for breath and drenched in cold sweat. He sat up, finding himself in the darkened room once more; lying on the small wooden bed with slats for restraints. A soft glow from across the room highlighted a shielded night light and Erik noticed a small trash can nearby with a sink above it, a water closet on the left with a small end table next to the bed that had a telephone on the edge and a pitcher of water. Standing weakly on unsteady feet, Erik shuffled for the door and found it had no handle.

"Hey!" he called, banging on the door with his palm. "Hey, open up!" A small window slid open, revealing a slat barely two hands wide with two-inch thick bulletproof glass.

Hardened dark eyes glared at Erik from the slat. "What?" sneered the guard on the other side.

"I want out of here," Erik proclaimed.

"You got all the amenities you want," the guard grumbled. "Toilet, phone, telly... so why are you complaining?"

"I don't need to be here."

"You're sick, kiddo, real sick, and you gotta stay here if you wanna get better." The slat slid close, cutting off the source of contact.

"They're still watching me," Erik thought, glancing up and around. *"I know there's cameras hidden in here somewhere..."* He knocked at the door again, rapping it with the knuckles on the back of his hand. The slat came open once more.

"What now?" the guard complained.

"How sick am I really?" Erik pressed.

"Enough to be quarantined!"

"What is it I've come down with?"

"It doesn't have a name yet."

The slat slammed shut. Sighing, Erik returned to the bed and sat on the edge, holding his head in his hands. His gaze fell upon the touchtone phone resting next to his lamp on the nightstand.

"There's a phone here," he realized, dumbfounded. *"But why would they allow me to call the outside if I'm not allowed to in the first place?"* Feeling hopeful, Erik grabbed for the phone and held it in his lap, shuddering with excitement. *"Maybe it is a real hospital and not a fake one like General!"* He picked up the receiver and dialed his home number, waiting for an answer.

After two rings, the voice of the doctor answered. "It's three in the morning," he moaned. "What is it you want?"

Erik quickly slammed down the receiver, shaken. *"Why is he answering Father Greenfield's phone?"* he wondered, terrified.

The phone rang moments later and Erik dropped all he held, crashing the telephone to the floor. The receiver became unhooked and the doctor's tinny voice called for him.

"Hello, hello?" called the doctor. "What's the matter? Is everything all right?" Erik lay back in bed, drawing the sheets to his chest. "Please tell me what's wrong. What is upsetting you? Remember, I am here to help. I only wish to help..." Erik shut his eyes and tensed when he heard the door open.

"We've got some medicine to make that scary feeling go away," said a low, soothing voice.

Erik gave no resistance when his arm was taken and he was injected. After the door closed again, Erik stared up at the darkened ceiling, listening to the buzzing of the dial tone flooding the air. He then clutched his head when his hearing warped, overwhelmed by the flash of pain in his head.

"My brain's on fire!" he wailed. "It's burning!"

Erik curled into the fetal position, rocking as he struggled to breathe. His heartbeat drummed in his ears, like a loud mechanical tick and everything he felt and heard faded into the shadows.

SEVENTEEN

After three weeks, Erik finally became used to the routine of The Center, faking his way through their constant tests of strength, endurance and agility, as well as interacting with others. Josef hardly spoke to him, instead, he unleashed his irritation upon the other patients there to show Erik how much tougher the punishment would be if he were ever crossed. Clayton hardly responded to Josef's antics, only humiliating him if he tried to be vindictive toward Erik.

After another afternoon of tests, followed by lunch, Erik made his habitual trek to the washroom he shared with Josef and vomited up the raw meat he had to eat for that period. Erik leaned against the stainless steel toilet after heaving, relishing the cool metal against his face. He sighed and shut his eyes, considering other possible ways he could deceive the staff for the remainder of the afternoon.

"Oh, that's how you're getting by, huh?" Josef's voice called. Erik looked up, finding Josef standing at the doorway. "I don't believe you!" Josef screamed and kicked Erik's face, forcing him spiraling back and strike the toilet. "I have to go through this shit day in and day out while you play them for fools!" Erik received another hard kick in his chest, cracking his ribs.

"Life's not fair, so accept it," Erik groaned and gripped the edge of the toilet for support, struggling to stand. "I liked my life just fine and the way things were before it was taken from me!" Erik stood unsteadily to his feet. "Outside this demented place, I had a nice family who loved me and good friends that cared about me!"

"That's all a fucking lie and you know it!" Josef kicked Erik down to the floor and stomped hard on his chest. Erik wheezed as blood quickly filled his lungs. "You piece of shit! I'll kill you, I swear!"

"That's enough!" Clayton's voice called and he entered the room. Clayton grabbed Josef by his hair before he geared for another kick and threw the young man back against the shower stall. Josef grunted when his head checked the partition and slid to the floor. "I dare you to get up!"

Erik gasped for breath and got up on his knees, lurching forward as he coughed up blood. "I told you not to worry about me," Erik moaned moments later. "I can handle myself fine!"

"I'm going to tell," Josef rasped. "They're going to find the right serum to control that son of a bitch!"

"Tell them," Clayton snarled, "and I'll destroy you."

Josef let out a weak laugh. "You can't!" he snapped. "You're bullshitting and you know it!"

"You wanna bet?" Clayton said in a low, even tone.

"Clayton, don't!" Erik begged.

"Come on, then!" Clayton growled, clenching his hands. The room's temperature abruptly dropped to freezing, icing over the regurgitated food-filled toilet water.

Erik shivered as he stood, watching in shock at his panting breath coming out as freezing puffs. "W-what's going on?" he sputtered. He reached forward, grabbing Clayton by the arm and gasped when his hand quickly turned bluish-white as instant frostbite swiftly traveled up his arm.

Clayton turned to Erik, his black eyes glowing in pale ice blue light. "Let me go," he sneered.

"I-I'm sorry," Erik sputtered, recoiling. His hand slowly began to warm, with the sensation returning as the frostbite faded.

"They will fix you both!" Josef crowed. Clayton stepped in and yanked Josef by the shirtfront. He threw Josef against the wall with his right hand, clenching his left at his side. A blue steel dagger formed in his free hand, surrounded by frosted light. "I don't claim it to be true because it *is*! They *will* fuck you up big time!"

"Shut up!" Clayton screamed and Erik quickly grabbed his arm before he could drive the dagger through Josef.

"Don't!" Erik said in Clayton's ear as he twisted his arm behind his back. "You'll be just like him if you hurt him!"

"You've got to be wary of him, Erik," Clayton growled. "They're going to use him against us, I just know it!"

"I'll keep that in mind and you too!" Erik released his hold and Clayton blew a hard sigh, dropping Josef to the floor.

"Come on," Clayton grumbled, "we've got Group Therapy." Clayton stomped out the room and Josef burst out laughing manically.

"Joe, I wish you'd stop trying to hurt me," Erik said to him. "I don't understand why you keep targeting me."

"Don't worry," Josef said cordially and let out a demented laugh. "You'll see!"

Erik backed away, cautious. "What's so funny?" he demanded.

"When you're not in your place, I'll put you where you need to be."

"We'll see about that." Erik backed away then bolted.

Erik still felt ill at ease and generally tense when Josef was nowhere to be found later that evening, though Clayton's reassurances that he should relish the times when Josef was not trying to hassle him made him feel less better.

The trays came up for dinner and Erik uncovered his plate while trying to prepare himself to vomit later, only to be met with surprise: the tray consisted of two pieces of French toast, two slices of bacon, two sausage links, and an egg omelet mixed with cheese, green and red bell peppers, black olives, green onions and shiitake mushrooms.

"What is this?" Erik asked as Clayton set his tray aside and picked up his mug of tea.

"Manipulation," he said simply while the other patients cheered and devoured their meals, talking happily and laughing amongst themselves.

"What do you mean?" Erik murmured. "Are you saying they're trying to get our guards down, to make us too comfortable?"

"I'm not confirming nor denying."

Erik glanced up, spotting Fenway standing offside, glaring back with his arms folded across his large chest.

"I think I'll settle for a biscuit," Erik said softly. "My stomach's been really upset lately."

Fenway approached the cart and extracted a roll wrapped in wax paper. He tossed it to Erik who caught it and looked away from his harsh gaze as he unfolded the wrapping paper from it.

"You need to keep up the changes," Clayton muttered from behind his mug. "They're gonna throw you curve balls and screw balls... you've got to keep ahead to continue faking them out."

"I don't know which way is the right way to 'fake them out'," Erik murmured and bit into the stale bread. "It makes my head hurt."

"At least it's only your head."

Josef entered the room moments later and picked up Erik's tray as he came around the table. Erik turned to Josef standing behind him, biting into a sausage link.

"This place is a total sausage factory," said Josef. "Let's escape and terrorize the girls across the yard." Erik's face flushed and Josef chuckled. "Oh, so that embarrasses you, huh?"

"That's just a little forward, is all," Erik replied. "I never thought you were into girls."

"I can go either way." Erik frowned and Josef laughed. "I don't care what the rest of them say; I'm still better than you."

"You just think that," Erik replied. "I *am* better than you and that's why you hate me so much!"

"Huh, really?" Josef said, grinning. "You don't know what truly drives me, Brother." He let the plate drop to the floor and quickly advanced. Erik quickly rose to his feet and Josef thrust forward his clenched hand, punching his side. Erik let out a cry in shock, doubling over when sharp pain pierced his flesh.

"You–!" Erik gasped and coughed up blood.

Josef bared his teeth and leaned forward to Erik's ear.

"You're still weak, you stupid fuck," Josef sneered. "I always get what I want and if it means destroying your body, then I will!"

"What are you talking about?" Erik wheezed. "You're not making any sense!"

"I'm sure you hate being violated, huh?" Josef grabbed Erik by the hair. "I told you, you're getting something much harsher!"

"Where did you–?" Erik groaned when the blade thrust deeper into his side and Erik grew faint, finding breathing difficult as dark spots clouded his vision.

"Answer the question," Josef growled.

"I'm not telling you what you want to hear," Erik hissed.

"I admit, I'm not confident in my own skill, but given the chance, I will betray you, just like I've done all my other 'friends'." Josef thrust the blade deeper, then turned it and released Erik, pushing him away.

"Why?" Erik moaned and slipped to his knees, clutching his side that bled profusely. He fell forward at Josef's feet and Josef smiled wickedly, licking the shank he held.

"Oh, so you're not defending him this time, aren't you Clayton?" Josef teased.

"You've got another thing coming," Clayton snapped, huddling over his mug.

Josef approached Clayton and draped an arm around his shoulders, leaning in. "I'm sure," he snarled. "Give it to me, eh? I want it real bad!"

"Listen up," Fenway barked, "it's time for Group Therapy you pieces of shit!" He stormed out of the room and everyone else scattered, immediately fleeing the dining area leaving behind just Erik, Josef, and Clayton.

Clayton shoved Josef away and rose to his feet with clenched hands that glimmered dimly in pale frosted light. "I've had enough of your shit, Joe," he spat. "You crossed the line."

"No!" Josef screamed. "You crossed the line!"

"Get out of here; I don't have time for your shit!"

"I'll get you to learn!" Josef roared. "You'll see!" He raced out the room and Clayton approached Erik's side, kneeling beside him.

"What are you doing?" Erik mewed as Clayton turned him over onto his back.

"You can't easily heal from this," Clayton muttered and pushed back Erik's arms. He nudged the cap on his head that threatened to fall forward, revealing worried black eyes.

"Don't touch me," Erik moaned. "I'm a mess."

"You're bleeding, man," Clayton complained. "I don't like blood, okay? The faster I fix you, the faster you can change your clothes!"

"Okay, whatever," Erik groaned and Clayton pressed his cold hands into Erik's side.

Clayton tensed when footsteps thundered outside in the hall and the door smashed open, revealing Blazejewelski accompanied by the nursing technician Nelson.

"That's fucking sick!" snapped Nelson as he entered the room.

"Nelson, shut the fuck up," Blazejewelski grumbled. "Just take them both downstairs."

"Hey!" Clayton yelled when yanked up by the collar. He swung at Nelson and the orderly parried, striking him on the side of his neck. Clayton staggered back and Erik scrambled to his feet.

"Leave him alone!" Erik shouted and shoved Nelson aside, sending him crashing to the floor.

"You son of a bitch!" Nelson yelped.

Blazejewelski advanced and Clayton put an arm out as he backed into Erik who clutched his wounded side.

"Leave us alone," Clayton demanded and drew a frosty blue steel short sword in his left hand, glaring at the surgeon.

Blazejewelski withdrew a pistol from a side holster he wore under his blazer and loaded a magazine cartridge into it. "It doesn't matter to me what the hell happens to you," he retorted and pulled back the safety. "I'm getting paid whether you monsters are dead or alive."

"Doctor Blazejewelski, don't!" Nelson cried and grabbed for his arm, pulling away.

Clayton charged and Blazejewelski shook free of Nelson, firing at Clayton. Clayton cried out when hit in his shoulder, forcing his arm lame. He grunted and stumbled rearward, seething in pain.

"Clayton!" Erik screeched, grabbing for him as his blade disappeared and protuberant lines formed from the wound under his skin.

"Come on!" Clayton called and took off running.

Erik raced after him, panicking as Nelson and Blazejewelski gave chase, barreling down the corridor. "Where are we going?" Erik wailed.

"Trust me!"

Reaching the exit at the end of the corridor, Erik turned around and backed into Clayton as Nelson and Blazejewelski approached.

"Without a key, you're fucked!" Blazejewelski spat. "I told you boy, I run you!"

"I told you, I'm fighting my way out of here!" Erik shrilled. "I don't care if I have to die over it!"

"Then die!"

"Damn you, Blazejewelski!" Nelson hollered and tackled the surgeon. They struck the ground, wrestling each other for control of the pistol.

Making use of their distraction, Clayton sprinted down the hall and Erik hurried along his side. They entered an open office and Clayton immediately shut the door, leaning against it as he panted hard for breath.

"How are we going to get out of here?" Erik moaned and sank against the wall. "The locks take three different keys just to get outside!"

"Trust me," Clayton reassured, "I got a plan."

Clayton left the door and picked up a heavy wooden chair. Moments later the door burst open and Clayton smashed the chair into his aggressor, bashing his head. Giving another swing, he brought down the body and gave another whack upside his head, forcing him still. Dropping the chair, Clayton panted hard for breath, standing over Nelson's lifeless body.

"How did you know it would be Nelson?" Erik asked as Clayton crouched down and sifted through the technician's pockets, taking his keys.

"I didn't," Clayton answered and stepped out into the hall.

Erik sank to his knees, drained. "I can't go anymore," he moaned.

"Come on!" Clayton protested. "We got this far!"

"Too dizzy..."

"Please, hold out a minute longer!" Clayton pleaded. "Once Fenway and Benedict get back from rec time, we're really going to get punished!"

Finding his resolve, Erik nodded and Clayton lent a hand, pulling him to his feet. Erik draped an arm around Clayton's shoulders, leaning against him.

Leading Erik back to the exit, Clayton ran the key card through the reader then tried the handle, only to find it didn't move.

"We need his thumb and palm print if we're getting off this floor," Erik said.

"Shit!" Clayton hissed.

"I'm sorry," Erik moaned and slipped from Clayton's side. "Just forget it. We're stuck here."

"Don't give up yet. We're going to make it!" Clayton left Erik's side, leaving him alone at the door.

Erik slumped to the floor, clutching his soaked shirt sticking to his skin. He glanced around; growing nervous when he realized Blazejewelski was nowhere to be found.

Erik cringed, hearing a harrowing scream and swallowed back the acrid burning in his throat when Clayton returned covered in blood, holding a severed hand and thumb.

"Get up!" Clayton ordered and swiped the card in the reader, then mashed the thumb into the verifier. After pressing the palm against the device, the door buzzed and Erik rose to his feet. Clayton tossed the digits aside and pushed open the door. "Come on!" Clayton grabbed Erik by the arm and dragged him out into the dimly lit corridor.

"Where are we going?" Erik complained. "There's no way out!"

"There is!"

"I can't reach it!"

"No, no, no!" Clayton urged as Erik collapsed on the ground. "Don't go out on me now!"

Erik's world grew dark when the pain became too much.

EIGHTEEN

A constant chirp rang in Erik's ears and he slowly roused, realizing he was still at the hospital and outside Kevin's room where the machines took note of his vitals. He could not hear Mahjin or John Greenfield speaking and grew nervous.

Footsteps came down the corridor and Erik looked up at a young man with short dark slicked back hair wearing a white consulting jacket over a dark brown suit and gold sunglasses with reflective lenses. Erik tensed when the young man stopped before him.

"You're looking for somebody?" Erik asked and the young man smirked.

"It's as I suspected," he replied.

"Who are you?"

"We should have rid of you two irritants from the beginning... otherwise you'll be a certain cause for trouble."

"Wait..." Erik immediately rose to his feet, alarmed. "Are you saying you're here to kill me?"

"Since your father's just started working for us, then I have no reason to get rid of you right now."

"Why are you telling me this?" Erik demanded. "If Dad's going to be mixed up with something this dangerous...!"

"The only reason I came to you in the first place is to warn you. If I were to just simply destroy you, his grief might interfere with his work."

"If Dad's dealing with classified stuff, I swear I won't tell anyone!"

"It's no matter. The home isn't really the sort of place to be exposed to such materials in the first place." The young man chortled. "I'm giving you a warning, boy: don't get in the way." He walked away and Erik gulped down his fear.

John Greenfield came down the corridor moments later. "What's wrong, Ace?" he asked. "You don't seem like yourself…"

"Nothing really," Erik murmured.

John Greenfield motioned Erik to follow him and they both walked the halls together. "If you're worried about your buddy Kevin, it'll be okay," John Greenfield said. "He's in very good hands and he's getting the best of care here."

Erik nodded numbly, not entirely hearing. "*I can't believe that guy,*" he thought as they exited the hospital and walked for the parking garage. "*Why would Dad work in a program that will kill if someone told their secrets?*"

"You seem deep in thought," John Greenfield interrupted.

"Dad," Erik said nervously, "what are you working on exactly with Gateway?"

"I told you…"

"But even if you're in the Defense Works program, would they really kill you if you told someone on the outside their secrets?"

"It's a Federal job," John Greenfield explained, "so I have to take an oath of secrecy."

"So if I'm understanding this right, Gateway is involved with the armed forces somehow?"

"Yes, we work directly with AMASTCOMS, or the Army Missile and Aviation Systems Troop Command Support. Both Gateway and their sister company, Gen-Tech work for them."

"What is Gen-Tech?"

"Genetic Technologies. They work on all sorts of biological and chemical applications, like cures for diseases and how to defend against biological weapon attacks."

"That's... well... How did you get mixed up in that sort of thing?"

John Greenfield chortled. "I've always been into engineering. Smiley and I used to work on cars and build things, though he's more the brains and I'm more the brawn of the operation. We had some good times building custom hotrods back then."

"They hired you because of that?"

"No, it was after The War. I worked in Engineering Support when I served my time in the Defense Forces while Smiley was in Aviation Logistics."

"So he wasn't a jet fighter?"

"He worked on their computers, like missile defense systems and such," John Greenfield said instead, avoiding the question. "Anyways, after we finished our tour, I decided to put my skills to good use." Finding the car, John Greenfield searched for his keys and huffed when he realized he did not have them.

"Where did you lose them?" Erik asked.

"Probably after fighting with Smiley." John Greenfield laughed. "He hasn't left yet, so let's go back for them."

Erik grunted and walked with him for the elevators at the lot's end leading upstairs into the main building.

"I don't feel all that great," Erik complained as they stepped onto the cable car.

"Rest rooms are at the end of the hall." John Greenfield struck a button and they moved upwards.

"I'll meet you at the elevators here, okay?" Erik said once the doors opened on the floor where Kevin stayed.

"I won't be long."

Erik walked in the opposite direction, finding the men's washrooms. He entered and approached the sinks. Running the tap, Erik splashed cold water on his face.

"I don't understand the meaning of this," he muttered. "If they're supposed to be so secretive, then why did that orderly slip me that card?" Erik shut off the water and grabbed the nearby paper towels, wiping at his face. The doors opened and the mysterious young doctor entered. "Hey," Erik snapped as he threw away the paper. "Who are you exactly and how are you with Gateway?"

The young man whirled around, surprised. "Sorry," he said, and put his hands in his pockets. "I can't tell you anything about that."

"Are you working with more than just the military?"

"It's a complicated situation, I can tell you that much," the young man retorted. "So it's really not worth it trying to explain to you." He shrugged his shoulders. "Besides, you're not meant to know and your father's still an outsider, so we have every right to be cautious."

"Why is that?" Erik demanded.

"He's involved with Genovera Zachary, a genius-level scientist. We're concerned that she may lean towards committing felonies by conducting hazardous illegal experiments, given her current situation."

"What's wrong with trying to save a life?" Erik yelled. "You act as if that's somehow wrong!"

"As she's a very ill son in critical condition, she might steal Federal secrets to use in her favor. Given her personality and looks, she may even manipulate others to gain classified information and that's not impossible to do."

"So you already dislike her because she's a lady scientist?" Erik scoffed. "The woman is smart, so don't be so jealous!"

"Oh, I'm not jealous, but women are just not to be trusted, simply put." The young man grinned darkly. "I've figured she will go to great lengths to use what she can at her disposal. That's why I'm not surprised she put in paperwork and vouched for your father to work with us. He too is quite gifted and I'm afraid if they team together, they may cause us much trouble in the future."

"Then why accept him?"

"We need his skills. No one has such impeccable ability as he has." The young man blew a hard sigh. "Of course, what he chooses to do with that skill is of his own will, but it'll be quite a pity if he's under that woman's influence."

"Why would that be a bad thing?"

The young man withdrew his hands from his slacks pockets and reached into his inside blazer pocket. "I'll just have to force him to make a choice," he snarled, revealing a double-barreled blunt-nose revolver. "Either he cut his ties with that woman or face certain consequences."

Erik put up his hands, intimidated when the man pointed the gun in his direction. "Where do I fit in this?" he cried.

"You may also prove a problem as well, so I'm telling you... don't interfere and I won't have to kill you and the woman both. But of course, if he chooses neither of you, then all is well, hm?"

"You're crazy!"

"I'm just telling you to tell your father to weigh his decisions carefully, is all."

"I'll tell him," Erik said faintly. "Just please, don't kill me!"

"I'll skip over the needless details and will just tell you my goal: you will be my safeguard to maintain the balance of your father's work. Should that balance collapse, I *will* come after you for the answers I seek."

"But I don't know anything!"

The young man laughed. "Statistically speaking, I wouldn't be surprised if he *didn't* hide anything with you. Given how close you two are, you *will* be a liability, but if I were to destroy you, he'd have no choice but to work for us once he came to collect you."

"What if he disagrees?"

"Then I'll destroy him too."

"Justin," John Greenfield called from outside. "Are you okay?"

"What's the point of killing him if he's so central to your program?" Erik demanded.

"A man of that great skill is bound to have an even greater memory. If he obtains top secret security clearance, he'll sell his soul to the highest bidder if he ever gets crossed."

"My father isn't anything like that!"

"We'll see."

"Justin!" called John Greenfield, his voice closer.

The young man lowered his gun and stalked over to one of the empty stalls. He stepped inside and Erik blew a shaky sigh, relaxing slightly when the door shut with a click.

Moments later, the restroom doors opened and John Greenfield poked his head in. "There you are!" he chirped. "I was getting worried."

"I'm okay," Erik grumbled.

"Are you sick?"

"I will be in a minute..."

"Want me to wait for you?"

"I just need some air..." Erik hurried over to John Greenfield's side. "Let's go, Dad."

"Okay..."

Erik grabbed John Greenfield by the arm and John Greenfield appeared concerned. He gently pet Erik on the head and kept pace as Erik hurried to the elevators.

Once returning to the elevators, on their way down, the car stopped at one of the lower floors and the doors opened, revealing the mysterious doctor. He stepped on, smiling maliciously at Erik.

"Schumacher," he greeted, ignoring Erik and faced the mirrored doors once they hushed close.

"Hello," John Greenfield said timidly.

"I want to congratulate you on working for Gateway."

John Greenfield gave a hesitant smile. "I heard the program is very difficult to enter."

"Yes, it takes a *very* special person..."

"Are you one of the technicians at Gateway?"

"I make various rounds between Gateway, Gen-Tech and General..."

"So you're in the Research Department?"

The young man chortled. "You can say that..." The doors opened at the parking garage and all three stepped out. "I just want to warn you, that in the work you're taking on, you *will* have to make difficult decisions."

John Greenfield raised an eyebrow. "How so?"

"I went over your military records... twice you saved a life."

John Greenfield blushed. "I'd love to finish talking this over," he said quickly, "but I have to get my son home... It's getting late."

"I'm sorry for keeping you and I'm sure you have to get going, but I want to continue our talk."

"I'll let you know when I have the time to listen to what you have to say," John Greenfield replied.

The young man went through his pockets and withdrew a matchbook. "If you possess the time to talk to me then visit me after work," he said, handing it to John Greenfield. "There we can discuss other options."

"Options regarding what?" John Greenfield asked, taking the matchbook.

"Another place of employment where your skills can be used for the greater good." The young man walked away. "I'm there at six-o'clock each evening," he called over his shoulder.

"See you then," John Greenfield called after him.

"Dad," Erik murmured as they headed back for the car. "I

don't like that guy. He's creepy."

John Greenfield blew a short sigh. "He doesn't seem to be a problem to me." He looked down at the matchbook he held. "It's important that I get to know all my coworkers."

"He never told you his name."

"Right, yet he seems to know me."

"What are you getting into exactly?"

"Only as much as I know and what I told you is what the little Genovera told me."

"But why apply if you have no clue about it?"

"Genovera entered my application for me and told me not to worry about the details. She said my skills were just wasting away and they're needed very much right now."

"Please, be careful…"

Approaching the car, John Greenfield unlocked the door and got in, then leaned over, unlocking the other door for Erik. "So, would you like to go out to eat or go home?" he asked, starting the engine.

Erik entered the car and pulled the door close. He let out a distressed moan and sank into his seat. "I just want to hide under the covers," he whined.

John Greenfield tousled Erik's hair. "I know the feeling, Ace," he said gently. "I honestly understand." He pulled out the lot and Erik watched the scenery pass on the long drive home. He later nodded off.

Erik groaned when he heard ringing. He reached over blindly and picked up the receiver.

"What is it?" he murmured.

"I'm surprised you're up this early," said the female voice over the line.

"My eyes are still closed," Erik snapped. "What do you want?"

"Don't you have work today?"

"I don't know. Do I?"

"They want you to come down to the office today and pick up your latest assignment."

"All right, give me an hour."

"I'll come by and pick you up."

"Thanks."

Erik put the receiver back on the cradle and blew a heavy sigh. Opening his eyes, he stared up at a pale yellow ceiling with a single wooden fan and a pair of frosted bulbs.

Sitting up, Erik took in his surroundings. The bedroom was small, with a full-sized bed covered by a pair of yellow and brown comforters. Across the room near the door was a closet with a mirror hanging on the wall and next to it was a stuffed chair in the corner with a white canvas bag filled with laundry on its side that had jeans and T-shirts falling out. The room was plain, with yellow walls and a window covered by a heavy brown curtain.

Erik stepped out of bed and shuffled over to the window, pulling aside the curtain. He saw the black-painted weather-beaten grated fire escape leading to the alley below. Moments later, a dark sedan pulled up and idled near the large chipped navy refuse bin.

Erik left the window and approached the laundry bag, picking through the clothes inside. He frowned when he found the clothing were unwashed and headed for the closets.

Opening them, he found several dark suits and pastel dress shirts. As he pushed the items aside, he noticed several dresses and blouses.

"These can't be mine," he murmured and grabbed a pair of dark blue slacks and a lavender shirt then headed to the bathroom down the hall to shower and change.

NINETEEN

Erik later entered the kitchen, finding a pack of cigarettes and a lighter left for him on the table next to the paint-stained teacup, a jar of instant coffee and a single white mug. He noticed the kettle on the stove and turned the dial on the range. Taking a seat at the table, Erik lit a cigarette, waiting for the water to boil.

After the kettle whistled, Erik searched the kitchen drawers for spoons and found a small amber bottle with no label. He opened the small white metal cap and poured out silver powder into his palm. Erik frowned and dumped the bottle in the sink, then grabbed a spoon for his coffee.

Moments later, he heard a knock at the door and hurried to answer it. Opening the door, he met a young woman with tanned skin and long red hair, wearing wide dark brown tinted sunglasses and a black overcoat.

"I'm surprised you're still here," she said, smiling. Erik shrugged and returned to the kitchen to resume his coffee. "Did you get into any trouble?"

"Not that I recall," Erik called back.

"Aren't you ready yet?"

"I want my coffee first," Erik spat.

The woman sighed and shut the door behind her, then

entered the kitchen. She leaned against the wall, watching Erik sip his drink while he held a lit cigarette in his free hand. "We're going to be late," she complained.

"Who are you?"

"Call me Gina."

"Whatever."

"Why are you being hostile toward me?"

Erik glared back at Gina and set down his mug with a firm bang. "What do you expect from me?" he snapped. "I'm nobody!"

"You're somebody," Gina said gently. "Somebody very important."

"Then why can't I remember?"

"Did you hit your head?" Gina withdrew a slender silver pen from her pocket and pressed a switch on the side. She approached, taking Erik's chin in a gentle hand and passed a blue light into his eyes.

"I'm not sure," Erik murmured as Gina checked his eyes.

"And you can't tell me how long you've been like this."

"Your guess is as good as mine."

"Maybe it's starting to get worse...?"

"What is?"

"Well, you haven't been home for three days." Gina switched off the light and frowned. "I was starting to worry."

"So I don't live here?" Erik asked, raising an eyebrow.

"I was surprised to find you were here. Happy accident, I suppose."

Erik narrowed his eyes. "So what is it I do, exactly?"

"You take care of problems." Gina turned on her heel. "Come on, let's not waste any further time."

"What kind of problems?" Erik demanded. "Do I kill people?"

Gina chuckled and turned around, facing Erik. "No, you don't kill people! In fact, you hate killing, remember?"

Erik looked down into his mug of coffee, distressed. "I don't know what to think," he murmured. "I wake up and I don't know where I am. I don't know who I am. I don't have anything with me - no wallet, no VitaStat card, anything."

"Your name won't matter. What matters is that you help me get rid of nasty problems."

"But how can I get rid of problems if it doesn't require killing?"

"All problems can be solved without bloodshed. That's what your father believed in." Gina waved at Erik to follow. "Now come on."

Erik put out his burning cigarette into the cup and rose to his feet. "What happens if someone dies?" he asked softly.

"Fate, I suppose, maybe Karma. I don't know what to call it."

Erik grunted and returned to the bedroom, collecting his coat from the floor. As he headed for the door, he noticed a faded sepia-toned photograph on the bureau, showing three young men and three young women in Defense Force uniforms posing in front of a stairwell.

Erik picked up the photograph and turned it over, finding only names listed: Ossie, Gina, Jerry, Smiley, Joe, Shana.

"Hey," Gina called. "Did you go back to sleep?"

Erik pulled into his coat and pocketed the photograph. "Yeah, I'm coming," he called back.

"Your shoes are near the couch."

Erik grunted and returned to the parlor, grabbing his loafers left on the floor. Stepping into them, he followed the woman out the door and they headed downstairs.

"Will you be all right today?" Gina asked once they made their way outdoors into the cold morning.

Erik nodded as he flipped up his collar and held his coat close. "I'll survive," he murmured.

Gina led Erik to the alley where the dark sedan awaited them. She opened the rear passenger door for him and Erik stepped inside. He looked up at the driver who wore a dark coat, cap and glasses and nodded to him. The driver smiled and nodded back.

"Where to?" asked the driver once Gina shut the door and entered the front passenger side.

"Let's stop by Mercado Corp," Gina answered.

The driver snorted and started the car, then pulled out the alley. "Planning to get a refill?" he teased.

Gina let out a short laugh. "Not exactly." She opened the glove compartment and withdrew a small booklet. "Here, take a look at this."

Erik grabbed the small leather booklet and opened it, finding a pair of photographs and several folded sheets of paper. One showed a bloodied bullet-riddled body slumped against a bloodstained wall and the other showed a smiling young man with dark brown hair in cornrows and bright gray eyes against a blue opaque background.

"That used to be Derrick Andrews, a Gen-Tech scientist," Gina explained. "He was working on a project code-named

'Divinity' that Kanbal Industries was interested in. We want you to sniff around and find out why he met a nasty end."

"Why go to Mercado?" Erik asked and set aside the photographs. "Didn't you want me to stop by the office first?"

Gina giggled. "We are in the office." Taking the folded sheets of paper tucked in the book, Erik unfolded them, finding a resume and research papers. "You're going to take his place, Mister Ferdian," Gina replied.

"I know nothing about science or engineering," Erik protested.

"You've got an uncanny photographic memory. Study what you have there and just fake your way at Mercado's labs. If you need anything else, feel free to call me."

"How can I have a photographic memory when my long term is shit?" Erik complained.

"Have you always wondered how you know a lot yet can't recall why?" Erik nodded. "For some reason, though you can't remember the previous day, you somehow retain what you read and anything involving bodily skill."

"What about people?"

"For some reason, you forget them after a day. Names, faces... Unless they stick around, they're not important to you."

"Did I have some kind of accident?" Erik murmured.

"It was a long time ago."

Erik set aside the paperwork and sat back in his seat, looking out the tinted windows at the passing cold city morning. "How long has it been like this?" he wondered aloud.

"It wouldn't make sense for me to tell you," Gina explained.

Erik blew a sigh and ran his hands through his hair. "After

I finish this assignment today, where will I go?"

"Where do you want to go?"

"Home." Tears suddenly streamed down Erik's cheeks and he held his head in his hands, sniffling.

"Hey," Gina said kindly and turned in her seat. "What's the matter?"

"I don't know," Erik moaned. "Just thinking about where home is... It makes me sad."

"You live alone in this big empty apartment," Gina noted. "You told me you didn't want anyone there because it would be difficult."

"That's not it." Erik shook his head and wiped at his eyes with the palms of his hands. "I don't know how to tell you how I feel."

"Let me know where you want to go when you're done with today, okay?"

"Yeah, sure," Erik murmured.

"Will you be aright?"

Erik nodded and picked up the papers, resuming his study of the material.

Later, the driver pulled up in front of a large glass and chrome office building with the name 'MERCADO' emblazoned in large bold steel letters atop its edifice. Gina handed Erik a small leather wallet and a cellular phone. He took the wallet and opened it, finding only a fifty dollar bill and his employee ID card, showing that his name was Ferdian Smith.

"Now feel free to call me if things get hairy," Gina said. "That number is secure."

Erik nodded and pocketed the wallet and the phone.

"Have a nice day, Mister Smith," said the driver as Erik stepped out the car.

"Call me after you're done with work," Gina called and Erik shut the door, then made his way up the stairs.

Opening the glass doors, he entered the building that had dark marble floors, dark yellow tiled walls, and walnut furniture. Approaching the front desk, Erik smiled at the receptionist who wore a chocolate brown blazer, chinos, and yellow shirt, filing his manicured nails. The young man glanced up, giving Erik a sour look.

"I'm the new assistant," Erik said brightly.

"Where's your ID?" the office worker snapped. "You're supposed to be wearing it at all times. Company policy."

"Well, I just started today." Erik dug through his wallet and withdrew his card. "Do you have something I can clip this to?"

"Ugh, why the pretty ones gotta be dumb?" the receptionist grumbled as he set down his nail file and opened a drawer, sifting through it. Pulling out a lanyard, he slammed it on the desk.

"Thanks," Erik said through gritted teeth. Putting the cord around his neck, he clipped on the tag and glanced up at the overhead clock. "Care to tell me where Floor Five-Ninety-Three is?"

"You can find it yourself," the receptionist snapped.

Erik frowned and reached over, grabbing the office worker by the shirtfront. The receptionist gasped and grabbed Erik's wrists as he leaned in. "Now listen, be nice," Erik snarled. "You don't know who might just end up dead if you upset the wrong person."

"I'm sorry!" the receptionist yelped and Erik let go, throwing him back into his chair.

"Now, where's Floor Five-Ninety-Three?" Erik demanded.

"Elevator Five, Hall Nine." The receptionist pointed to the right. "Elevators are that way."

"Thanks," Erik chirped and made his way in the direction for the elevators.

Upon entry, Erik noticed a mocha-skinned young man with a silver thin line mustache wearing a gray jumpsuit and black cap over his shaggy white hair. Hanging from his rear pocket lingered a navy towel and the man carried a beaten red toolbox. On his face, he wore wide dark brown sunglasses and had a slender scar across his right cheek.

Erik frowned and the young man grinned.

"Something wrong?" the man asked.

"I'm not sure," Erik murmured.

"Why, what is it?"

Erik shook his head. "I shouldn't."

"That's okay."

"Maintenance?" Erik asked instead.

"Somewhat," replied the man. "I'm also known as 'The Mechanic'."

"So you're good at fixing things?"

"Why shouldn't I be?" The man chortled. "Which floor?"

"Fifth."

The man pressed the button and the elevators began its ascent. "Nice day, is it?"

"It's cold," Erik replied and blew a short sigh. "So, where's your ID card?"

"Pocket."

"Shouldn't you be wearing it though?"

"They know me well here."

Erik grunted. "What's broken?"

"All sorts of things." The maintenance worker snorted. "New guy, huh?"

"Er, sure," Erik murmured.

"Be careful. There's a high turnover rate here."

The bell pinged once the elevator reached the fifth floor. Erik stepped off and turned to the man who waved at him before the doors closed.

Erik shrugged and followed the signs, leading him to room ninety-three. Trying the handle, he opened the door, revealing a small office with wall cabinets. Many papers surrounded a desk and a tower computer. A single chair rest in the corner behind the door.

"Hello?" Erik called. "I'm the new assistant."

Shutting the door, Erik took off his overcoat and put it on the hook embedded in the door. Approaching the desk, he picked up a paper at random, finding notes about purchase orders.

Tapping the keyboard, the screen came to life, revealing an open database. Scanning the screen and the paper, Erik saw the data was being inputted. He sat down and began work.

Moments later, the door opened. "Hey, what do you want for lunch?" a voice asked.

"Something cheap," Erik replied, never once turning away from the computer.

"How's Chinese take-away sound?"

"That's fine."

"I'm getting me an egg foo on bun. Want one?"

"Sure."

The door shut and Erik continued working in silence.

TWENTY

After taking the morning of typing data and filing the used paperwork, Erik stretched and yawned. He glanced at the clock, noting it was a quarter to noon.

Leaving his desk, he opened the door and bumped into a woman with wavy blond hair and blue eyes, wearing a black skirt, pink blouse and red heels holding a cup of coffee and a stack of forms. Erik let out a yelp when hot liquid splashed on his chest and the papers went falling to the floor.

"Oops!" the young woman cried and Erik grabbed her by the arm before she staggered back on her heels.

Erik grabbed the cup of coffee she held before she dropped it and gave a derisive smile. "Don't tell me you got this for me," he snapped.

"I'm sorry," the woman said and pulled out of Erik's grip. "Thanks though... I almost broke a heel."

"Sure, no problem." Erik handed back her coffee and unbuttoned his shirt.

"Hey," the woman wailed in horror as Erik pulled out of his shirt, "what are you doing?"

"You're buying me a new shirt."

"Just rub out the stain."

"Then tell me where the restrooms are."

"End of the hall." Erik snorted and took her coffee then left her side, stomping down the corridor. "What a weirdo," she muttered and crouched on the floor, picking up the fallen papers.

Erik entered the restrooms and came to a pause when he heard water running. He turned around, surprised by the mirrors on the walls. On one end were a marble counter and two stainless steel sinks with a soap dispenser and automatic hand dryer. Stepping beyond the partition, Erik found several stalls containing urinals and a pair of toilets. On the other side was a small adjoining shower with locker room.

Erik took a seat on the locker room bench and set aside the coffee then withdrew the small phone he had in his pocket. Turning it on, Erik waited for the startup sequence and took note of his surroundings. The walls matched the floor with plain white tiles and the lockers were all solid gray, spray painted with red numbers. Several had locks on them and others were empty.

Erik glanced at his phone and pressed a button, going to his contact list. He only had a single number listed with no name and called it.

"Hello?" answered Gina.

"You didn't tell me you had me processing data all day," Erik snapped into the line. "What is it you're looking for exactly?"

"What?" Gina yelped. "That's not what you were supposed to be doing!"

"I don't know if this is of any interest to you, but while I was putting in the numbers, I noticed some of the orders seemed off - they weren't adding up."

"What's it regarding?"

"I need to look some more and see what's the correlation. If it has anything to do with that Andrews, I'll let you know."

"All right, be careful."

"Wait, before you go..."

"What is it?"

"What about the labs you initially planned before?"

"Don't worry about it. I'm sure it was just a minor filing error." Gina cut off the line and Erik glared at his phone.

"The nerve!" he grumbled and took up the cup of coffee. Taking a sip, he tasted sugar and gagged, dropping the cup. Erik stood and let out a gasp when he faced a naked barrel-chested middle-aged man with short dark brown hair graying on the sides and green eyes standing in front of him.

"I thought I was the only one here," the man replied.

"What do you want?" Erik yelped.

"You're in front of my locker."

Erik backed away and pocketed the phone he held. "Sorry," he murmured.

"Don't worry about it," the man said as he padded over to where Erik once stood and opened the locker. "I'll call Maintenance."

"I didn't know they had a shower here," Erik said, looking down at the floor.

"Yeah, all the floors got one. It's useful if you ride to work instead of driving." The middle-aged man withdrew a bag and took out a change of clothes, pulling into them.

"You bike?"

"Yeah."

"Are the restrooms always this empty?"

"Nah, the IT department's a mess. Always busy, full of towels... Full of dirty young dogs, filthy animals if you ask me. Now the clerical pool - it's nice, quiet. Lots of pretty young things to drool over too."

Erik felt his face burning as the middle-aged man sat on the bench and pulled into his tie. "I just started here," murmured Erik. "I don't know everyone on this floor."

"What's the name?"

"Smith... Ferdian."

"I'm Avers, Brodie."

"Er, Mister Avers..."

"Brodie, call me Brodie."

"Alright, Mister Brodie..."

"Just Brodie."

"Sure, Mister Brodie."

Brodie snorted and tied on his shoes. "Hey, Feddy, what's so interesting about your shoes?" he joked as he approached and gave Erik's back a firm pat. "Unless you came for something else?"

"I, um, no..." Erik glanced up and Brodie grinned brightly. "I had a stain on my shirt..."

"If you send it down to Laundry, it won't get dropped off 'til Friday."

"What's today?"

"Tuesday!" Brodie let out robust laugh and jarred Erik with a crushing shoulder hug. "I like you Feddy - you're something else." Brodie left Erik's side and approached his locker, withdrawing a shirt. "Here, take mine. I'll send yours down with mine and you can stop by and pick it up later."

"Thanks, I suppose?"

Brodie tossed Erik his shirt and Erik took it, then pulled into Brodie's larger shirt. Erik tossed the soiled shirt to Brodie who caught it and put in the bag at his feet. Shoving the bag inside the locker, Brodie locked it and waved at Erik to follow him.

"What you feel like for lunch?" Brodie inquired.

"Someone's bringing me Chinese," Erik replied after he finished the last of the buttons and followed Brodie's stride.

"So, eating at the desk today?"

Erik nodded. "It seems like it."

"Care if I join ya?"

Erik shrugged. "I really don't care."

"You're really going to love working here," Brodie went on. "The canteen is great, there's little coffee shops dotted here and there and we even got a little gift shop on the second floor." Brodie jabbed Erik's chest with his elbow. "They have these cute little stuffed microbes! You ever seen what The Clam looks like?"

Entering the corridor, Erik passed the young blonde he bumped into earlier. "Your coffee skills are horrible," he said to her.

The blonde-haired woman whirled around, stunned. "Don't tell me you drank it!" she yelped.

"I let the floor have it." Erik continued walking ahead and Brodie laughed.

"You owe me three-fifty, Mister!" the woman shouted.

"Aw, Kass, here, let me pay for it," Brodie said and came to a stop. He withdrew his wallet and Kass approached, glaring at Erik. "Is five okay?"

"Yeah," Kass muttered and frowned when she took the money from him.

"What's with that look?" Erik asked.

"Ugh, you bastard!" Kass suddenly yelped and slapped Brodie's arm. "Really?" Brodie flinched when she slapped him again.

"Hey!" Brodie yelped and Kass stormed down the hall.

"What was that about?" Erik asked.

"I don't know," Brodie said, shrugging. "I don't understand women sometimes."

"I'm holed up in here," Erik said, leading Brodie into his cramped office.

"Oh, so they finally sacked Eisenheimer," Brodie noted as he stepped in. "Hey, open the window, will ya?"

Erik nodded and reached over his desk, pulling up the shade. He unlatched the panel and Brodie approached Erik's desk, opening the bottom drawer.

"Do you smoke?" Brodie asked, withdrawing a glass ashtray and set it on the edge.

"I do," Erik replied. "I don't mind a little chill."

"Good, then you won't tell on me."

Erik snorted. "Why, it's not allowed or something?"

"Not around computers."

"I see." Erik waved at Brodie. "Hand me my cigarettes from my coat pocket, will you?"

"Sure."

Brodie left the desk and dug through Erik's coat, withdrawing the pack and the lighter. The photograph fell out and he picked it up. "What's this?" he murmured.

"What now?" Erik implored, taking a seat at his desk. Brodie picked up the chair behind the door and set it before the desk.

"Here," Brodie said, passing the cigarettes. "You know Joe?"

"Joe?" Erik shook his head. "Clarify, please?"

Brodie tossed the photograph across the table. "Joseph Stone?"

"Name doesn't sound familiar to me at all."

"Giuseppe Petra then?"

Erik gasped when pain flashed behind his eyes. He closed his eyes and rubbed at his abruptly throbbing temples. "I'm not sure," Erik murmured. "It seems familiar, but I can't put my finger on it."

"Yeah, we were in the same unit when we fought in The War back then," Brodie went on. "We both were in the Communications Division. Had to deal with the ComSat so the boys in Aviation Logistics could plan their routes and not get blasted to smithereens." Brodie dug through his pants and frowned when he withdrew his wallet. "Hey, care if I bummed one off ya?"

"Sure, go ahead."

Brodie put his wallet back and took Erik's pack of cigarettes, withdrawing one. "So how long did ya serve in the Defense Forces?"

"What?" Erik opened his eyes, staring at Brodie as he lit his cigarette.

"Were you a Tenner?"

"Tenner...?"

"Did you do your ten-year stint?"

"No."

"Quin then?" Erik gave Brodie a lost expression. "Did you do your five?"

"I…"

Brodie laughed and wagged his finger at Erik. "Ah, I see, you're a Duce. No wonder you're so skinny! Just wanted to hurry up and get home, eh?"

"Sure," Erik murmured. "I did my two years and went home."

"Don't be embarrassed by it. Not everybody's cut out for that sort of thing." Brodie grinned and sat back in his chair, tapping the ashes into the nearby glass tray. "I'm telling ya, War ain't what it used to be. Back in my granddaddy's day, they actually sent *live* ones out there! Guns and everything… It was a real bloody mess."

"How horrific."

"Yeah, but when I went, that's when they started out with those newfangled combat androids. They weren't too smart then. You still needed a guy to handle the controls behind the lines."

The door opened moments later. "Hey, here's your lunch," said the mysterious voice.

Brodie turned in his chair and grinned. "Oh, hey Sangita," he said brightly as the door opened wider, revealing a dark-skinned woman with long raven hair and wide brown eyes. She wore a short navy skirt and a sky-blue blouse with black knee socks and leather shoes.

"He ordered the egg foo sandwich," she said, handing Brodie a paper sack with Chinese characters in red emblazoned across the face. "Your total's three-seventy-five."

Erik dug in his pocket and withdrew his wallet. Opening it,

he found the fifty-dollar bill. "Do you have change for fifty?" he asked sheepishly.

"Don't worry, I'll take care of it," Brodie said and Erik set his wallet aside. Brodie passed Erik his lunch and Erik nodded. Opening the bag, Erik withdrew a napkin and an egg and vegetable paddy on white bread with pickles and onions wrapped in wax paper. Brodie took out his wallet and counted out four bills. "Get me something with the change."

"You can't get nothing for a quarter anymore!" Sangita protested, taking the money.

Brodie grinned. "How about your silence about us breaking the rules?"

"Sure, I won't say anything. But if the fire alarms go off, I *will* tell on you."

Brodie chortled and Sangita shut the door after her.

"The girls seem to like you," Erik murmured.

"It's just my charming personality," Brodie replied and put out his tapering cigarette.

"Do you want half?" Erik asked, unwrapping the sandwich. "It's already been cut."

"Sure."

Erik took his half and passed Brodie the rest. "What else does Mercado do?" he asked and bit into his sandwich.

"Mainly a manufacturer of pharmaceuticals. We're in the processing division, obviously."

Erik nodded. "I see."

After finishing their lunches in silence, Brodie rose to his feet. "Want a soda or anything?" he asked.

"Thanks," Erik answered.

"Preference?"

"Cherry."

"Do they still make that?" Brodie murmured, raising an eyebrow. Erik leaned forward, pressing his fingers to his forehead as he furrowed his brow. "Hey, you okay Feddy?"

"I'm not sure."

"Onions giving ya trouble? I'll bring up a clear soda if ya want."

"Sure, go ahead."

Brodie left his office and Erik moaned, putting his head on the desk.

TWENTY-ONE

Erik slowly roused and opened his eyes, finding himself lying on the floor of a small room with a desk and chair surrounded by file cabinets, bookcases, a multi-line phone and several computers. Behind the desk and office chair, rest a large picture window with a folding bamboo screen in front of it, blocking out the evening sky.

Erik groaned when the fiery pain returned, searing in his side. He sat up, clutching his side and noticed he had blood on his clothes. Pulling up his shirt, he saw several scars across his torso and wondered how he arrived in the mysterious office.

Getting to his feet, Erik approached the window and paused when he heard a soft moan. Turning, he found Clayton slumped on the floor next to the desk, clutching his bloodied shoulder. Cold sweat beaded on his face and neck.

The door to the office suddenly opened, revealing Schnell. "Oh!" the doctor said in surprise and dropped the charts he held in his arm. "What happened?" He quickly shut the door and ran up to Erik.

"Doctor Blazejewelski shot him," Erik answered as Schnell approached and knelt at Clayton's side. "What's going on? How did we get here?"

"I don't know who brought you here," answered Schnell as

he ripped Clayton's shirt collar and examined his shoulder further. "Hand me my bag in the second lower desk drawer."

Erik opened the nearby drawer as told, revealing a small black bag with a red cross on the front. He pulled it out and tossed it to Schnell. The doctor caught it and opened it, withdrawing a leather book containing a scalpel, surgical tweezers, a pair of different sized scissors, a bottle of antiseptic and a flat roll of gauze.

"I'm not sure what's going on anymore," Erik murmured as Schnell used the flathead scissors, cutting away Clayton's shirt and then used the tweezers to dig around in Clayton's wound. Erik clenched his teeth when Clayton groaned in pain and the veins threatening to jump from underneath his skin seemed close to breaking. "What was in that thing?" he demanded. "What's happened to him?"

"Almost," Schnell muttered while he continued digging. Erik wrung his hands as Schnell concentrated, narrowing his eyes when cold sweat appeared over his forehead and nose. "Hold on a little longer!" Clayton gasped as Schnell extracted a black shard with a green sheen.

"What is that thing?" Erik asked when Schnell dug through his pocket and withdrew a small glass vial. Thumbing off the rubber stopper, the doctor dropped the shard into it and the fragment clunked softly.

"They're a kind of fragmentation bullet," Schnell explained, setting the tweezers aside. "I'm lucky to get the bulk of it... Most times they shatter like glass and they're impossible to extract."

"What happens if the remaining stay inside him?"

Schnell picked up the roll of gauze and packed Clayton's

wound, then opened the leather book's side pocket. He withdrew surgical tape and fixed the gauze to Clayton's shoulder. "He'll get sick from the poison," Schnell answered, "but it won't kill him."

"What's their purpose? I thought bullets were made to kill."

Schnell opened the other pocket and withdrew a small vial of clear liquid and a syringe. "This is to help you recover, understand?" he said softly to Clayton. "I'm sorry I don't have anything else for the pain."

Clayton numbly nodded and Schnell uncapped the needle then filled it with the colorless serum. After injecting the drug into the side of Clayton's neck, Clayton fainted and slumped over on his side. Schnell blew a hard sigh and set the used needle aside, then sat back on his knees.

"Why do you help us?" Erik implored. "Will you get in trouble?"

"It doesn't matter," Schnell replied. "Are you injured?"

"I was..." Erik shrugged his shoulders. "I don't know what happened; I don't remember getting here."

"That probably explains why Suber called me," Schnell murmured, "and the reason behind the Code Orange..."

"What?"

"There's a change of clothes in the white file cabinet," Schnell said instead. "The clothes are sealed in plastic storage bags and are marked with various sizes by letters."

Erik left Schnell's side and approached the cabinet on the room's far end, surrounded by computers. "And to think you kept papers in here," Erik quipped as he opened the drawers and searched for clothing that fit. Pulling out a set of scrub shirt and pants, Erik tore off the plastic and quickly changed.

"It's proving useful," Schnell wearily replied.

Erik approached Schnell's side and nudged the doctor gently with his foot. "Why do you help us?" he asked again.

"Do you want the truth or another lie?"

"What kind of answer is that?" Erik spat. "Either way, I'm eventually going to die, so stop talking circles around me and just tell me!"

"They only see and hear what they want," Schnell retorted, "but I can tell you this - if you tell them what they want to hear, they'll know you're lying."

"You're not making any sense!" Erik shouted. "You just want me to deteriorate, is that it?" He kicked the desk and Schnell stiffened. "I don't want to forget everything! I want to remember my friends and my family, the Greenfields!"

"You don't have a family, not anymore."

"Then what are you saying?"

The desk phone began ringing and Schnell grunted. He rose from his place on the floor and struck a button before dropping into his leather desk chair. "Yes?" he grumbled.

"Doctor Schnell," said Hayden's voice over the line, "Number Three's lab results keep returning 'normal' or 'average'."

"What do you want me to do?" Schnell snapped bitterly. "He's most likely just reverted back to baseline."

"That's not possible, Doctor. If he's a part of the CENTRA Program, he should still have–!"

"Have you forgotten the 'X' factor?" Schnell interjected. "We can't force certain qualities, because mutations still happen, no matter how perfect we deem the material we create!"

"We have orders from Corbin to change the trials."

"No."

"Doctor Schnell!"

"It's too risky!" Schnell spat and struck the desk's edge with the flat of his hand. "If his body has reverted, then forcing any more changes will have dire consequences!"

"Corbin insists. We have those orders from Gateway–"

"Don't even think of injecting him with any more enhancement serums!" Schnell snapped. "I'm through talking about this."

"But the potential he may have..."

"Good night."

"Doctor Schnell, wait!" Hayden cried. "You don't sound right... what's going on?"

"It's nothing," Schnell griped and blew a distressed sigh. "I'm overworked, that's all."

"Don't you have vacation time coming?"

"About a good three months worth!"

"Why don't you take time off?"

"I have a lot to do..."

"Corbin insists."

Schnell snorted. "Then I'm taking the charts with me."

"Doctor Schnell...!" Schnell struck the 'end call' button and dial tone flooded the air.

"What's going on?" Erik asked worriedly. "You mean they're *trying* to force changes within me?"

"After you leave this room, you *will* be drugged," Schnell warned. "They've called a Code Orange and everything is on lock down. That I can't save you from, since you will be punished for coming here."

"I don't remember getting here!" Erik protested.

"That's not my problem."

Erik left the desk and approached the bamboo screen, pushing it aside. Across the commons lay the tan building with three floors above street level. "It was Clayton's idea to escape," he murmured.

"Why did you go along with it then?" asked Schnell.

"The staff won't do anything about my roommate. He has plans to either rape or kill me while I sleep." Erik let out a short laugh. "Given how unhinged he is, probably both."

Hearing Schnell's chair squeak, Erik turned around, facing him. The doctor leaned back in his chair, crossing his legs at the knee while he rest his hands on the armrests.

"So running away was your only choice?" inquired Schnell.

"I've even been threatened with death from the other doctor here!" Erik protested. "All he has to do is tell the nurse to put air in my veins and lie to my parents about it!"

"Why do you think they're trying to kill you?"

Erik shook his head. "Your guess is as good as mine."

"There has to be a reason, otherwise you wouldn't be here."

"You're not making sense." Erik left Schnell's side and returned to the window, looking out into the dark of night. "There are some things here and there," he said softly. "But sometimes they're just dreams... Maybe disjointed memories I really don't know much about."

"How much do you remember?"

"Not enough..."

"But what *do* you know?"

Erik blew a hard sigh when the pain began again in his head. "Something about Core Irons and Corite and schematics," he murmured, "and weapons and some papers that look like notes about alchemy and this woman I always see in my dreams and her voice I always hear and her face..."

"What about those things?" Schnell pressed.

Erik shrugged his shoulders. "Forget everything, he told me," he murmured. "They're only going to use him too he said. Trust no one..."

Erik heard Schnell abruptly stand to his feet as a knock resonated at his door.

"Enter," Schnell called.

Erik turned around, watching two large guardsmen enter the office armed with their long-range shotguns slung over their backs. In their hands, they wielded automatic pistols.

Schnell's expression turned stony. "Put that away," he snarled. "There's no need for that here."

"We don't want no problems," said one of the guardsmen and the other stepped over the doctor's dropped charts as he advanced toward them. "You know a Code Orange's been called, so we can't be too lax."

"Don't fight," Schnell said sternly as Erik readied on the defensive. "Not yet, not now."

Erik slackened when the guard grabbed him and dragged him out the room. He grunted once thrown down in the corridor, striking his head against the wall.

"Hold him down," Nelson's voice called. "He's feisty."

Erik scrambled to his feet and whirled around, facing

Nelson who approached with a blackened eye and swollen face. "You're supposed to be dead!" he screeched.

Nelson grinned darkly as he withdrew a syringe full of green serum. "I can take a few to the chin," Nelson replied and the guard pointed his pistol at Erik's head. Erik tensed when Nelson grabbed his arm. "That should get the fight out of you, eh?" Nelson cracked as he injected Erik. "Now don't get me wrong, I like it rough, but I'm making sure you're gonna be the one doing the kicking and screaming." Nelson withdrew the needle and pushed Erik against the wall.

"What about my life?" Erik snapped.

"What does it matter? You're our property now, my pretty young thing." Erik pushed him back and received a hard kick in the groin in return. Erik grunted and slipped to his knees. "I'm skinning your ass alive, boy."

"I don't believe you," Erik hissed.

"Oh, really now?" Nelson grabbed Erik by his shirtfront and leaned in close. "I've got bills to pay, see, and if that means I'll have to cut you a little, then I will!"

"Get out of my face, you piece of trash!" Erik snapped and spat at Nelson.

Nelson's eyes narrowed. "I see," he growled and wiped away the spittle with the back of his free hand. "You're going to be my favorite troublemaker worth punishing!" Nelson grabbed Erik by the face and smashed his head against the wall, knocking him out.

Erik began to rouse, hearing voices nearby.

"You made it," a male voice said softly.

"Well, I had to make sure he was well asleep," said a female voice, "otherwise he's a monster!"

Erik sat up, finding he was back in the room with the comfortable bed and the posters of various actors and bands on the wall. Noticing the bedroom door ajar, he stepped out of bed and silently made his way down the hall. Reaching the edge, he looked over the banister, spotting Genovera on the couch speaking to John Greenfield.

"You look like you can use a drink," John Greenfield said. "I know I do after today!"

"I'm fine," replied Genovera, "I just need a rest."

"How do you deal with him?"

"The same way you deal with him."

John Greenfield chuckled. "I'm so sorry for what happened..."

"I'm sorry too. I hope Melvin didn't rough up Justin too badly..."

"He's a strong kid." John Greenfield went through his pocket and withdrew the matchbook. "So have you heard of this place?"

Erik backed away for his room and cursed himself when a floorboard squeaked as he neared his door.

"He seems to be up," Genovera murmured.

"This isn't the place to talk... let's go elsewhere while we still have plenty of time."

"Last I need is for Melvin to wake up and find that I'm not in bed."

"Where else would he think you'd be?"

"In bed with you."

John Greenfield laughed and he stepped outside with Genovera.

Hearing the front door shut and the locks turn, Erik hurried back into his room and grabbed his reserve skates hanging on the bedpost. He raced down the steps and peered out the window, catching sight of Genovera and John Greenfield in her car parked across the street.

Erik quickly slipped on his skates and waited until Genovera pulled away to step outdoors. Shutting the door behind him, Erik jumped the stoop and skated after them. Keeping out of sight on the sidewalk, once Genovera idled at a stop sign, Erik crouched low once he approached and grabbed the bumper.

"What was that?" John Greenfield yelped, startled. Erik ducked down, sweating profusely.

"I probably hit a cat," Genovera replied.

"Or the curb," John Greenfield teased.

Erik blew a sigh of relief as Genovera turned the corner and he followed with them.

TWENTY-TWO

Pulling up to a diner, Erik let go and skated behind another car, watching them park several car-lengths ahead. John Greenfield and Genovera left the vehicle moments later and entered the restaurant, taking a window booth near the rear.

Erik left his hiding place and entered the diner, taking a seat several tables away. He picked up a menu, hiding behind it and listened to their conversation. A server approached moments later, setting down a glass of water and silverware.

"Just water," Erik said quickly and the server nodded before moving on. Erik pulled out his spoon and set it on the table, watching their reflection.

"Aren't you cold?" John Greenfield asked and took off his jacket.

"It just seems so crazy," Genovera murmured as John Greenfield handed her his blazer and she draped it over her shoulders. "I can't believe you're finally working with me!"

"Well, I've tried my best. I can't bear to be too far from you, you know."

Genovera giggled as John Greenfield reached across the table and took her hand. "At least this way, Melvin won't be too suspicious," she said wryly. "Now we have a legitimate excuse."

"Now you're the one to talk!" John Greenfield rolled his

eyes. "He can just leave you and take off, but on the other hand, he'd *kill* me, whether or not I'm his friend!"

"It's useless to try now; we're in it too deep with Kevin and all..."

"I'm just happy he looks more like you. Otherwise, there'd be tons of questions..."

Genovera flushed. "Enough about the past. We're here in the present now."

"Don't fret... I *will* find a way to save him. I care about him too, you know."

Genovera smiled sadly. "I know."

John Greenfield gave Genovera's hand a gentle squeeze in return. "I'm sure there's a third option," he murmured. "If we put our heads together we can come up with something!"

"But we don't know if it'll be a good or bad decision..."

"Don't be so afraid of the unknown, Gina!" John Greenfield protested. "We won't know unless we try!"

"But what if we get penalized for even trying?"

"If all we do is worry, then we won't know. First we have to understand, and then we won't make the same mistake twice."

"If you think it'll be okay, then I'll go with you."

John Greenfield smiled. "Thanks for being brave... After all, we don't have a lot of time. We have to work quickly."

"That's right; his status can change at any time..."

"After all, you have the power to make this happen and find some kind of breakthrough..."

Genovera shook her head. "I can't help but worry," she demurred. "What if they use our ideas for other programs?"

"Why do you say that?"

A server approached them and Erik took a gulp of water, stunned and trembling in shock. "*Is he saying what I think he's saying?*" he thought. "*Is Kevin really my half-brother?*" Erik left his table and skated away, heading back for home.

Skating up sidewalk upon approach to his house, Erik spotted Mahjin sitting on the stoop in an olive overcoat and his shaggy blond hair hung disheveled in his face. Draped across his lap lay his white wax staff.

"What are you doing here?" Erik demanded, startled.

"Where have you been?" Mahjin snapped in return.

"I was out and about..."

"Where's Jerry?"

"I'm not sure..."

"Out with my wife, eh?" he grumbled. "She's gone too!"

"I... well...!" Erik backed away when Mahjin stood unsteadily to his feet.

"I've tried ringing and no one answered, so I came here, finding the damn place empty!" Mahjin struck out at Erik and he dodged the blow. "That swine...!" Erik turned out of another fierce swing. "I'll kill him, I swear!"

"Please don't!" Erik cried. "It's not like that!"

"What would you know?" Mahjin roared as his face reddened in rage. "I should've known he was like that from beginning..." He tightened his grip around his staff. "Some friend he is!"

"They were just talking, that's all!" Erik skated out of Mahjin's path, keeping his distance. "I skitched behind them and followed them. They're just talking, really! Please believe me." Mahjin raised his staff in both hands and held it at ready. "Dad's a good guy, isn't he? He helped you a long time ago, didn't he? Wasn't he worth saving?"

Mahjin sighed heavily and lowered his staff. "I shouldn't blame ya, lad," he grumbled. "I'm just broken up, is all." Mahjin plopped back down on the steps and leaned against his staff. "Kevin will be fine, he keeps tellin' me." He glanced up at Erik. "I owe you a debt of gratitude... Without you doin' what you did in that, his unpleasant disposition probably would've been worse."

"Isn't he on the verge of death?"

"He's got a fighting chance, Jerry says."

"Aren't Public Security involved?"

"What do you mean?" Erik explained the events leading to the accident. Mahjin shook his head. "It's best not to involve them... it seems something greater than us at play and we've mixed up in it."

"What will we do then?" Erik wondered aloud.

"Other than be careful?" Mahjin scoffed. "We won't know until the time comes."

"Will you be alright?"

"Just leave me here to sober up some more..."

Erik took off his skates and walked past him for the porch light. Unscrewing the cover, he took out an extra key and entered the house. Erik dropped his skates near the door and set the porch light cover aside on the table with the key. Making a straight line for the couch, Erik dropped on the edge and fainted from exhaustion.

Erik groaned when the darkness of the world slowly faded back into the white-walled room and he heard a ticking clock in the background, with the noise almost deafening to the ambient silence around him. He shut his eyes again from the smartness, seething.

"Shall we start over?" asked the doctor.

"Start with what?" Erik muttered, glancing up at the doctor who sat across from him, notepad in hand. The tape recorder rest nearby on the desk, hissing softly with its gears turning moderately.

"You were going to tell me something."

"Nothing. I'm telling you nothing."

"Please, let's not get agitated again," said the doctor gently. "The sooner we start, the better you'll be."

Erik spat at the doctor with contempt. "Bullshit," he hissed.

"You must relax," murmured the doctor. He withdrew a handkerchief from his suit pocket and wiped the spittle from his cheek. "Please, don't do that again."

"I want out of this place."

"You're very sick, you see."

"I'm not and you know it."

"Please, calm yourself. We can get more medicine..."

"No!" Erik clenched his hands. "You do that again and I *will* kill you!"

"Please..."

"Shut up!"

"You must relax."

"Why?"

"You must..."

Erik struggled against the restraints around his wrists. "Say that again!" he snarled. The pain entered his face and his head whipped back from a heavy blow, striking out his world.

"Hey, Feddy," Brodie's voice called. "Wake up, buddy."

Erik groaned and sat up, disoriented. He felt a cold wind at his back and looked up, finding himself on the floor underneath his desk and Brodie standing over him with a can of cola. Behind him, the window was cracked open, letting in the icy winter air.

"What happened to me?" Erik moaned and ran his hands through his hair. "How did I get down here?"

"Did you fall out your chair?" Brodie inquired.

Erik glanced over, noticing his office chair pushed against the wall and several papers and folders scattered at its feet, blown from the frigid breeze. He blew a hard sigh and stood.

"I don't remember," Erik murmured. "I have a headache..."

"You feel like calling it in early?" Brodie sipped the cola he held and Erik saw another can of soda on the edge of his desk.

"Why do you ask?" Erik inquired. "Was I sleepwalking or something?"

"No, just talking in your sleep, I suppose."

"Was I saying anything?"

"Sangita tried to tell me but I brushed her off. I said you're trying to get back to Normy with us plebeians." Brodie chortled. "I told her I'd take care of you. I'm a vet too, ya know, so I totally get it - the nightmares, the cold sweats, the whole thing."

"You seem so adjusted."

"That's what pills are for." Brodie laughed and pat Erik's back. "Let's skip and hit up a nice place for the evening. What do you say?"

"I really need to get these forms done."

"Fine, but I'll pick you up after work, okay?"

"Sure." Brodie left Erik's desk and headed for the door. "Hey, Mister Avers," Erik called.

"Yeah?" Brodie paused near the door.

"Get me some vodka, will you?" Erik requested and pulled up his chair.

"Oh, I got the wrong kind?" Brodie turned around as Erik picked up the papers and set them aside.

"No," Erik answered sourly, "I need it for my nerves."

Brodie chortled and wagged a finger at Erik. "After work, Feddy. It's important that you don't screw up the numbers."

"Fine, I'll wait." Erik popped the tab on his soda and sipped it, tasting lemon and lime. He raised his can toward Brodie and Brodie nodded, then left the room. His phone rang moments later and Erik withdrew the cellular. "What is it?" he answered.

"Where do you plan to go tonight?" Gina's voice asked.

"I'm going out with a friend," Erik answered. "I'll call you to pick me up afterwards."

"Be safe."

Erik set the phone aside and resumed sorting the papers, then input the data into the computer database.

After filing the last stack Erik had on his desk into his cabinet, he noted his changes from his database in his logbook, writing in red pencil next to the columns in blue.

"Oxygen, Hydrogen, Nitrogen, Potassium, Chlorine, Magnesium, Calcium...?" Erik muttered and tapped the pencil against his teeth. "Does he mean Fluoride, Carbide, Carbonate, Chloride, Hydroxide, Cyanide, Hypochlorite, Nitrate, Oxide, Phosphate or Cyanamide?" He grunted and rubbed at his temples. "That's some interesting stuff they're moving around, Andrews," Erik murmured. "What part did you play?"

Placing his logbook in his cabinet, Erik then shut his window and put away the ashtray in the bottom drawer. The door to his office opened and Brodie stepped in, grinning.

"I can't wait to get out of here," said Brodie brightly. "Let's hurry."

"Where are you taking me?" Erik asked and collected his phone and wallet as Brodie reached over, taking the coat off the hook behind the door.

"There's this nice steakhouse I wanted to try out and now's a perfect time."

"Whatever."

Erik took his coat from Brodie and put in his belongings then pulled into it. Following the older man out, they entered the corridor, meeting with other young men and women leaving their offices.

Erik ignored the cacophony of others who readied for the evening, mulling about the data he processed while Brodie talked on about nothing in particular when they headed for the elevators. Erik put his hands in his slacks pockets, grasping the phone there and nodded, giving non-committal answers once they left the office building.

Stepping outside into the cold winter evening, Erik followed Brodie, walking with him down sidewalks and crossing various streets before entering a modestly furnished Japanese steakhouse.

Erik took a seat across from Brodie at a small table for two near the large pane window showing the outdoors and glanced at the menu he was given. "Give me the special," he replied, "and the strongest vodka you have."

"We don't have vodka," said the server and gave a polite bow. "Would you like *shochu* instead?"

"Sure," Erik answered.

Brodie then told the waitress his order and Erik gave him a lost expression when he couldn't understand what was said between the two. The older man whispered something to the server, making her giggle in response.

"What did you tell her?" Erik asked once the menus were taken away.

Brodie grinned and tapped the edge of his nose. "My secret," he teased. "Let's enjoy ourselves, eh?"

Later their meals came and Erik looked at his plate of roasted chicken in gravy with a side of soya beans then to Brodie's consisting of grilled beefsteak and peppers with a side of wild rice.

"You're okay, Feddy?" Brodie asked as he picked up his wooden chopsticks and broke them apart. "Hell, you still got your coat on!"

"Sure," Erik murmured and picked up his fork. "I'm fine."

After eating in silence for several moments, Brodie spoke up. "You know, quarterlies are coming up and I might need your help."

"Oh?" Erik continued staring down at his plate as he ate his meal.

"Yeah, I need to compare documents and make sure we've got everything squared away."

"Sure."

Brodie frowned and put aside his chopsticks. "Something on your mind, Feddy?"

"No, everything's fine."

The waitress approached with a bottle of rice liquor and two serving cups. She set it on the table and flashed a bright smile as she gave a brief bow.

"The food's good," Erik replied, glancing at her.

"Thank you!" The server left and Erik pushed around the food on his plate.

"Why won't you open up, Feddy?" Brodie protested. "I'm not a bad guy here; I'm worried about you."

"You're not going to do anything to me, are you?"

Brodie snorted. "Why?" he asked. "How the hell you get that thought in your head?"

"There's no reason for you to be this nice to me."

"What's wrong with being nice?"

"I'm not used to it."

"Well, get used to it!" Brodie opened the bottle of wine and poured some for Erik first, then himself. "You should enjoy yourself more often, Feddy!"

"If you say so." Erik took up the drink and downed it, wincing as the alcohol burned his throat. "This is different," he murmured.

"Good stuff, yeah?"

"Sure."

TWENTY-THREE

Erik wavered as he became drunk and laughed loudly at Brodie's jokes. "You're hilarious," he said, waving his fork at his companion. "How could you mix up perikaryon with peptonization? They're two different things!"

"Hey, they were the ones who came up with that code," Brodie complained. "If it weren't for Mell's adjustments, it would've been a lot messier than what it was."

"That's great." Erik pushed back from the table and stood. He let out a yelp when his world tilted and he struck the floor on his rear. Erik fell back laughing and Brodie cracked a smile as he also stood.

"I think you're done, buddy," Brodie chirped.

"I think I might take a nap," Erik said from his place on the ground. "The floor feels nice."

"Not here," Brodie said and approached. "Come on; let me get ya a cab or something."

"Can't I stay with you?" Erik asked as Brodie perched down and grabbed his sleeve, pulling him upright. "I just need to sleep this off."

"How far are you from here?"

Erik shrugged and hiccupped. "Search me," he said.

"Oh, can't remember where you live when you have too

much in ya, eh?" Brodie chortled. "That's bad, real bad."

"How come?" Brodie stood and pulled Erik by the wrist to his feet. Erik staggered forward and fell against Brodie then giggled as he wrapped his arms around the older man's neck. "You're so strong," Erik slurred. "Reminds me of my dad..."

Brodie paled and pat him gingerly on the back. "Okay, Feddy," he murmured, "we're calling it a night."

"Let me pay for it," Erik said and pulled away. He staggered and slumped into his chair, then dug into his coat pockets, withdrawing his wallet. "Here, this should be enough." Erik withdrew the fifty-dollar bill and set the note on the table. "Off to the races!" He rose to his feet and Brodie caught him before he spiraled to the floor.

"Is there anything wrong?" called a server when Erik burst out laughing and pushed Brodie away.

"Call a taxi, will ya?" Brodie asked, grabbing for Erik before he fell again. "I'm afraid of my wasted friend here walking it off tonight."

"I'm not that sloshed!" Erik complained and pulled away from Brodie. "See?" He took one step forward and hit the floor face-first.

"Shit, Feddy!" Brodie yelped and Erik fell into a fit of giggles.

Brodie knelt beside him and Erik turned over on his back. He looked up and pat Brodie on the cheek. "Don't be scared," Erik cooed. "I'm not going to remember in the morning anyway."

"Do you always get this weird when you're drunk, Feddy?" Brodie asked apprehensively and picked up Erik's fallen wallet.

"I never got this drunk in the first place."

"The cab is on its way," called the server.

"Thanks," Brodie called back and tucked the wallet back into Erik's coat pocket. "Don't lose that, buddy."

"Hey, hey," Erik whispered and grabbed Brodie by the shirtfront. Brodie gasped when Erik pulled him closer. "Do you like me?"

"Of course I do," Brodie answered and raised an eyebrow. "Why else would I invite you out to eat with me?"

"On a date you mean?"

Brodie's eyes widened. "What? No!"

"Why else would you feed me drinks?" Erik held Brodie's face in his hands and pulled against his cheeks. "You want my body, don't you? You think I'm cute."

"Hey, it's not like that." Brodie gently pried off Erik's hands. "You seemed like a friendly guy. I just didn't want to eat at home with cold take-away again tonight."

"Am I the first guy you asked out?"

"You're the first one who didn't say 'no'."

"The taxi's here," called the server.

"Come on, up we go," Brodie murmured and pulled Erik to his feet as he stood. He then hoisted Erik over his shoulder and Erik let out a gleeful whoop. "I'm sorry," Brodie said apologetically to the waiter. "I didn't know."

"It's okay," said the server and waved as Brodie hauled Erik out the restaurant. "Please visit us again!"

Brodie stepped outdoors and huffed when met with rain.

"Hey!" Erik called. "It's raining!"

"Just one?" asked the driver once Brodie opened the door

and slipped Erik inside.

"No, two," Brodie said and stepped in the rear passenger, then shut the door. "Downtown Lofts."

"Sure thing."

The driver pulled away from the curb and began its journey through the wet dark streets.

"You're all wet," Erik murmured and hiccupped again. "It's raining out there."

"I know," Brodie replied and blew a short sigh.

"How are you going to get to work? You left your bike."

"I'll call for a cab."

"It's okay, I can call for one." Erik dug through his pockets and withdrew his phone. "I'm sorry for making you do this." He punched the buttons and waited for the call to go through. "Hey!" Erik said brightly.

"You don't have to do that," Brodie protested and reached over for Erik. "We're already in a cab!"

"I can reserve one in the morning, right?" Erik asked and held the phone out of reach. "Just tell her!"

"Come on, stop!" Brodie struggled with Erik for the phone and Erik giggled, pulling away and tossing the cellular from one hand to the other. Brodie grew frustrated and grabbed Erik by the wrists, slamming them over his head against the seat. Erik's eyes widened as Brodie leaned over him, panting hard for breath. "That's enough," Brodie snapped. "You're getting annoying now."

"Are you going to beat me?" Erik grinned. "You like rough games?"

"Argh, you're crazy." Brodie let go and pushed away, then

hunched over on his side of the seat in the cab's rear. "I've met my share of drunks," he muttered and held his chin in his hand as he leaned against the window, "but never crazy drunk."

"I'll call you in the morning," Erik said into the phone and turned it off. He sat up and pocketed his cellular then smoothed out his coat. "What are you thinking about?" Erik asked and grinned, glancing to Brodie.

"My regrets."

Erik scooted over to Brodie. "Regretting meeting me?" he wheedled.

"I hardly know you, Feddy."

"That's right." Erik suddenly grabbed Brodie by the tie and Brodie stiffened when Erik pushed down on his chest and straddled him with his knees. "Why, are you afraid of me?"

"I–!"

"Afraid I might do something?" Erik let go and draped an arm around Brodie's shoulders as his other hand pressed against Brodie's chest. "Would you rather I did?"

"Feddy–!"

Erik ran his hand through Brodie's hair and Brodie closed his eyes, taking a shallow breath. Erik pressed forward and leaned in, whispering in his ear, "Ah, ha, I tease!"

"Shit!" Brodie yelped and hurled off Erik across the seat. Erik struck the door and suddenly broke out into hysterical laughter.

The taxi came to a stop moments later. "Twenty-two eighty," said the driver.

Brodie clambered out the car and stood in the rain, shaking and heaving for breath as his face burned bright red. "You son of a bitch!" he squawked and dug through his pants, withdrawing his wallet. "Is twenty-five okay?"

"Thanks."

Brodie handed over the bills to the driver then reached in, grabbing Erik by the sleeve. "Come on, you bastard," he muttered and Erik stumbled out into the rain with him.

"You really thought I was going to do something!" Erik crowed. "You're getting a stiffy, aren't you?" He collapsed against Brodie who grunted and pulled him along up the apartment steps toward a set of glass doors. "Don't you need to adjust yourself at all?" Brodie held Erik back against the wall and sifted through his pockets, searching for his keys. "Will you be able to sleep tonight?"

"You're a horrible piece of shit," Brodie grumbled, finding his keys and unlocked the front door. Erik stumbled forward and entered the carpeted corridor. He gasped, in awe of the blue and creamed marbled walls.

"This place is great!" Erik hooted and giggled. He stumbled down the hall, running his hands along the tiles. "Feel how nice it is!"

"Come on, Feddy," Brodie called, "I'm upstairs." He headed for the elevators and pushed the button.

Erik returned, standing next to Brodie and leaned against him. Brodie grabbed for Erik before he slipped forward, holding an arm around Erik's waist while he draped the young man's arm over his shoulders.

"I'm drunk," Erik murmured.

"Yep," Brodie answered, "you are."

The doors opened and Brodie stepped on, taking Erik with

him. Erik moaned and pulled away, slumping against the wall.

"Why are you nice to me?" Erik mewed as he slid to the floor. "There's no need for you to be nice."

"I *want* to be nice, Feddy," Brodie said, frowning. "Now come on, get up."

"Let me sleep."

Brodie grunted and pushed the button for his floor. "Why do you drink so heavily?" he asked. "What is it you're trying to escape from?" He glanced over to Erik slumped forward on the floor. "Oh, Feddy, you're tiring me out here." The doors pinged and Brodie bent down, hoisting Erik over his back.

Brodie stepped off the elevator and headed to his apartment at the hall's end. He opened the door and stepped inside the darkness, heading for his bedroom.

Dumping Erik onto his bed, Brodie removed Erik's shoes and rolled him over, taking him out of his coat. He set the shoes at the end of the bed and draped the coat on a nearby chair near the bedroom door.

Leaving the room, Brodie shut his door and dropped into a chair in the parlor, moaning in exhaustion. He later nodded off.

Erik grunted when thrown with force onto a hard surface and he opened his eyes as the sounds of a door locking penetrated the air. Erik looked around, finding he was in a room with titanium walls and floors and a steel door with locks on the outside. Inside were four blue-plate lights shining harsh light in the enclosed room's interior, washing everything in white.

"Why do you put me here?" Erik yelled.

"You're a threat to everyone's safety," a hollow voice called to him. "You're a threat to your own safety."

"That's a flat out lie!" Erik screamed. "You're just trying to destroy me!"

"We're not here to do destroy you, Number Three. We're here to help you."

"Stop lying to me."

"If you have a problem with your treatment here, then you can talk this over with our superiors."

"Why should I bother?"

"We don't want to really hurt you, Number Three. You have to work with us if you want to get well."

"I'm not sick! I want to go home with the Greenfields and hang with my friends!"

"*Here* is where you belong. The Greenfields are nothing but a faint memory. Your friends are nothing but a faint memory."

"I *don't* belong here!"

"You are sick, Number Three. If you do these special tests for us, we can give you some freedoms."

"How free are these freedoms?"

"Unless you want a window of the world you so wish to see, then you're staying here in solitary confinement!"

"You're mad! All of it, everything!"

"Very well..."

The blue-plate lights flickered out, leaving Erik in perpetual darkness. He drew up his knees, waiting for when the doctors would take him away to do whatever they called testing. He eventually nodded off when weariness overcame him.

Erik grunted when punched in the face and he spiraled onto his back, stunned. Erik's eyes snapped open and he faced the young man with his likeness standing over him, wielding a long-range rifle aimed at his head.

"I thought you were gone!" Erik yelped.

What makes you think I'll ever disappear? The counterpart kicked Erik's side. *Wake the hell up!*

"I didn't hear you call my name," Erik replied and gave a facetious grin. "What did you expect me to do?"

The young man narrowed his eyes and pulled back the bolt. *Are you trying to make a fool of me?*

"Are you planning on fighting me here?"

Did you really think they would have medicated me away?

"Sure! Why not? I'm already crazy!"

Are you implying that I can't defeat you?

"I'm implying that you're in my head and you can't hurt me!"

Then let me show you how I treat those who make fools of me!

Erik quickly rolled out the way once the young man fired, blasting a hole in the floor. He swiftly jumped to his feet as his mirror image turned the rifle around.

"Don't tell me it only had one shot!" Erik jeered.

Hurry up and get with it, or else the next thing I'll destroy is where you're standing! Erik stepped back as the young man pressed forward. He let out a yowl when his counterpart twirled the rifle and slammed the gunstock against his head, knocking him against the wall. *You're easily replaceable, did you know that?*

Erik groaned and sagged to the floor, stunned. "I don't know how you found me," he moaned, "and of all things, smacking me around. You're not real and you know it! You're just a figment of my dreams!"

How pathetic! Erik's counterpart jammed the butt of the rifle against his throat and pressed hard. *I'm going to kick your ass and make you disappear for good! I'll destroy you!*

Erik grabbed the rifle and pushed back. "Get out of here," he snapped. "This is your final warning."

There's nothing else for you to do here; it's useless. The young man pushed forward and flipped the rifle around as it charged with bright light. *Kenzan Ugate!* Erik screamed as the force blasted into him and he fell back, seizing. *It hurts, doesn't it? You feel it down into your nerves, your soul, your core... But relax and let me kill you. Then I won't have to chase you anymore...*

"I'm just dreaming," Erik moaned as his counterpart picked him up by the collar. "This can't be real...!"

I understand how you feel - really, I do. But I simply can't just let you go like this.

"Why not?" Erik asked weakly. "You have me where you want me, right?"

You already know. I don't need to say it.

Erik's reflection dropped him to the floor and turned away. "Then what is it?" Erik demanded and staggered to his feet.

I see where your strength lies... You'll only return and fight me again and again, forever and ever! Erik froze when the young man swiftly turned around, piercing his side with a violet saber.

It's that dirty filthy woman who has complete control over you!

"What are you talking about?" Erik wailed.

She's always on your mind... Over and over... it's all you ever think about! Releasing his blade, Erik slipped to his knees and his counterpart grabbed him by the hair. *I guess I have no choice, but to wipe that out and destroy everything!*

"Unless I kill you first," Erik wheezed, "you'll never stop... am I right?"

You're just telling me what I want to hear. I will just destroy you instantly.

"I guess it's unavoidable... It looks like checkmate..."

Giving up already? You're not fighting me anymore? The young man yanked Erik back by the head, forcing him grimacing in pain. *Why? Why is it even after all the things I do to you, you just give up?*

"You've seen it, haven't you?"

Don't hold so much kindness in your heart for me!

"I don't know why... it's just how I feel..."

What a sickening sight... I'll just have to kill you and revive you a hundred times and keep piling up the pain and suffering on you as punishment for all the times you made a fool of me until now!

Erik took in a weak breath and his counterpart swiftly swung the saber across, marking out his world.

TWENTY-FOUR

Faint jazzy dance music and the scent of chocolate and cookies jarred Erik from the darkness. He struggled to get free from the binds constraining him and his limbs refused to move.

"Justin," John Greenfield's cheerful voice called from afar. "Justin, yoo-hoo!"

Erik felt his head becoming clearer and the dance music turned louder, the scent of cookies growing stronger and he finally released himself from the world of sleep, opening his eyes and finding himself in a familiar world altogether.

"Where am I?" Erik asked himself, noting the large airy house, the bay windows overlooking a suburban street that had other children playing outside, and the sound of their joyous laughter filtering in.

Noticing the front door propped open with the screen door ajar on a chain, letting in the summer afternoon air, Erik saw the houses across the street in the neighborhood were worn-down from use but seemed lively and well lived-in.

Tall palms and willows lined the sidewalks spottily, granting shade on one side of the street then would unexpectedly break for shade on the other side. Erik held his head, overwhelmed.

"Come on, Justin," John Greenfield called again. "I'm making cookies!"

Erik glanced around the parlor he sat in, noting the large brown couch with yellow flowers embroidered into the cloth, the large oak wide-screened floor-model television against the far wall, and the redwood paneling all around the house, including the staircase leading to the upper rooms.

On his left, rest an end table that held a lamp shaped into a woman's leg with a fishnet stocking. On the room's other side rest a record player that blared jazzy lounge music next to a cherry and glass mini-bar that had a shaker and empty silver bucket for ice atop its surface.

Erik took notice of the parlor, noting many photographs hanging on the walls, with several pictures over the television depicting a redheaded boy with bright violet eyes and freckled cheeks in a variety of sports.

"That can't be me," Erik thought, rising to his feet. *"I'm not much of a sports kind of guy..."* He studied other photographs in the room, finding that they had pictures of a young man with shaggy brown hair and a comb-style mustache with bright brown eyes and a long red-haired young woman with freckled cream-colored skin and bright violet eyes posing for various scenes. *"That's Father Greenfield without his glasses,"* Erik mused. *"But who is that woman...?"* Erik noticed in some of the other pictures were a young man with frizzy blond hair and large sideburns wearing oversized sunglasses with the younger John Greenfield, making outrageous poses. *"That's Mahjin..."* He paused at a framed photograph of both John Greenfield and Mahjin with shorter hair wearing tan uniforms, standing with several other uniformed men and women outside a black helicopter that had a large silver jet in the background. *"Were*

they in the Air Corps together...?"

"I'll keep these cookies all to myself if you won't help!" John Greenfield's voice called and Erik left the parlor, racing to the kitchen.

He spotted his father in T-shirt and jeans, dancing around the kitchen while stirring a large bowl of cream. Erik laughed and clapped his hands, watching the much younger John Greenfield without eyeglasses wipe his brow, throwing back his shaggy brown hair that fell into his face as he sang along to the song blaring from the parlor. Surprised at his vibrancy and youth, especially in the casual clothing he wore, Erik found slightly disconcerting since most of the time he knew him, he never strayed far from his suits and dress shirts.

"What are you doing, Dad?" Erik asked, grinning.

"I'm trying to make butter-cream frosting," John Greenfield replied. "I could use your help frosting these cookies, since Sir Duke declined and Satchmo can't do it."

"Sure thing!" Erik said and danced over to him, taking a butter knife in hand and dipping it into the bowl. He grabbed a cookie cooling on the counter and spread the frosting over it.

John Greenfield chuckled, tousling his hair. "How many strokes was that now?" he asked.

"I don't know, five-hundred something!" John Greenfield laughed heartily and dipped a finger into the frosting mixture, dabbing a bit on his nose. "Hey!" Erik dipped his finger in and spread it across John Greenfield's mustache.

"Now I'll have to shave it!" John Greenfield joked and Erik giggled. Moments later, the telephone rang. "Take care of that, will you?" John Greenfield asked, pulling away. "The frosting's still lumpy."

Leaving the kitchen, Erik wiped his nose and licked his finger. He picked up the receiver with his free hand in the hall.

"Justin," a pleasant female voice said over the line.

"Hey, Mom," Erik greeted cheerfully.

"There's a meeting at the office, so let your father know about it."

"I will."

"Don't forget to go shopping for new outfits; school starts next week!"

"Sure thing, Mom!"

Suddenly, pots crashed in the kitchen.

"Hoo-boy!" John Greenfield yelped.

"What was that?"

"I gotta go, Mom," Erik said hastily as banging resumed. "Dad's burning down the house!"

"Wait!"

Erik dropped the receiver and rushed into the kitchen, watching John Greenfield throw a pitcher of dark water onto the flaming pan and a loud sizzle emerged, hissing as cloudy smoke filtered the air.

"Nice catch, Dad!" Erik called.

"But the tea's ruined!" John Greenfield complained. "It sat in the sun all day, coming out rightly perfect!"

Erik laughed. "It's alright," he said gently. "We can always make more!"

"I just wanted to enjoy my only week off with you before you go back to school and I start my new job!" John Greenfield fussed.

Erik ran up to his father and hugged him tightly about the waist. "It's all right, Dad," Erik said brightly. "We're having fun now, right?"

John Greenfield chuckled, rustling Erik's hair. "Right!"

A loud screech of the tires came from outside and Erik turned around, glancing out the kitchen archway. He saw a shiny yellow convertible parked out front with several young men clustered inside wearing assorted athletic gear, with one who had a floppy hat and wide aviator sunglasses holding a large boom-box blasting dance music into the street. Erik recognized the one tall lanky man with frizzy blond hair and pork chop sideburns wearing tight jeans and a denim vest with cowboy boots to be Mahjin.

Mahjin tumbled out and his friends laughed in return when his left leg suddenly became crooked. Mahjin readjusted the leg and scrambled to his feet, dusting himself off.

"Oi, you stupid git," Mahjin snapped, shaking his fist. "I oughta run ya through for laughin' like that!"

"Right, right," one drawled.

"Wha'cha gonna do, kick us to death?" another responded and they roared harder. Mahjin gripped the front of his pants and sharply pumped his hand.

"Yeah, we love you too!"

Mahjin huffed and left the car, sauntering toward stoop as the rowdy men continued to hoot and jeer.

"Come on, Jerry!" a very inebriated Mahjin complained. "You silly cow, get a wiggle on!" John Greenfield pet Erik's head and grabbed a nearby towel, wiping at his face then put it in his pocket. He hurried for the door once Mahjin yanked against it, grumbling curses. "A bloody chain! Hell, where do you think you live, at the bloody fuckin' border?"

"Smiley!" John Greenfield said brightly, unlocking the door for him.

"Coo, Jerry, about time!" Mahjin snapped once he yanked open the door. He fell into his arms and they both laughed as John Greenfield dragged him indoors and set him on the couch.

"Sorry I took so long," John Greenfield said and Mahjin snorted, pulling off his boots.

Mahjin unscrewed the bolts and slipped out the artificial leg he owned, slamming it on the cocktail table while John Greenfield returned to the door and waved at Mahjin's friends in the car. He gained a honk in return and the car sped away, tires squealing.

"Man, Jerry, aren't I happy to see you, ducks!" Mahjin said and reclined back, sighing heavily. Erik clenched his teeth, staring at him in disbelief. "You absolutely missed a raging party, love!" Mahjin carried on. "The best wine you've ever tasted... straight from the gardens of Paradise itself!"

"Don't you have your son to be bothered with now?" John Greenfield retorted, locking the screen door behind him.

"Bah, he can take care of himself," Mahjin replied and hiccupped.

"*How can he be so glib?*" Erik thought, clenching his hands. "*Kevin's in a coma for crying out loud!*"

"Smiley, you ought to take it easy with those friends of yours," John Greenfield replied. "It's not like how it used to be!"

"Come on, baby," Mahjin complained. "It's beautiful enough as it is without your square self spoiling it!"

"That's why I stopped hanging with that crew of yours." John Greenfield left his place near the door, returning to the kitchen. Passing Erik, he touched his shoulder. "Make yourself useful, Ace," he said.

"How?" Erik asked. John Greenfield grinned and Erik smiled back, knowing. "Yes!" He hurried upstairs to his bedroom, throwing clothing about while searching for his favored outdoor skates. "About time, roller skating like he promised!" Erik said to himself. "He's finally going to show me how to do that triple axle!"

Finding the bag that held them, he slung it over his shoulder and hurried downstairs. Erik paused at the middle of the staircase, spotting John Greenfield holding a highball glass in hand, chatting away to Mahjin who sat on the couch's arm, listening with interest.

"I must be daft," Mahjin protested, digging through his vest pocket and withdrew a packet of cigarettes that had several unfiltered tips standing up, "letting you take over that project alone..." He pulled one out with his lips and searched his pockets.

"Here," John Greenfield said, taking a box of matches that lay nearby the mini-bar. He tossed them over to Mahjin and he caught it.

"You'd better be right, bucko," Mahjin murmured as he opened the box and struck a match on the side. "You'd make a monster out of that and we'd both be hung out to dry!"

"Dad..." Erik said timidly.

John Greenfield turned around, slightly startled. "Ready to go, Ace?" he asked.

"Are you talking about that new job at Gateway?" Erik

asked, descending the stairs.

"What I tell you about listening in on adult matters, eh?" Mahjin snapped, narrowing his eyes at Erik. "Teach your boy some better manners, Jerry!"

"Sure," Erik said warily. "Sorry." He approached John Greenfield and pulled at his sleeve. "Let's go!" he protested.

"Oh, going out to party, eh?" Mahjin drawled, puffing smoke through his nose. "Out to the roller rink, is ya? How 'bout them levers holdin' up, pal?"

"Don't be so jealous!" John Greenfield quipped, laughing heartily. "My leg will be fine."

"Not mine so much!" Mahjin grumbled, gesturing toward the artificial leg on the table. "That hunk of metal's really rubbin' into me!"

"Well here, this will ease the pain." John Greenfield grinned brightly and handed Mahjin the drink. Mahjin snatched it from hand, glaring at John Greenfield in return.

"If that baby face of yours wasn't so cute," Mahjin growled, "you poncy arrogant stuck-up snob..."

John Greenfield grinned, patting Mahjin's cheek. "You swine!" He promptly leaned out of a slap and laughed harder.

"Who do you think you are," Mahjin shouted, biting the end of his cigarette as he picked up his leg and poked at John Greenfield's chest, "throwing your weight around like that, eh?" John Greenfield fell into a fit of giggles, pushing away the false foot with a weak hand. "Stand still and lemme kick ya some more!"

"Come on, Dad!" Erik complained.

"Yeah, Popsy, come on! Stand still!"

"You two can play later!"

"Go to the car, Ace," John Greenfield gasped between giggles. "He's killing me here!"

"Right he is!" Mahjin said mockingly. "On your guard, you yellow pansy turkey-feathered waterfowl!"

Erik shook his head and headed outdoors after unlocking the screen. He paused as he came out onto the porch, noticing a large dark van with tinted windows parked across the street.

John Greenfield exited the house moments later, wiping the tears from his eyes from laughing and bumped into Erik. "My," he said, taking his shoulder in hand to keep his balance. "Hey, Ace, what's wrong?"

Erik looked up at his father and John Greenfield stared ahead, his grip on his shoulder tightening. "Dad..." Erik started.

"Let's go," John Greenfield commanded and took Erik's arm, hurrying down the sidewalk.

"But, Dad," Erik protested. "The car's over there..."

"Let's walk instead," John Greenfield said brightly. "This nice August afternoon air... Smell it; it's wonderful for the lungs!"

"But the roller rink's that way..."

"I know, but why not take a detour?"

Erik felt John Greenfield hurrying his stride, pulling him along. "*Does he know what we're running from?*" he wondered as their pace increased. "*Does he know about those guys in the black van? Are they really going to finish what they started?*"

They crossed the street and headed for the nearby park where several families were gathered. Erik noticed a large dark-skinned muscular man in chinos and white-sport shirt wearing an apron and baseball cap barbecuing meat on a grill.

He felt chilled when the man glanced in their direction and withdrew a large mobile phone from his apron pocket.

"Dad," Erik said worriedly, "is everything all right?"

"Let's race," John Greenfield said instead and took off in a sprint.

Erik ran after him, overwhelmed by the wind blowing through his hair, the skates thumping over his shoulder and the grass underneath his shoes as they headed deeper into the park against the disconcerting dread coursing through him.

Crashing through shrubbery and tripping over fallen branches and tree limbs, they hurried deeper into the woods. Moments later, John Greenfield paused near a tree, panting for breath with his hands on his knees.

"You won," Erik said and leaned against the tree, gasping for breath.

John Greenfield looked up, smiling faintly. "You're a good sport, Ace," he replied and tousled Erik's hair, then patted his cheek.

A rustle came from behind and John Greenfield urgently stood on full alert, his body rigid and tense. He put a finger to his lips and Erik nodded as John Greenfield slowly backed away, searching for the sound's source. Another rustle came, louder than before.

Unsettled when one woman and two men in dark suits appeared from the greenery, all wearing dark glasses and caps with headsets, with leather gloves and calf-high boots, Erik grew ill at the sight of the large man who stood across from John Greenfield.

"He was cooking at the grill not too long ago!" Erik

thought, stunned. *"Were they waiting on us?"*

"This is ridiculous," John Greenfield grumbled as the pale-skinned slender young woman approached, poking his chest with a gloved finger.

"Out for an afternoon jog, Gerald?" she asked with disdain in her voice.

"These people," Erik mused, breaking out in nervous sweat. *"They look capable of violence, even though they're not carrying any weapons... Hopefully..."*

"Don't attack me here," John Greenfield said weakly.

"Now why'd we want to do that?" drawled the olive-skinned slender young man to the woman's right, grinning sardonically. "We don't want any trouble, Gerald. Am I right, Rene?"

"Right," grumbled the large coffee-colored young man who stood apart from them, standing out with his large frame and wide-set shoulders and chest.

"Father Greenfield can't take him down!" Erik thought in terror. *"He's going to get pulverized!"*

"Let's back up a little," John Greenfield said nervously.

Erik gasped and cringed as their movement brought the large man named Rene to put a hand to his hip.

"Now, I wouldn't do that, Gerald," the woman said evenly.

"Sharon's right, Gerald," growled Rene.

"It was bound to happen, Gerald," said the thin man, holding out a hand. "We've been waiting most impatiently for you..."

"But Lukas thinks you've forgotten about us, Gerald," Sharon said sweetly as John Greenfield leaned out of Lukas's grasp. Erik swallowed hard, pained as his heart skittered wildly in his chest.

"Look, Justin," John Greenfield said in a strained tone and took a step back, clenching his hands. "We've got to do something about this…"

"No, you won't, Gerald," sneered Lukas.

"What can I do, Dad?" Erik asked and struggled to stay awake as the sensation of faint from sheer terror slowly came on.

"Firstly, I want you to get out of here," John Greenfield commanded. "It's me they want."

"But, Dad!"

"Right that, sonny boy," Rene grumbled. "This is men's business. No time for little boys to play around, otherwise, they'd get hurt!"

"I don't want to leave you here, Dad," Erik complained. "Let me stay with you."

"Look, they're only going to let one of us go," John Greenfield said through gritted teeth. "Don't upset these beasts by changing their minds!"

Erik took a hesitant step back. "Where will I go?"

"Anywhere but here."

"But what about you?"

"I can handle it alone."

"I want to help!"

"You'll help by not worrying your mother," John Greenfield growled. "Now, go!" Shaken by the finality in his voice, Erik retreated sullenly. "What do you want with me for?" John Greenfield demanded.

"You know the reason," Sharon snapped.

"But if you run away again, we won't quit until we've got what we come for," Lukas growled, taking John Greenfield by the arm.

John Greenfield pulled out of the grab and kicked Lukas away with a side kick, then followed through with a jumping roundhouse kick, smashing his foot into Sharon's head, throwing her down.

Lukas charged and tackled John Greenfield who slipped out of his grasp and whirled around, unleashing a forward stomp, only to get his foot grabbed. He turned with the throw, coming up with a leg sweep that tripped Lukas back, forcing him down on the ground.

John Greenfield took a step back, crouching low as he panted for breath, clenching his hands. "Come on, you son of a bitch!" he roared.

Rene charged and John Greenfield made a rushing tackle, grappling the man by the waist and barreled him into a nearby tree. Rene slumped forward and John Greenfield let go, delivering two sharp blows into Rene's side with clenched fists.

Rene grunted and struck back with an elbow to John Greenfield's chin, forcing him staggering back. Rene then grabbed John Greenfield by the arm before he fell, throwing him off balance. Throwing him aside, John Greenfield hurtled onto the ground several feet away, bowling over into the dirt. John Greenfield let out a cry when landing on his back awkwardly, moaning in pain.

"That's what you get when you leave," Rene sneered, standing with ease and stormed up to him, chortling darkly. "You have a lifetime contract with us, naughty boy." He stood over John Greenfield's downed body, withdrawing a golden semi-automatic pistol from at his back. "It's not ethical, it's not right for you to break it the way you did."

"Ethical?" John Greenfield spat. "Right? Bullshit!" John Greenfield struggled to sit up. "I'm not going to be a slave to you monsters. I am a free person, no matter what the cost!"

"*I need to do something,*" Erik thought, stunned. Breaking out of his stupefied fear, he raced forward. "You beast!" he screamed. "Leave him alone!" Erik threw a punch, only to get rammed back with a heavy blow to his face.

"Sneaky boy, aren't you?" Rene sneered as Erik staggered back, clutching his bloodied nose. "Now you don't have a choice, Gerald!"

"No," John Greenfield wailed, "don't take him away from me!"

Rene turned the pistol at Erik and pulled back the safety. A loud blast followed and Erik screamed, clutching his head in pain. His world slipped from his grasp.

TWENTY-FIVE

Erik's eyes snapped open and he found himself back in the small white room, curled into a chair. The rays of the morning sun filtered through Erik's small window from the room's far end, a diminutive square barely the size of a pocket paperback book.

Looking around, he saw he faced the small portable television across from the chair playing a video about teamwork, resting on a small corner case with two shelves for books and papers. On the wall behind it were three shelves for clothing containing several sets of blue scrub suits. Erik tensed, hearing footsteps and the door to his room later unlocked.

"You are looking well this morning," the doctor said brightly as the door opened.

"Who is he?" Erik demanded once the doctor entered the room.

"What do you mean?" the doctor asked as he pulled in a chair to sit on. "Let me get seated first and we'll discuss whatever's bothering you."

"Whatever."

Erik glanced over the doctor's shoulder, spotting the guard standing outside the door with a rifle strapped to his back. The doctor went through his blazer pocket, extracting a small dictation machine and struck a button, forcing the gears whirring softly as the tape began recording.

"Right," said the doctor, "as you were." Erik glared at him, silent. "We are making excellent progress so far, don't you think so? Aren't things getting much clearer now due to our discussions?" Erik frowned and turned away, staring blankly at the television. "You seem troubled. Is anything the matter?"

"The other boy," Erik snapped. "The one named Justin Schumacher."

"I don't know who he is."

"You do, you liar!" Erik shouted, glaring at him. "You do know him and Ferdian too!"

"Maybe this line of questioning disturbs you," the doctor said coolly. "Why not talk freely and discuss something else..."

"No, I'm through with this!"

"We have come so far to this point. We can't back away now that we've so far to go..."

"How far are you willing to take this?" Erik demanded, standing to his feet.

"It all depends on you."

"What do you mean, 'it all depends on me'?" Erik asked caustically.

"Well, the medications help, as well as these sessions..." Erik clenched his teeth, growing enraged. "Why are you staring at me that way?"

"Why are you so intent on getting information out of me?" Erik hissed. "I told you, I don't know anything!"

"Whenever we get close to the truth... that anger of yours flashes again. You're trying to deny or hide something,

something that is preventing you from getting better from your psychotic illness. You turn on me as a coping skill because I'm the only one available."

"What do you mean, 'turn on you'?" Erik spat, incredulous. "I'm tired of dealing with you! You're so horribly irritating!"

"Well, then, let's not discuss Justin Schumacher for now. What about your father?"

Erik paled, shuffling back. "What about my father?" he spat.

"Tell me what you can about your father."

"Maybe I turn on you because you already know him," Erik sneered.

"Now you're twisting my words."

"You do know him and you're that Lukas guy who attacked my father!"

"No need to get angry and shout," the doctor calmly replied.

"I saw you before!" Erik screamed. "You hurt Father Greenfield!"

"Maybe medication is in order."

Erik clenched his hands, shaking intensely. "Get out, you monster!" he bellowed and rushed forward to throw a punch. The doctor leaned out the attack and Erik struck the floor. The doctor withdrew a small device from his pocket and switched a button as Erik scrambled to his feet, gearing for another attack. A loud screech abruptly squelched in the air and Erik screamed, clutching his head.

"That's enough," the doctor snapped as Erik stumbled rearwards and doubled over.

"Please," Erik wailed, "make it stop!"

"Then don't do that again." The doctor switched off the

device and Erik moaned, stumbling for the chair. He collapsed into it, dazed. "If you relax, then the tension wouldn't get to you."

"You're trying my patience," Erik muttered.

"I understand how your anxiety throws you off balance. You must stay calm and take everything one step at a time..."

"Shut up."

"Well, if you don't wish to discuss your father, that's just fine." The doctor set aside the machine and leaned forward in his seat. "Now, what about your mother? Can you tell me anything about her?"

"What do you mean?" Erik griped. "You never asked me about my mother before!"

"I'm sure she had some sort of impact on your life."

"You were never interested in her before."

"Well, you never spoke about her, but I am quite curious."

"I thought you're just a guide, not someone who leads me on."

"I'm only making suggestions is all."

"Then I suggest you leave."

"Please, tell me why you're so irritated at the mere mention about your mother? Did something happen?" Erik blinked slowly, staring blankly at the doctor in return. He clutched the arms of the chair, feeling his chest tighten as his heart raced like a trapped caged bird.

"*I can't remember who she is,*" Erik thought in dismay. "*Who is she really?*"

"Why the silence all of a sudden?" pressed the doctor. "Remember, relax and breathe and let it all come. She is there, a part of your being..."

"I can't remember her," Erik said faintly.

"But you do, you do."

"Please," Erik pleaded, shaking his head. He stared at the floor as tears streamed down his face.

"She will come to you, just relax for me."

Erik took in a shallow breath as he focused on her face, her scent, the way she moved, her laugh. The harder he tried to recall, the more the sensation of paralyzing fear crept through his bones.

Justin...!

"*What happened to her?*" Erik thought. "*Why was she erased from me?*"

Justin, run! Save yourself...!

"There is panic in your eyes," the doctor said firmly as Erik increased his grip around the arms of the chair. "You're trembling like a leaf in the wind. You remember, you remember and it disturbs you, right?"

"I don't know," Erik said faintly and sucked in a shallow breath.

"What is it that comes to mind?"

"I..." Erik clenched his teeth, afraid to answer.

"You must tell me now," the doctor demanded.

"I barely remember..." Erik said softly. "It's there, at the edges..." He shook his head, wheezing. "I can't do it... It'll break me for sure!"

"Tell me, what's going on?"

Watch closely as I break you...

Erik stiffened as the color drained from his face and pain

radiated in his arm and shoulder. He quickly left his chair and ran across the room toward the wastebasket.

"What's the matter?" the doctor asked, mildly alarmed when Erik vomited. "Something came to you, is that it?"

"What happens next?" Erik wailed, slipping to his knees. "What happens now? What happened back then?"

The doctor rose from his seat. "You must relax..."

"I don't know, I don't know!"

"Don't let the terror consume you..."

"What's happened to them? Where is my mother?"

"You must not become agitated," said the doctor as he approached. "Perhaps a pill will help you relax..."

Erik pushed the doctor away as he stood unsteadily to his feet. "Where is she?" he demanded. "Why was she taken from me?"

"Please, control yourself. You must calm down!"

"What's going on? Why am I here? Why are you here? Where is Father Greenfield? Why can't he save me?"

"Shall we suspend for now?" asked the doctor gently. "We'll get to the business of Justin Schumacher later..."

"No, no," Erik moaned, slumping against the wall.

"Shall we continue, then?"

Erik slid to the floor, exhausted. "I don't know..."

"Do you feel unwell?"

"Just stop it, please," Erik cried, drawing up his knees. "Your questions..."

"You seem distracted."

"Why is everything so different?" Erik wrapped his arms around his knees and shut his eyes.

"Please, tell me."

"I don't know…" Erik rapped his head back against the wall, seething.

"Maybe I should have medication administered…"

"Please, not again." Erik buried his head onto his knees. "*It makes no sense,*" he mused. "*It has to be a dream. All of it a terrible dream…*"

"What dream?"

"Stay out of my head!" Erik screeched.

"You have to tell me," the doctor urged. "Please, it's for your benefit. You have to tell me if you wish to get well."

"I'm tired of this…"

"It's early. We have a lot to cover today."

"I don't know what to think. What I saw…"

The doctor knelt beside Erik, clearly interested. "What did you see?"

"It was so long ago… In some other time, in some other place…"

"What do you mean?"

"The house, the décor… It was somewhere else, I was somebody else…"

"Where? What?"

"Please!" Erik shrieked.

"I think medication is best for you right now until you can better control yourself."

"Stop trying to control me!" Erik screamed.

"It'll calm you and take away the fear…" Erik clamped his hands over his ears and began counting aloud. "You have to talk to me," the doctor called over his voice. "Don't play games like this. Do not retreat!" Erik slammed his head against the wall, forcing his vision flashing red behind his eyes. "Don't do this!" Erik rammed his head again. "Come back to the present!"

Erik gave no fight when rough hands pulled him apart from his folded position and held him down, injecting him with a serum.

TWENTY-SIX

Erik woke up with a start, moaning when his head pound fiercely in pain. He ran his hands through his hair and staggered out of bed. After peeling out of his clothes, he stumbled around in the dark, searching for the bathroom.

"Damn it, shit, fuck," Erik growled as he blundered and crashed into things. Finding a door handle, he leaned against it and fell down to the floor as the panel gave way to cool tiles.

Crawling across the floor, Erik felt around and touched porcelain. He moaned when his stomach lurched and put his head in the toilet, vomiting.

Erik smelled cigarette smoke as he spat in the commode and looked up, squinting when the lights suddenly turned on. He saw Brodie standing at the door in opened dress shirt and tie loosened about his neck, wearing checkered blue and black boxers and trouser socks with garters. He had a lit cigarette dangling from his lips and ran a hand through his disheveled dark brown hair.

"Hey, Feddy," Brodie greeted and stepped in. "Move it, will ya? I rather not piss in the sink." Erik grunted and pushed away from the toilet, leaning against the shower stall as Brodie approached the toilet. "That girlie of yers kept calling," Brodie said while he urinated. "She's really freaking out, buddy. I told her you're in good hands but she didn't trust me." Brodie flushed the toilet with his toe and washed his hands. "Will you be able to clock in tomorrow?" When Erik didn't answer, Brodie approached and crouched before the young man. "Hey, what's the matter?"

"Gimmie," Erik grumbled and took the cigarette from Brodie. He tapped the ashes from it on the floor and took a hard drag, inhaling deeply. Erik shut his eyes and leaned back, pressing against the stall.

Brodie frowned as he stood. "I'm worried about you, Feddy," he said softly. "You want anything?"

"Vodka, please," Erik muttered, blowing smoke over his head.

"You can't live off that alone."

"Something for the pain then?"

"I'll see what I can find."

Brodie left Erik's side and Erik moaned.

Later, Erik finished smoking and dropped the dead cigarette into the toilet, then got to his feet and rummaged through the bathroom closet, withdrawing towels.

After taking a hot shower, Erik wrapped the bath towel about his waist after drying off and returned to the parlor. He saw Brodie dressed in a dark blue and white bathrobe sitting on the couch, smoking. On the cocktail table, rest his phone, a pack of cigarettes with butane lighter and a ceramic ashtray.

Erik approached and picked up the pack, withdrawing a cigarette.

"You know they're going to talk about us tomorrow," Brodie

said as Erik sat next to him and put up his feet on the table.

"I stopped caring what people thought," Erik murmured. Brodie leaned over and grabbed the lighter. Erik held his cigarette as Brodie lit it for him, then lit another for himself. "I won't be able to remember anyway."

"So it's true with what you said?" Brodie asked.

"What did I say?"

"That you won't remember in the morning if we did anything?"

Erik glanced at Brodie, repulsed. "You didn't-!" he cried.

Brodie smiled and held up his hands, chortling. "Never, I hardly touched you at all!" he said brightly. "Did I think about it? Sure, but you're a scary kid when you're drunk. I'm getting too old for that!"

"Shit, shit, shit," Erik moaned and held his head in his hand as he leaned forward.

"Look, Feddy, don't worry about it," Brodie said gently. "I know you don't believe me because why would you? You wouldn't remember if I did, didn't, or said anything otherwise."

"You just said you thought about it," Erik grumbled. "How do I know you didn't at least try?"

"I couldn't..." Brodie blew a hard sigh and continued smoking in silence.

"Did I hurt you?" Erik asked softly moments later.

"No," Brodie answered. "I just felt bad."

"Guilty, you mean?"

"No..." Brodie shut his eyes as he sat back. "I was sitting outside the door, hearing you scream... I don't know what they did to you, but I'm sorry. I wish I could do something."

"Why didn't you wake me up if I was making such horrible noise?"

"I tried, but you belted me a good one," Brodie answered. "Right in the chest."

"I hope I didn't break any ribs," Erik murmured, flushing slightly.

"Nah, I'm holding up fine. Just so you know, you're crazy strong for a kid as small as you are."

"Sorry."

Brodie chortled and stood, then tousled Erik's hair. "Want some coffee?" he asked. "We have to get up in a few hours anyway."

Erik nodded. "Sure," he answered.

Brodie left his side and Erik picked up the phone left on the table. Turning it on, he saw he missed several dozen calls from the number, ending at two in the morning. He pressed the button and put the phone to his ear, waiting for the line to pick up.

After several rings, Gina's groggy voice came over the line. "Are you all right?" she sleepily asked.

"I'm fine," Erik replied. "Hung over though."

"Please don't scare us like that. Ossie's worried sick."

"Ossie...?"

"Osphena?" When Erik said nothing else, Gina sighed. "Anyway, she was worried about you too. After you get off work, I'm picking you up so you can come straight home."

"I want to stay here," Erik said.

"What? What are you talking about?" Brodie approached moments later with a mug of coffee and Erik nodded when he set it down on the table. "Who are you staying with?"

"Is it all right if I stay here awhile?" Erik asked.

"What?" Brodie yelped and his face flushed beet red. "Don't tell me you're serious, Feddy!"

"Just a little while then?" Erik pressed.

"Sure, as long as you want," Brodie answered apprehensively. "I don't care."

"Who is he?" Gina squawked. "What is he doing?"

"Don't pick me up tomorrow," Erik said into the line. "I'll be fine."

"But your apartment!"

"I'm not staying here forever, if that's what you're worried about."

"Then what are you planning?"

"I don't know... Something's driving me for some reason. I'll figure it out and let you know." Erik pressed the button, ending the call before Gina could say more.

Brodie crouched before Erik, concerned. Erik smiled down at Brodie as he set the phone aside on the table.

"What's with that look?" Erik asked gently.

"I'm afraid," Brodie said softly.

"Don't tell me you're scared of me." Erik ran a hand through Brodie's hair. Brodie shut his eyes, blowing a nervous sigh. "I'll never hurt you."

"Please, don't."

"Unless you ask me to." Erik leaned in, holding Brodie by the back of the head. Brodie opened his eyes and Erik grinned, poking the wing of his nose. "Ah, ah, I tease."

"Shit!" Brodie growled and shoved Erik away. Erik giggled

and Brodie stood, shaking as he held his hands clenched at his sides. "You're a cruel bastard," he snapped while Erik bit his fist and curled over on the end of the couch, overcome by short spasmodic laughs. "Get the fuck out of my house!"

"Sorry," Erik murmured once he calmed. "Before you do that, would you tell me your name?"

Brodie's countenance softened and he blew a hard sigh. "Forget it, Feddy," he muttered. "You're still drunk." He gestured to the coffee. "Here, sober up and if you need anything, call me."

"Oh, going to let off some steam?" Erik teased as Brodie stormed for the bathroom.

"Fuck you, man," Brodie called over his shoulder.

"You wish!" Erik called back. The door slammed shut and Erik put out his cigarette then left his place from the table, returning to the bedroom.

Erik turned on the light and headed for the nightstand, rummaging through the drawers. Finding nothing of importance, he headed for the chest and picked through it, finding discarded computer parts, old cellular phones and pieces of jewelry.

Leaving the dresser, Erik approached the closet and opened it, noticing an old battered shoebox on the top shelf. Pulling it down, Erik opened it, finding a smaller black box and several yellowed papers.

"*It's his service papers from the Defense Forces,*" Erik mused as he thumbed through the work. Setting the box aside, he withdrew the smaller box and opened it, revealing three medals: a bronze star, a silver star, and a purple heart.

"I was a Lifer," Brodie's voice cut in. Erik gasped and turned, finding the man standing at the door with his bathrobe loosely tied about his body. "I did twenty years for the Defense Forces."

"Sorry," Erik murmured and immediately put the box away.

"Were you looking for something?"

"I forgot now."

"Something about Joe then?" Erik gave Brodie a blank look as the older man approached the bed and sat on the edge. "You had a headache after I mentioned the guy and now you're going through my Service stuff."

"Sorry."

"I'll call him up in the morning. Maybe a meeting might help you remember something?"

"Sure."

"Well, I'm taking a nap. I'm exhausted."

"Again, I'm sorry."

"Don't be."

Erik left the room and shut out the light then returned to the couch. He noticed a bottle of pills next to his mug of coffee and opened them, shaking out several tablets. Sitting on the couch's edge, Erik swallowed the medicines and sipped his cooling coffee. He then nodded off into darkness.

TWENTY-SEVEN

A heavy stomp on Erik's chest rattled him awake and he opened his eyes, finding Fenway standing above him, highly irritated.

"What is it?" Erik snapped.

"You're out of Solitary for a while," Fenway growled. "They've ended the Code Orange and deem you stable enough to return."

"Thanks," Erik said dryly.

"You've got another test run coming up and the doctors want to exam you before it gets underway."

"I don't care," Erik grumbled and turned on his side away from him. "I don't want anything to do with tests anyway..."

"Just do what we say," Fenway grumbled, "and you can leave this hell."

"I don't believe you."

Fenway grabbed Erik's arm and yanked him to his feet. Erik pushed him away and brought up his foot to kick Fenway, only to get caught and flipped to the floor.

"You can't kill someone with that kind of lame shit," Fenway snapped. "Stop playing around and follow me, or I'll make sure you'll never come upstairs again!"

"You'd like that, wouldn't you?" Erik spat and rose to his

feet. Blowing a heavy sigh, he followed Fenway leading toward the elevators. After stepping on, Erik heard Hayden's voice call for Fenway.

"Please wait!" Hayden cried and put a foot into the door before they slid shut. The doors opened and Hayden smiled faintly at Fenway who appeared annoyed. "I've got Number Eight from the C-O-one-ninety-two-C Project."

"Yeah?" Fenway groused as Hayden stepped inside the elevator.

"I found something disturbing with his results."

"What about it?"

"You ought to alert Doctor Rosenthal and anyone else involved in the project because this finding may terminate our contract with AMASTCOMS and Gen-Tech."

Fenway banged his fist on the cable car's side. "Out with it before I fucking strangle you!" he thundered.

"The reason Number Eight is so unstable is because of the incompatibility of his Dyna-Widget to his E-Sys."

"What the fuck?" Fenway yelped, surprised. "Wasn't Zachary and Schnell on the Research and Development team?"

Hayden nodded. "If we release the models given the data we have now, they're going to trigger a war we can't win!"

"Why didn't they warn anybody?" Fenway griped.

"My best guess is that they somehow tampered with the projects themselves!"

"The only one who created that damn chip was that bastard Schumacher!"

"I'll get on the horn and alert Colbert."

"What are you doing?" Erik shouted at Hayden.

"What does it look like I'm doing?" Hayden retorted. "Your unstable condition could kill us all!"

"I didn't ask to be put here!"

"You are a no-sponsor, so technically you don't exist!"

"I can prove that fact otherwise!" Erik hurled a punch, slamming into Hayden's side. Hayden grunted and staggered against the wall. Fenway grabbed Erik by the arm, throwing him to the floor before he swung again. Hayden struck a button and the car began moving upwards. "I'm real!" Erik screamed, kicking at Fenway. Fenway growled and stomped on Erik's chest.

"Yeah, real dangerous!" Hayden squawked.

"I'm not letting you destroy me!" Erik jumped to his feet and Fenway punched Erik's face, throwing him into the corner.

"Why the fuck you have to set him off?" Fenway bellowed. "You don't have to deal with his shit - I do!"

"Then scrap him; it should be easy!"

"You're not going to destroy me!" Erik cried and shoved past Fenway and Hayden once the doors opened on the upper floor.

"Hey!" Fenway roared after Erik as he raced out of the elevator.

"You'd better check on him to see what brains he has left," Hayden called as Fenway rushed after Erik, "if he hasn't had it all cut out by now!"

Erik hurried down the corridors and entered the dining area, spotting Clayton making another mug of tea.

"Clayton," Erik yelped, "you won't believe this!"

"Believe what?" Clayton asked.

"You don't say shit," Fenway growled as he came to the door, panting for breath. "One word and I'll make sure your ass never talk again!" Erik swallowed hard and nodded, sinking into a seat at the rear plank table. "I swear to fucking god, I'll send your ass to the scrap heap with my own damn hand!"

"You can't keep me quiet forever," Erik spat.

"Watch me boy." Fenway stomped away and Erik moaned, running a hand through his hair.

Clayton suddenly chortled and Erik raised an eyebrow at him. "How are you today?" Erik asked timidly.

"Good," Clayton answered and dipped his tea bag into the steaming mug of hot water.

"You didn't get hurt from the last run, did you?"

"I'm fine, really."

"Did they give you a serum or something?"

"It helped a lot. It made me feel better."

Erik left his place at the table and approached Clayton, touching his arm gently. "Clayton, look at me." Clayton looked up and Erik took in a shallow breath, noticing the young man's dark eyes were foggy. "Clayton... what did they do to you?"

"When you're sky high, it's alright," Clayton replied. "It's when you fall down that you get in trouble." He broke away from Erik and approached the table, sitting down with his mug of tea.

"It was because of that Code Orange, wasn't it?" Erik continued. Clayton didn't respond, sipping his tea carefully. "Why do these people try so hard to control and manipulate us?"

When Clayton said nothing else, Erik left his side and returned to his room. He froze at the doorway when he spotted Josef wiping down a sleek automatic pistol with a bloodstained towel at his bed.

"Oh, they deemed you stable enough to return," Josef said without turning around. "That's too bad."

"Joe, what's that you have there?" Erik asked nervously.

"Something I shouldn't have," Josef nonchalantly acknowledged and grinned as he finished polishing. "But then again, it's something to kill you with." Josef pointed the pistol at Erik and Erik put up his hands.

"I'd rather keep my life, thank you!" Erik countered.

"You don't need it!"

Erik dashed inside and dropped low for a tackle, only to get kneed in the chest and slapped back with the pistol cracking across his jaw. Erik fell back to the floor, stunned and Josef stomped on his chest, standing over him.

"If you really want to shoot me, go ahead," Erik snarled. "Isn't that what you want?"

"No," Josef snapped. "I want to see you suffer."

Erik punched Josef in his inner thigh and Josef staggered back. Erik kicked Josef in the groin and scrambled to his feet then lunged for Josef's wrist, struggling to wrestle the gun out of his hand.

Josef kneed Erik in the groin and bashed the pistol aside Erik's temple, forcing him dazed. He grabbed Erik by the arm and hurled him overhead, slamming him down onto the bed.

Josef straddled Erik before he could get up and dug his knees into his side. Erik stiffened when Josef pointed the pistol at his head and fell slack.

"It seems I have no choice," Erik muttered.

"You really don't want to test me," Josef sneered. He leaned in close, nuzzling Erik's cheek. "But you seem so set to see what I can do, aren't you?" Erik winced when Josef licked the side of his neck. "I wonder what your blood tastes like," Josef murmured in Erik's ear.

"Please, don't," pleaded Erik. "You already had that chance when you stabbed me." His eyes widened and he broke out into cold sweat when Josef sat back and caressed the pistol down his cheek.

"You hate it when I tease you, don't you?" Josef said gaily. "Hurry and get it over with already, right?" Josef chortled then stuffed the towel in Erik's mouth. "If I let you go, will you tell on me?"

"This nutcase will kill me if I don't tell him what he wants," Erik thought and shook his head, pushing against Josef's chest. He froze when Josef pressed the head of the pistol to his temple.

"You're walking a thin line, Brother," Josef hissed. "Do you really want me to hurt you?" Erik shook his head again and Josef laughed. "You're so cute when you're scared," Josef teased, grinning brightly. "It's so sexy." Josef ran a hand through Erik's hair. "You sit right here and I'll maybe consider sparing your life!"

Josef pulled away and sat on the bed's edge, twirling the gun he held. Erik pulled out the towel and coughed, gasping for breath. He sat up and Josef glared back at him.

"What do you plan to do to me?" Erik asked weakly. "Besides killing me of course?"

"Oh, wouldn't you like to know?" Josef replied. "You wouldn't understand what Hell I go through, with the voices telling me this and that and the other!"

"Joe," Erik said softly, "Joe, I hear them too. I can hear them sometimes."

"I don't believe you!" Josef pulled back the safety.

"Joe, please! I heard them, everyone... there's all sorts of others in my head..." Erik gulped for breath as Josef's grip tightened around the handle. "Maybe they're trying to get help for us, to get us out of here and away from these sick people!"

"I don't believe you!"

"They're all in this together!"

"Liar!"

"We're not alone in this," Erik said quickly. "There's others on the outside that's trying to help us."

"Like who would bother?"

"There's Mahjin and Arizeh and Mister Greenfield...!"

"Greenfield..." Josef lowered the gun, his hardened eyes softening. "Yeah, that's right..."

"You know him?" Erik asked softly, relaxing slightly.

Josef reset the safety then set the pistol aside on the nightstand and Erik sighed in relief. Josef suddenly smirked, gesturing toward the nightstand. "I suggest you hide that where they can't find it," he said cordially. "I don't want to go through another messy ordeal stealing that thing."

"I see we have no qualms about killing others," Erik said flatly.

Josef chuckled and pat Erik's head. "It comes to me as easily as breathing, Brother." Erik winced when grabbed by the hair. "Remember, they made me that way."

"I'll keep that in mind," Erik mewed. Josef let go and stalked out the room. Erik let out a shaky sigh and ran his hands through his hair. *"I need to get out of here,"* he mused, glancing back at the door. *"He's going to hurt me for real tonight, I know it!"*

TWENTY-EIGHT

Erik grabbed the pistol and headed into the washroom. Studying his surroundings, he noticed a vent high in the wall. Tucking the gun into his waistband, he climbed on the sink and reached for the bolts, finding one loosened.

Using his fingers, Erik unscrewed one and palmed it, then tried the others. He clenched his teeth as his skin ripped when he applied strength against the screws, twisting them out with his fingers.

After working the other three bolts free, Erik held the loose screws between his lips and pulled against the grate, opening it with ease. He set the handgun inside and placed the vent back in place, then wiped the blood away with the end of his shirt.

Jumping down off the sink, Erik rinsed his hands in the cold water and sat on the toilet's edge, exhausted. "*My hands look like raw hamburger,*" he thought, looking at his cut and mutilated fingers. "*They'll surely punish me for real!*"

"Number Three," Fenway barked outside his door, "you've got another test run."

Erik left the washroom and stepped out into the corridor, watching Rosenthal approach, holding a mid-sized case in one hand and leaning against his rosewood cane with the other. Fenway stood at the hall's end, arms folded across his broad chest.

"What's that?" Erik grumbled.

"We need to get your vital statistics before this particular test," Rosenthal answered. "Come with me."

Erik followed the doctor down the hall into a room with a single plate on the door labeled 'Consulting'. He unlocked the door with his key card and Erik stepped inside, taking in the sight of the variety of small machines and an examination table. Rosenthal set the case aside on the end table near the door and stepped back out.

Turning around, Erik watched the doctor enter with a chart and he set it aside on the nearby table. Pushing the door shut with his shoulder, he ordered Erik on the examination table.

Erik sat on the table's edge as Rosenthal hooked his cane on the doorknob then approached, frowning.

"What happened to your hands?" the doctor snapped.

"What does it look like?" Erik spat back. "I had rats gnawing on my fingers while I napped. Apparently they like the awful food you send up."

Rosenthal grunted. "If you're being mouthy, then you must be doing better."

Erik shrugged in response. Rosenthal then went through the routine of checking Erik's blood pressure with the adjacent cuff, followed by an electrocardiogram from the portable he carried, and lastly asserted Erik's weight on an electronic scale, after having his height checked with the height gauge.

"What's the point of all this?" Erik complained as Rosenthal wrote the statistics into the chart he held. "If I reverted back to baseline, then there's not much you can do about it, is there?"

"We're planning to make some changes to your treatment program," Rosenthal replied.

"What kind of changes?" Erik demanded. "Shouldn't I be involved in my own care? You're tinkering with my body after all."

"You're too sick to be an active participant in your care," Rosenthal snapped. "You wouldn't understand if we told you."

"I want a new roommate," Erik snapped. "The one I have is dangerous and he plans to kill me tonight."

"There's nothing I can do about room assignments."

"You're just going to wait until he does something then?" Erik shrilled. "Fine, be that way!"

Erik jumped off the table and snatched up the cane, swinging it at Rosenthal. The doctor ducked and Erik swung again, bashing it over his head. Rosenthal let out a cry in agony and Erik kicked him rearwards on the floor, sending him crashing into the desk.

"Tell him to back off!" Erik hollered. "Otherwise, I might have to do something I really don't want to do!"

"What's the point of this?" Rosenthal demanded and staggered to his feet.

Erik held firm to the cane, tensing when he sensed a mechanism clicking. He turned the pewter handle and pulled apart the redwood cane, revealing a saber.

Rosenthal advanced and Erik quickly slashed into the doctor, lashing deeply into his arm. Rosenthal cried out, holding his wound as he stepped away in shock when blood ran between his fingers.

"I told you!" Erik shrieked. "Do you really want me to hurt

you?"

"You can't fight your way out of here."

"Watch me cut you monsters down!"

"You don't have the guts!"

Erik pointed the blade's edge at Rosenthal's throat. "If you're out to destroy me, then I have to get you out of my way," he threatened. "I'm done with this."

Erik lowered the blade and turned away. Tucking the redwood sheath under his arm, he opened the door and stepped out, coming to a pause when he faced Josef.

Josef smiled brightly at Erik. "I see you do understand, Brother," he said brightly. "Let me borrow that toy you have, eh?"

"Forget it!" Erik shouted and swung at Josef.

Josef immediately stepped out of Erik's path and pushed back, hurling Erik against the wall. The redwood sheath clattered to the floor and Josef kicked it up, grasping it as Erik swung the blade again, cutting into the hardwood.

"You're sloppy," Josef teased and kicked Erik hard in the groin, forcing him down. Josef pulled the staff away and bashed Erik upside the head, stunning him. Josef dropped the redwood to the floor and kicked away the pewter-handled saber. "You don't need that. Let me have it."

"No!"

Erik scrambled to his feet as Josef grabbed the blade. Erik put up an arm, shielding his face as Josef returned with a lunging thrust and seethed when the blade cut into his skin. Erik reversed Josef then ducked down, taking his leg and flipped him onto his back.

Josef's head smashed against the tile while Erik kicked the sword away. He clutched his burning arm and the flaring pain immediately spread from his hand, traveling up his arm.

"What's wrong with you?" Erik demanded as he backed away, taking up the hardwood staff.

Josef chuckled darkly once he sat up. "Do you really have to ask?" He jumped to his feet and charged Erik, tackling him by the waist. Erik yelped in pain when thrown against the wall and beat Josef on the back with the staff.

Josef threw a hard blow into Erik's side, stunning him. Then grabbing Erik by the face, Josef smashed his head against the wall. Erik groaned, slipping against the partition once let go.

Josef stamped down with his heel and Erik immediately rolled out the way, watching in alarm when the tiles beneath Josef's foot cracked from impact. Erik scrambled to his feet, panting hard for breath as he stood at ready for another attack.

"Stop fighting me!" Erik yelled.

"Getting tired, eh?" Josef teased. "You can't run from me for long like this, you know!"

"Do you *want* me to kill you?"

"Give it your best!"

Josef ran for the sword left on the floor and Erik chased after him. Grabbing for the blade, Josef came up with a hard diagonal slash, slicing across Erik's chest. Erik turned out and Josef pressed ahead with a one-handed forward pierce. The saber struck the wall, snapping in half.

"You're through!" Erik shouted and swung the cane into Josef's side, striking the wind out of him, then brought around the other end, hitting Josef square in his face.

Knocking Josef dazed, Erik jumped out of his savage return swipe with the broken blade and hurled the tapered end into Josef as he turned for another swing, taking out his eye. Josef screamed, clutching his hand to his face.

"You bastard!" Josef wailed, staggering rearward in shock and pain.

"Leave me alone!" Erik roared.

Josef hurled the blade at Erik and he ducked. Hearing a stunned cry, Erik turned, finding Rosenthal at the open door before the consulting office.

The doctor clutched his throat, his fingers weakly around the blade stuck through his skin. Rosenthal collapsed and Erik let out a yelp when Josef jumped on his back and wrapped his arms around his neck.

"Why are you doing this?" Erik wheezed and gasped as Josef's grip increased. Erik staggered then smashed his back into the wall in a vain attempt to throw Josef off.

"Why do you want him to live?" Josef thundered, batting Erik upside the head with a heavy fist. The force rattled Erik and his vision doubled, tinting in red. "They want to destroy us! I thought you were better than that!" Erik slipped to his knees and Josef jumped off Erik's back. Grabbing Erik by the hair, he slammed his head against the wall, forcing him seeing dark spots amidst the red. "Look at it this way, Brother!" Erik cried out in agony as Josef let him go and he slid to the floor, clutching the back of his head. "You must understand why I would do this... You know it's not right with what they do to us!"

"Killing me isn't helping your cause," Erik moaned.

"You're right. I just realized how useful you can be to me."

Josef perched before Erik, grasping his collar. "I'm sick of the torture they do to us and the outside never knowing!"

"Then why hurt me instead?"

"Oh, I just love watching you squirm. It turns me on."

"Please don't torture me," Erik pleaded. "They've already got the lead on that!"

"You're right, they're the ones causing our pain and suffering, you see," Josef said. "They drove me to this!"

"Don't punish me!"

Josef picked up Erik and struck him heavy-handedly across the face with a hard left. Erik let out a howl in pain as his tinted and spotted vision grew murky.

"I can't keep you alive if you vouch for them!" Josef bellowed.

"I don't!" Erik wailed.

"Do you hate me, Brother?" Josef said wryly as he shoved Erik into the examination room. Erik stumbled over Rosenthal's body and crashed to the floor. "I bet you do... especially after all those horrible tests you had to endure!"

"I hate the people who made you this way," Erik said weakly. "I don't hate you, just the things you do."

A hard kick brought back Erik's vision and he faced Josef holding the doctor's bloodied cane, tapping it into his palm.

"You don't hate me enough to face me yet," Josef growled.

"You're not making any sense!"

"Wake up and truly see!" Josef pressed the cane's tip against Erik's forehead. "Come on, be a good boy."

"I don't understand!"

"How rough do you think they'll punish you this time?" Josef asked smugly. "Do you think it'll be worse than what I can give you?"

"I don't know," Erik whimpered.

"Then I've a suggestion?"

"Sure, anything."

"I suggest you keep yourself alive and we'll meet again under better circumstances." Josef grinned. "I'm sure you want your revenge, right?"

"I–!"

Josef slammed the cane over Erik's head, forcing his vision flashing in red. The agony rushed at his mind and his doubled vision worsened. The discordant voices started in Erik's head, calling out to him.

They're going to destroy you...

Falling off the edge of madness and despair...

Seeing will drive you cold and numb...

Until there's nothing left...

Never to return...

"I don't have enough hate..." Erik seethed as he struggled against the cold seeping in, "and you know what? I'm nothing like you, Joe! I will never be like you!"

"Oh?"

Erik hissed in pain when the skin on his back slowly split open, the tears traveling to his shoulders, arms, and hands. The agony in his shoulder where the burn-like bruise lay seared intensely. Erik screamed and Josef chortled darkly.

"You're right," Josef said then turned on his heel. "You can never be like me..."

"Wait!" Erik called and Josef came to a pause. "What are the voices saying to you?"

"You hear them too?" Josef glanced back at Erik. "Why do you want to know?"

"Please tell me what they're saying, Joe. I don't understand them."

"Prevail, fight, destroy..." Josef suddenly laughed and he doubled over, clutching his sides. "I have to kill them all, everyone, everything, including you."

"Please don't kill me. I'll help you."

"You're weak, Brother." Josef suddenly stood upright, smiling brightly as a manic glaze glassed over in his eyes. "You're too weak. You don't have the heart in you to kill - you never did."

"Show me then?"

"Of course!"

"But you know doing that will put us all in danger, Joe!"

"I've stopped caring a long time ago!"

"Wait it out, Joe! It will get better!"

"Never as long as these fiends exist!" Josef approached, standing over Erik. He pressed the cane against Erik's chest and Erik grasped the wood with a weakened hand. "Please don't beg me anymore. I might not control myself."

"I'm sorry," Erik moaned.

"Lie down and die for me. Will you do that, please?"

Erik struggled against the suffocating cold overpowering him. Josef stood over him, smiling and Erik moaned when he lost the battle against the darkness taking out his world.

TWENTY-NINE

Erik roused to the sounds of pounding outside. Sitting up with a start, he realized he rest in the room again with the comfortable bed and walls adorned with posters of famous bands and actors. Erik stiffened, hearing the front door handle turn, followed by more knocking.

"How did I get here?" he muttered and seethed as his ears rang.

"Get up, Jerry," Mahjin bellowed from outside. "Come on; wake the blazes up, why don't you?"

Erik slipped out of bed and padded downstairs to the parlor. He turned on the table lamp near the couch along the way and unlocked the door, revealing Mahjin had his frizzy blond hair pulled back by a black band and wore a slate gray suit over a white dress shirt and black tie.

"What are you doing here?" Erik demanded as Mahjin pushed past him.

"Jerry, get up you swine!" the older man thundered, walking unsteadily against his cane. Mahjin collapsed onto the nearby couch before he lost his balance, heaving for breath.

"What's the matter?" Erik asked softly as Mahjin clutched tightly to his white wax staff. Mahjin leaned forward and shut his eyes, struggling for breath as his body trembled slightly.

"*He's so pale,*" Erik thought, studying him. "*He's wearing a suit too... What gives?*"

"There's an emergency..." Mahjin said in a controlled voice. "I need his help..."

"Dad's not here," Erik murmured. "What's this about?"

Mahjin glanced up at Erik with a worried look shadowing his face. "Then do you think he's working late again at the office?" Mahjin said instead and Erik shook his head in response. "Fix me a drink, will ya, lad?" Mahjin requested.

"What do you want?"

"Whiskey."

Erik approached the mini-bar, tense. "How did I get here?" he demanded.

Mahjin raised an eyebrow. "What do you mean?"

"We were attacked at the park earlier."

Mahjin's face became unreadable and he stiffened when the phone in the hall suddenly rang. Erik ran for it and picked it up, giving his usual greeting.

"Twenty minutes," a mysterious voice said and the line suddenly cut off.

Erik stared down at the receiver, stunned. "What does that mean?" he muttered, hanging the receiver back in the cradle. He drifted back into the parlor, finding Mahjin leaning against the cherry and glass mini-bar, mixing himself a drink.

"What's that all about?" Mahjin grumbled.

"It's weird..." Erik murmured. After explaining the message he heard, Mahjin dropped his glass, shattering it against the hardwood floor. He whirled around when the doorbell suddenly rang.

"Upstairs, now!" Mahjin ordered.

Erik nodded and scurried upstairs to his bedroom. He closed it partway and crouched near the entrance, peeping out. Through the crevice, he spotted Mahjin speaking to a young man in a dark suit who gestured wildly. Erik shrank back once Mahjin pushed past him and the young man entered the house, heading upstairs. Erik quickly shut the door and locked it, backing away once the handle turned.

"Open up," the voice of the young man said on the other side. "You need to get out of here. It's for your own protection."

"Who are you?" Erik demanded.

"There's no time to explain." The handle turned again. "We have to get you out of here!"

"What about my dad?"

"He's safe, but you need to be safe as well so that he can be kept safe."

"How can I trust you?" Erik shouted. "I don't know you!"

"Your father's friend Melvin Zachary sent me to get you. You know he can't do it alone."

Erik hastily searched around his room for a weapon as his panic rose. He hurried for his closets and threw out articles. A case fell from the top shelf, smacking him aside the head and Erik yelped, startled when it banged on the floor. Wondering how the case got there, he sprung it open and gasped, finding plain clothing in his size packed inside.

"You should have a suitcase on the top shelf of your closet," said the mysterious young man. "Take it, grab a pair of shoes, and let's go!"

Erik grew increasingly terrified regarding how much the

stranger knew, fearing he may have sinister intentions. Slipping into a pair of his flat-soled laceless sneakers, Erik hurried for his bedroom window and pushed it open. He climbed out and jumped onto the ground then stepped carefully around the house's side, peering around the corner.

Erik spotted several dark cars with tinted windows lined out front and Mahjin sat on the stoop, smoking a cigarette. Erik backed away and let out a scream when hands grabbed for him. Elbowing into his attacker, Erik turned out, kicking the person who wore all black: wool cap, gloves, turtleneck and jeans, in the groin before racing away.

"Justin!" Mahjin called after him.

"Leave me alone!" Erik cried and quickly hopped the fence. *"They're going to kill me,"* he thought frantically as he ran down the street, escaping his would-be pursuers. *"I can't let them kill me!"*

Slipping into the local park, Erik took the walking trail toward the edge leading to a forested area close to the nearby highway. He gasped for breath as he crashed through the branches and foliage, finally stopping to rest near a large log leaning against another tree underneath dense shrubbery.

Erik crawled below and cowered, shivering from the cool night air, waiting for time to pass. He heard indistinct voices shouting and people running in various directions.

Erik held his breath, watching beams of light flash around, searching for him. He drew up his knees to his chest, rocking slowly as he counted to himself from one-thousand to one, trying to slow his breathing in an effort to subside his panic.

"Justin," a faint voice whispered to him. "Justin, come on." Erik craned his neck, searching for the source. "Justin, it's me, Genovera!"

Coming out of his folded position, Erik got on his haunches, slowly turning in the cramped space and peered out. He spotted the woman in dark flats and her frame hidden underneath an overcoat halfway hiding behind a large tree, waving to him.

"Why are they here?" Erik hissed back.

"Some bad people want to use your father for very bad things and he won't have any of it," she whispered back. "He wants me to make sure you stay safe!"

"What about Smiley?"

"They already got to him."

"How can I trust you?"

"I found you out at the park earlier..."

"How did you know we were there?"

Genovera put a finger to her lips and reached into her coat, withdrawing a pistol with an attached silencer. Erik froze as she pointed it ahead and fired a muffled shot, forcing a groan from behind followed by a crash to the ground.

Erik whirled around, spotting a body dead at his feet, with blood running from between his eyes. In his stiff hands, he held a wire. Erik turned back to Genovera who beckoned to him.

"Come with me," Genovera urged, "before they get suspicious!"

Erik scrambled out of his hiding place and she took him by the arm, pulling him up along her side.

"There he goes!" a voice shouted once they both raced out the woods together. The sounds of several others followed them, their feet striking the ground unevenly.

Erik tripped over a gnarled branch and stumbled forward, losing his shoe. He scrambled to keep pace as they climbed up a steep incline near a hill. His head banged in pain and he fought the sensation of faint as his lungs burned from the crisp cool nighttime air, struggling for breath with each weak gasp. Coming onto a divide in the woods, Erik banked left while Genovera turned to the right.

"No, not that way!" she cried and Erik yelped in terror as the ground suddenly slipped from beneath him. He felt himself falling freely before instantly splashing into frigid cold, knocking his reality out into a watery underworld.

Bobbing up to the surface, Erik wheezed for breath, helpless when the current took him away from the park. He looked up, spotting Genovera standing at the edge of the path. Her silhouetted form against the navy starlit sky grew smaller the more distanced he became as the river carried him away. She ran a hand through her long hair blowing in the breeze, watching in dismay.

Erik relaxed and let his body float and bob as the current took him down river until he eventually landed at a sandbar. Crawling onto the banks, Erik fell forward, exhausted and drained.

Relishing the cool earth beneath him, he felt himself fading into the earth, becoming one with it, then suspended and unable to touch the ground.

Surrounded by frigid air, Erik struggled for breath, gasping as his lungs contracted in protest. His head reeled from the many voices he heard speaking to him at once.

I understand it best...

I made that decision myself...

It still hurts...

"Help me," Erik cried out in the darkness. "Somebody please...!"

This is why I hate them so...

They tinker on us without reserve...

They think they're gods...

We are forever broken, never to truly heal...

THIRTY

Erik had no idea how long he slept. He was dozing fitfully, but suddenly found himself pulled from slumber by the slight bounce of the couch, followed by a startled gasp as a soft hand came in contact with him and pushed down firmly on his chest.

Erik coughed and took in a weak breath, sensing the person belonging to the hand was very startled to be touching another warm body and was on the verge of screaming.

"I'm sorry," Erik murmured and immediately sat up then scoot back, knocking into the couch's arm. He looked up and around, finding he was in an unfamiliar parlor with its heavy curtains pulled close. "Please don't scream. I'm more afraid of you hurting me than me hurting you."

In the filtered light from the curtained window, he saw the hand move towards the small table lamp and switch it on. His eyes adjusted to the dim light and there sat a young woman with long thick red hair, a mass of curls hanging below the middle of her back slightly damp and frizzy from the rain, and dark green eyes. Her skin was flawless and she wore no makeup, even without lipstick her lips were a deep red. Erik gulped, noticing she stood slightly taller than he in stockinged feet, assessing she may be six feet tall.

The young woman wore an oversized University T-shirt that

hardly hid the curves of her body. Erik glanced down at her long legs, noting the hugging material of the sea foam green jeans she wore were snug across her hips and bottom.

"What are you doing here?" the woman asked. Erik returned his attention to her and felt his face burning hotly. "Don't tell me you're one of my father's new friends?"

"I–!" Erik took in a shallow breath and unexpectedly found it difficult to speak. "W-w-wait, what? No!" He noticed the young woman's T-shirt was sensuously clinging to her upper body and swallowed hard when he began to feel strange sensations stirring in his groin.

Erik's face burned brighter when he realized he had only a towel and knew what the arousal meant. He forced himself to remember he wasn't even in his own house and that she assumed he *her father's friend*.

"Are you alright?" the young woman asked, raising an eyebrow.

"I, well–!"

Erik felt strange, also completely out of his element and had no idea what to say to a breathtakingly beautiful woman who sat merely inches from him. Erik brought up his legs and leaned forward, vainly trying to hide his interest by holding tightly to his knees as he hugged them to his chest.

"Did I spook you?" the young woman asked when Erik broke out in cold sweat. "I'm Clairese."

"H-hello Clairese." Erik swallowed hard. "I-I would tell you my name, but I don't remember it..."

"Are you that hammered?"

"S-sure..."

"I usually try not to drop in on my father out the blue, since he can be a total perv sometimes..." Clairese left the couch and Erik breathed a sigh of relief. "But this is the only place I could think of when I had to get away from that asshole chicken-shit dumbfuck!"

Erik unfurled from his position, listening intently to Clairese talk about her formerly abusive boyfriend. He felt strange, hearing the horrific stories she had to tell about all the times he beat her, raped her and tortured her and she felt powerless to do anything, since he came from money and her mother didn't want her to end the relationship. Clairese told Erik how she felt scared and alone, unheard by her mother and too afraid to tell her father.

"I just had enough," Clairese concluded. "After that bastard made me miscarry, I had to come up with a way out."

Erik reached over and grabbed for his cigarettes. "What way did you come up with?" he asked.

"I talked to this insurance salesman and he told me how houses could be dangerous... Many accidents happen at home."

"I see..."

Erik lit his cigarette and glanced up at her staring down at him. Clairese's cheeks were pink and her chest rose and fell in indignant anger. Erik swallowed hard, somehow finding himself turned on by it. He knew he should excuse himself and run into the bathroom and drown himself in cold water, but was very tired yet felt energized in her presence.

Clairese smiled sweetly at him. "Thanks for listening to me," she said gently. "I just had to get it out of my system. I was afraid you might judge me."

"That's all right," Erik murmured. "I really should get going. You can have the couch and what have you..."

Erik stood and made his way across the floor. He froze when he saw Clairese was still staring at him and he remembered he only had a towel on. Not only that, but his hard-on was rearing up stiffly in the front and creating a very noticeable bulge.

Mortified, Erik looked at Clairese, and she was looking back. However, not at his face - she was staring at his crotch with an indecipherable expression in her eyes. She smiled gently at him and Erik rapidly grew hot.

"Don't you want me?" Clairese asked.

"I...!" Erik backed away when she approached and he grunted when she pushed him back, forcing him plopping on the couch's end. Clairese pushed Erik down by the shoulder and took a seat in his lap.

"What's your name again?" Clairese murmured in his ear.

Erik closed his eyes and struggled to breathe as his heart pound hard in his chest. "I must be dreaming," he moaned.

"No, you're not," Clairese said and took the burning cigarette he held, putting it out on the nearby ashtray. "How old are you?"

"I'm not sure..."

"You seem to be younger than the usual guys he usually brings over." Clairese twirled a finger in Erik's hair and he shuddered. "All those scars on your chest and arms... You seem so tough and rugged."

"I-is that a bad thing?" Erik stammered.

"I don't know. Maybe he's going through a mid-life crisis?"

"I-I don't know..."

"So, have you ever gotten laid?"

Erik shook his head wildly as his face burned hotly. "N-no," he struggled to say. "T-this can't be happening..."

"Don't you want to?" Erik tensed when Clairese stroked his chest. "Or is it you don't like girls?"

Erik nodded. "I-I like girls... T-they just don't like me."

"Why is that?" Clairese asked coyly. "You're so cute!" She poked Erik's hard-on and he grunted.

"Please don't do that," Erik mewed. "That hurt..."

"I don't see how girls could not like you," Clairese continued. "You're one well-hung guy."

"I-I never thought about it."

"Your little friend seems to be thinking about it." Clairese giggled. "Do you want me as much as he does?"

Erik's face burned beet red and he sweat profusely. "Wh-wh-what are you going to do?" he pleaded.

"What would you like for me to do?"

"Please, don't," Erik moaned and took in a shallow breath, smelling her scent of faint musk from the rain and flowery perfume.

The overhead light abruptly turned on and Erik's eyes snapped open. He let out a strangled sound, surprised at Brodie standing at the parlor archway from the rear hall leading to the bathroom.

"What's going on?" Brodie snapped.

"Hi," Clairese said, waving at Brodie. "I was thinking about borrowing him if you were done."

Brodie bit the inside of his cheeks, unable to speak.

Erik looked to Clairese who had an arm draped around his

shoulders, then to Brodie who wore his bathrobe, his expression stony. Suddenly intimidated, Erik pushed off Clairese and she let out a squeak when she struck the floor on her rear. He jumped from the couch and raced to the bathroom, slamming the door behind him.

Erik turned on the cold water full blast and stepped into the stall. He slipped to his knees, panting hard for breath as he knelt underneath the stream. Suddenly he found it hard to keep awake and fell forward.

Erik woke up gasping when cold water splashed on his face and opened his eyes, squinting when sheets of frigid rain pelt down around him as thunder rumbled overhead in the dark gray sky.

"Is it morning or afternoon?" he wondered, scrambling to his feet.

Running alongside the river's edge, Erik escaped into the woods once he heard indistinct shouts and barking dogs in the distance. Tearing through the forest, Erik tripped over a large tree root, throwing him forward onto the ground and knocked off the other shoe he had.

Pulling himself up, Erik raced forward, ignoring the low hanging branches ripping into him and trying to keep his balance as he slipped through mud and moss before finding an opening once he came across jutting rocks leading to a canyon.

Erik shivered, running his hands over his arms covered in clinging soaked flannel while facing the assorted rocks below.

"The longer I stay out here in the rain," he mused as he pushed forward, *"the more slippery those rocks get and I won't*

be able to get away..."

Taking a small foothold, Erik pulled himself up and climbed carefully over the numerous rocks, swinging to find a gap with stinging feet cut from the rough stone. Coming onto a small flat surface with a thin trail where animals prowled, Erik rose to his feet and looked back as he caught his breath, staring out onto the canyon hillside dotted by trees with the river below.

In the distance, Erik saw several men in tan jumpsuits and heavy leather gloves, boots, and wool caps combing the rocks with German Shepherds and Bloodhounds wearing red vests running ahead of them, barking.

Erik looked up, noticing the cliff's edge jutting before him had a small cave created by one large flat boulder resting against the surface from the canyon's side. Finding two small twisted pines clustered nearby and a thorny bush in front partly blocking the cave's entrance, Erik searched for another foothold and let out a cry as his nails scratched against rock when fiery pain shot through the palm of his hand.

Yanking back, Erik quickly threw himself against the surface side to keep from falling off the extreme narrow ledge he stood upon and seethed in agony at the many spines from a cactus in his hand. Thunder rumbled loudly overhead and Erik felt the hairs stand on end as bright light flashed overhead.

Another large crack followed and a spray of rock struck Erik's face, throwing him aside as the stones gave way. Tumbling down, Erik's back struck a gnarled thin wind-twisted pine tree, knocking the breath out of his lungs. The brittle wood cracked, bending beneath his weight.

"I need to get out of here," Erik thought in despair, gazing

up at the edge looming before him. *"There's got to be something up there on the other side..."* His body refused to respond to mental commands, disobeying orders to move and stiffening instead, turning into icy leaden blocks. Dread overwhelmed him as the barking dogs and the men's voices came closer. *"I know I can't go with them,"* Erik realized, closing his eyes. *"But who am I kidding? I'm no survivalist!"*

Feeling himself drift, he heard the high winds howling and the rushing rain turned hollowed and diffused once the pain enveloped him completely.

THIRTY-ONE

Erik let out a cry and gasped for breath as remnants of his dreams began to fade. He opened his eyes, seeing nothing but shifting shadows.

"Are you ready now?" called the doctor's voice from afar.

"It's hazy," Erik moaned.

"What is?"

Erik shook his head, clearing the fog. Looking up, he faced the doctor who sat with his hands resting atop the desk's surface in the empty white room. The tape in the machine whirred softly and Erik noticed the pad of paper now gone, with a stack of cassettes nearby in its place.

"I've got nothing to tell you," Erik spat sourly.

"Tell me," pressed the doctor, "what it is you're thinking?"

"There's nothing to think," Erik grumbled.

The doctor chortled. "Now, that's impossible."

"My impression of you is very poor right now."

"That's okay... if you're uncomfortable; we can do this another time. There is no rush here."

"But you want *something* from me, is that it?"

The doctor smiled faintly. "Why yes, we do."

"What is it you want?"

"You're here to tell us."

Erik shut his eyes, sensing himself drift. "I don't have to stand for this mess."

"Now, don't withdraw," said the doctor sternly. "Just tell me, right now, on how you feel."

"Honestly?" Erik snorted. "I want to get out of here."

"Not what you want, but how you *feel*."

"I feel..." Erik sighed heavily, feeling himself separate from his body, standing in the kitchen he always had known, yet it seemed different from all the others. "These imprints..."

"Yes, go on," said the doctor's voice from afar. "What is it you see and feel and hear?"

"Lights..." Erik looked at himself in the finish of the stainless steel refrigerator, staring back at a redheaded teenager with freckles across the cheeks and sad violet eyes. "*Who is that?*" he thought, touching the surface.

"Why are you hesitating?" the doctor called. "What is it you're doubtful about?"

"Who is he?" Erik asked.

"Whom are you referring to?"

"The red-headed boy."

"What red-headed boy...?"

"The one that looks like me."

"I'm not quite sure..."

Erik blew a hard sigh as his resolve slackened. "He's always there, watching me..."

"Don't go back now. Stay here."

"I'm tired..."

"Please, stay."

"Don't press me."

"I understand…"

"I'm through with this."

"There's plenty of time; everything will be all right tomorrow."

Erik gave up fighting and drifted into darkness.

Erik sat up with a start, disoriented. Before he could make out where he was, Erik felt a gentle hand on his shoulder, pushing him back down.

"It's okay," Clayton said softly from overhead. "It's not real."

"Sure," Erik moaned and sat forward, running a hand through his hair. Sudden grogginess took over and Erik rubbed at his eyes. "What would you call what they're doing to us?"

Clayton snorted and returned to the room's other side and sat on his bed's edge, picking up a thick anthology of thriller stories left there. "It's real enough," he murmured. "Real enough…"

Erik lay back in the hard bed with its regular gray sheets, resting his head on the worn flat pillow underneath. He gingerly turned on his side, seething as the searing pain shot through his shoulder and back.

"I feel like dirt," Erik moaned, clutching his arm close to his aching body. He glanced at it, finding only a faint scar across the top.

"Feel okay otherwise?" Clayton inquired, turning a page in his book.

"What kind of question is that?" Erik spat. "You'd feel great too if you got the beating of a lifetime like I did!"

"I guess you're right," answered Clayton. "Just so you know, you're under watch by those sick bastards."

"Lock down again?"

"Yeah, though I don't know what code they called this time."
Clayton shrugged his shoulders. "Not that it matters anyway."

"What do you mean?" Clayton scoffed in response, rolling
his eyes. "Why are you here?" Erik wondered aloud. "Where's
Joe?"

"You're rooming with me for now," Clayton replied. "He got
sent away to the downstairs for reprogramming..."

"Reprogramming...?"

"To make you into a more compliant and productive citizen
of society," Clayton filled in. "That's the reason you're here. They
assume you're dangerous."

"I'm not a psychotic monster like Joe."

Clayton chortled. "I hope that bed's softer than the one you
had," he said gently.

"Not really..." Erik sighed. "What's going to happen to him?"

Clayton turned another page in his book. "You really don't
want to know," he muttered.

"When will they be back with him?"

"Whenever the next meal is called, I suppose... so I suggest
you rest."

"I don't think I can."

A knock resonated outside the door moments later.

"Doctor Schnell wants to see you," a nurse called and left
the doorway.

"I heard them mention another test," Clayton said. "Erik,
you can always say no! You don't have to go along anymore!"

"What are you saying?"

"They know."

"Know what?"

Clayton shook his head as Schnell appeared at the door, knocking.

"Are you ready?" asked the doctor.

Erik groaned and got out of bed then followed Schnell into another consulting room. He sat on the examination table while the doctor stood across from him, holding his chart containing his information.

"What is it you want with me?" Erik grumbled as Schnell continued to stand there unflinchingly with his gray eyes blank, staring out into dead space. Erik stiffened, immediately nervous and concerned. "Doctor Schnell...? Are you okay?"

A slow smile appeared over the doctor's face and Erik quickly stepped down off the table. Rushing toward the door, Schnell sidestepped Erik and shut it before his hand reached the knob.

"What does it mean when one says 'a stitch in time will save you nine'?" Schnell inquired.

Erik shrank back, giving the doctor a blank stare in return. "I don't know," replied Erik slowly. "I really never heard of that saying before."

"How does a transmitter and a receiver work?"

"What?" Erik continued to stare at the vacantly smiling Schnell who made no other movements. As he stood there facing him, Erik noticed the smile seemed strained and his face twitched slightly. "Doctor Schnell, what's wrong?"

"What special abilities do you have?" Schnell asked in response.

"I'm not special in *any* sense, Doctor Schnell!" Erik snapped. "Are you trying for bullshit answers or something because the questions you're asking are really stupid!"

"Then explain what happened to Doctor Rosenthal."

"I didn't cut him up that way," Erik protested.

"Please, Number Three."

Erik sucked in a breath and clenched his hands. "What do you want me to do?" he exploded. "You're blaming me for what that psychotic monster did!"

"What is it about pain and death that you don't like?"

Erik shook his head. "I just..." He suddenly found it hard to breathe. "I just can't explain..."

"Have you seen it in life? Is that why you're resistant to such?"

"I'm not understanding what you're asking."

"Please, Erik," Schnell went on. "I promise not to share what you say in confidence in me. No one will have access to this data."

Erik grew annoyed. "It's just not in me to hurt others!" he snapped. "How else do you want me to explain it? I just hate it!"

"Is that so?"

"What are you trying to mold me into," Erik shrilled, "some demented killing machine? You people are sick!"

"That's not what we're trying to do."

"Then tell me what happened to Joe?" Erik demanded. "Why does he act the way he does?"

Schnell blinked slowly before answering. "He is really sick," the doctor replied with careful words, "and he needs to stay alone for the time being to fight his personal demons under careful observation."

"It's because you people *made* him that way!"

"Well, how about I keep talking and you can answer however you wish?" Schnell said suddenly.

Erik folded his arms across his chest and glanced warily at the doctor. "Are you trying to trap me?" he retorted. "This place is probably bugged and they might use what I say against me!"

"We must obtain some blood and urine samples," Schnell said, ignoring Erik and pulled out a plastic cup with a sticker over the top. Handing it to Erik, Erik glanced at the label, expecting it blank to mark where the urine came from and instead found a note written in small cramped handwriting on the side. "First give me the urine sample, and then I can take your blood."

"I, ah, hadn't enough to drink today," Erik said nervously, scanning the label on the cup. He clenched his teeth when he saw the note: *'John Greenfield reassigned to Centerville'*. He set it aside, shaking slightly. Schnell grabbed the plastic cup after pulling free a label sticker from his chart and placed it over the note.

"Well, then," murmured Schnell. "I have some release forms for you to fill out. It shouldn't take long." He handed Erik a clipboard with blank paper and a pen.

'What does this mean?' Erik wrote. *'Please don't let them kill Mister Greenfield. He's all I've got!'*

'I don't know how soon I can get him released,' Schnell wrote back in response. *'Centerville's a very punishing place and is the first step toward Termination. However, we have*

some very special friends working on it. Hopefully they won't brainwash him too hard.'

"What's the point of all this?" Erik asked as Schnell took the paper and folded it then placed in his vest pocket.

Schnell glanced through Erik's chart. "Well, we need permission if we're going to run risky tests that haven't been approved," he answered, writing another note on the clipboard. Erik blanched when he read the handwriting: *'I apologize beforehand, but Greenfield may not even remember you anymore after his forced corrective treatments.'*

"You're already doing things to me against my will," Erik protested and slumped into a nearby chair. He held a hand to his face, hiding the tears that suddenly came to.

"It's because you've shown to be a danger to yourself and others," Schnell replied. "Until you can pass psychiatric examination, you don't have a say."

"What is it you're looking for?"

"You remember, do you not?" Schnell implored. He took the second sheet and folded it, then placed in his slacks pocket.

"Just barely..."

"Though most likely the trauma erased your memory, your body always remembers. It still exists, deep within at the cellular level... We just need to find the right method to bring it to the surface."

Erik glared at the doctor who continued writing in his chart. "Wait, so you mean they're doing this to me to force something they know I forgot on purpose?" he thundered. "Then I'll keep fighting and die if it comes down to it!"

"Then you must hate your father, don't you?"

"He told me not to at any given cost!" Schnell paused in his writing and gasped, dropping his pen. "Doctor Schnell!" Erik wailed as Schnell grunted and cupped a hand to his face. He rose to his feet when Schnell staggered back and moaned, faltering.

Erik immediately grabbed for the man when he lost his balance, settling him gently on the floor. The chart clattered to the floor beside them and Erik frowned, noticing the blood running from Schnell's nose. Erik glanced over the chart, finding notes about his psychological profile.

"Ferdian, third revision?" Erik murmured and stiffened when he heard the door handle turn. He immediately stood on guard as the exit opened, revealing Fenway.

"Hey," Fenway said sharply, "what the fuck happened here?"

"He just fainted," responded Erik nervously. "I didn't do anything to him, I swear!"

Fenway glared at Erik and turned back out to the hall. "Tsenninger," he barked, "do we still have that blood order?"

"I didn't even get examined yet!" Erik protested.

"No matter," called Nelson as Fenway stepped away and the technician entered. Erik backed into the wall, cringing at the sight of the young man who had dark bruises on his face and under his left eye. "I can take care of it."

"I'd rather you not," Erik spat.

Fenway entered behind Nelson and picked up Schnell, hauling him away. Erik cowered as Nelson approached, grinning slyly.

"What are you staring at, huh?" Nelson snapped and shoved Erik backward into the nearby desk chair. Erik grunted and let out a yelp when Nelson grabbed him by the face in a firm hand. "You like me, yeah? Think I'm pretty cute, huh?"

"No!" Erik yelled and gripped Nelson's wrist. "Like I told Joe, I only like girls!"

"Then don't stare at me, you freak!"

"I got it." Erik pushed against Nelson and he let go.

"I've got to draw your blood," Nelson replied nonchalantly.

"It's not going to change," Erik said defiantly as Nelson pulled out the desk's drawer holding various sized needles from a tray. "Type O and all that jazz."

Nelson snorted. "Oh really?" he said wryly and pulled out six long vials from his pocket.

Erik stiffened when Nelson grabbed his arm and tied it down with a rubber tourniquet then drew a sharp breath once struck with the needle into the vein that appeared. Nelson stuck the vial on the end and blood filed the tube.

"What do they need my blood for?" Erik grumbled.

"Do you really want to know," acknowledged Nelson, "or are you just making conversation?"

Erik bared his teeth. "I just love talking with you," he said through gritted teeth.

"They're cloning you," Nelson replied, withdrawing the vial and started on the second sampling. "After they get the answers they want, they're going to kill you and send the Replicant to your father and have him killed."

Erik's eyes widened in disbelief and Nelson chortled. "You can't be serious!" he yelped.

"Oh dear, that's not what you've expected, huh?" Nelson jeered. "You couldn't have thought –!" A small ring penetrated the air and Nelson grunted after he pulled out the second vial and started on the third.

"Why they want to kill my father?" Erik demanded as Nelson reached into his pocket and withdrew a small cellular phone. Flipping it open, he held it in place with his shoulder against his ear.

"What is it?" Nelson snapped. "I'm busy right now." He glanced to Erik. "They want to get rid of him because he tampered with Agency property," he explained. "That's akin to going against Policy."

"So you mean...!"

"Huh?" Nelson said into the phone after he finished the last remaining samples, then followed with an injection before Erik could protest, flushing the serum within the drawing needle. "No, Greenfield's the one getting whacked. You're still fine. Sure, I'll see if I can get more of the stuff, but if you get caught selling it, I'm not bailing your ass outta jail!"

Nelson flipped the phone shut and pulled out the drawing needle, then threw both used needle and syringe into a hazardous materials bin above the desk.

"What did he do exactly?" Erik asked timidly.

"What, Greenfield?" Nelson responded, untying the tourniquet.

"How did he go against Policy?"

"He let the buggy chips through into our products," Nelson answered. "We don't know what they'll do until they go online." Nelson scooped up the six vials of blood samples and pocketed them along with his phone then glanced out the examination room door.

"Not a big deal!"

"It *is* a very big deal, little boy," Nelson growled, checking his watch. "But first, I'm going to have some fun with you."

Erik turned to the nearby waste bin, gagging. "*I don't believe it!*" he thought, fighting the compulsion to retch. "*But he seems serious! I can't let them go through with their plans...*"

Nelson abruptly kicked the door shut as Erik leaned back against the chair, drained and overcome with faint. Nelson approached and grabbed at his hair, pulling back his head as he wrapped a leg around the chair's arm, trapping Erik's limb. Nelson put a knee on Erik's thigh and leaned in close, trapping his other arm against the chair.

"I've been keeping an eye on you," Nelson said and grinned deviously. "You just love causing trouble around here, eh?"

"What are you going to do to me?" Erik asked weakly.

"That all depends on how I feel at the moment." Erik sucked in a breath as Nelson pulled out a pocketknife from his back pocket with his free hand and flipped it open with his thumb. "I might cut your eyelids off so you can't help but watch what I do to you, whatever it may be..."

"You're the sick freak around here!"

Nelson chortled. "Is that so?" Erik clenched his teeth as Nelson cut near his jaw line, drawing a small line of blood. "I could fillet you like a fish, cutting your skin layer by layer..."

"Please!" Erik whimpered as Nelson cut deeper.

Nelson laughed darkly, leaning in to his ear. "You look good like this," he whispered, withdrawing the knife. "Nobody's going to miss you if you let me put you out of your misery. You're replaceable, remember?" Erik stiffened when Nelson ran the knife on the back of his neck. "I told you you're going to be punished. So relax for me and just take it!"

"I...!" Erik pushed Nelson back, sending him crashing to the floor. Erik stood as Nelson sprang to his feet and grunted when slashed across the chest.

Turning out of another stab, Erik grabbed Nelson by the wrist and Nelson turned with a swift roundhouse, throwing him backwards over the chair. Erik staggered to his feet as Nelson stood over him, holding his switchblade at ready.

"Stop fighting and just give up," Nelson spat. "You're through!"

"Put your hands on me again," Erik declared and put up his fists on guard, "and I'll make sure they don't exist!"

"We'll see about that!" Nelson advanced, swiping at Erik. Erik backed out of the slash and jumped on the desk.

Nelson turned, jamming the blade into Erik's thigh and Erik screamed. Nelson yanked Erik down and climbed atop him, holding his hands around Erik's throat. Erik pushed back against Nelson's chest and the young man froze when a sharp knock came at the door.

"He's got dinner," Fenway called from the other side.

"Shit," Nelson grumbled and socked Erik across the face with a heavy hand, snapping back his head. Erik groaned, seeing stars. "When's the test?" he called back.

"He's got it in an hour."

Erik yowled when Nelson withdrew the blade embedded in his thigh and got off. Erik curled up, clutching his wound.

"You beast," Erik moaned as Nelson grabbed the first aid kit on the nearby wall and tossed it at Erik, bouncing it off his head.

"Hurry it up," Nelson snapped and Erik clenched his teeth when the kit clattered aside on the desk. "Either patch it up yourself or let me, your choice."

"I don't want you touching me," Erik snapped.

"There's always next time," Nelson said brightly and chortled, grinning craftily. "Your punishment is coming."

Erik shuddered and took off his pants, immediately attending to the deep cut on his thigh. After applying antibiotic cream and taping down a pad of gauze, he heard the door open and looked up at Nelson sauntering out the room. Erik swallowed the acrid burning that came up and readjusted his clothing then also left the room, returning to the dining area.

THIRTY-TWO

Upon entry, Erik ground his teeth when he saw the meals consisted of bloody steaks. Taking his usual seat at the rear, Erik pushed away his tray and put his head down on the table.

"What's the matter?" Clayton asked moments later.

"I'm dying," Erik moaned.

"I sometimes pretend it's something else, like a slice of chicken-fried steak, a spoonful of buttered rice, seasoned green beans and cranberry sauce." He chortled and Erik cracked a smile. "Besides, keep playing a fake and you'll always keep them guessing."

"How long have you been here?"

"Too long... but long enough to fool them and avoid Nelson's physicals."

Erik shuddered at the mere mention. "Don't tell me there's more than him getting stabbity," he said wryly.

"You just now noticed?" Erik sat up, facing Clayton who sat with his back against the table, holding his mug of tea in one hand. He had one leg crossed at the knee and draped his free arm against the table. "There isn't much you can do about Nelson getting too close to you. I heard he likes the pretty ones."

"Don't tell me he's pretty sweet on you too," Erik retorted.

"He used to mess with me, but I'm getting too old, I suppose."

"Does it ever bother you?" Erik asked.

"The drugs help sometimes," Clayton murmured and looked down into his mug. "It's better if I were so zonked that I couldn't tell left from right."

"I'm sorry..."

"Don't be. It happens in corrupted places like this."

"I don't understand what they're trying to fix," Erik groused. "Joe's messed up due to some chip or something it seems. But I don't see how it has anything to do with me."

"What chip?" implored Clayton.

"Dyna-Sys or E-widget or something..."

"Oh, you mean the Dyna-Widgets and the E-Sys. They're important chips - Dyna-Widgets hold DNA samples and are integral to Homunculus production," Clayton explained. "E-Sys is short for Emotion System. They're AI chips for the Snythoids to express and calculate emotion."

"Homunculus...?" Erik muttered.

"Yeah, that's the old term they gave the androids. Now they're called Snythoids."

"Android...?"

"Yeah, Combat Androids. They're machines who appear Human used in place of soldiers now. Saves lives and gives the IT sector more reason to come up with new tech. Military loves that stuff."

"If you say so..." Erik held his chin in his hand and blew a heavy sigh. "*So that's how they're going to do it,*" Erik mused. "*Study me, get my range of emotions, kill me off and send a Combat Android to do him in.*" Erik suddenly broke out laughing and Clayton raised an eyebrow.

"I'm not going to ask you if you're okay," Clayton said softly. "Obviously you're not."

"I don't understand what's the point of all this testing!" Erik protested. "If we're that dangerous, then why continue with the poking and the prodding?" He glanced to Clayton who sipped his tea. "My friend Chico said they're taking away a bit of our soul each time, trying to bring out the worst in us. Now I understand!"

"Chico, hm?"

"Do you know him?" Clayton shook his head. "So, why don't we have a choice?"

"If they made it voluntary, then they won't get their answers for their so-called progress!"

"Answers to what?" Erik grunted. "Why with so much force?"

"It's the only way for them," Clayton said sadly. "They know no other way..."

"But does it have to be?" Erik argued. Clayton said nothing and Erik put his head back on the table. *"That's why they're trying to make me remember something,"* he pondered. *"They need all the memories they can use to make a flawless reproduction so he won't know he's marked as a target!"*

"Feel like tea or anything?" Clayton asked after several moments of silence between them.

"Sure," Erik answered, "thanks."

After dinner, everyone left the dining area and headed for the lounge. Erik played a game of billiards with Clayton and while Clayton studied his next shot, Erik felt a tap on his shoulder. He turned, facing Fenway who held a paper-covered plate.

"Here," Fenway grumbled, handing the plate to Erik. Erik took it and removed the napkin covering it, revealing several sugar cookies. "Here's the deal: you improve on your teamwork skills and I won't have to knock you around like the mindless shit you are, understand?"

"Whatever," Erik huffed and set the plate aside on the table.

"If you won't comply, I'll get Tsenninger to do it."

"Sure you will."

Fenway stalked away and Erik picked up a cookie, biting into it. He frowned when his tongue burned slightly and tasted metallic powder.

"Damn, I scratched," muttered Clayton, knocking the cue ball into the pocket after nudging another colored ceramic ball in.

"I don't want to deal with that Nelson," Erik said nervously and set the cookie aside.

"He's a freak; we know this," Clayton replied, rolling his eyes. "So, is Fenway getting sweet on you or Nelson sent it up to apologize?"

"They're messing with me, for sure!" Erik complained and grabbed the cue ball, returning it to the table.

"What are you going to do about it?" Clayton asked as Erik lined up his next shot with the cue stick, studying the dynamics of how to sink more than one ball into the pockets.

"I could just toss it but I might get punished later."

"True, that." Clayton left the table and approached the plate, taking up a cookie.

"It tastes like that medicine they used to control my dad

with."

"Oh?" Clayton snorted. "Then just let them punish you if you're that worried about it."

"Hey!"

"Number Three," Benedict called. Erik looked up, watching the director approach. "You've a phone call," he said gently. "Make it quick... patients are not allowed to have phone calls."

"It must be important," Erik murmured as he set his pool cue aside and followed Benedict out into the corridor.

In the middle of the hall, rest a telephone receiver hanging from the wall and Erik approached it, picking it up. Glancing to his side, he spotted Benedict standing several feet away, listening.

"Go ahead," said Benedict.

Erik nodded and put the receiver to his ear. "Hello," he answered.

"Good evening, Number Three," an unfamiliar friendly male voice greeted on the line. "Now, just listen to what I have to say, okay?"

"Why should I?"

"Right now, Mister Benedict is watching for your reactions due to this phone call. Most likely, he is logging in minutes as well trying to hear your responses. So due to the facts of that, do not say much and keep your expressions minimal."

"What do you want?"

"I have your work from the Lab and I must say, it's good to hear you are in good health," the friendly voice continued. "Most likely you have received some cookies before this call, correct?"

"Yes, sugar."

"Do you know how Emerald Dust works?"

"Yes, unfortunately."

"Have you eaten the cookies already?"

"No."

The mysterious caller blew a sigh of relief. "Good, so enough small talk. Listen carefully and do not say anything." Erik twisted the cord around his fingers, waiting intently. "I am a friend of your mother's and she asked me to keep watch over you. I will do the best I can to aid you, but that means you may be at added risk of Termination. Do you still wish to listen to what I have to say?"

Erik swallowed hard. "*My mother?*" he thought. "*What does Mother Greenfield have to do with my being in here?*"

"Well?" the friendly voice questioned, worried.

"Yes," Erik answered slowly.

"Very well... the lead doctor will come to the floor tomorrow afternoon and he will be addressed as Doctor Colbert, but we know of course that is not his real name. He will speak to everyone there as a group, then later as individuals." Erik clenched his teeth, growing worried. "Are you familiar how the questions are asked?"

"Not really..."

"Some questions may be about sports, electronics, even common sayings though not limited to just the English language."

"Is it like the one about the stitch in time?"

"Yes," continued the voice. "Now, when you speak to the floor doctor, answer the following exactly..." Erik listened and nodded once told a set of canned answers that made no sense to him. "Now do not try to make sense of them for it is a trap for that test."

"I understand."

"Now, my time has run out and it is most likely that Benedict is checking his watch." Erik glanced at Benedict writing into a chart, then glanced at his titanium wristwatch and wrote more. "Listen, you're going to be forced to eat the cookies, so ask for some milk to go with it. If you're able to regurgitate, please do."

"What if I'm unable?"

"I don't want to incite violence, but make a scene. They'll probably give you Fair Jewel serum to calm you and that'll cause an adverse reaction."

"Why is it important for me to do that?"

"They're looking for something that you know and we can't have you talking about it."

"I don't remember, regardless!"

"You might not consciously, but you still do. It's for your safety, and your father's."

Erik tensed when Benedict approached and Erik heard the faint clattering of keys while the mysterious caller typed at a keyboard. "In the case they ask and most likely they will, tell them that I just wished to ask about your general health to verify the lab data."

"I'll tell them."

"Good night, Number Three. I shall call again soon."

Erik hung the receiver back on the cradle, overwhelmed. "*What is it they're trying to make me remember?*" he wondered. "*What did Father Greenfield tell me?*"

"What was that about?" Benedict demanded.

"Someone from the lab wanted to verify my data," Erik replied in response. "He just asked me about my health, is all."

"That's fine." Benedict nodded. "Go back to the lounge."

"May I have some milk?"

Benedict glared at Erik. "What, you haven't eaten dessert yet?" he spat.

"What's the point of cookies without milk?"

Benedict snorted and waved at Erik to follow him back to the lounge. "Oh, like to savor the flavor, eh?" he chided.

"Something like that..."

Erik approached Clayton who waited patiently for him at the billiards table. Picking up his cue stick, Erik measured his shot and struck the cue ball. It struck two balls after bouncing off the edge, and then struck one more resting near the corner, sinking all three before stopping.

"Damn, you're good," Clayton said, grinning.

"It's simple geometry and physics," Erik said, returning with goofy smile.

"You're bullshitting me now," Clayton retorted. "Just a lucky shot, that's all!"

Benedict returned with a carton of milk and Erik nodded to him, taking it out of hand. He opened the carton and took one cookie before dipping into the milk then bit into it. Benedict gave Erik a wary look as Erik continued to smile as he chewed.

"Good stuff," Erik replied.

Clayton started laughing, catching on. "You're bad," he said and Erik chuckled.

"What can I say?" Erik replied, shrugging.

"You're a strange one," Benedict murmured and Erik resumed his game, measuring his next play. Benedict left the room with his chart.

THIRTY-THREE

After playing several games, Erik cried out when jarred with a hard kick at his lower back and fell forward on his hands and knees. Clayton backed away, holding the pool cue defensively as Erik scrambled to his feet, facing Fenway standing over him with his clipboard.

"What's your issue?" Erik yelled.

"You're up for your test." Fenway grumbled and narrowed his hazel eyes at Erik. "Don't even think of acting up. At this point I don't care if you end up dead!"

Erik clenched his hands, growing enraged. "Get out of my face," he growled. "I'm through with you and your tests and this place altogether!"

"First order of the evening is to move your bed!"

"No."

"Number Three," Fenway barked, "move your bed!"

"I said 'no'!" Erik bellowed and yowled in pain when rapped across the head with the clipboard.

"Orders here state you've got to disassemble your bed and move it three doors down," Fenway spat. "Move it or else!"

"Or else!" Erik snapped, rubbing at his head.

"Is that a refusal?"

Erik folded his arms across his chest, glaring back. "Flat

out," he snarled.

"Stein, straighten him out."

Erik paled when Josef entered the lounge, wearing a navy jumpsuit with silver buttons and white canvas shoes, armed with a simple leather harness containing a decorated saber slung low around his hips. Erik took a step away; putting up his hands in guard when he noticed Josef had one green eye and the other blue.

"I thought I put out your eye," Erik spat.

Josef bared his teeth. "They gave me a new one," he sneered. "My first order of business is taking out yours!"

"Don't bother," Clayton snapped. "You and me got some unfinished business, Joe."

"We'll play later," retorted Josef. "This is between me and Blondie."

"Don't make me hurt you, Joe," Erik warned. "I'm thin on my patience."

"Too bad," Josef answered and kicked Erik hard in his knee. Erik screamed as the ligaments tore and he struck the floor. Clayton stepped forward and Josef withdrew the sword, pointing it in his direction. "Don't think about it."

"You sick bastard!" Erik wheezed, glaring up at Josef.

Josef glowered down at Erik. "No, Brother," he hissed through gritted teeth. "You're the one that's sick and I'm here to cure you!"

"Now," Fenway groused, "let me say for the final time: disassemble your bed and move that piece of shit three doors down!"

"I need some help!" Erik complained.

"You're quite able!"

Clayton drew back, holding tightly to the pool cue. "I'm done pretending," he growled.

"Don't bother yourself," Josef spat. "He's not that important to you."

"If you don't get your crazy ass out of here," Clayton thundered, "I'll throw you out my damn self!"

"Do it!" Josef held the saber at ready as Clayton approached. He swung at Clayton and Clayton sidestepped the attack, crashing the pool cue over his head, snapping the wood in half.

Clayton grabbed Josef's arm when he returned with a swift thrust and hurled him over on the floor. He stepped on Josef's wrist and his hands glowed dimly in pale white light. "*Shika Kouri*," Clayton hissed and formed a blue steeled broadsword in his hand.

"Shit!" Fenway snapped and backed away, then hurried out of the lounge. "Benedict!" he called in the hall. "We got a Code Red back here!"

"Look Joe, you gotta make a choice," Clayton grumbled. "You keep fucking around and we'll never get out of here!"

"You promised me for years!" Josef shouted. "Every time you and I escaped, we failed!"

"This time I got a sealed-tight plan; you just have to keep your fool self in line!"

"I don't believe you anymore - I'm through listening to you!"

"I'll cut you down!" Clayton thundered.

"Try me!" Josef roared and pushed Clayton away. Clayton staggered rearward as Josef scrambled to his feet, slashing at Clayton who whirled away. Clayton blocked his overhead strike and grunted when forced against the wall. His arms shook as he struggled against the saber cutting through and into his head.

A tall slender broad-shouldered man with dark beard stubble on his face entered the room. He wore a black fedora with a dark violet band over his short dark brown hair.

The mysterious man, dressed in black blazer, oxfords and slacks with a dark violet dress shirt and lavender tie underneath a white consulting jacket, pushed up the large silver-tinted aviator-style sunglasses hiding his eyes before they slipped off his nose. Erik noticed his hands had dark brown mottled spots as he folded his arms across his chest, watching silently as Clayton kneed Josef's groin, forcing him down. Clayton then kicked Josef away, slashing him across the chest.

Clayton glared up at the doctor and grabbed Erik by the collar, putting the blade under his throat. "Let me go," he growled, "or he's dead!"

"That's fine," the mysterious doctor replied and searched his pockets, withdrawing a nametag labeled 'Dr. Colbert' then clipped it to his consulting jacket.

Clayton dropped Erik then raced out the room and Erik stood unsteadily to his feet. He staggered over to Josef who slashed back at him once he approached.

"You," Josef rasped, clutching his chest, "stay away!"

"Fine," Erik snapped and hobbled past Colbert, only to have Colbert grab him by the arm and throw him rearward against the billiards table. "I want to leave," he spat.

Colbert stood there motionless for several moments, saying nothing. Erik sighed and attempted to walk past him again, only to get arrested by a heavy hand clamping on his shoulder.

Erik grunted when his left shoulder flared in pain as Colbert tightened his grip. "You're not leaving yet," Colbert grumbled in a low tone. "Tell me, do you enjoy playing team sports?" Erik swallowed hard, recalling the conversation with the mysterious voice and gave junk answers in return. Colbert sneered and let Erik go. "Move your bedding as told into your newly assigned room and go immediately to the dining hall."

"I refuse to eat that horrid mess they call food," Erik retorted. The man socked Erik's face, corkscrewing him to the floor with a hard thud. Erik clutched his stinging cheek as Colbert stood over him with clenched hands.

"You obey what I instruct you to do," the doctor snarled.

"It's not happening!" Erik objected.

"Since you refuse, you now will be placed in solitary confinement!"

"I don't care!" Erik rose to his feet, clutching his lame leg. "It's not like it hadn't happened before!"

"Do as I say!" Colbert barked.

"Never!"

Erik yowled once punched in his face again and hit the floor with a bang. He moaned and clutched his sore face, growing numb from pain.

Colbert gave a sadistic grin in return and Erik struggled to his feet. He backed away and cried out when searing pain struck his back. Whirling around, he faced Josef wielding the bloodied saber.

"You're not going anywhere," Josef threatened.

"Don't tell me you're under his control!" Erik cried and jumped out of Josef's attack.

Colbert grabbed Erik roughly by the arm and Erik pulled away, struggling against Colbert who wrestled him down. The doctor slammed his knee into Erik's spine and pinned his arms behind his back. Erik fell slack when the onslaught of pain overwhelmed him.

"I will be conducting your final test soon and I want you in top shape," Colbert uttered in Erik's ear, leaning forward. Erik let out a weak cry, sensing Colbert increase his weight against his knee into his lower back. "But it seems you're already at a disadvantage..."

"The test is to see which one is the better fighter." Josef nudged Erik's face with his toe. "If one of us fails, that one dies."

"I'm not a fighter!" Erik cried.

"Then you're dead!"

Colbert sifted through his pockets and withdrew a syringe. Pulling off the cap with his teeth, he injected the dark green serum into the side of Erik's neck. Erik screamed when the burning contents drained into his system and his vision flashed brightly before growing dark. His vision then altered, highlighting his surroundings in disjointed harsh colors.

"Once we get what we need from you," Colbert growled, "you'll be dropped in a vat of acid and all traces of your existence will be erased!"

"I'm not telling you anything," Erik screeched, "no matter what you do to me!"

"Doctor Colbert," called a voice over the announcement system. "Doctor Colbert, you are needed downstairs."

"Stein, take care of him," Colbert grumbled as he let go.

"Gladly, Sir," Josef responded and pointed the saber's edge

at Erik's throat.

Erik's eyes rolled to the back of his head and the acid-washed colors faded into complete darkness.

Erik hissed through clenched his teeth, sweating profusely when suddenly overcome by nausea while his head pound in thudding agony. The beating headache later gave way to the ticking clock and Erik looked up, realizing he was again in the bright white room, facing the desk with the tape recorder resting on the edge.

Erik found himself restrained in the stiff-backed chair, with leather restraints and heavy padlocks on his wrists and ankles. The door opened moments later, revealing the doctor who held an armful of charts in hand.

"Good morning," the doctor greeted breezily.

"You're overly cheerful," Erik muttered as the doctor set the charts on the desk and struck a button on the machine, turning on the recording device. "Are you high or something? Drunk perhaps?"

"I'm sorry," said the doctor, mildly surprised, "come again?"

"I'd rather be drunk. It's more enjoyable than rotting in here!"

The doctor chuckled. "Well, it's a beautiful day today," he went on. "I'm sorry you're missing out on it."

"Right," Erik spat.

"Maybe if you're a good boy today, you'll be allowed to sit on the patio with supervision."

"Not likely."

"Oh, well... So," the doctor gave a short sigh, smiling

brightly. "How do you feel?" The doctor loosened his blazer's front buttons and took a seat behind the desk. "You seem quite alert nonetheless. Your skin tones are quite fleshy, not as pallid as before and your eyes are bright and focused..."

"Cut the crap, Doctor," Erik cut in. "Do I look all that well to you?" He jerked in his chair. "Look at me!" he screamed. "You're not blind, are you?" The doctor stared blankly at him in return and Erik blew a hard sigh. "I feel ready to puke!" he griped. "Looking at you makes my stomach turn!"

"They tell me you're more compliant today," the doctor replied. "That's good..."

Erik narrowed his eyes. "Are you done?" he snarled.

"Do you wish to converse?"

"Not really."

"We can speak about anything you wish. Family, friends, school..."

Erik scoffed, rolling his eyes. "You probably already know it."

"I leave it up to you." The doctor placed his hands atop the desk.

"What are you getting at?" Erik accused, eying him warily.

"There is no need to discuss Justin Schumacher today. We can talk about anything at all, anything you want."

"Like what?"

"Ferdian perhaps."

"Let's not."

"Why not?"

Erik ground his teeth when the pain drilled through his head, knocking hard behind his eyes. "Everything hurts," he

322

complained and shut his eyes tightly. "My head, my body, my arms, my hands, my legs, my hips, my thighs... I'm sick of all these damn needles you put into me and the constant beatings!"

The doctor chortled. "I'm sorry about that," he replied gently. "I'll make sure to ask them to shift the area of penetration. I'm sure you understand why it's necessary, right?"

"I've got to hear your best excuse."

"You withdrew completely and we had to take drastic measures."

"At my expense!"

"Don't you realize how ill you are?" Erik glared at him, unresponsive. "You must understand..."

"I get it," Erik drawled icily, "really I do."

"Listen, it's quite possible you retreated from reality because you came close to recalling a very painful event. You realize that, don't you?"

"I don't know..."

"It's possible that this Justin Schumacher is the key to who you are and why your memory has so many blank spots."

"You want me to tell you everything, is that it?" Erik shouted, bristling.

"Yes," the doctor said calmly. "You have to tell me and get it out in the open, otherwise, you will always be sick, always be struggling with the past that obviously hurt you! These psychotic episodes won't stop until you confront it."

"Who is Justin Schumacher?" Erik demanded.

"He is a key to the puzzle that you refuse to place; I don't know him. You do."

"Liar!" Erik screeched, yanking against the restraints. "Why are you trying to get me to admit to something I clearly can't remember?"

"He is your answer to why you are ill and the key to your wellness. So we have these sessions to recover why and help you get better."

"You liar!" Erik screeched. "You're a filthy liar!"

"I have no reason to lie to you."

"Then what is the point in all these questions?"

"Like I said..." Erik began counting aloud at the top of his voice, bellowing out the words. "Don't do that!" the doctor shouted over him then rose indignantly to his feet. "Stop that this instant!" He slapped a hand across the top of his desk, flaring in rage. "Shut your face right now!" Huffing, the doctor picked up the phone and angrily dialed a number. "Yes," he said after several moments. "I need my patient sedated right now. He is retreating yet again." The doctor glowered sternly at Erik. "Yes, I believe it is better to suspend questioning for now and wait until he heals."

The doctor slammed down the receiver and cut off the tape machine. Switching out the cassette, he replaced it with a new one and struck the playback button, forcing the melody Erik hated blaring through its single speaker.

Erik thrashed about as the doctor turned up the volume. "Shut that racket off!" Erik shrilled.

"You cheeky son of a bitch," the doctor growled. "You don't like that, now do you?" The door opened moments later, revealing a pair of orderlies, one with blond hair and brown eyes and the other with black hair and blue eyes.

"Mister Carlsbad, Mister Johnston," the doctor greeted.

"Please take care of this."

"Sure, right," Johnston said as Carlsbad entered with a small medical bag. "What medicine do you suggest, Doctor?"

"The full cocktail," the doctor sneered, glaring hatefully at Erik.

"I'm not giving you answers," Erik spat back vehemently. "You want difficulty, you'll get it!"

"You're only hurting yourself doing this," the doctor snapped irritably while Carlsbad sifted through his kit containing various syringes and vials of serums.

"Tell me a new one," Erik said sourly.

Johnston approached Erik and checked his bruised arms. "You've got collapsed veins everywhere," he murmured.

"Try the carotid," the doctor responded.

Johnston glanced up, startled. "Damn, you're trying to kill him or what?"

"Don't tell me you're seriously thinking about it!" Erik hollered as Carlsbad prepped the serum.

The doctor waved a hand in dismissal. "I kid," he said, smiling maliciously. "Go easy on him."

Johnston held Erik's head in place once Carlsbad thumped the hypodermic needle with his finger, taking out the air.

"Here we go," said Carlsbad. "We got something that's gonna make you all nice and fuzzy!" Erik snapped at him, biting at his hand. "Fuck, man!" Carlsbad wailed and dropped what he held. "The shit broke skin!"

"Let's do it the old fashioned way, then!" Johnston snapped and plowed his fist into Erik's temple, knocking him out.

THIRTY-FOUR

Erik slowly roused, finding himself in a soft bed. He groaned and rubbed at his throbbing temples then looked around, noticing the room was dark. Outside the door, he heard voices arguing.

"Dad, what the hell were you thinking?" Clairese's voice shouted. "He's my age; that's gross!"

"I didn't do anything with him, Sweetheart!" Brodie's voice protested. "Honest!"

"Ugh, I can see why Mom left you! You just couldn't keep it together!"

"I still care about Darling and you too, but please, don't make a scene!"

"Then why is he here?"

"He got hammered and I brought him over to sleep it off. He couldn't remember where he lived!"

"Oh, tell me a new one!"

"Damn it, Sweetheart, don't do this to me!"

"Is that his phone? Couldn't he call someone to get him?"

"He told them he didn't want to go home!"

"You should have made him go!"

"He can make his own decisions!"

"You're just trying to take advantage! Ugh, how can I be

related to such a perv?"

Erik switched on the nearby light, listening to Clairese continue her shouting match with Brodie. He found a pair of flannel pants draped on the bed's edge and a matching bathrobe. Pulling into the clothes, Erik then padded toward the door, opening it wide and glared at Brodie who sat on the couch, smoking and Clairese who paced over him, drink in hand.

"Shut up, both of you," Erik growled. "You're making my headache worse!"

"Shut up!" Clairese snapped.

"You're the one to talk, lady!" Erik spat. "You wanted to rape me!" Clairese opened her mouth to speak then shut it as her face burned bright red. "You want to talk about being related to a perv, you should call yourself Junior!" Erik stormed over and snatched her drink away then downed it. He screwed up his face in disgust. "This is weak," Erik said and handed back the glass to her then returned to the couch, picking up the cigarettes.

"What are we going to do with him?" Brodie asked softly while Erik lit his cigarette and took a seat on the couch's other side, fuming.

"He's your problem," Clairese complained, "not mine."

"You're just as involved."

"How?"

"Look you two," Erik grumbled. "I'm not going to remember tomorrow, so don't worry yourselves."

"I want to help you," Brodie protested. "You shouldn't suffer like that."

"I already got somebody watching out for me," Erik

muttered.

"At least let me help you with the current problem you have," Brodie pressed. "You wanna talk to my old friend Joe, right? He could be a piece to the puzzle you need."

"Oh no, not Joey," Clairese moaned and held a hand to her head. "Don't tell me he's involved!"

"Hey, hey, it's not like that!" Brodie snapped, glaring sharply at her. "This is Defense Forces related stuff."

"Now I'm going to be sick. You're making this worse!"

"Shut up!"

"I'm leaving," Erik grumbled and rose from the couch.

"Go make yourself useful, please?" Brodie demanded and held out an arm to Erik, barring movement. "Go to the Dub and buy me more cigarettes and vodka."

Erik grunted and plopped back on the couch then put up his feet. Clairese gave a contemptuous smile as she approached behind Erik and bent forward, setting the glass she held on the table. Erik tensed when she held him by the shoulders.

"Don't worry," Clairese cooed in his ear. "I'll make you forget all about that dirty old man."

"Stop messing with him and go!" Brodie spat.

Clairese chortled and grabbed for her coat draped on a chair near the door and stepped into her shoes. "Laters," she called and exited, shutting the door behind her.

"How...?" Erik started.

"I thought I could pray it away," Brodie muttered, lighting another cigarette. "I did everything I was supposed to do... But I guess you can't fight nature."

"And the ex-wife?"

"Oh, there's no ex," Brodie griped. "She doesn't believe in divorce."

"So, then...?"

"I live here and she lives across town. The woman is terrible. She always scares off any boyfriends I have." Brodie let out a bitter laugh. "Even if they're resilient, some get spooked when they find I have a grown daughter..."

"Let alone a battering ram for a wife."

Brodie burst out laughing and slapped his knee. "That's why I like you, Feddy," he said brightly. "You're something else!"

"So you said..."

"Hey, if you still want to stick around, it's fine by me. I won't fondle you while you sleep or anything, promise." Erik paled and Brodie laughed harder. "Don't be so serious!" he crowed. "Loosen up a little!"

"About this Joey then...?" Erik started, changing the subject.

"Oh, same fella, Joseph Stone. We goof off sometimes, but it's not serious."

"Not about *that*."

"Oh, right." Brodie waved at Erik. "I doubt he's up this early. It's only five."

"What time do we need to get to the office?"

"A few hours."

"Call him anyway?"

"If he wants to beat someone, I'll let him whale on you first."

"That's fine, I can take it."

Brodie left the couch and drifted into the kitchen, picking up the phone there. Erik continued smoking in silence, listening to Brodie speak cordially over the line.

"Say, Feddy," Brodie called later. "He wants to holla at ya."

Erik groaned and left his place on the couch, stomping into the kitchen. Brodie handed him the receiver and left his side, attending to the automatic coffee maker. "Hello?" Erik greeted. "Giuseppe, is it?"

"It's Joseph, Mister Ferdian," a warm voice said over the line. Erik gasped when his skin abruptly grew cold. "It's been a long, long time."

"Has it?" Erik asked weakly.

"If you're looking for me, and especially by that name, then that causes concern."

"Why would it?"

"You know what it means, so don't act as if you don't know!"

"I'm sorry, I don't understand... I'm suffering from memory problems, you see."

"If you say so."

Erik leaned against the wall, clutching tightly to the handset. "Look, he just mentioned you and I had a bad reaction," he snapped. "I don't know why and I just wanted to know."

"Don't tell me you're starting to feel guilt!"

"I just take care of problems," Erik said defiantly. "If people die, then it was meant to happen."

"Well then, I'll be seeing you soon?"

"I don't know, will you?"

"Let me speak with Mister Avers."

"Sure." Erik turned around, finding Brodie gone. "Mister Avers?" he called.

"I got it," Brodie called from the bedroom. Erik palmed the mouthpiece and listened to the call.

"Don't tell me you actually jumped his bones," Giuseppe said in annoyance.

"No, Joey, damn!" Brodie complained. "Sure he's a nice piece of ass to look at, but I've got standards. He's a scary kid."

"Scary is an understatement," Giuseppe snapped. "It was no accident that he replaced Eisenheimer and suddenly appeared to work in your same department."

"Oh?"

"He's a Cleaner."

"Oh, shit..."

"Be careful around him."

"But he doesn't remember anything the next day," Brodie protested. "He couldn't even remember my name after he woke up."

"Does he have a cell with him?"

Brodie scoffed. "Doesn't everybody?"

"How many numbers does he have?" Giuseppe demanded.

"I only saw one..."

"That's his Collector. They get his info he accumulated during the day and wipe him out, so in the case he gets captured, he can't say anything."

"Shit..."

"You need to get rid of him."

"What did I do to get something this heavy on my ass?"

Erik heard the front door opening and carefully hung up the line. Clairese entered, calling for Brodie.

"He's on the phone," Erik called back and took a seat at the kitchen table. Clairese stepped in, holding a small shopping bag and a box of pastries.

"I got some crullers for the coffee," she said brightly.

"That's nice," Erik murmured.

"What's the matter?"

Erik shook his head. "I don't feel well."

"Maybe you ought to call in sick?"

"No, I've got a lot of work today."

"I'll make some coffee?"

"Sure, thanks."

Brodie entered the kitchen moments later as Clairese set down the bags and headed for the cabinets, rummaging through them. Erik sorted through the bags and withdrew a pack of cigarettes. He tossed Brodie the other one and grabbed the pint of vodka at the bottom, then twisted off the top.

"You got to clock in later," Brodie protested, catching the pack.

"Sue me," Erik spat and took a gulp.

"He's still in a bad mood," Clairese replied. "I think he's confused because we both want his body."

Brodie unexpectedly laughed, finding it hilarious. "You really think so?" he asked and left the room, laughing harder.

Clairese later approached the table, sitting across from Erik and held her chin in her hand, gazing at him.

"What do you want?" Erik spat.

"So if you had to choose," she said, "which would you prefer?"

Erik capped the vodka and set the bottle aside. He leaned forward on the table and gestured Clairese to come closer. She left her seat and knelt over to Erik, listening intently. "Do you really want me to pick?" he murmured in her ear. Clairese nodded. "I'm never telling."

Clairese turned to Erik, stunned and he grinned as he unwrapped the cellophane off his cigarettes.

"You bastard!" she pouted.

Erik let out a short laugh and passed her the pack. "Want one?"

"I don't smoke."

"Too bad."

Clairese left his side and later returned with the lighter and ashtray. "What do you do for a living?" she asked.

"Same as your father does," Erik responded. "You?"

"I'm a technician at Kanbal Industries." Erik dropped the pack of cigarettes he held and Clairese frowned when she saw the color drain from his face. "What's the matter?"

"It's nothing," Erik said quickly. "What is it you do there, exactly?"

"Oh, some high level Federal stuff that I can't talk about."

"Oh..." Erik moaned and held his head in his hands.

Clairese appeared concerned. "Was it something I said?" she murmured.

"He gets like that sometimes," Brodie said near the door. "Just leave him be."

"Well, I was going to take a nap," Clairese replied, turning to him, "but it's already six."

"Take a shower and have some coffee. You can always check out at lunch and take a quick nap."

"If I took a nap, then I'd never get up!"

Brodie chortled and entered the kitchen, holding a lit cigarette in hand. "Go on. I'll keep him company."

"I already asked him," Clairese said upon passing. "He won't tell me."

Brodie snorted and wagged a finger at Erik. "You're such a tease," he chided.

Erik hastily smiled and grinned as he sat up, dropping his hands in his lap. "That's right," he said brightly. "I was mean to you earlier."

"Oh, don't start," Clairese protested and stormed out. "I don't want to hear it!"

Erik laughed and Brodie sniggered.

"So, what are your plans for today?" Brodie asked, taking a seat across from Erik.

"I have to work," Erik said. "What kind of question is that?"

"But didn't you start drinking again?"

"Just a bit of hair off the dog," Erik replied. "I know my limits."

"I wonder..."

Erik reached over, picking up the cigarettes he dropped on the floor. He stiffened when Brodie kicked at his chair. "What is it?" he asked apprehensively.

"I'm thinking..." Brodie muttered.

"Please, it's not what you think."

"Then what is it?"

Erik shook his head. "I wouldn't know."

"So how long do I have to wait?" Brodie demanded.

"Please be nice," Erik pleaded.

Brodie frowned and put out his cigarette in the ashtray. He stood and approached Erik, placing his hands on his shoulders then bent forward, looking directly into Erik's eyes. "I'll be nice," Brodie said in a firm tone, "but don't do something that you'll regret." Erik stiffened when Brodie squeezed his shoulders. "Do you understand?"

"I understand," Erik murmured.

"Good. As long as you're here, I promise to play nice."

"Please?"

"But if you cross me, I'll have to get mean."

"I know."

"Don't make me have to get mean. I like you a lot."

"I promise."

Brodie smiled and pet Erik's head then left his side, returning for his bedroom. Erik moaned and held his sides as he doubled over, suddenly finding breathing difficult.

THIRTY-FIVE

After Clairese showered and had coffee with Brodie and Erik, Erik borrowed a shirt and socks from Brodie, opting to shake out and spray his slacks.

"At least it's wash and wear," Brodie noted and Erik snorted, saying nothing. They later clamored into Clairese's compact car and she dropped them off at the Mercado Corp offices.

The two made their way to the fifth floor and Brodie waved off Erik, heading for his office down the hall. Erik then entered his assigned room, setting aside a small paper sack with two crullers inside.

Putting away his coat, he opened his drawers and withdrew more files, then started the task of inputting data. Once noon came, Erik opened his window and withdrew his ashtray from the bottom desk drawer.

"Was he really that bad in bed?" Sangita's voice called to Erik. He looked up, noticing she stood at his door.

"I already have my own lunch today," Erik replied. "Besides, it's a little late, isn't it?"

"I had a meeting to sit through, sorry," Sangita apologized. "How about I make it up with some coffee to go with your donuts?"

"I'm broke today, sorry," Erik responded. "I spent it all on

Mister Avers last night."

"And you didn't even get a good screw out of it!" Erik snorted and Sangita grinned. "It's on me, okay?"

"Only if you want to."

"What do you want in it?"

"Three creams, no sugar. Make it Irish."

"I'll try my best." Sangita left Erik's door and he heard her voice down the hall. "I'm telling ya, Kass. He's majorly pissed!"

"Damn, and I thought for sure he was straight!" Kass responded. "I don't like him anyway. He's a weirdo meanie."

"He's nice to me."

"Maybe he's got a thing for chocolate?"

"Ooh, stop!"

The women giggled and their voices faded down the corridor.

Erik snorted and withdrew his cigarettes and phone from his slacks pocket. Turning it on, he dialed the number and withdrew a cigarette to light with his other hand.

"Are you okay?" Gina's voice answered.

"Can you talk long?" Erik asked.

"Sure, I can make time for you."

"Do you know about any scientists at Kanbal working on the same project with Andrews?"

"I'll look into it. So does this mean you're coming home later then?"

"Until I finish this project, I'll be staying with a friend."

"Well, at least let me stop by. I'm sure you're starving."

Erik snorted. "I've managed."

"Oh, going by your looks again?" Gina said dryly.

"Hey!" Erik protested. "I can't help it if they find me pretty!"

"Okay, Mister Pretty Cute, don't call for help if you get in some deep shit."

Erik grinned. "If I need money, I'll just hit you up, right?"

"This isn't a bank!" Gina protested.

"Fine then." Erik turned off the phone and frowned when he saw Brodie standing at the door. "What do you want?"

"Something important?" Brodie asked. "Was it that girlie of yers?"

"She wanted me to come home."

"Oh, got a battle axe to deal with as well, eh?"

"I'm sure you understand."

Brodie gave a thin smile. "Right, I do."

"Look, I don't want to cause you trouble. I'll wander off and you can go home and we can forget whatever's happened, happened."

"I told you that you can stay as long as you wanted."

"You also warned me what would happen if I didn't play nice." Erik waved Brodie away. "I don't want to test you."

"Aw, you think I'm going to do something to you?" Brodie snorted. "*I* should be more concerned - *you're* the crazy drunk, not me."

"Then how can I show you I'm not a threat?" Brodie smiled brightly and Erik frowned, turning away in his chair. "Not happening," he spat. "Get that thought out of your head, you dirty old man!"

"Hey, you're the one who asked!"

"The gals are gossiping about us already," Erik moaned.

Brodie entered the office and took the seat on the desk's other side. "I warned you that would happen," he teased. "Does it bother you at all?"

"Given the oranges to bananas ratio here, I'm not that concerned," Erik murmured. "It'll make it easier on me for my job."

"Oh? So you mean clerical isn't the only job you have?"

Erik glanced back at Brodie who smirked. "Why are you giving me grief?" he demanded.

"Why am I a target?" Brodie snapped.

"I don't know what you're talking about," Erik retorted.

"Then why else would you be here?"

"I don't know!"

Brodie rose to his feet, his expression stony. "If you have to do something, spare my Sweetheart, would you?"

"I can't guarantee that," Erik murmured.

Brodie blew a hard sigh and looked down at the floor. "Same time tonight, then?"

"Only if you want to."

Brodie left the office and shut the door after him. Erik grunted when his cigarette burned down to the filter and he discarded the remnants into the ashtray. He resumed his work, dreading the day's end.

Erik grew tense once he put away his materials and set the last of his filing. Taking out his logbook, he scribbled the database changes and downed the remainder of his cold coffee.

"Water, Ammonia, Lime, Sulfur, Iron, Silicon, Sodium...?" Erik grunted and tapped the pencil against his teeth. "Is it Chloride or Bicarbonate?" Erik put down his pencil and rubbed his temples. "Shit, there's so many kinds of Sodium, you bastard! Alginate, Barbital, Benzoate, Ammonium Phosphate, Borate, Tetraborate Decahydrate, Peroxide, Carbonate, Hydrogen Carbonate, Hydrosulfite, Thiosulfate, Hydroxide, Hypochlorite, Chlorate, Chloride, Citrate, Nitrate, Cyclamate, Dichromate, Glutamate, Fluoride, Cyanide, Pentothal, Silicate, Perborate, Phosphate, Propionate, Sulfate, Sulfide, Sulfite and Hyposulfite..." Erik gazed at his list of purchases. "What were they trying to build, Andrews?"

Putting away the logbook, Erik left his desk and grabbed his coat, pulling into it. Exiting his office, he headed for the elevators and stepped on with several others, including Sangita and Kass.

"Oh," Kass teased, "so not going out with your boyfriend tonight?"

"I'd never thought you had a thing for older men," another coworker replied.

"This pretty face needs money," Erik said, grinning wryly.

"But you have a steady job for that!" Sangita protested, appalled. "Mercado pays more than Federal for clerical processing!"

"It doesn't pay enough for my habit."

"Oh no, you're a junkie too?"

Erik laughed when Kass held onto Sangita's arm in shock.

"He has to be!" Kass went on. "See how skinny he is? There's no way that's natural at all!"

Once the doors opened, Erik stepped out and turned to the group, bowing deeply. "Have a good evening, ladies," he said cheerfully. "I'll see you tomorrow."

"Your drunk ass better not screw up the quarterlies come

Friday!" Kass shouted at Erik's back as he stalked outdoors.

Erik came to a pause when he saw a dark sedan parked in Mercado Corp's front lot. The door opened and Erik cautiously approached as the driver stepped out.

"Your ride, Mister Smith," said the coachman, opening the rear passenger door. Erik nodded and stepped inside then gasped when he saw the tanned young woman with long red hair. He stiffened when she embraced him firmly.

"You've got me worried about you!" Gina protested and Erik slackened, unable to respond. "I know I shouldn't worry so much, but I can't help it."

"If you say so," Erik murmured.

Gina pulled away and blew a short sigh. "Well, I did some digging around and I couldn't find too many names without setting off alarms," she said. "However, I did find this." Gina picked up a small case at her feet and opened it, revealing a folder. "It's tied to Health Control and I need you to stop by Osphena's to do a little digging there. She won't tell me and I can't exactly ask her."

"Do I have to sleep with her?" Erik murmured, glancing over the paperwork.

"What?" Gina yelped, aghast. "No, why? What made you think of such a thing?"

"Never mind about it. So is there anything specific you want me to dig up?"

"Just find the correlation, that's all."

"I'll try my best."

"Is something on your mind?"

"No, why?"

"You seem distracted..."

Erik gave the best smile he could muster. "I couldn't be more great."

Once dropped off in front of Osphena's apartment across town, Gina walked with Erik upstairs and let herself in, taking Erik with her.

"She must trust you enough to have a key," Erik said as he took off his coat.

"Please take care," Gina pleaded. "I don't like how strange you're acting."

"I'm drinking too much..."

"Slow down, please? I need you here."

"I'll try." Erik waved Gina goodbye. "I'll see you later."

Gina frowned and let herself out. Erik dropped his coat on the couch then peeled out of his clothes and headed into the shower.

After showering and wrapping himself in a towel, Erik rummaged through Osphena's bedroom, going through drawers and her closets. Finding nothing of importance, he lastly returned to the home office and approached her computer. He heard the locks turn and left the room, hurrying down the hall. He took a seat on the lumpy couch once Osphena entered.

"Oh!" Osphena said, stunned. "What are you doing back?"

"I missed it," Erik replied.

"Don't you have another home you could curl up to?" Osphena snapped and removed her coat. "I don't want any disease from whatever fleas you've picked up."

"Oh, calling me a stray dog, eh?" Erik spat. "I don't

remember ever falling for you in the first place, so I don't see why this is a problem."

Osphena put away her coat and returned to the couch near Erik. She struggled to form her words and clenched her hands at her sides, growing steadily enraged. Erik smirked and said nothing as he withdrew his cigarettes from his coat pocket, casually lighting one. Osphena gave up and stormed off in a huff.

Later, Erik shared a light dinner of pan-fried vegetables and rice with Osphena then grew tired, retiring for the parlor and settled against the couch. He started to nod off then sat up, tense and afraid once the house became quiet.

Osphena padded out her room with a blanket and draped it over Erik. Erik moaned and she caressed a gentle hand through his hair, murmuring soothing words. Erik began to calm and blew a sigh of relief, then closed his eyes. Osphena returned to her room once Erik drifted back to sleep.

THIRTY-SIX

Erik shot bolt upright, gasping for breath that came as frosty puffs. He shivered in cold from the sweat that dried in the chilled air, though he felt feverish and perspired heavily as a dull ache consumed his entire being.

Looking down at the damp blanket gathered at his waist, Erik numbly ran his hands over the fabric, trying to piece together where he sat. He paused, noticing his right hand had been bandaged and the palm had specks of blood on the front.

"What happened to my hand?" Erik muttered and pulled at his clothing clinging to him, soaked with sweat.

Searching around his surroundings, Erik found himself inside a van with large windows covered by thin red curtains. Pushing the cloth aside, he stared out at grass, rocks, desert plants, and a canyon with a winding river below.

Erik grunted and held his head as he disassociated from the overwhelming pain attacking without remorse, coursing through his back and feet, his arms and legs, stinging, biting, searing, and burning all at once. Erik gulped for breath when his fear rose and no matter how many times he mentally told himself to calm and lie still and stop the shivering, the worse he felt.

Erik rubbed at his face, moaning in fear and dismay as he

looked back at a stranger with his looks under the light of the moon shining partly behind thin clouds. The sound escaping him turned louder, into a scream and the voices shouted at him questions he couldn't answer while the ghostly version of himself hovering outside near the van answered back.

Who am I?

I don't know.

Who are you?

I don't know.

But isn't your name Justin?

I don't know.

Isn't my name Justin?

I don't know.

Why are we Justin Schumacher?

Maybe we learned it, because we have to be.

Who is Justin Schumacher?

He is somebody's beloved son...

What are we?

We are nothing.

Why are we nothing?

We have no life.

Where did our life go?

They took it away from us...

The door to the van opened moments later and Erik gasped for breath, coughing and wheezing once the other ghostly self vanished. Before him stood a young man with shaggy nape-length dark brown hair and dark brown eyes behind wire-framed glasses wearing a red quilted baseball jacket, black jeans, and worn short boots.

"Hey it's okay," the young man said gently. "You're safe

now."

"Who are you?" Erik rasped.

"I'm Sully," he said brightly, climbing in. "I'm gonna get you somewhere safe, okay?" Erik clenched his teeth. "You okay?" Sully inquired when Erik said nothing.

"How did you get here?" Erik asked weakly. "How did I get here?"

"I found you passed out in the hillside." Sully pulled close the door and leaned against it, stretching out his legs.

"Are you one of those guys looking for me?"

Sully looked back at Erik in revulsion. "What kind of question is that?" he spat.

"Who sent you?" Erik demanded.

"I can't tell you in case I lose track of you to the bad guys…"

"Who's trying to hurt me?" Erik leaned against the wall of the van, pulling up the blanket to his chest and tucked it over his shoulders.

"Some real bad guys that are up to no good."

"That's not enough!" Erik wailed. "Don't be so vague!"

"I can't rush into details about this…" Sully blew a short sigh. "Look, you'll just have to trust me. Relax and let me take care of it."

"Who wants to hurt my dad?"

"Like I said…"

"Are you not telling me because *you're* one of the bad guys?"

Sully chortled. "Now what would make you think I'm one of them?" He grinned. "If I were, you'd be dead now!"

"Why are they after me?"

"To use as leverage, simply put."

"What did my dad do?"

"He didn't do anything that I know of. Heard he got mixed up in some terrible stuff, is all." Sully sighed. "It's late. You ought to get to sleep."

"I can't... I'm worried."

"Why?"

"I don't know..."

"Perhaps you're just tired and that can make you confused."

"No, no, that's not it..."

"Maybe you haven't eaten." Sully reached over, removing other blankets and revealed a small cooler. "I have some soda pop and jerky and nuts..." He opened the top, sifting through the contents.

"No, that's not it either..."

Sully shut the cooler and reclined back, using his belt buckle to pull the cap off one small glass bottle of soda. "Then what is it?" Erik clenched his teeth and shook his head. "Well, whatever you wanna know, ask away."

"Why do they hate me?" Erik asked slowly.

"Who's 'they' and why do they hate you?"

"The people who want me dead. Killing me isn't going to make much difference to them. Even if my dad works for them, it won't be his best because he'll be grieving for me."

"Why should they hate you?" Sully pressed and took a drink of his soda.

"I don't know... maybe it's because they thought I saw something I shouldn't have."

"What did you see?"

"I don't know..."

"We'll figure it out in the morning." Sully shook the half-empty bottle of soda in Erik's direction. "They're still cold. You sure you don't want one?"

"I'll be fine."

"Your choice."

Erik felt himself drifting, feeling the panic slowly dissipating and later his eyes grew heavy. Before he nodded off, a sudden crash startled him and Erik let out a cry in fright, noticing a large baseball-sized stone in the interior of the van.

Sully dropped the bottle he held and got on his haunches, withdrawing his pants leg and revealed a four-chambered blunt-nosed revolver strapped to his ankle. The font door rattled and Erik held his breath, watching a shadowy figure come around, trying the handle on the front passenger as Sully withdrew and readied his handgun. The door came open and Sully fired twice.

"Son of a bitch!" a voice cried and the intruder fell back.

The back door came open and Sully kicked them back, grabbing the handle and flung it shut. Automatic gunfire followed and Erik and Sully pressed themselves to the floor as bullets sprayed the back and sides.

After a pause in gunfire, Sully clamored over the seats and dropped into the section between the front driver and rear passenger seats. Pressing against the front passenger seat, he opened the door, peering around the corner.

"Come on, you bitches!" Sully screamed. He fired twice through the slat in the side from his vantage point and ducked back, quickly reloading before firing again.

On the floor, Erik held his breath as he broke out in cold

sweat and trembled in fear. Another round of automatic gunfire followed and Erik squeaked when searing pain cut above his right ear. Reaching up with his shaking hand, he felt sticky warmth.

"Damn it!" Sully seethed after several bullets punched through, shattering his windows. "Those bastards are serious!" He withdrew his keys and climbed into the driver's seat, starting the van with a roar. "We're going on a wild ride, all right?" Sully called, shifting gears and hurtled the vehicle in reverse, despite the gunfire around him. A loud thump followed moments later and Sully laughed as he switched gears again, peeling forward.

Erik's eyes widened and he got up, peering out the curtain from the rear window as Sully made a wide left turn, forcing the door hanging open freely swinging shut. Erik spotted one body on the ground with a submachine gun near him and several men in dark clothing scattering for their cars.

"You just killed somebody!" Erik yelped.

"No shit!" Sully snapped back. "They're trying to kill me first!" Erik turned back to Sully who reached underneath his seat with one hand, withdrawing a high-powered hunting rifle while the other rolled down the window with the manual handle. "And this one's for good measure!" Sully whooped as another thump followed when he ran over the body he struck.

"Be careful!" Erik shrieked when Sully kicked the seat back and leaned out his window with his rifle tucked under one arm while keeping one hand on the wheel as he sped around, firing potshots at the runaway sedans.

"Yeah!" Sully whooped. "Run for the hills like the bitches

you are!"

Erik watched in awed silence, scared mute as Sully shot out tires with deadly accuracy. He ducked, hunkering back down to the van's flooring when one car exploded after getting several shots into the sides when Sully circled around.

The van suddenly lurched forward and Erik glanced up, watching Sully smash his van into a dark sedan. He kept on its side, trying to run it off the road. Erik gasped as they met a curve and Sully gunned the engine, keeping the nose of the van into the sedan's side as it tried in vain to turn.

When the sedan slowed and tried to back out, Sully threw the van into reverse and turned into the enemy car, forcing the sedan off the edge. The car tumbled overhead on the cliff, crashing into metal and glass fragments as it crashed down the side before exploding into a fireball.

"One more..." Sully muttered, turning the van around in the field. He idled and reached over to the glove compartment, opening it.

Erik left his place on the floor and came closer to the front seats as Sully withdrew more shells and reloaded his rifle, staring out the cracked windshield. A dark sedan with tinted windows drove up several feet away on the field across from the van and its headlamps turned on.

"Why is it waiting?" Erik asked. Sully pulled the bolt, suspending a bullet and clenched his teeth as he narrowed his eyes. "Sully!"

"Back there should be a suitcase," Sully said quickly. "Take it and run."

"Why?" Erik yelped.

"They're going to blow our asses to Hell!"

Erik left his seat and hastily searched the van's interior, throwing around blankets, clothing, and camping gear. "I can't see in the dark!" he wailed frantically. "Forget it! You'll just have to hate me..." Approaching the door handle, Erik pulled at it and screamed in frustration as he yanked back on it and the mechanism refused to move.

"The lever goes down," Sully called when Erik kicked at the window, "not up!"

Pulling down, the door popped open and Erik tumbled out onto the ground, kicking up dust. Scrambling to his feet, Erik made his way across the tract of sand, rocks, and an array of desert plants, hobbling forward on weakened legs and achy feet.

Clamoring once he lost his balance, Sully appeared as he raced up to his side with the rifle tucked under his arm and the case in his hand.

"Get down!" Sully called when a sudden high whistle whined overhead, becoming instantly louder, followed by a loud screech.

Sully scooped up Erik and threw him to the ground as he dove into the earth when a deafening roar of crunching metal and crackling fires gave way to silent darkness.

THIRTY-SEVEN

Erik woke up with a start, screaming and Osphena hurried into the room, startled. Erik looked to her wild-eyed and scrambled to his feet, tripping over his steps as he stumbled from the couch.

"No, please!" Erik pleaded. "Don't hurt me!"

"I won't," Osphena said gently.

"Please, please, please..."

Erik fell back on his rear and clamored to his feet as he backed away. He turned and ran for the door, opening it wide. Erik screamed when he met a man on the other side in a black riding coat and charcoal gray suit, who had bobbed dark brown hair peppered with silver and circular glasses.

The middle-aged man appeared alarmed and watched Erik race for the bathroom, slamming the door shut behind him.

"What's going on?" the man murmured.

Erik crawled under the standing sink, shaking and holding his knees. He rocked, listening to Osphena and her friend on the other side.

"He had another nightmare," Osphena replied. "Come in."

"I'm a bit concerned about this new boyfriend of yours," the man said as he entered and pulled out of his duster, and then took a seat on the couch, draping his riding coat on the arm.

"He's not much of a boyfriend," Osphena answered dryly as she shut the door. "I'm sure you'd understand that, Giuseppe."

"Don't be mean," groused Giuseppe.

"That boy's more like a crazy old dog. He shows up whenever he feels like for a meal and maybe a stomach rub."

"Heh," Giuseppe murmured.

"So what did you stop by for?"

"There were some spikes in your records access and I wanted to know personally what's going on before I had to file."

Osphena gasped. "Are you saying Federal's involved?" she asked weakly.

"Not yet, but you know I'm in Database Management. I'm giving you a heads-up."

"I have no reason to access my records." Osphena shrugged her shoulders. "That's stupid."

"Then who would be poking around?"

"Beats me."

"Is it your new part-time pet then?"

"I don't know what he does."

"Ask him."

Osphena approached the door and knocked. "Are you all right in there?" she called from the other side.

"Yeah," Erik called back. "Give me my smokes, will you?"

"Anything else?"

"A strong drink?"

"Sure."

Erik blew a hard sigh then grew concerned when he heard nothing on the other side. Suddenly the door opened and Giuseppe glanced inside, then behind the door.

"Oh, there you are!" Giuseppe said brightly. "Care to have a drink with me?"

Erik rose to his feet, frowning as he studied the man. He took in a shallow breath when his head pound hard in pain. "You...!" Erik gasped, clutching his head. "No!" He backed away and Giuseppe entered the room, concerned.

Giuseppe reached forward and Erik swung at him. Giuseppe stepped out of the blow and grabbed Erik by the arm, turning him around. He immediately arrested Erik's other arm and locked Erik's neck beneath his elbow, pulling back. Giuseppe pressed against Erik's head, pushing at a painful angle and Erik cried out when Giuseppe leaned into the headlock.

"What are you fighting me for?" Giuseppe hissed in Erik's ear. "I'm on your side, aren't I?"

"No..." Erik mewed.

"I thought you were dead," Giuseppe snarled. "It would be useless to ask who brought you back."

"I'm just a ghost then, huh?" Erik rasped. "You must be a very bad man..." He let out a strangled laugh and Giuseppe dropped Erik to the floor. Erik clutched his neck, gasping for breath.

"I better not see you," Giuseppe snapped.

"I'm sorry," Erik grumbled. "You're going to see more of this face whether or not you like it."

"Don't tell me you're doing a quickie in there," Osphena complained as she came to the door. "Lay off him, Giuseppe, he's my toy to play with."

"I was just asking him a few questions," Giuseppe muttered

and stalked out the room.

Osphena approached and knelt at Erik's side as he ran his hands through his hair. "Will you be okay?" she asked timidly.

Erik sat back against the shower stall and took the glass of vodka she handed him. "Thanks," he murmured.

"Are you going to be all right?" Erik nodded. "Good. Now whenever you feel like it, I'm up front."

"I won't be in the way."

"It's fine."

Osphena left the bathroom and Erik drew up his knees, sipping his drink.

After finishing his cocktail, Erik left his place on the floor and stepped out, finding Osphena and Giuseppe speaking softly to each other on the couch. Erik picked up his cigarettes off the cocktail table and headed for the painted table in the kitchenette's corner, lighting his cigarette. He slouched in his chair, hunched over his cigarette as he smoked and fumed in silence.

Giuseppe left the couch moments later and took a seat across from Erik. "Do you have nightmares like this all the time?" he asked.

"Unfortunately," Erik murmured.

"What are they about?"

"People trying to kill me."

"I don't recall you ever serving in the Defense Forces."

"I was a Duce," Erik replied.

"How old are you? I'm a Lifer and for sure I would've seen you around Base."

"Your best guess is as good as mine. My memory is shit."

"I see..."

Osphena returned moments later with Erik's discarded glass and approached the refrigerator, taking out an ice tray. "Do you want anything?" she asked.

"Gin and tonic if you have any," Giuseppe replied.

"All I have is tap, if that's okay."

"Fine by me."

"What is it you want from me?" Erik snapped, glowering at Giuseppe.

"I should ask you why you're snooping around my friends?" Giuseppe said evenly. "They're nervous since you've showed up out the blue like that."

Erik gave a dismissive shrug. "That's their prerogative then."

Osphena set down two lowball glasses filled with clear liquid in ice. "Vodka on the rocks for the dog," she said wryly, "and gin and water for the lecherous old man."

"He's too young for me anyway," Giuseppe said, cracking a crooked smile. "You can have him." He picked up his glass and Osphena chortled.

"So is that okay with you?" she pressed.

"You're asking me?" Erik asked, raising an eyebrow. "I don't see what you want me for..."

"I have my reasons." Osphena rubbed Erik's shoulder and leaned over. "I'm sure you can give a solid guess," she whispered in his ear. Erik stiffened and Osphena left his side.

"I don't see what else we have to talk about," Erik complained, taking up his drink. "I don't know you and I don't remember her, but apparently we have a history."

"You and I have a history as well, unfortunately," Giuseppe said flatly.

Erik shook his head. "There's no point in my remembering."

"I suggest you remember. It'll make me feel better."

"It's not anything I can just turn on and off. It comes and goes. Sometimes it hurt..." Erik gulped his drink and looked down at the ice. "I wonder if I really am crazy and people put up with me because they're scared I'm some kind of monster."

"Sometimes people put up with you because you're likeable."

"Oh?"

"You can be nice when you want to be. They're drawn to that, that innocence..."

"I'm not innocent at all." Erik set aside his glass and looked down at his hands. "These hands aren't clean at all. Dirty, filthy, broken... I'm an outright mess."

"Yet you have such a pure soul. What a rare quality it is to have these days."

"I'm rotten," Erik complained.

"Then where did you get that sense of justice?"

"What?" Erik looked up and moaned when his vision suddenly blurred and shifted. He held his head in his hands, groaning. "Shit, not again..."

"What's the matter?" Giuseppe's voice called from afar.

"The bitch drugged me," Erik lamented.

"I just want to know who you really are, open you up a bit."

"Don't hurt me..."

"I won't hurt you, Ferdian. That's your name, right?"

"That's what it says on my VitaStat card, right?"

"No, on your employee ID for Mercado Corp."

Erik slumped forward at the table, rapping his head against the worn painted wood. "What do you want?" Erik whined. "I told you everything I possibly can..."

"Not everything, Ferdian," Giuseppe said darkly. "You didn't tell me who you're working with."

"I don't know my supervisor's name."

"She's your caretaker, isn't she? She keeps up your apartment, your finances, right?"

"How do you know it's a woman?" Erik muttered. "What if it was a man?"

"Oh, I know it's a woman. Mister Avers told me about her. She called you several times the other night, asking about you, wondering about you..." Giuseppe left his chair and stood over Erik. He grabbed the young man by the shoulder, pulling Erik upright.

Erik stared blankly up in space, seeing Giuseppe as a blurred dark mass. "You're not going to hurt her, are you?" Erik slurred. "Please don't... I won't live if you did that to me."

"That's the point, Ferdian - you're a danger to us all. We have to protect ourselves."

"She gave me a secure number..."

"Oh? Call her, bring her over then."

"If I sound like this, then she'll know something's wrong..."

"What is she to you?" Giuseppe let go and Erik grunted when he fell forward out of his chair, striking the floor.

Erik struggled to get up on his knees. He found it difficult on his elbows, shuddering as his body grew weaker. "I don't know why she means a lot to me," Erik murmured. "Apparently I mean a lot to her."

"Oh?" Giuseppe kicked Erik's side and he cried out. "You know her name, don't you?"

"I don't remember!" Erik yelped.

"Liar!" Giuseppe kicked Erik again and he screamed. "Tell me her name!"

"I can't!"

"Do you want me to beat you into submission?" Giuseppe thundered. "I have all night!"

"Try your worst!" Erik wheezed. "It's not the first time!"

Giuseppe let off a swift boot into Erik's ribs and he yowled, curling into a ball on his side. "Where's the phone?" Giuseppe demanded.

"In my coat pocket," Erik moaned.

"It better be there!" Giuseppe kicked Erik again and Erik howled in agony.

Osphena peered around the partition, frowning at Giuseppe standing over Erik, heaving for breath. "Cut that out," she complained. "If you break him, I won't have any fun with him later!"

"He's a major threat to us," Giuseppe snapped and pulled out of his blazer. Osphena entered, taking it from him. "I need to get answers before the end of the week."

"If you beat the crap out of him and he goes to work looking like that, people will talk!"

"I'm sure he can come up with a good excuse. He's very good at lying!" Giuseppe yanked Erik up by the arm and threw him into the chair. Erik groaned and fell back slackened, unable to focus. "Wake up in there!" Giuseppe shouted and slapped Erik across the face.

Erik grunted when his head whipped to the side. "I thought you wanted to make a phone call," he muttered.

"Go check his coat," Giuseppe ordered.

"What are you looking for?" inquired Osphena.

"His contact list."

"All right." Osphena left the room and Erik suddenly laughed as Giuseppe unbuttoned his cuffs and rolled up his sleeves.

"Is that the best you have?" Erik crowed. "I've had better beat downs that felt like a walk in the park!"

Giuseppe growled and slapped Erik again. Erik let out a laugh and Giuseppe continued slapping him across the face, grunting with effort. Growing enraged when Erik continued laughing at him, he threw a powerful punch, knocking Erik out of his chair.

Erik struck the tiles, stunned and wheezing for breath as blood flowed from his nose, leaving a large red stain on the floor.

"Is that enough for you?" Giuseppe snarled, massaging his sore hand.

"Leave him alone," Osphena complained. "He's not going to talk."

"Fine, I'll try again another night. Let me know when he stops by." Giuseppe grabbed his drink and swallowed it quickly. "Did you find his phone?"

"Pockets are empty." Osphena answered. "He probably ditched it."

"You!" Giuseppe roared and kicked Erik hard in his guts. Erik moaned, clutching his side and curled over, struggling to breathe.

"What makes you think he'll say anything to you?" Osphena demanded.

"He had a bad reaction when he first saw me," Giuseppe explained. "Something loosened in that corrupted memory bank and he's going to be fiending for medicines to forget."

"There's no reason for him to come to me for that."

"You work for County Health Control. You have access to all sorts of powders and pills."

"You're going to get me in so much trouble!" Osphena protested and walked with Giuseppe back into the parlor.

"I'll cover it up, promise." Giuseppe took his coat and gave Osphena a friendly kiss on the cheek.

"I'll see you later," Osphena said and waved Giuseppe goodbye once he stepped out. After locking the door behind him, Osphena returned to Erik lying on the floor in a daze. "I'm sure you want some painkillers, huh?" Erik slowly nodded. "How far gone are you on a scale of one to five?" Erik nodded again. "Oh, you poor thing..."

Osphena knelt at his side and Erik shut his eyes when he felt a gentle cool hand on his face. "Please," he whispered.

"I'll be gentle, promise..."

Erik let himself drift in the fog, confused and unsure as his body alternated between signals of pain and pleasure.

Immense heat burned on Erik's back and his eyes snapped open, looking at sand. Hearing a hiss, Erik slowly rose to his knees and froze when he saw a diamondback rattlesnake at his side. He clenched his fists on his knees, sweating profusely when the snake hissed again before slithering past.

"At least it's just a warning," Erik thought and blew a relieved sigh.

Getting to his feet, Erik ran a hand over his face covered with granules of sand and turned around, finding himself surrounded by endless hot dry sand and no indication of civilization nearby. Coming full circle, he saw nothing but vast dry wasteland, devoid of people or many plants and grew dismayed when he found no traces of footprints or tire tracks. Shading his eyes, Erik looked skyward at the blazing sun glaring down with its harsh rays beating onto the land below and noted its position.

"It's not high noon, but it may be before," Erik muttered. "I know it's dangerous, but I should start walking in one direction than dying out here..."

Erik walked across the sands, struggling to put one foot in front of the other as he sweat profusely. The winds kicked up and Erik looked at the endless reaches of sky, catching sight of low-hanging dark gray clouds rolling in. He continued his slow trek and later a distant rumble rolled across the skies. A loud crack of thunder resonated loudly throughout as a streak of chain lightning lit the sky. Suddenly cold showers pelted down around him.

"Some rain at last!" Erik whooped and ran his hands on his face, relishing the water falling on him. He cupped his hands, drawing water and gulped it down his parched throat.

His resolve strengthened, Erik continued forward, his thoughts returning to his family with hope they missed him enough to send someone searching for him.

In the thick muggy haze, Erik spotted a white object in the distance and broke into a run, ignoring his achy feet and burned body as he willed himself onward. Coming closer, he noticed a large white tent, surrounded by tan jeeps.

A young man dressed in beige T-shirt, khaki slacks, short leather boots, a pith hat and dark aviator style sunglasses with binoculars hanging around his neck waved at Erik and Erik tentatively waved back. Approaching offside several paces away, Erik ran a hand through his hair, panting hard for breath.

"Hey!" the young man greeted. "Nice day, eh?"

"You're getting soaked out here!" Erik said.

"So are you."

"I'm enjoying it right now."

"How long have you been wandering around?"

"I don't know..."

"It's amazing how long you survived... Were you ever a Scout?"

"I don't remember..." Erik squinted at the young man grinning back at him. "So why are you here?"

"We're the search party looking for *you*," he replied, "but it seems that you've found *us*!"

"Nice..."

Exhaustion rushed to Erik's head and everything quickly slipped from beneath him in an instant.

THIRTY-EIGHT

Erik slowly came to, hearing indistinct noise around him. The rush of light and sound startled him and he felt a supportive hand hold him by the arm.

"Hey, it's cool now," murmured Clayton.

Erik blinked and his vision cleared. Turning his head, he spotted Clayton kneeling over him and the young man gave a gentle smile. Erik noticed his pants leg pulled up and elastic bandage around his left knee.

"Where am I?" Erik demanded, cuffing his trousers. "How did I get here?"

"In Doc Schnell's office," Clayton answered then rolled his eyes. "How else, man?"

Erik looked around his surroundings, noticing he sat on the floor of the small office with the surrounding file cabinets, bookcases and several computers outlined in a psychotropic color. The moonlight barely came through the large picture window, partially blocked by the folding bamboo screen in front of it.

Erik moaned, holding his head in his hands. "What's wrong with me?" he complained, rubbing at his eyes with his knuckles. "Why is everything so bright and colorful?"

"I don't know how zonked out they're trying to make you,"

Clayton said gently. "I'm afraid they might make you into some psycho killing machine like Joe."

"He went on talking about some battle to the death or some nonsense," Erik grumbled. "But they aim to erase me."

"That's why I'm trying to save you here!"

Erik glanced warily at Clayton. "Why bother with me?" he complained. "What about Joe?"

"We'll deal with him later. I'm more concerned about you."

"You keep acting as if you know me..."

"We did meet before, a long time ago." Erik appeared lost and Clayton chortled. "Man, any more close calls like this and we won't be around anymore!" Clayton ran a hand through Erik's hair and Erik winced.

"Is it true what that Colbert said," Erik inquired as Clayton stood, "about being dropped in acid and our records erased?"

Clayton nodded and stiffened once the door to the office opened. Erik scrambled to his feet, watching Schnell enter the room with a stupefied smile plastered on his face. His usual clear gray eyes were now foggy and inattentive.

"Shit!" Clayton growled. "They drugged him!"

"For what?" Erik approached, taking the doctor gently by the arm. He waved a hand in front of Schnell's face and the man barely flinched in response. "Doctor Schnell," Erik called and increased his hold.

Schnell blinked slowly and turned to Erik. "Hm?" he responded.

"How are you today?"

"The Gods are happy in the palace in the sky and I'm happy on this wonderful Earth and everything's just super when you're gay!"

Erik recoiled, not expecting his answer. "Um..." Erik turned to Clayton who paced and cursed under his breath. "Why would they drug him like this?" he questioned nervously.

"They're trying to control him," Clayton snapped. "If he was a threat, he would've been Terminated a long time ago." Erik fell silent, unsure what to say in return. "We better get out of here before they catch us!"

Erik nodded and released the doctor. "I have to get going, Doctor Schnell," he said gently. "They're going to erase me and I'm going to suck it up."

"Oh?" Schnell murmured.

"Really. I don't know if I'll make it this time."

"Don't forget this."

Erik watched the doctor leave his side and approach his desk. Schnell opened a drawer then withdrew a key card and a sheet of paper with opaque raised lines.

"What's that?" Erik wondered aloud.

"Second skin with my imprint," Schnell replied. "Don't you want it?"

Clayton's mouth dropped open in shock when Schnell grabbed Erik's left hand and pressed it into the paper. Erik hissed in pain when his skin seared from the chemical contact. He pulled away, stunned and withdrew his raw hand, clutching it close to his chest.

"The hell is wrong with you, man?" Erik wailed. "Beatings I can take, but chemical burns? You're out of your damn mind!"

"We need to get going before they find you're not where you're supposed to be," Clayton pressed as Erik pushed away

Schnell who looked at him blankly.

"You shouldn't leave like that," the doctor said.

"What do you want me to do?" Erik retorted.

Schnell took Erik's right hand and Erik struggled against the man as he held it down on the desk. Erik pushed back when Schnell withdrew a vial of yellow-green liquid from his vest pocket and thumbed it open, then poured it on Erik's hand. Erik screamed when the liquid burned his skin and Schnell thrust open his fingers.

"Take it," Schnell snarled and Erik bat Schnell in the face with his fist.

"Stop it, old man!" Erik wailed. "Let me go!"

Clayton withdrew a steel blue stiletto and pointed it at the doctor's throat. "That's enough," he snarled. "He can't take any more."

Schnell let go and Erik slumped to the floor, clutching his wrist as he rocked, fighting the tears streaming down his face. Clayton forced the blade to vanish and headed for the office door.

"Why are you doing this to me?" Erik moaned, unable to look away from his badly burned right hand with the skin puckered and blistered in places.

"I'm just trying to help," answered Schnell.

"Thanks, I suppose," muttered Erik.

"You'll need this." Schnell tapped at the desk. "It's imprinted on the card. Hopefully it'll take."

"Whatever." Erik rose to his feet and snatched up the key card with his left hand then hurried alongside Clayton who exited the room.

They ran down corridors, ducking out into doorways to bypass the guards who made their rounds. When they encountered another set of doors, Erik used his key card imaged with Schnell's right thumbprint, pressing it into the reader and his altered left hand. Making their way back safely to their floor without further incident, Erik and Clayton entered the dining area, finding the plank tables empty.

"Now's not the time for tea!" Erik spat when Clayton approached the cupboards and withdrew a chipped mug and a bowl. "We're in major trouble here!"

"*I'm* in trouble, *you're* not," Clayton retorted, finding a tea bag. "You're not the one hacking off hands and using their keys to get over there. Soon they're going to call a code when they find that sack of beef stuffed in the john and we're on lock down again."

"What do you expect me to do?" Erik protested.

"I want you to get out of here." Clayton dropped the bag into the cup and headed over to the sink, filling it with water. "The doc's given you the key - the reward for following the rules. The ones who have us locked away, they have the key and can do whatever they want with us."

"I didn't do anything to deserve it," Erik said, dumbfounded. "I want you to have it."

"You're full of too much hate to die in this cesspool." Clayton poured the contents into the bowl then put in more water. "I've accepted that I'm going to die a slow horrible death in this place."

"Don't sound like some useless loser," Erik spat. "You're not beyond the reach of vengeance, are you?"

"I don't know."

"Come with me, and get back at those bastards who hurt you. I'm sure there's plenty of people on that list you'd like to knock down a few notches…"

"You think escape is that simple?" Clayton muttered. He passed Erik the bowl of green tinted water and Erik put in his right hand, relishing the coolness over his burns. "I can't simply escape like you can. You have somewhere to go. I don't. I've long been forgotten!"

"You aren't forgotten!" Erik protested and wilted under Clayton's irate glare. "I'm sorry… I blame the constant beatings for my poor memory."

"Don't worry about it." Clayton placed his filled mug into the microwave and pressed several buttons.

"Where should I go once I break free from here?"

"Cicero Park's your first option. That's all I got."

"One more question?"

"Sure."

"What's the meaning of the testing?"

"Rumor has it that they want to make us into super soldiers."

Erik doubled over, laughing. "You can't be serious!" he crowed. "That doesn't make any sense, with the way they keep drugging me until I can't remember and they turn me into some blank-headed zombie. I don't believe you at all!"

"Have you heard anything about Termination lately?" Clayton requested.

"What about it?" Erik complained once he calmed. "I've heard some things here and there, but I don't know what it's all about."

"If they mention Termination and your name in the same

sentence, just know you're never seeing your family and friends again... or even the outside world."

"What are you saying?"

"Just like Colbert said: they will destroy you and erase your records to put it simply."

"Please tell me you're lying!" Erik cried. "There's no way they'll allow that!"

"Get real here, Erik!" The microwave beeped and Clayton removed the cup then set the mug aside, letting the tea steep. "The Agency rubs shoulders with The Corporation. Hell, you're tagged and given a Federal number once you're born! They can fuck you up until you die, or they kill you before your time, whichever comes first."

"How chilling..." Erik murmured. "But why...? I didn't do anything wrong!"

"You don't have to *do anything* wrong," Clayton explained. "You just have to *be* wrong and that's enough grounds to eliminate you!"

"What do you mean?"

Clayton shook his head. "I can't say anything about *that*. I've spoken too much already."

"So say if someone *else* made a mistake, like going against company Policy, and used *me* as a means of leverage?" Clayton glanced to Erik, giving him a lost expression. Erik blew a hard sigh as Clayton resumed sipping his tea. "Have you always had that ability?" Erik asked moments later.

"What ability?" Clayton murmured. "Don't bother asking me. It's nothing important."

"Why acid then?" Erik pressed.

"Burning you from the inside out, chemically trashed..." Clayton snorted. "That way if someone somehow finds your remains - which is highly unlikely - nobody can identify you, from your skin to your hair, even your teeth."

"How disheartening..."

THIRTY-NINE

While conversing with Clayton, Erik stiffened when Fenway entered the room. The man paused in step, stunned at the sight of them both. Clayton fell silent, dropping his cup to the floor and it crashed, splattering tea everywhere. Erik immediately tensed as Clayton stood by his side, clenching his hands.

"You're supposed to have a session with Doctor Colbert," Fenway grumbled. "How the fuck you escaped Solitary?"

"It doesn't matter," Erik snapped. "I'm not going."

"I'll be back for you soon!" Clayton said as his hands glowed in pale blue light.

"Not that trick again!" Fenway growled and withdrew an oversized silver pistol from his rear holster. He shot at Clayton and Clayton screamed when white-hot light surged through his body. Clayton fell to his knees, gasping once the electricity faded. Fenway depressed a button, retracting the metal barbs and sheathed the gun back.

"You monster!" Erik yelled and threw the bowl of water at Fenway, crashing the ceramic at his head. Fenway staggered back bewildered as Erik knelt at Clayton's side and Fenway shook off his initial daze then advanced, throwing a hard blow to the back of Erik's head.

Spiraling to the floor, Erik struck his face against the table and Fenway held down Erik's head with a locking hold. Erik gagged and rasped for breath when Fenway bore down, making it harder to breathe.

"What's going on is that you're due for more aggressive treatments," the man growled in Erik's ear. "Your constant non-participation is making the rest of the group irritable and therefore, more troublesome for me!"

"It's not my fault!" Erik wheezed.

"It's more work for me!" Fenway snapped. "The more work I get, the more Hell I rain down on *you*, understand?" He readjusted his grip and slammed Erik against the table again.

Erik coughed and groaned. "Why don't you find something else to do with your time?" he griped. "Like play with that freaky bastard Nelson?"

Fenway chuckled. "You're suitable enough!" He let go and wrapped a strong arm around Erik's neck as he leaned in. "For now, you do as ordered if you don't like being doped up!"

"Why?"

"It's for your best interest."

"Why is that?"

"Because you have to!"

"But *why*?"

"I just said...!"

"Why is it that I have to do as you say?" Fenway tightened his grip and Erik grabbed his arm with his injured right hand, struggling to pull him off. "What's with this 'have to, got to, need to' mess? Why must we be so heavily sedated, placed under this strict social scheme and ordered around?"

"Because, Number Three!"

"Saying just 'because' isn't a suitable answer!" Erik screamed.

Fenway let go and slammed Erik's face against the table with much force, breaking his nose and fracturing his cheek. Fenway leaned in, growling in his ear. "Keep this up and I'll do more than shut your face for you," he seethed. "I'll punish you severely myself!"

"Then keep on punishing me," Erik muttered and spat blood at him. "Join the line!"

Fenway yanked Erik out of his seat and wrestled him to the floor, crushing Erik's arms behind his back. "Tsenninger!" Fenway called as Erik struggled. "We've got a Code Orange!"

Clayton staggered to his feet and looked down at Erik, shaking his head. "Man," he muttered as Erik continued to struggling against Fenway, "Why don't you just pull a fake and save yourself the trouble?"

"What's the point?" Erik hissed. "They can see right through me!"

"Remember, the moves make the man and the fakes you pull off in here can make or break you!"

"What are you planning?" Fenway barked at Clayton. "Either help me hold him down or go back to your room!"

"I'll help," Clayton said and kicked at Erik in the head. Erik yowled and bucked, throwing Fenway off. Fenway grunted when he struck the floor and Clayton grabbed Erik once he scrambled to his feet, taking him by the arm. "Now calm down," Clayton said sternly. "You're only making it worse for yourself." Clayton took Erik's hand, palming the key card and kicked him to the floor.

Erik grunted when he fell on all fours as Nelson entered the room moments later with a hypodermic needle filled with a dark red serum.

"What about you?" Erik complained, sitting up on his knees. "You can't get out of here!"

"I'll just give them the same song and dance," Clayton answered and shrugged his shoulders. "That's all they want: obedient zombie children."

"Oh, it's the little scrappy fighter, eh?" Nelson said brightly upon approach. "It seems that we need a whole cocktail on you!"

"Shut up!" Erik screeched and swung at Nelson.

Nelson stomped on his chest, and then dropped down once Erik hit the floor on his back, holding back his head at a painful angle. Fenway stepped on Erik's left hand and Erik screamed when his fingers crushed under his weight. Using his free hand, Erik grabbed at Nelson's braid and yanked on his hair.

Nelson pulled off the cover with his teeth and jabbed the needle in the side of Erik's neck, injecting him. "Shut up!" Nelson snapped. "You scream like a damn girl!"

"With someone as problematic as you are," Fenway sneered, "your scrawny ass is getting sent directly downstairs *right now!*"

"Of course," Nelson replied as he withdrew the needle and flipped the protective cap back on with his thumb then pocketed it. "It would've been simpler on you if you just went along with the plan!"

"I don't care," Erik rasped and grunted once his muscles began to stiffen and his skin numbed. He loosened his hold on Nelson's hair and the young man stood, kicking Erik hard in the chest, rattling him.

"I'm fucking tired of waiting on those suits finishing their test preps," Fenway groused. "You're getting outta my face *tonight!*"

"Want me to hurry things along?" Nelson asked in false cheer.

Fenway glared at him as he grabbed Erik by the arms and pulled him up. "Tsenninger, let's take him down," he grumbled, ignoring Nelson's comment.

Nelson sighed, grabbing Erik by the legs and they both carried him out the dining area. Taking him down the corridor into an unused room, they strapped him immobile into an empty gurney with leather restraints on the edges.

Pushing the bed to the elevator, Fenway struck the button, waiting for the signal to change. Once it turned green, they boarded along with Erik and Nelson pressed the button with the single circle and bar underneath.

"I want to do something, anything," Nelson complained. "Just leave me alone with him, just this once!"

"You stay out of it," Fenway barked. "I've got enough complications."

"Let me try?"

Fenway glared at Nelson. "Last I need is you breaking him!" he spat. "Forget it!"

"He might just become compliant..." Nelson shrugged his shoulders. "You never know."

"Shut up."

Arriving onto the next lower floor, Nelson and Fenway wheeled Erik through a darkened corridor into another empty room where he was promptly untied and dumped. Fenway gave

Erik a swift kick to the face for good measure and both he and Nelson left the room, locking the door behind them.

Erik searched his surroundings, finding he lay in a dimly lit room with white ceiling, walls, and floors. Its only door across from him had five locks bolted on the outside. The room's lighting flickered once static filled the room.

"You must do as we say," Colbert's voice grumbled, echoing into the room. "You are our property and what we say has precedence!"

"You don't own me," Erik screamed, "no one does! I'm a free person!"

"The dream will surely kill you," Colbert snapped back. "There is no such thing as personal freedom, just allowances. What is given can easily be taken away!" Colbert gave a short laugh. "Keep believing such a false dream and you will be sorely disappointed!"

"Let me go! I don't have to stand for your demented rules!"

"Impossible, Number Three. Your resistance causes irritation for us, as well as agitation for the group. We must keep everyone nice and happy... I'm sure you'd dislike ruining everyone's happiness, now do you?"

"No one in their right mind is happy here!" Erik screeched. "You poison everyone's mind to make them believe..." He struggled to get up, grinding his teeth from the sharp pain assaulting his joints, making it hard to stand. Erik seethed as he got to his knees. "They're nothing more than mindless drones, just empty-headed sheep!" A short laugh escaped the communication speakers and Erik grew immediately chilled. "You're erasing them all, replacing them with monsters because of someone related to them did something you don't agree with!"

"We cannot have you upset," Colbert grumbled. "You must be happy."

"I'm fine the way I am!" Erik hollered. "I'm not letting you erase me! I'm not going to forget!"

"No, you are *not* fine!" Colbert said sharply. "You are *very* sick and we aim to make you well again!"

"There's *nothing wrong* with me!"

"There is *plenty* wrong... something *profoundly* wrong, *deep* inside of you!" More static came over the system. "You have to follow orders if you wish for the treatments to work effectively, for it is your best interest and safety in mind. Do so and the pain will stop."

"No!"

"You will get more aggressive treatments whether or not you comply!"

"I don't care!" Erik wailed. "I'm tired of you treating me like this!" He tensed when the flickering lights worsened and the bulbs buzzed and crackled. "I'm sick of it and I'm not going to take it any more!"

Colbert said more over the intercommunication system, only to have his voice drowned out by excessive static. Erik heaved for breath as his rage took over and he struggled to his feet.

Erik clenched his sore, blistered hands at his sides and screamed. "I can't take it!" he screeched. "If you don't let me go, I *will* break out of here! I will expose you for the monsters you are!"

Rushing for the door, Erik threw a punch with all his might, denting the steel. Sudden pain jarred through his fist and he continued striking, sending more fiery agony up his arms and cutting his skin. His vision wavered as he continued hitting the door, causing more dents. Footsteps later pattered on the door's other side, followed by indistinct talking.

The killing stroke will come naturally, in time...

Erik screamed as he threw another solid strike, breaking his fist through one layer of the steel and cut the back of his hand. The scent of his blood caused strong thudding ache behind his eyes as his dimmed vision flashed red.

Remember, you must make the first cut...

"*What is it they want me to remember?*" Erik thought. "*What is it they want me to forget?*"

Erik continued punching repeatedly, letting out his frustrations against the door and screaming curses. Suddenly the lights brightened brilliantly before crashing out forcing Erik blind and the fiery agony snatched his body from the world he knew, pulling him into oblivion.

FORTY

A constant chirp filled Erik's head and suddenly the faint scent of antiseptic roused him. He opened his eyes, finding himself in a clean bed inside a warm hospital room, facing a window covered by white linen curtains with a view of a garden of wildflowers. Erik glanced aside, noticing several monitors keeping track of his vitals.

"Oh, you're awake!" a voice said happily. "I'm so glad!"

Erik looked up, spotting Genovera entering the room, wearing a blue and white spotted sundress and white sandals, smiling sadly. "Why are you here?" he asked. "Where's Dad?"

"He's away for a bit and is terribly busy," Genovera murmured as she approached Erik's bedside. "How are you feeling?"

Erik shook his head. "Why did they bring me back here?" he demanded.

"I worry terribly about you!"

"You're not my mother!" Genovera opened her mouth to speak, then bit her hand as the words refused to come out. She looked down at the floor, fighting tears. "What's with that reaction?" Erik snapped.

Genovera shook her head and took in a weak breath. "Once they think you're ready to go home, I'll take you," she said slowly. "Your father will come in late."

"Why are you hurting Smiley like this?" Erik shouted. "What an ugly thing to do!"

"It's not like that!" Genovera cried and straightened her stance, narrowing her eyes at Erik. "I don't have to speak to you about this!"

"I won't tell Mom," Erik grumbled. "I won't tell Smiley either."

"Justin..."

"Please, go away."

Genovera blew a hard sigh and left the room. Erik clenched his teeth when he heard her sobbing softly outside the door. "Damn it," Erik groaned and kicked back the sheets. Gingerly stepping out of bed, he winced when the intravenous line yanked against him. Erik seethed and ripped out the cords, then stepped toward the door. "Missus Zachary..." he said softly at the doorway. Genovera's crying began to cease and Erik leaned against the frame as he held his bleeding arm. "I'm sorry..."

"It's fine," Genovera murmured from the other side. "I deserve to be chastised."

"It's none of my business..."

"But it does involve you."

"How so?"

"I can't tell you now... when you're older, you'll understand."

"Or would you rather wait until Smiley dies?" Genovera stepped into the room, her face red and appearing cross. "Or would you rather have the guilt drive you insane and kill yourself and let him know by leaving a note?"

Erik grunted once slapped harshly across the face. "Don't

say things like that!" Genovera hissed. "I love Melvin just as much!"

"What kind of response is that?" Erik spat and Genovera slapped him again.

"I care about both him and Gerald, as well as Kevin and you!" Genovera huffed. "Say something like that again and I'll slap you even harder!"

"So is it true that Kevin's my blood brother?"

Genovera's eyes widened, stunned then her expression softened. "Forgive me," she murmured and embraced Erik. Erik stiffened, astonished and she stroked his hair. "I'm under a lot of stress, dealing with my husband, my son, and worried about you..."

"Please don't worry about me," Erik muttered. "Dad's got that area covered."

"I can't help but worry." Letting go, Genovera placed her hands on Erik's shoulders and looked seriously at him. "Don't ever forget that I love you very much and don't want anything horrible happening to you."

"If you say so..."

"Now get back in bed and get some rest!"

"Are you going to yell at me for running away?" Erik asked instead.

Genovera smiled and shook her head. "If you stayed with me, we'd be somewhere else now," she responded.

"Where else?"

"Montana or perhaps Canada."

Erik snorted. "Seriously?" Genovera nodded and Erik chuckled. "You're silly."

Genovera gave a tight smile and led Erik toward the bed. "Please, rest," she pressed. "Your father's working himself to death trying not to worry over you!"

"Will you call him and let him know I'm alive?"

Genovera cringed. "Yes," she said in a strained tone. "Yes, I'll tell him."

Genovera followed Erik into the room and tucked him in once he returned to bed. Genovera caressed his face before leaving and Erik touched his cheek, growing slightly warm.

"*My own mother doesn't touch me this way,*" he thought. "*Why does she care so much...?*" Erik groaned when he abruptly grew lightheaded and looked down at his arm, seeing the sheets soaked in crimson. "*Why isn't the bleeding stopping by now?*"

The machines chirped wildly and Erik moaned when the lightheadedness worsened. He clutched his arm as he stepped out of bed and struck the floor, unable to move. Moments later, many voices abruptly talked frantically around him as he fell into the darkness.

Erik woke up in agony, his skin on fire and spreading through his entire being. He screamed, fighting the sheets twisted about his body.

Sensing someone grab for his arm, Erik sat up, facing a dark shadow standing over him. He reached out, grasping them by the sleeve and threw them down onto the bed. Flipping over, he pounced on the body beneath him and straddled the stranger, throttling the threat with all his strength as he panted hard for breath.

"Hey!" Osphena gasped and reached out with a weak hand,

grasping for a lamp. She crashed it over Erik's head and kicked him off, sending him bowling head over heels onto the floor.

Erik struck his head against the door and moaned, slumping forward on his side. Osphena curled on the bedside and clutched the sheets to her chest, frightened as Erik slowly came to.

"Ugh," Erik moaned, holding his head. He staggered to his feet and stumbled out into the hall.

"At the end," Osphena called.

"Thanks," Erik called over his shoulder. Osphena sighed in relief when she heard the door close.

After Erik showered, he stepped out, finding a pack of cigarettes and lighter left for him on the sink's edge. He wrapped himself in a towel and picked up the cigarettes, taking out one to light. Leaving the bath, he entered the dimly lit parlor, finding a change of clothes left for him draped on the couch.

"You're up early," Osphena murmured from the bedroom door as Erik sat on the couch's edge and pulled into a pair of athletic socks.

"What time is it?" Erik muttered, grabbing the tweed trousers.

"It's five."

"What time do you go to work?"

"I leave out of here at seven. I don't know what time you go to work."

"Then what do you want?" He shook out the pants. "No undies?"

"I didn't know your size." Osphena shrugged. "You were

fighting in your sleep again."

"Sorry about that." Erik pointed to the door behind him. "I can go if you want."

"It's not your fault that you're sick."

Erik pulled into his slacks. "What do you want from me?" he groused.

"Other than a good screw?" Osphena teased. Erik raised an eyebrow and looked up, shocked and disgusted when he noticed the woman only wrapped in bed sheets. "I don't want anything unless you want to."

"I'm not sure what to think," Erik replied and Osphena left her place at the door. She returned to the kitchenette, switching on the overhead light. Erik left the couch and took his seat at the painted table in the corner, tapping his ashes in the chipped stained cup. "Are we a long-term thing? Married? What?"

"You come over sometimes." Osphena withdrew the kettle and filled it with water. "It's nothing serious."

"Because I can't remember..."

"I prefer it that way."

"Am I horrible person?"

"No, you're a nice, sweet person."

Erik felt his face flush slightly as Osphena put the kettle on the stove and switched on the gas. "I'm sorry," he said softly. "I'm sorry I can't do anything else for you."

"It's fine," Osphena said gently and opened her cabinets, pulling out a jar of instant creamer and coffee. She set both containers on the table then leaned forward, looking deeply into Erik's eyes. "Hey," she purred.

"Yeah?" Erik murmured and took another drag of his

cigarette.

"Why is it you always cry?"

"Huh?" Erik's face burned hotly and Osphena grinned, poking his bare chest with the tip of her finger. "What are you talking about?"

"After we fool around, you cry. Any other man would just drop off to sleep or light a cigarette and talk about nothing. You, Mister, curl up and cry."

"I'm really messed up in the head, apparently," Erik said flatly. "I don't remember what we do anyway if anything at all."

"I see that. You tried to kill me this morning and you act like you don't have a care in the world!" Erik continued to give her a lost expression and Osphena chortled, petting his head. "That's okay. I should know what I'm getting myself into."

"Don't."

"I'm not worried. I find it quite exciting, to be frank."

"Please don't touch me," Erik managed to say, immediately growing uncomfortable.

"Don't you want a quick one before I go to work?" Erik shook his head, thoroughly daunted. "Oh well, will I see you tonight?"

"I don't know."

"Oh well..." Osphena left the table once the kettle whistled.

Erik groaned and put his head on the table, holding his cigarette above him. Osphena took the burning stick and put it out in the nearby cup. "Why are you doing this to me?" he murmured.

"Because, I find it fun." Osphena rubbed at Erik's back. "Here, wake up with some java. Come on."

"You didn't add anything extra to my coffee, did you?"

"No, just hot water. Come on."

Erik sat up, glaring at Osphena as she sat across from him, smiling. Before them, rest two mugs of hot water and a spoon.

"Pick one," he snarled.

Osphena pointed to the mug on her right and Erik took the one on her left. He added three spoons of whitener and one spoonful of coffee to his mug and stirred it.

"You're acting like I'm trying to poison you or something!" Osphena protested.

"I don't trust you," Erik muttered, sipping his coffee.

"Why don't you punish me then?"

"I have no reason to be."

"Oh, but haven't I been a bad girl?" Osphena giggled when Erik raised an eyebrow.

"Leave me alone, lady," he spat. "I don't need this shit early in the day."

"Fine, I'll leave you be." Osphena pat Erik's cheek as she stood. "I'm so going to wreck you when you come in tonight."

Erik paled and Osphena giggled again. "Get out of my face, lady," he grumbled.

Osphena left the table and Erik grunted, stewing in silence as he resumed his drink. Once he finished his coffee, Erik set down the mug with a firm bang and moaned when the walls began moving.

"What's the matter?" Osphena called from the next room.

"Damn it, woman!" Erik roared. "You tricked me!"

"I'm sorry," Osphena said and entered the kitchen as Erik slumped forward on the table. "You're irresistible."

"There's another reason," Erik moaned when Osphena pushed him upright. He looked up at her with bleary eyes and gasped when he noticed she was naked. "You're trying to make me forget…"

"Maybe, maybe not…"

Erik whimpered when Osphena kissed him deeply, and then fell into darkness.

FORTY-ONE

"Missus Zachary," a voice called, breaking into the darkness. "Missus Zachary!"

Erik's eyes snapped open and he faced an athletic young man who had blond hair styled into a mullet and steel blue eyes behind navy horn-rimmed glasses, wearing white scrub shirt and slacks standing near the hospital bed, glancing at his silver wristwatch.

"Who are you?" Erik grumbled.

"I work with Missus Zachary," he explained. "I'm her assistant Stearne."

"Stearne?" Erik asked. "That's a strange name."

Stearne grinned. "My mother was a Nautical Officer in the Defense Forces and my father loved sailing."

"Why are you here?"

Before Stearne could answer, Genovera entered the room moments later, wearing a white lab coat over a red sundress patterned with small yellow flowers and cream-colored sandals.

"Sorry to keep you waiting, Mister Gelnika," she said. "We've only ten minutes before rounds start."

"On it," Stearne replied and shut off the various machines monitoring Erik's vitals. Erik punched Stearne's chest when reached for and Stearne grunted, mildly surprised by his reaction.

"I'm not going with you," Erik snapped.

"You have to," Stearne said evenly. "Missus Zachary's orders."

"What?" Erik cried, astonished.

"Please, Justin," Genovera pleaded. "Just come along."

"Am I going home?" Erik inquired, hopeful.

"In a bit."

Erik cried out once scooped up and hoisted over Stearne's shoulder in a fireman's carry. "Hey, put me down!" Erik yelled and punched at Stearne's back.

"Calm down," Stearne grumbled as he pulled up the sheeting and tossed it over Erik's head. "Now be still!"

Erik clenched his teeth as Stearne began walking. He calmed slightly when he smelled Genovera's perfume as she followed closely behind him.

"Time," demanded Genovera moments later.

"Seven minutes," Stearne answered.

"We're taking the stairs. The elevators will be too long."

Erik lifted the sheet covering him and peered out behind Stearne. He spotted Genovera walking several paces behind and in the distance; he noticed several men and women in dark suits heading down the corridor where they left.

Stearne pushed open the side door and descended the staircase. Genovera waited at the top of the staircase then descended down after Stearne took a flight ahead.

"What do you assist Missus Zachary with?" Erik asked.

Stearne grunted. "You're supposed to be laundry," he grumbled.

"Well, you're going to get kicked in a minute if you don't tell me," Erik threatened.

"I work with her at the labs at Gateway by helping with the heavy lifting."

"This included?" Erik snapped, incredulous. "Last I checked, I'm no Public Defense Works project!"

"Don't get smart, kid," Stearne grumbled. "She asked me to work directly with her and I got a pay rise since then, much more than Gen-Tech was giving me when I used to work for them." Stearne snorted. "I needed the money and she's better to work for. I ask no questions."

"She *is* pretty."

Stearne chuckled. "That doesn't hurt either."

"So are you a scientist or something?"

"I work with chemicals, yes."

Stepping out of another door, Stearne entered a parking garage. A large powder blue sedan with a white hardtop, chrome fenders and grill pulled up to Stearne containing two young men in the front.

The driver with shoulder-length dark brown hair and round glasses wore a tan suit and yellow dress shirt. The passenger, with curly sandy hair and blue eyes wore a light gray suit with pale violet dress shirt.

"Good timing," said the curly-haired young man and leaned over, opening the door for Stearne.

Stearne dumped Erik inside and pushed him over as he stepped in; then shut the door once the driver took off.

Erik quickly took off the sheets and glared at Stearne. "Where are we going?" he demanded. "Who are these guys?"

"Roland Schneider," said the curly-headed man brightly. "That's our friend Giuseppe Petra." The driver raised a hand in acknowledgement before placing it back on the steering wheel. "So you're the infamous Justin Schumacher Missus Zachary won't shut up about."

Erik grunted and folded his arms across his chest. "Why isn't she here?" He glanced out the window as Giuseppe pulled out the garage and entered the busy street.

"So, Roland," Stearne said, ignoring Erik completely. "What do you think Missus Zachary has planned?"

"She told us to meet her at the library."

"We're to go around for about twenty minutes to give her time to get there," Giuseppe interjected.

"So we're not stopping anywhere?" Stearne wondered aloud.

"Hopefully not," Roland replied.

Coming to a roadblock, Giuseppe cursed under his breath and switched gears to back up, only to hear a horn blast from behind. Erik turned around, spotting another car behind them, blocking them in.

"What's with this?" Roland grumbled.

"This can't be right," Stearne snapped, growing tense.

Erik glanced out his window, seeing several dark cars ahead and officers in navy and black uniforms walking around, peering into cars and speaking to drivers.

"That doesn't look like County," Giuseppe murmured.

"You're right," Stearne answered and reached under the seat. He withdrew a pistol and tucked it in his waistband at his back.

An officer armed with a shotgun later approached

Giuseppe's vehicle and tapped the window. Erik tensed, taking in a shallow breath as Giuseppe rolled it down.

"What's going on up there?" Giuseppe asked innocently.

"We've been told of a kidnapping by terrorists," replied the officer, "and that they're trying to cross county lines."

"That's news to us."

"The boy was taken from a hospital..."

"Really now?" Stearne shifted in his seat and the officer tightened his grip on his weapon. "What's this boy look like?"

"Tall, thin, red hair..." The officer leaned in, glaring through the glass. "Kinda like this boy you got here."

"We're his caretakers," Roland said quickly. "He's very sick..."

"We're taking him to the cancer research center in East Alscesca," Giuseppe added.

"Cancer Center's that way." The officer gestured with his shotgun in the opposite direction. "Now I've got to ask you boys to get out and come with me."

Stearne hastily unleashed his pistol and grabbed Erik by the hair, pointing it at his head. Erik let out a frightened yelp when Stearne pressed the pistol against his skull. "You let us go," Stearne snarled, "or this kid winds up dead and it's all over!"

"I'll blow your hand off first!" The officer snapped.

"Do you really want to see who's faster?" Stearne challenged.

Giuseppe gestured to the officer. "Give us your gun," he snapped.

The officer snorted. "Not likely."

"Then you must not want him bad enough." Erik cried out when Stearne fired and the window shattered. Erik ducked down, seething as his ears rang and the officer staggered back with blood running between his eyes. He struck lifeless to the ground and Stearne tossed Roland the pistol then quickly climbed over Erik, opening the door.

"Punch it!" Stearne shouted, grabbing the fallen rifle when several more several more officers ran toward their car.

Giuseppe slammed back into the car behind him after Stearne yanked the door shut, crunching metal and pulled away with squealing tires, speeding off down a side street.

"She's going to kill us," Stearne moaned as Giuseppe ran lights and barely missed other vehicles nearly running into him.

"It couldn't be helped," Roland muttered and took the shotgun Stearne passed to him, then placed the longarm under the seat.

"Are the cops going to come after us?" Erik asked. "I hope we don't end up on the news!"

"That's not going to happen," Roland said. "No one saw or heard anything."

"What are you saying?" Erik mewed.

"We're saying 'shut up'," Stearne growled.

"Are you going to kill me?"

"Would you rather we did?" Roland jeered.

Erik drew up his knees and held his head down when Stearne laughed and Roland guffawed in response.

Later pulling up into a library parking lot, Giuseppe put the car in park and stepped out, stretching. Genovera exited from within the building moments later holding a briefcase, her hair pinned up in a loose chignon and violet-tinted glasses on her face. Erik noticed she had changed her clothing, wearing a pleated pale rose skirt with matching blazer, sleeveless white blouse and pink flats.

"I didn't know you were a sexy librarian on your off time," Giuseppe quipped as he came around and opened the rear passenger side door on Stearne's side.

Genovera giggled and stepped in as Stearne scoot over and Erik unfolded from his huddled position. "I didn't have time for the lipstick," she replied and leaned over the seat, setting the briefcase in Erik's lap. "I know this is probably quite scary," she said as Giuseppe shut the door, "but you'll have to trust me."

"It might not look like it, but I'm really scared to death!" Erik snapped. "What's going on? Just tell me, please!"

"When we have more time," Genovera said as Giuseppe returned to the driver's side. "Please just change your clothes." Giuseppe switched gears then pulled out the library lot and Erik glared at Genovera as she smiled sadly in return. "Please?" she pleaded.

Erik huffed and opened the briefcase, finding stonewashed jeans, blue T-shirt, black slip-on sneakers and a red baseball cap. "Now?" he complained.

"Yes, right now."

Erik grunted and hurried out of his scrubs and pulled into the jeans and shirt. After placing the cap backwards on his head and pulling into the shoes, he stuffed the old articles inside the case.

"Does Dad know about all this?" Erik demanded and Genovera nodded. "Is all this related to that new project they started him on?" Genovera nodded again, saying nothing. "Then why would he put up with this dangerous stuff?"

"It's because of you," Roland said gently from the front passenger seat. "Now don't feel guilty. Your father would even go to Hell and back again if it means keeping you safe."

"What about Kevin?" Erik murmured. "It all started because of me getting Kevin seriously hurt..."

"It's not your fault," Genovera said in a dead tone. "It was bound to happen either way... It just happened sooner than we thought."

Erik glanced to her, noticing she appeared distant.

"We ran into a little trouble along the way, Missus Zachary," Stearne said softly.

"It was bound to happen." Genovera glanced back at Stearne and gave a strained smile, patting him on the thigh. "Thank you for keeping him safe for me."

Stearne flushed slightly in response.

The busy city streets became longer and less populated with businesses as they entered the suburbs, bypassing large houses. Soon the houses gave way to empty lots and more trees and the roads had no signs.

"Why are we so far out?" Erik asked once they reached a two-lane road.

"We're taking a break from city life for a while," Roland answered.

"What could be out here?"

"Monsters," Stearne gibed.

Giuseppe later pulled up to a large tract of gravel road and approached a barn where rock music blasted from an unknown source. Pulling onto the building's side, they approached a young man working underneath the hood of another older-model sedan. Giuseppe depressed the horn and the young man wearing coveralls and a black bandana glanced up from behind the car.

"Hey," he called and wiped his hands on a towel he had hanging from his rear pocket. "You guys almost had me worried when I heard of that blockade downtown!"

"Do you have anything for us?" Stearne answered.

"Leave all that stuff you've got there," said the mechanic. "I'll clean it for you guys later."

"Let's go," Stearne called and they all clamored out the car.

The mechanic approached a large bin near the barn door as Roland and Genovera entered inside. The mechanic opened the lid and withdrew another case.

"Is she ready to go yet?" Giuseppe asked and entered the other car.

"Was checking the fluids," the mechanic called, handing Stearne the case as he approached from behind. "There's two twenty-two's in there and five stacks. That's all I could get..."

"That's fine," Stearne said.

"I asked for some thirty-eights," Giuseppe complained. "They'll fragment and with the noise it makes, it'll wake the dead!"

"Hey, thirty-eights are fucking popular right now, okay?" the mechanic protested. "That's the best I could get my hands on short notice!"

"The flash will alert anyone in the vicinity!" Giuseppe ranted.

"We probably won't need them soon," Stearne interjected.

"Let's hope not."

Stearne waved off the mechanic and Erik followed him to the car. He took the rear passenger and Stearne sat in the front. Roland appeared moments later and approached the mechanic, conversing softly with him. Genovera came over to the car and disappeared behind the hood.

"I hope you fixed that fuel line," she said and several metallic knocks came from the other side. She stepped back moments later and dropped the hood with a clang. "You had the air filter on wrong again."

"I'm not used to working with a car like that," the mechanic said sheepishly.

"You just like to see a woman working on cars, that's all," Genovera chided and slipped into the back seat with Erik. Giuseppe started the car with a roar and gunned the engine.

"I'll follow," Roland called and Giuseppe switched gears, then pulled away from the barn.

Entering a one-lane road, Giuseppe eventually approached a secluded lot surrounded by numerous rocks and tall pines. He parked at the bottom of the hill and stepped out, stretching.

"What time do you have?" Giuseppe asked as Stearne opened the door and squinted at his watch.

"It's stopped working again," Stearne answered.

"Why don't you get an atomic one?"

"They cost too much!" Stearne took the case and shut the door with his hip then followed Giuseppe uphill on a small track.

"What's going to happen?" Erik asked after the men left his field of vision.

Genovera turned to Erik. "You're in safe capable hands," she said softly.

"I don't know," Erik murmured. "When will I see Dad again?"

"Once all the mess and confusion dies down, then we'll go back."

"So what are we doing out here?"

Genovera smiled. "Camping."

Erik grunted and got out of the car. He waited for Genovera to exit and she walked with him up the hill.

"Are we in tents or something?" Erik asked.

"There's a lake for swimming in and we've got a nice cabin with all sorts of enmities," Genovera explained. "You'll like it very much."

"So where are we exactly?"

"I can't tell you."

"Why not?"

Genovera grinned brightly. "We don't want others stealing such a nice spot, now do we?"

FORTY-TWO

After walking for a time through shaded trails and switchbacks, they came across an enclosed canopy of trees sheltering a redwood cabin. Stearne sat on the plank deck, scratching at the ground with a stick and Erik saw Giuseppe's shadow moving about inside through the glass pane windows.

"Feel like going for a swim?" Genovera called. "I'm about to hit the lake."

Stearne looked up, smiling wolfishly. "Really now?" he called back.

"Hurry up!" Genovera waved him away and Stearne threw the stick aside as he clamored to his feet, then ran inside the cabin. Genovera chortled and turned to Erik, smiling brightly. "Let's go swimming together!" she exclaimed. "It'll be nice and relaxing."

"I'm only coming along because I want to swim," Erik snapped and stomped up the path toward the cabin.

Upon entry, Erik noticed several generators scattered around and several tables and chairs set up along the walls. One had a radio and transmitter on the side where Giuseppe sat at with one hand cradling part of a headset's earpiece while turning dials and trying to gain a signal with the other. At the other table were several single electric and propane burners, with trays of vials while a third table held a compact computer.

Erik approached Giuseppe, looking over his shoulder. "What are you listening for?" he asked.

"I'm checking the news channels," Giuseppe replied.

Genovera entered moments later and picked up the small case left on the table near the door then headed into another room. Erik heard a shriek and whirled around, spotting Stearne in yellow swim trunks with a camera in hand, running out the room with clothes and books flying at him. He laughed as he wound the dial.

"You're going to get it, buster!" Genovera shouted and a parasol smacked Stearne in the chest before clattering to the floor.

"I'm keeping that one in my personal collection," Stearne called back, grinning and the door slammed shut.

"She's going to light all your stuff on fire," Giuseppe teased, cracking a smile.

Stearne chuckled and looped the camera's straps around his neck. "Want me to take a picture of you?" he asked.

Erik pointed to himself and Stearne nodded. Erik shook his head and Stearne held up his camera as he moved near Giuseppe. "Smile, Joey," he sang. Giuseppe waved him away as Stearne snapped a photo.

"Alright boys, let's hit the water," Genovera called as she exited moments later in a cherry red sundress. "Some of us need to cool off some."

Giuseppe chortled and set down the headset as he rose from the table. "We're all clear," he replied.

"Come on!" Genovera grabbed for Erik's hand and bounded

outdoors, dragging him along. Stearne followed after and Giuseppe left last, picking up the fallen parasol along the way from the floor.

At the lakefront beach, Genovera ran along the sands, playing catch with Stearne's camera against Giuseppe as they tossed it back and forth out of his reach. Stearne jumped and caught it then began snapping random pictures.

"Stop it!" Genovera cried, laughing as she grabbed for the camera.

Stearne snapped a shot and quickly stepped out her way. "I can't help it," he replied, rewinding the film for another take.

"If I pose for you, will you stop?"

"Yes!" Genovera approached the rock where Erik sat watching them under the parasol's shade tucked between the stone crevices and picked it up. Taking several paces forward, Genovera hoisted the parasol on her shoulder then gave a seductive smile. "Hey, let's turn this way to get you in better light."

"Okay."

Genovera stood with her back to Erik and Stearne stood in front of her with the camera. He adjusted his aim, took a picture then Genovera hastily took the camera from him and pushed him back into the water.

Giuseppe hooted at Stearne. "That's what you get for being fresh," he jeered.

"I'll take a break here," Genovera said and approached Erik, taking a seat on the rock's ledge. "Aren't you going to take a swim?"

"I will in a minute," Erik replied.

"Don't worry about ruining your clothes. We have more."

"It is pretty hot today…" Erik murmured in agreement and blew a sigh. Leaving the rocks, he climbed up and took the stony path overlooking the lake. Reaching the top, he took off his cap and tossed it down, watching it tumble into the rough sands below.

"Jump in," Stearne called, treading water near the shore. "The water's great!"

Erik stepped back then ran forward, jumping in with a big splash. Down in the murky watery world, he noticed something shimmering in the deep and swam for it. Before he could grasp it, his lungs protested and he swam up to the surface to catch his breath. Erik spotted Genovera swimming lazy strokes nearby and Giuseppe standing at the shoreline, holding onto the camera.

"Where's Stearne?" Erik asked when he noticed the young man missing.

Genovera screamed when Stearne suddenly surfaced and splashed water on her. "You bully!" she shrieked and splashed water back.

Erik stifled a laugh as Genovera swam away and Stearne came after her. Moments later Roland came down the path, wearing a yellow short-sleeved dress shirt, green short pants and brown sandals.

"Hey," he called, waving, "let's get back."

"So soon?" Giuseppe called. "We just got here!"

"We've got a lot of work to do!"

"In this awful heat?"

"Well, we can take a break later if it gets too hot." Roland waved off Giuseppe and headed back up the hill.

"Alright, let's get to business," Genovera said as she came to the shore. Throwing back her wet hair, she approached Giuseppe at the bottom of the hill for a short exchange. Stearne waved to Erik and Erik sighed, also exiting the lake. "I'll let you know if I need any help," Genovera called and made her way toward the house with Giuseppe following her.

"How long do I have to stay here," Erik asked as Stearne watched Genovera leave.

"No longer than a week at best," Stearne replied. "Your father will worry and we don't want him to."

"Will I be safe here?"

Stearne nodded. "I'll protect you." He tousled Erik's hair. "You'll be like my little brother."

Erik shrugged. "So what are you going to do now?" he inquired, following Stearne up the hill toward the cabin.

"I'm going to develop those pictures," Stearne said, grinning. "I got some good ones."

"Especially *that* one, right?" Erik teased and Stearne chortled.

Once Stearne and Erik entered the cabin, they found everyone else inside working on various projects, with Giuseppe operating the radio and Roland in front of a miniature laboratory mixing chemicals while Genovera in bare feet wearing a dry white sundress with blue flowers sat on the floor surrounded by mechanical parts, putting together a machine. Stearne pet Genovera's head as he passed her and she glanced up.

"Stop that!" she snapped and threw a wrench at him. Stearne sidestepped the attack, chuckling. "I'm married and you're much too young for me!"

"I can keep trying," Stearne said and picked up the camera on a nearby table before exiting into one of the rear rooms.

"Might as well relax for awhile," Genovera said to Erik. "You can sleep in my room. There's a change of clothes for you on the bed."

"Thanks," Erik murmured and headed for the room.

"Oh, and Justin...?"

Erik paused near the door, tense. "What is it?"

"Please keep what happened to yourself. We don't want Gerald to get in trouble."

"What about you?"

"That's for me to worry about."

"Why do this if it'll get my dad in trouble?"

"I do this to get him *out* of trouble." Erik turned to face Genovera who sat huddled over her machine she worked on. "No one suspects much out of me, being the only woman there, so I have to use it to my advantage."

"That's a stupid idea."

"Most men are stupid."

Erik clenched his teeth and stomped for the bedroom. He slammed the door shut behind him, then peeled out of his damp clothes. Picking up the cargo shorts left for him, Erik pulled into it and tossed the other t-shirt aside on the nightstand before crawling into bed.

Staring at the ceiling, Erik placed his arms behind his head, listening to the various hammering and clangs of Genovera's work, the static off the radio Giuseppe tuned into and the clinking and crackling of Roland's beakers and burners. A knock suddenly resonated at the door.

"Hey," Stearne's voice called from the other side. The door opened, revealing Stearne in loosened shorts and open short-sleeved sport shirt baring his broad chest and lean stomach. He stepped in, holding a small metal case. "Would you like to hang out?"

"And do what?" Erik spat sourly. "There's nothing here to do!"

"We can break a few rules." Stearne grinned devilishly as he held up the small case. "You might never get a chance to do this again."

"What rules are that?" Erik sat up as Stearne entered the room and shut the door behind him.

"You're a good kid, I can tell," Stearne said. "You might not get another chance like this again." He approached the bed and sat next to Erik. Opening the case, Stearne revealed a flask of vodka and two shot glasses.

"I'm just not that interested in drinking," Erik murmured. "My dad does enough of that with all the stress he's under and my best friend's dad stays drunk. He gets scary sometimes."

"It's just a drinking game." Stearne dug through his pockets and produced a quarter. "It's easy. Toss a quarter into the shooter. You get it in; you don't drink. Miss and you take a shot."

"Are you picking on me because Missus Zachary won't play with you?" Erik accused.

Stearne let out a short laugh. "I'm playing with you, Justin, because I *want* to!" he replied.

Erik quirked an eyebrow and glanced warily at Stearne. "You're not trying to get me drunk for *other* reasons, are you?" he pressed.

Stearne let out a rolling laugh. "What makes you think that?" he crowed.

"If I play a few games with you," Erik groused, "will you leave and let me sleep?"

"Agreed!"

Stearne tossed Erik the quarter and he caught it. Erik glanced down at the coin, noting its age. "Why keep such an old piece?" he inquired. "You can make money off this... it's almost a hundred years old!"

"I don't need the money."

"Did Missus Zachary give it to you?"

"It was before we met." Stearne leaned over and pulled up the nightstand, then picked up Erik's shirt and dropped it in his lap. "Hold on to that, you'll need it!"

"For what?"

"You'll see." Stearne set up the first shot glass on the table and set the secondary aside with the flask of vodka. "Now, this is how it works." Stearne held out his hand and Erik handed him the quarter. "Just flip it in like this." Stearne flicked the coin and it landed in the glass with a small ring. Sliding out the quarter with his fingers, he passed it to Erik. "Give it a try." Erik copied Stearne and flipped the coin into the shot glass. He grinned when the coin landed.

"That's not so hard!"

"Wait until you start missing a few!" After taking several

turns back and forth, Erik flipped the coin and it nicked the side of the glass, landing on the nightstand. "Oh my, time for a drink!" Stearne teased. He uncapped the bottle, poured the alcohol into the empty glass, and handed it to Erik.

Erik took it warily and sniffed it, smelling nothing. "This won't kill me, will it?" he asked.

Stearne let out a robust laugh. "Like I would do something as bad as that!" he protested. "You know she'd kill me first!"

Erik shrugged. "Down the hatch," he murmured and took a large gulp. Erik cried out as the burning liquid ran down his throat and dropped the glass, immediately clutching his hands to his neck. "It burns!" he wailed, gagging. "What's in that stuff? Gasoline?"

"Close," Stearne said and chortled. "It's two-hundred proof vodka, imported from Poland!"

"You lie!"

"Let me show you." Stearne dug through his pockets and withdrew a cigarette case. He opened it, displaying a set of unfiltered cigarettes and a small lighter inside. "Hand me that glass there." Erik picked up the fallen glass as Stearne took out the lighter. "Hold it." Erik held the glass and Stearne flicked the switch near the used glass. Erik gasped when the glass flared immediately before quickly burning out. "It's enough to light on fumes alone!"

"Who would drink such awful stuff?" Erik said in amazement and put the glass back on the nightstand.

"Born losers." Stearne picked up the quarter and flicked it with his thumb. The coin missed its mark entirely, striking the floor.

"You did that on purpose!" Erik said as Stearne poured himself a serving and downed it easily. "How can you handle it?"

Stearne flashed a devilish smile. "By starting early," he said darkly. Stearne reached over on the floor and tossed Erik the quarter. Erik swiftly caught it. "I'm holding onto this." Stearne waved the lighter. "Kids shouldn't play with fire."

"Hey, I'm no kid!" Erik snapped. "I'm almost sixteen you know!"

"Then show me."

Erik flipped the coin and missed again, having it bounce off the edge and roll on the floor. He groaned when Stearne poured him another serving and handed it to him gleefully.

"You're evil," Erik complained and Stearne grinned.

"That's how the penalty game works," Stearne teased. Erik shuddered as he swallowed the contents. "Let's see how far we can go... Hopefully we can finish this bottle and nobody finds out."

"You're just trying to get me in trouble so Missus Zachary can yell at you!" Erik protested.

"Any kind of attention is good attention!" Stearne chirped.

"Evil!" Stearne laughed and Erik hiccupped, immediately growing warm and picked up the quarter off the floor. "When my turn comes next, I'm not missing!" Erik declared, handing the coin back to Stearne.

Stearne snorted and tossed the coin at Erik. It bounced off his chest and struck the nightstand, then bounced into the glass with a clink. Erik's jaw dropped and Stearne turned to Erik, poking the wing of his nose.

"We'll see," he challenged.

Erik poked Stearne back against his chest. "Evil!" he spat.

Stearne laughed again.

FORTY-THREE

After playing several rounds, Erik felt himself sweating profusely when he downed his sixth shot. He giggled when the room tilted slightly and Stearne laughed at him.

"Weakling!" Stearne teased.

"You're not drunk yet!" Erik slurred.

"But you are!"

"What are you, master of the game?"

"I have to admit, I am."

Erik hastily stood and wavered as he put his hands on Stearne's shoulders. "I pronounce you 'Shot Glass' Stearne," Erik declared, "master of whatever this game is..."

"I call it Booze Roulette," Stearne clarified and Erik fell into a fit of giggles.

"That's funny!" he crowed and staggered back against the wall. Stearne tossed the coin at Erik and it bounced off his chest. "Hey, you missed! You take a drink!"

Stearne calmly poured himself a serving and downed it with ease. "You're so cute when you're drunk," he needled.

"Hey, hey!" Erik protested. "I only like girls!"

"I know!" Stearne dug through his pocket and withdrew a single photograph. He waved at Erik to come over. "Take a gander at this!"

Erik staggered forward and plopped on the bed, then laid back, resting an arm behind his head. "Give it here," Erik grumbled and hiccupped. He snatched the photograph from Stearne as he leaned on his elbow and held his head in hand. "She's pretty," Erik murmured, staring at the picture of Genovera reaching for the camera on the lakefront beach.

"Now you're one of us," Stearne said, grinning, "because she's one of us."

"And how's that?" Erik asked.

Stearne pointed to the photo, then back at himself and Erik. "We're the same as her," he explained.

Erik furrowed his brow. "I'm not getting it."

"Just know that I'm your brother and don't you ever forget it!"

Erik glanced to Stearne who continued smiling brightly. "Will you protect me?" he asked.

Stearne nodded. "Always!"

"But we look nothing alike!" Erik protested.

"You'll understand later."

"Now you're just messing with me!" Erik turned on his side, clutching the picture to his chest. "I'm keeping this one. You can have the rest."

"Now..." Stearne snatched the photograph away and slipped it back into his pocket. "If you win the game, you can have it."

"What if I lose?"

"What do you think?"

"Hey, what happened with those other pictures you made?"

Stearne chortled and tapped the tip of his nose. "You'll get to see them if you can stand up!" he chided.

Erik pushed Stearne away and sat up, groaning. "I'm not done yet!" he spat and stood. Erik stumbled and caught himself against the wall across the room, then tossed the coin back at Stearne who caught it.

"You missed." Stearne poured a shot for Erik and held it out to him. "You know how the game works."

Erik took an unsteady step forward and slipped to his knees. He pushed Stearne's hand away and rose on shaky footing. "Is it hot in here to you?" Erik moaned.

"Just you," Stearne replied and stiffened when Erik grabbed his shirt, wiping at his drenched face. "Hey, your shirt's over there!"

"I didn't know this stuff would make you sweat so badly!" Erik complained.

"That's why folks up North drink this all the time." Stearne chuckled and reached over for Erik's shirt. "It keeps them warm." He tossed the garment at Erik and he caught it.

"What about during the summer?" Erik slipped the shirt over his head through the opening and let it drape down his back.

"I wouldn't advise going swimming after all this!"

"Give it here!" Erik snatched the glass from Stearne's hand and gulped it down. He groaned as his vision split and he saw everything in doubles. "It's way too hot in here..."

"Justin, you're so red...!"

"I think I'm going to be sick..." Dropping the glass from hand, Erik collapsed to the floor, landing on his back. "Ouch..."

"Justin!" Stearne cried and left the bed, immediately kneeling at Erik's side.

"My head hurts so much," Erik moaned.

"Can you get up?"

"I can't feel anything," Erik said weakly. "I can't move my legs."

"I'll help you up..."

Darkness came quickly.

"Shall we continue?" a voice called from afar.

Erik slowly roused, finding himself in a pale blue room with a large bay window behind a large oak desk with several colored folders stacked on the sides.

"What...?" Erik muttered, turning to face the mysterious doctor who entered the room, holding a thick medical chart under his arm. He came around the desk and set the chart nearby on the edge then sat in the leather chair behind the polished wood.

"Do you feel well?" asked the doctor.

"Not exactly..." Erik glanced down at his arms, finding them bruised and scarred with many needle tracks. He saw he had a line attached to his wrist and followed it with his eyes, noticing the intravenous drip holding a satchel of blue serum administered into his veins.

"You appear quite unhappy," said the doctor.

"I want to leave this place," Erik grumbled. "I want to return home with my family."

"What about your family?"

Erik glared at the doctor. "Why do I have to do this? Why are you asking me these stupid questions?"

"These sessions are for your benefit, you see. When you are

well enough, then you can return home."

"Where is home?" Erik spat.

"I don't know." The doctor shrugged. "You will have to tell me if you wish to return."

"Otherwise I'm a no-sponsor, right?"

The doctor paled and cleared his throat. "Tell me about that."

"No, Doctor, you tell me."

"I'm afraid I don't know."

"Fine..."

"Is there a problem you wish to discuss?"

Erik shut his eyes as he felt himself departing from his body, standing beside himself. He looked down at his cut and burned hands as the doctor kept asking questions he could barely hear, then watched him reach for the phone and dial a number. Erik clenched his burned hands when a pair of orderlies entered the office, recognizing both men at once.

"Perhaps you should postpone the inducement procedure, Mister Carlsbad," the doctor said to the blond-haired, brown-eyed orderly who checked Erik's limp wrist.

"Still beating," Carlsbad answered, "just weak."

"Can you confirm, Mister Johnston?"

The other dark-haired, blue-eyed orderly withdrew a silver pen and switched a button on its side, revealing a yellow light. He pushed back Erik's lids, peering into his eyes. "Yeah," he replied. "I mean, there ain't no rush, so why hurry now into this?" Erik crept around and looked at his bruised and bloodied body sitting in the chair unresponsive.

"Am I dead?" Erik asked.

"I'm just following orders," the doctor said flatly.

Erik tensed when sudden pain shot through the back of his neck. He staggered back, slipping to his knees and held his head in his hands when a dull ache entered, thrumming behind his eyes.

"What you want us to do?" Johnston asked, shutting off the pen and pocketed it.

"Let's suspend for now."

Erik moaned when the fuzziness in his head increased and the dull pounding gave away to ringing in his ears.

"Alright, Johnston, let's haul ass," Carlsbad grumbled and Johnston grabbed Erik by the arm. Erik fell forward, unable to keep hold of the world around him.

Erik later awakened at the painted table, hearing knocking at the front door. He grunted when pain radiated in his face and chest as he ran his hands through his hair. Looking down, Erik noticed his slacks loosened and stood, adjusting his pants. Heading for the parlor, the front door opened moments later, revealing Gina. She gasped at the sight of Erik as he pulled into a pale green dress shirt.

"What happened?" she cried.

"What are you talking about?" Erik muttered.

"You look like you got the crap beaten out of you!"

"No wonder I feel like shit," Erik cracked.

"And there's no way for me to find out either!" Gina groused and blew a distressed sigh. "Anyways, here's some spending money and a new lifeline. Don't lose it, okay?"

"What?" Gina handed Erik a small black gift bag with silver

gothic-lettered 'M' as the running pattern. Erik opened it, finding a small cellular phone, a copper money clip holding a pair of fifty-dollar bills and a small ashen figure-eight shaped stuffed plush toy with blank blue eyes. "The hell's this?"

"The Clap," Gina said dryly. Erik looked up at Gina, repulsed and she grinned. "Would you've preferred The Pox then?" she retorted. "You're crazy enough without that."

"You're nasty," Erik said, flushing slightly.

"They were out of the miniatures," Gina explained while Erik took the money and put it in his wallet. "They came in a little petri dish with yellow biohazard tape."

"You're a sick individual," Erik griped and Gina giggled. Pocketing the phone and wallet, he nodded to Gina and grabbed his coat, then walked with her downstairs to the car waiting for them in the alley.

"I have no changes in your assignment," Gina said after they entered the car. "Just continue what you're doing and you should be fine. No more fights at the bar, all right?"

"I'll try to keep my nose clean," Erik promised.

"So, Mister Smith," said the driver, "what are you going to do with the stuffy?"

"I'll put it on my desk," Erik said. "It's kinda disgusting and creepy, but cute."

The driver snorted, but said nothing.

Arriving at the offices, Erik greeted the desk clerk who appeared unsettled at his presence and headed to room 93 on the fifth floor. He took out the stuffed microbe and set it next to his computer, then dumped the bag in his waste bin. Putting away his coat, Erik started his routine of filing papers and correcting the database. At a quarter to noon, Sangita opened the door.

"What would you like?" she asked.

"Whatever you're having is fine," Erik responded and opened the lower drawer to his desk, withdrawing his ashtray.

"So fish and crisps okay with you?"

"Sure." Erik set the glass ashtray aside on the desk and Sangita gasped once he sat up.

"What happened?" she yelped.

"What do you think?" Erik asked, grinning.

Sangita hurried away and Erik turned in his seat, unlatching the window. Erik withdrew his cigarettes and lit one, tossing the pack on the desk. He leaned back in his chair when the door opened, revealing Brodie.

"Shit, Feddy," Brodie said, stunned. "You okay?"

"Never better." Erik gestured to the chair. "Take a break with me."

"Sure." Brodie shut the door and approached the chair. He withdrew his pack of cigarettes and sat across from Erik. Erik handed him his lighter and Brodie nodded as he leaned forward, lighting his cigarette. He raised an eyebrow when he noticed the stuffed microbe leaning against his computer monitor. "What's that you got there?" he asked, blowing smoke through his nose.

"The Clap," Erik responded.

"Who gave it to you?"

"My girl."

Brodie suddenly choked and coughed, clutching his chest.

He gripped the edge of the desk, heaving for breath. "Wait, what?" he rasped. "Did she say why?"

"No explanation," Erik replied. "Just left it for me on my doorstep this morning."

"How do you know it was her?"

"She's the only one I see the majority of the time."

"The *majority* of the time...?"

"I see other people too."

Brodie looked up at Erik, horrified. "You're going to The Clinic," he spat.

"What?" Erik complained. "Why?"

"She's trying to break it to you easy, man. She probably had a checkup and they called her with the results. She didn't want Health Control blowing up your line and probably told them she'll do it herself. That's her message, buddy."

"Huh, how ingenious." Erik shrugged and casually dragged on his cigarette.

"Anyone else you been with?" Brodie demanded.

"You mean lately?"

"Yes."

"Aside from the guy who likes it a little rough?"

"Shit." Brodie shook out his hand when the cigarette he held burned him. He stood, stamping out the lit cigarette on the carpet.

"Now you're going to get me in trouble," Erik protested.

"I'll take care of it," Brodie said. "Look, come with me after work, okay?"

"Sure, no problem."

Brodie picked up the damaged butt and put it in the ashtray

419

then stalked out the room. Moments later, Sangita returned with a greasy white sack.

"Got change for a fifty?" Erik asked, withdrawing his wallet.

"Big baller, aren't you?" Sangita teased, smiling. "Sorry, I don't."

"Hey, ask my buddy Mister Avers if he'll cover me. Tell him I'll pay him back tonight." Sangita clucked her tongue and wagged her finger at Erik. He grinned brightly and she left his office, shutting the door behind her.

Erik withdrew the small paper basket and put the included condiments on his meal, then picked up the plastic fork. Eating his lunch in silence, Erik relished the crisp battered cod and seasoned thinly-sliced fried potato slices. He glanced to the blue-eyed periwinkle-gray microbe staring lifelessly back and smirked.

FORTY-FOUR

After another uneventful day of filing and merging databases, Erik made annotations in his logbook.

"Saltpeter? The hell?" Erik murmured as he scribbled his notes. "Is it Niter?" Erik tapped his pencil against his teeth, mulling the information he knew about Saltpeter. "Does he mean Potassium Nitrate or Sodium Nitrate?" Erik then glanced at his other notes he kept near his computer while compiling the database. "This is getting weird, Andrews. Why do they need that along with Carbon, Phosphorus, Fluorine, Boron, Cobalt, Tin, Copper, and Iodine?"

Erik set the book back in his drawer and shut his window, then straightened his office. Grabbing his coat, his cell phone rang and Erik stepped out his office, hurrying down the corridor.

Entering the restrooms, he found an empty stall and sat on the toilet's edge once he picked up. "What is it?" Erik answered.

"What are your plans tonight?" asked Gina.

"I'm going to be out this evening," Erik replied. "Mister Avers is dragging me to the clinic. Apparently I'm quite sick."

"Oh, that's good. Then you can look up something for me there."

"Oh?"

"Ask for Doctor Swift; he handles your kinds of cases."

"You mean he's a VD specialist?" Erik spat. "What, can't they just give me some antibiotics and be on my way?"

"Please, do that for me."

"All right, fine. I'll ask for him."

"Take care."

Erik hung up the line and exited the stall. He bumped into another coworker, a bald young man with dark coal-colored skin, hazel eyes, and goatee.

"What is it?" Erik asked, raising an eyebrow as he pulled into his coat.

"Venereal Disease, huh?" the young man said. "They don't say that anymore. Hadn't said that in almost fifty years."

"What's it to you?" Erik spat. "So, I'm a little old-fashioned. Sue me."

"You're a weird guy."

"And?" Erik gave a malicious grin. "You want something from me?"

The young man narrowed his eyes. "I don't want anything to do with you."

"Of course you do!" Erik crowed. "Everyone does - ladies, gents, the whole thing. They just can't resist me." He stepped forward and the young man backed away, apprehensive. "You're following me for some reason. Now unless you don't want me for anything specific, then what are you doing listening to my conversation?"

"It's not like you were talking quietly," the young man declared and stiffened when he bumped into the nearby wall.

Erik slammed a hand over the man's head, baring his teeth as he stood over him. The coworker tried to step away and Erik put his other hand near his head, trapping the man beneath him. "You're not going anywhere," Erik sneered, "until you tell me what you want."

The young man set his jaw and thrust his knee into Erik's groin, forcing him to groan and cough, staggering back. "Lay off me, you sick piece of shit!" the man snapped. "I don't see why the hell anyone wants to fuck your infected ass!"

Erik sank to his knees, clutching his sides as he crumpled forward, moaning. The young man stalked out and the doors swung open.

Brodie entered moments later, concerned. "Hey, buddy," he called and approached Erik, standing over him. "Are you high or something?"

"No," Erik groaned.

"Then the hell you hitting up Sinclair for? Guy's straighter than a straight arrow."

"I decided to try my luck."

"Look, don't make the office hate you, okay?" Brodie held out a hand and Erik took it, getting pulled to his feet. "Though it's been legal on the books, don't mean they can make up an excuse to fire ya if you keep harassing everyone," Brodie continued. "With computers these days, they can tinker with data and make it seem like whatever they want!"

"Of course..."

"You gonna be all right, Feddy," Brodie said, walking with Erik down the corridor. Erik leaned against him, draping an arm around his shoulders. Brodie held an arm around his waist and a hand to his chest, steadying him.

"I'm sorry," Erik murmured once they approached the

elevators and Brodie pushed the button.

"You're fine," Brodie acknowledged. "Maybe you should detox and get your head clear," he went on. "You've been hitting the bottle pretty hard."

"I didn't screw up the numbers," Erik protested, "honest!"

"Yeah, the quarterlies are tomorrow. I'll stop by in the morning to run a merge check."

"Sure."

Stepping on the car once the doors opened, the elevators took them downstairs and Brodie walked with Erik outdoors to a taxi waiting on them. Brodie helped Erik inside and stepped in, shutting the door. "Downtown Clinic," he said and the driver nodded, taking off.

"Why do you put up with me?" Erik moaned. He slumped over, putting his head in Brodie's lap. Brodie stiffened and nervously ran a hand through Erik's hair. Erik sighed, shutting his eyes.

"Like I told you before," Brodie answered, "you deserve someone nice."

"You don't have to be nice."

"Would you rather I be mean to you?" Brodie chortled. "Don't ask me to do that."

"Why, are you really a monster under that sweet exterior?"

Brodie said nothing, continuing to run his hands through Erik's hair.

Later, the cab arrived at the downtown medical clinic and Erik frowned as he stepped out, noticing it was under the auspices of the County Health Control. Brodie paid the driver and took Erik by the hand, leading him up the stairs of the foreboding glass and brick building. They entered the waiting room dotted with small blue hard plastic chairs and Brodie approached the serving desk's window, tapping at the glass.

"Pardon me," Brodie called. "I've got an appointment for Ferdian Smith."

"I'm here to see Doctor Swift," Erik interjected.

"Oh?" said the check-in charge nurse. "I'll let him know." She handed him a number tag and Brodie took it.

"Let's sit over here," Brodie called, leading Erik to the waiting room's corner. Erik took a seat in the small chair and grunted when he found it difficult to get comfortable. After his legs grew numb, he got up and kicked the chair, sending it sailing several feet. It crashed into another row and Erik sat on the floor, leaning his back against the wall. "Hey, lean against me, will ya?" Brodie asked gently.

Erik snorted and scoot over, sitting between Brodie's knees. Brodie leaned forward, running his hands through Erik's hair. Erik mewed, shutting his eyes as he leaned back. "That feels nice," he murmured.

"You seem stressed out," Brodie said softly.

"I don't like hospitals," Erik muttered.

"This is just the clinic."

"It's all the same to me, the white walls, the bight lights, the antiseptic... The whole thing."

"Were you hurt in the hospital before?"

"I..."

"Ferdian?" a voice called to Erik, startled.

Erik opened his eyes, facing a thin man with long white hair and pale gray eyes behind thick square wire-framed bifocals. The man wore a white dress shirt, pale blue vest and matching slacks over oxfords, with a tarnished silver pocket watch hanging from the vest pocket. Attached to his consulting jacket was a nametag labeled 'Jonathan Swift'.

Erik scrambled to his feet, gasping raggedly for breath and clutched his chest. "Doctor Schnell–!" he cried and took a step rearward.

Suddenly Erik's world darkened when he lost his balance, striking the floor as a crumpled heap.

"Time to wake up, beautiful dreamer!" Josef's haunting voice called. "It's time to play!"

Erik's eyes snapped open and he stared up a white ceiling. He sat up slowly, seething from the soreness throughout his body and noticed a camera fixed over the bed. Examining his surroundings, he found the bed has slats on the sides with restraining leather belts hanging from the edges, and worn gray sheets over a hard green mattress. The camera above flashed a small red light as its head swept back and forth every few moments.

Josef stormed in, wearing the blue jumpsuit with the top unbuttoned and the sleeves tucked into the waist, offset by white canvas shoes on his narrow feet. He wore a simple harness holding the decorated saber and glared at Erik with burning hating eyes.

"Didn't mean to intrude," Josef sneered and withdrew the sleek pistol Erik had hidden earlier in the vent. Erik quickly scrambled to his feet and dodged the shot Josef fired, blowing away part of the tiled floor.

"Hey, Joe," Erik said nervously as he backed away and Josef advanced. "Why is there a gun in your hand?"

"To put it simply," growled Josef, "I'm here to kill you."

"I promised to help you get rid of those monsters, remember?" Josef lowered the pistol, appearing confused and Erik kept talking. "You stole that gun so we can escape, remember?" he continued. "You had me hide it in the vent so after Clayton cut down their numbers we could run, remember? I even stole a key card!"

"So the plan…"

Erik nodded fervently. "Yeah, it's coming along great! We're almost there! You just have to keep it together a little longer."

Josef smiled and Erik reached for Josef's hand. Josef ducked down, grabbing Erik by the leg and hurled him over his back. Erik cried out when flipped overhead and struck the floor, stunned.

Josef pointed the pistol at Erik, releasing a shot and Erik screamed when searing pain tore through his right shoulder. "I don't believe you," Josef snarled, narrowing his eyes as Erik clutched his blown shoulder and curled up on the floor, moaning in pain. "You're lying to me!" Josef knelt over him, pointing the smoking muzzle at Erik's forehead.

Erik pushed against Josef's chest, smearing blood. "Look at my hands!" he wailed. "Doctor Schnell burned his imprint in my hand so the key card can work! Look!" Josef grabbed Erik's bloodstained hand and peered close at it.

"You're lying!" Josef screamed and slammed Erik's hand aside. "They're just burns; you're just making it up!"

"Why would I lie?" Erik wailed and grabbed at Josef's wrist, struggling for the handgun.

"There can only be one of us!" Josef thundered. "You're nothing!"

Erik cried out when Josef kneed his groin and punched Josef in the face, then shoved him back. Josef staggered rearward and Erik clamored to his feet before sinking to his knees, clutching his profusely bleeding shoulder.

"All that hate you have for me," Erik wheezed as Josef pointed the gun at him again. "Use that and turn it against them; they're the ones truly deserving!" Josef bared his teeth. "You're innocent, Joe and they're wrong!"

"Liar!" Josef screeched.

"Don't hate me for being right," Erik yelped. "You know I'm telling the truth!"

Josef's hand shook and he backed away, heaving for breath. "Shut up!" Josef screamed and used his other hand to steady his aim then fired off several shots.

Erik howled in agony when the bullets tore into his arm, in his thigh and in his side. He struck the wall, seizing in pain when repeatedly shot until the gun clicked on empty. Erik gasped raggedly for breath and slipped to the floor, astonished and frightened at his blood splattered everywhere against the wall and floor.

Josef dropped the pistol he held and withdrew the golden saber from his harness. Erik struggled to keep awake as Josef approached.

"Are you going to kill me now?" Erik rasped as Josef pointed the blade at Erik's throat. Josef bared his teeth, his heterochromatic eyes staring blankly down at him.

"Yes," Josef snarled, drawing back.

Erik grabbed the blade with his burned right hand, grinding his teeth as the steel cut into his skin and blood ran down his wrist. "Why are you doing this, Joe?" he pleaded, struggling to hold him back.

"As you've noticed, I'm quite deadly." Josef let out a short laugh. "But apparently I enjoyed killing too much. I needed correction, they said."

"What are you doing this for?" Erik pleaded and winced when the pain in his left shoulder seared in response. "You kill me and you're stuck here."

"Liar! All lies!"

"Surely, you're right," Erik said caustically, "but then they'll eventually kill you once they get the results. You're already destined to the scrap heap because the outcome was wrong!" Josef growled and stomped on Erik's chest then wrenched the blade away.

"What about you?" Josef snapped.

"They're getting rid of me too," Erik admitted. "They're going to send someone with my face to destroy my father and I don't want that to happen."

"Maybe he was a bad man."

"No, he was a good man!" Erik cried. "He makes things to save people!" Josef stepped on Erik's shoulder and Erik grabbed his ankle with his bloodied hand. "Can't you see what they did to you?" Erik pleaded. "They're turning you into an automaton, filling your head with their ideas, their lies!" Josef grunted and pressed the blade on the side of Erik's neck. "Joe," Erik begged, "you need to get past the previous scars!"

"Prove it!" Josef hissed, shaking off his grip.

"I... I can't."

Erik shut his eyes and let go, expecting the final blow, only to tense when he heard Josef drop the saber with a clatter. Erik opened his eyes and glanced up, watching Josef walk away.

Erik groaned as he staggered to his feet and flinched when Josef returned moments later with a first aid kit. Josef gestured to the bed and Erik approached, sitting gingerly on the edge.

Erik said nothing as Josef attended to his wounds, wincing when Josef cleaned and taped his injuries. After wrapping his shoulder and his hands, Erik muttered his thanks and stood.

"Wait," Josef grumbled and Erik stiffened when Josef leaned against him, resting his head on his chest.

Unsure what else to do, Erik gave a tentative pat on the head. "What's the matter?" he murmured.

"See what they did to me," Josef moaned in an exhausted tone. "All this shit they did to me, all the hell they put me through..."

"I see it," Erik murmured. "I'm sorry..."

"All this, in the name of perfection!" Josef snorted. "All this... for nothing..."

"It doesn't have to be!"

"It's fine..." Josef pulled back, smiling faintly. "What you said was the truth." He cupped Erik's face in his hands. "The true essence of what really is, unaltered by ego."

"Sure." Erik pried off Josef's hands. "If you say so..."

Josef's eyes darkened and he increased his grip around Erik's hands. "Now if you don't mind," he snarled, "I want to get into your head and see if you're truly telling a tale!"

"No!" Erik cried and pushed him away. "Don't start with me again!"

"Stop resisting!" Josef roared and lurched after Erik.

Erik turned out of his grasp and bolted out the room then came to a dead stop when he bumped into Schnell in the corridor. Josef exited the room and immediately stood on guard.

Erik turned and threw a hard punch into Josef, corkscrewing him to the floor. Josef let out a pained wail when he struck the ground and Erik kicked his side, forcing him coughing and gasping for breath.

"Leave me alone, you maniac!" Erik screeched. He wound up for another blow and Schnell grabbed Erik by the arm.

"That's enough," Schnell snapped.

"Doctor!" Erik cried in shock and shook out of his grip.

"Your orders were changed," Schnell said plainly to Erik. "You have to come with me."

"What's going on?" Erik demanded, stepping over Josef and walked with Schnell down the corridor. "What happened to the test they wanted me to take so badly? What are they going to do now?"

"I'm unsure..."

"Please, Doctor Schnell, don't lie to me!" They approached the elevator and Schnell depressed the button. "What happened to you earlier?"

The green signal brightened and they stepped on once the doors opened. After the doors shut, Schnell turned to Erik. "That's for me to worry about," he murmured and put a hand on Erik's uninjured shoulder. "They are going to make you hungry for something that can never be quenched. You will hurt for something that can never be satisfied."

"What are you going on about?"

"Pray that the serum they are about to inject you with will fail, for living like a monster is such a sad existence."

"How much time do I have?" Erik asked timidly as Schnell withdrew his key card and placed it into a side slot.

The doctor turned the key and the orange buttons turned turquoise. Striking a button with two circles and one bar, the car lurched and slowly moved upwards.

"Not much," Schnell answered solemnly. "Until then, make the best of what you have for now... for once it's lost, you may never have it returned."

Erik blew a hard sigh, unable to say anything else in response.

FORTY-FIVE

Exiting the elevator, Erik turned around, watching the steel doors hush close with a click and heard the metal cable car continue its ascent onto the upper floors. He reached out, touching the finish, then at his face, smearing blood on the reflection of a pale redheaded teenager with tired violet eyes.

"Oh, you're here," Suber's voice called to Erik. "Let me finish my lunch and I'll be with you."

Erik turned about face, staring down a lone corridor adorned with colorless plate lights buzzing softly, washing the stark bland walls with a harsh brightness.

"*Oye, amigo!*" Hernando called as he stepped into the corridor and approached. Erik blew a sigh of relief when he saw no flanking guard. Hernando waved at Erik to follow him. "*Vámonos!*"

Erik grunted and followed Hernando when he entered through a side door and went through another corridor before coming into a sparsely decorated dining area.

"This looks nice," Erik noted, checking his surroundings and grew slightly ill at ease once he took a seat in a comfortable-appearing cushioned folding chair.

"Well, it's the employee cafeteria," Hernando explained as he stood across from Erik on table's other side.

Erik folded his arms across his chest and stared directly at Hernando. "I'm sick of this," he grumbled.

"I know I can't promise much, however..."

"Please," spat Erik bitterly. "Look, let's get to the heart of the matter: is it true with what they're going to do to me?"

Hernando snorted. "Then there's nothing else for me to say, is there?" he commented dryly, rolling his eyes.

"So you're just going to *let* them go through with it?" Erik roared. "I thought you gave a damn!" He slammed his fist on the table.

"My hands are tied, Erik!" Hernando complained.

"Some of you say you're going to help me and it never comes!" Erik ranted, standing angrily. "I swear; you must enjoy this sick experimentation!"

"I don't, Erik!" Hernando exploded. "I'm not like that and never will be after what those scheming sons of bitches had done to me as a means of leverage!" He banged his fist into the table and Erik stepped back in shock, watching the doctor's eyes watering at the corners as he shook in rage. "I hate them as much as you do, Erik! I just have to play my roles so they don't punish me as harshly..."

"I didn't mean...!"

"Don't you understand?" Erik shook his head, afraid to answer. "We're running on *borrowed time* here!"

"And you think I'm not?"

"Already I'm at a high risk of Termination by talking to you this frankly right now!"

"So, don't talk to me!"

Erik let out a yelp as Hernando reached across the table and grabbed at his shirt collar.

"Erik!" Hernando bellowed, shaking him. "Wake up!"

Erik winced and shied away, shrinking back in fear. "What are they trying to get from me?" Erik wailed. "I can't remember, I won't remember - Father Greenfield told me not to!"

Hernando let Erik go and he fell back into his chair. Hernando gripped the table's edges, breathing unevenly. "Erik," he said in a controlled tone, "tell me. Tell me and I'll save you."

"Bullshit," Erik retorted. "I'll keep the information to myself and die with it."

"That's selfish of you. They'll kill him."

"Even if I told you, they'll *still* kill him!"

Hernando clenched his teeth as his face reddened. "Erik," he strained through gritted teeth, "you're making a grave mistake."

"Sue me," Erik spat.

Hernando let out a strangled sound and Erik cried out in fright as Hernando grabbed at him again. Erik immediately leaned back, forcing Hernando's hands gripping at nothing but air.

"Damn it, Erik!" Hernando thundered and socked Erik in the chest with a hard left hook, throwing him to the floor. Erik grunted when he struck the chair and slumped on the floor on his side.

Erik staggered onto his knees, heaving for breath as his rage took over. "You want me dead?" he shouted, glaring up at Hernando. "Here, here's my neck!" Erik pointed at his throat. "Have at it, Mister! You want my body too? Take it! It's yours!"

"You don't understand at all!" Hernando snapped. "Your

old man screwed over the Corporation - that costly mistake he caused is punishable by death!"

"Why can't you save him?" Erik wailed and clenched his hands at his sides as he sat back on his knees. "He's doing this to stop them from killing more people!"

Hernando blew a heavy sigh. "The process already started," he muttered. "There's nothing I can do."

"Is there a way you can stop it?" Erik pleaded. "Is there something you can do stop his transfer to Centerville?"

Hernando raised an eyebrow. "Centerville?" he murmured.

"Schnell told me it's the first stop toward Termination..."

"Then maybe he has a chance. It's known as one of the best mental health institutions around."

"Are they going to kill him there?"

"If one dies there, it's nobody's fault but the induced illness."

"Oh my goodness," Erik moaned, gripping his hair in despair. "What kind of sick mess is this?" He hunched forward on the floor, fighting tears.

"It's how everything works here, like a well-oiled machine. We are given orders and we execute them. Those who disobey are Terminated, or driven crazy if they're too valuable to be destroyed." Hernando sighed, placing a hand on Erik's shoulder and Erik winced from the pain generated by the bruise-like burn. "The Corporation creates products for The Agency, which in turn makes them available for use by The Industry, which is controlled by The Establishment."

"Can you be more vague?" Erik grumbled and pushed Hernando away.

"What's the matter?" Hernando murmured when Erik

gripped his shoulder, seething once the pain became bothersome.

"That sore I have... I think it's getting worse."

"How long have you had it?"

"A few months or so now, I think."

"Let me see." Erik grunted in pain when he pulled out of his shirt, letting it gather at his wrists. Hernando stepped behind him, inspecting closely. "That's bad," he murmured.

"Erik?" Suber's voice called.

Erik put his shirt back on once Suber entered the cafeteria and rose upright as Suber motioned Erik to follow him. "I'll see you later?" Erik said to Hernando. Hernando waved Erik away and Erik blew a sigh then approached Suber's side. "How was lunch?" he muttered.

"Good," Suber replied. "Yours?"

"I've been too sick to eat."

"That's too bad."

Suber opened the door and let Erik step out first, then walked ahead of him back to his office. Erik followed several paces behind, looking down at the floor. Suber withdrew a cloth napkin from his pocket and wiped his hands.

"What did you have for lunch?" Erik murmured.

"Tuna salad sandwich."

"I wish they'd serve that. They're keen on serving raw meat."

"Oh, you prefer sushi then?" Suber chuckled. "Maybe I could sneak you some sometime?"

Once they approached Suber's office, the surgeon pushed the door open and stepped aside to let Erik entry. Erik entered a modestly furnished office, similar in layout to Schnell's. Suber pocketed the napkin he held, blowing a short sigh.

"What...?" Before Erik could finish his question, Suber shut the door and placed a hand on Erik's shoulder. Erik winced in pain and Suber let go.

"Listen," Suber said sternly, "after you leave my office, from this point on, you will be heavily medicated or sedated... maybe both, since the labs found what serums work best for you."

"What do they take me for," Erik yelled and pushed Suber away, "something to just be thrown away? I have a soul the last time I've checked!"

"Number Three, what other methods do you want?" Suber grumbled irritably. "I'm just telling you what to expect!"

"I'm sick of this!" Erik complained.

Suber scoffed. "And you think I'm not?" He approached his desk cluttered with papers and sat on the edge.

Erik sighed and sat across from Suber in the nearby stuffed plush chair. "I already have a plan," he murmured. "I just need to execute it at the right time."

"Time isn't what you have a lot of."

"I know."

Suber wrung his thin hands as a painful expression appeared on his face. He muttered incomprehensibly under his breath, shaking his head and looked down at the floor.

"What?" Erik asked, leaning forward to hear him better. The doctor shoved him back into his seat and Erik gasped when he noticed bruises on Suber's hand. Grabbing for it, Erik examined closely, turning the palm downward. "Why?" he demanded, looking at the bruised nail beds in ugly black, blue, and dark green with crusted dark reddish-black underneath. On some of

Suber's swollen fingers, no nails existed at all.

"I..."

"You mean they ripped out your nails as punishment?" Erik cried and Suber nodded in response, withdrawing his hand. "First they shoot you, then they do this!" Erik snapped. "That's sick, hurting you like that over some senseless directive!"

"It's not like it's broken and deformed," Suber muttered. "I'm a surgeon. Without my hands, I'm nothing."

"Those barbarians!" Erik snarled. "I'm putting an end to their madness!"

"How?" Suber spat. "You're just hacking at branches - you can't affect anything!"

"I *will* stop them! They're hurting people, they're hurting my friends, my family, and I'm not standing for it anymore!"

"There's not a damn thing you can do!"

"They have a weak point somewhere!" Erik declared. "I'll find it and destroy it! I don't care how long it takes to find the heart of the monster; I've had enough of their abuse!"

"That's a pretty heavy project," Suber murmured. "If you think you can put an end to their madness, by all means, try."

"Will you help me?" Erik asked.

Suber nodded. "I'll try as much as I can, but I can't promise a lot."

"I understand."

Moments later, loud rapping on the door startled Suber. Erik stiffened in his seat when the knock turned to banging. Erik turned in his seat, facing Hayden and another technician who stomped in, followed by a well-armed guard, bearing a pistol with a rifle laced across his back at ready given a moment's notice.

"What are you doing barging in here like that?" Suber demanded.

"We had a call that a G-seven-forty-five project was in here, making noise," retorted the technician. "We're under Code Brown and had to make a sweep."

Hayden grabbed at the guard's sleeve and gestured wildly. "He's one of the defectors in violation of Agency Policy," Hayden declared, pointing to Suber.

"That's a flat out lie, Hayden!" Suber shouted, striking the desk with the palm of his hand.

"We take all complaints seriously," the guard snapped and pulled out his two-way radio.

Erik gripped the arms of his chair, growing tense while the guard called in several codes over his radio. The other technician peered closely at Erik, sneering. "Did it threaten you or try to hurt you?" demanded the technician.

"You mean, did *he* yank out my nails with needle-nosed pliers," Suber retorted, "and gave my hands a good whack with a four-pound sledgehammer?" He snorted and sat up straighter in his seat. "No, Number Three here did no such thing, but by the fantastic courtesy of your lousy boss, it seems to be why!"

The guard pointed his pistol at Suber and the doctor glared back, completely unfazed. "Check this, wise guy," the guard snarled, poking Suber's bulge of taped gauze padding on his sore shoulder. Suber winced in pain from the severe injury. "Shut your face or I'll do it for you!"

"You make me ill," Suber seethed, pushing the gun out of his face with the side of his hand.

Another guard in similar attire, with the exception of two pistols holstered over his back, approached the door. "So which one's trying to defect?" he asked.

Hayden pointed to Suber and the doctor rose upright, placing his hands on the desk's edge.

"Touch me and I'll order Number Three to attack," Suber snarled. "You know he will."

The gunman struck Suber across the face with his pistol before the doctor had a chance to react, sending him over his desk and spiraling out onto the floor. Suber laughed and the rifleman stormed to Erik, yanking him out of his seat.

"What's so damn funny?" the technician demanded as the guard armed with two pistols dragged Erik to the door.

"Don't lie to us, Suber!" Hayden snapped.

"You're going to be sorry!" Suber crowed. "He's like a mad dog - he's going to latch on and never let you go; he's going to destroy you and burn this place to the ground!"

"You're talking shit!" Hayden shrilled. "Shut his face!"

The rifleman over Suber sheathed his pistol and unlaced his shotgun from across his back then struck Suber with the stock, forcing him silent. The technician stepped out of the office with the pistol-toting guard pulling Erik along.

"Prevail at any cost, Number Three," Suber called weakly as they continued down the corridor. "Show them you're not a dead, incompetent product!"

"I swear...!" Hayden yelled.

They approached a room in the corridor with a solid iron-cast door marked 'Caution: Hazardous Storage' stamped in green. The guard tightened his grip, holding Erik down and

Erik moaned when his head flashed in pain.

Erik yanked against the man's hold, pulling his arm. "Let me go!" he growled. "I'm going to be sick."

"Tough shit," snapped the guard and bat Erik upside his head. "Puke for all I care. You're dying anyway."

The technician pulled out a key card and swiped it in the reader, then followed by pressing his left hand into the palm reader then his right thumb in the verifier. The door slowly groaned open and the guard tossed Erik into the small bare room, forcing him tumbling head over heels.

Erik struck the wall and sat up, watching the gunman point both pistols at him as the door slid close. Erik immediately stood when static enveloped the room, followed by a cough over the intercommunications system.

"Number Three," a familiar voice said into the room, "this is Reinswitzer."

"I want out of here!" Erik screamed.

"You'll have to be detained in here for a bit until we get the various tests straightened out."

"You'll regret it!"

"It'll be over quickly, promise."

After a series of tones, silence followed and Erik sat on the floor, drawing his knees to his chest while he waited. The pain increased behind his eyes and he moaned, holding his head in his hands. The voices he hated to hear stirred again, ringing in his ears.

If you stopped now, you'll no longer survive...
Punish them, destroy them, hate them...
Forever and ever...

Until we meet again...

With everything you have...

Wipe them out...

Keep piling on the pain and suffering...

Make them suffer...

Until there's nothing left...

Erik cried out as the raging agony consumed him, taking out his world.

FORTY-SIX

Rousing, Erik found himself in the white room again, tied to the chair with the continuous intravenous drip releasing clear medication into him. Across from him sat the doctor at the desk. Nearby, the tape machine whirred softly and the overhead clock ticked loudly behind him. Erik noticed instead of a pad of paper and a set of cassettes stacked nearby, he had a glass of water.

"Are you willing to cooperate?" the doctor asked dully. "We gave you freedoms and you routinely disobey."

"What freedoms?" Erik snapped. "Constant monitoring isn't a freedom."

"We have to watch you. You are a risk... a danger to yourself and others!"

"Who says?"

"So tell me," the doctor muttered, bypassing Erik's question. "Are you ready to speak about Justin Schumacher?"

"I don't know who he is."

"You said he's the boy who looks like you."

"Forget it."

"What about Kevin Zachary?"

"Don't know him either."

"Why would we be sitting here discussing it if you didn't mention it?"

"What about Ferdian?" Erik shot back. "Why do people keep addressing me by that name?"

The doctor puffed an annoyed sigh and rolled his eyes. "Obviously he's of great importance to you," he said in annoyance.

"Rather, he's important to *you*," Erik retorted.

"How so?"

"You tell me."

The doctor blew an exasperated sigh and laid out his hands on the desk. "I only want you well so that you can leave and return home. Obviously this Justin Schumacher gives you a terrible fright; otherwise you wouldn't be having these dreams."

"I don't remember exactly," Erik grumbled. "Besides, what difference does it make what I tell you? You're killing me anyway."

The doctor scoffed. "Where did you get such a silly idea?"

"I don't remember my dreams," Erik complained. "I don't trust my memories, because it's like mine yet not mine, and I'm living and experiencing what he feels and I don't feel, and I see someone who looks like my father but isn't my father and everyone's reacting to me in one way and another way altogether."

"Why do you think it's like this?"

"I don't know why everything is so different now than then…"

"How did you come to this conclusion?" Erik shook his head and ground his teeth in frustration. "I need you to answer me," the doctor pressed.

"I'm tired and I've got a headache," Erik muttered. "So just dope me up and let me pass out. Everyone can agree to that, can't they?"

The doctor snorted. "Is that what you really want?"

"Sure."

"But don't you *want* to get well?"

"It doesn't matter what I say anymore."

"Please, tell me," the doctor pleaded. "Just tell me and we can start your recovery process."

Erik blew a heavy sigh. "It's too hazy to figure," he murmured.

"Please..."

"I don't remember!" Erik screamed, growing irate.

"You *do* remember!" the doctor snapped, bristling.

"Why make me go through this?" Erik demanded. "I can't tell you what you want! I don't even know what you want!"

"I told you..." Erik shut his eyes, tuning him out as he counted loudly. "Don't withdraw now! Don't withdraw..."

Erik cried out when slapped across the face. He glared back at the doctor who rubbed at his palm, wincing in pain.

"Stop retreating when it gets too painful," the doctor chastised. "You need to face it and deal with it, or you'll never get any better!"

"There isn't much to tell!" Erik protested. "So bank on that!"

"Please, tell me as much as you can..."

Erik blew a heavy sigh. "I'm dying anyway, right?" He let out a weak laugh. "Then what does it matter?"

"You need to relax," said the doctor. "The reason for the nightmares and the disjointed memories is because you're too tense."

"You would be too in an awful place like that."

"Let's start with an exercise to get you to relax. How's that sound?"

Erik snorted. "Whatever," he grumbled.

"Close your eyes and take a deep breath." Erik did as told, letting out a heavy sigh. "Good, now do that again, just like that, just breathe in and let it out, slowly, easy." Erik took in another deep breath and let it out slowly. "Just let your feet relax and your legs relax," the doctor said in a soothing voice. "Feel your hips relaxing and your waist relaxing. Feel your chest relaxing and your arms relaxing. Your shoulders relaxing and your neck and head relaxing. Feel your body relaxing all over."

Erik moaned when he started losing feeling in his body. "I don't like this," he mewed. "I can't feel anything…"

"It's okay," the doctor said softly. "You're relaxing. You're feeling yourself free yourself of stress and worry. A heavy relaxed feeling is coming over you as I speak. As I continue to talk, that heavy relaxed feeling will get stronger and stronger, until it carries you into a deep peaceful state."

"No," Erik moaned. "No, please…"

"Every word that I utter is putting you faster and deeper, faster and deeper, into a deep peaceful state. Sinking down, shutting down, further you go. Sinking and sinking into the darkness, shutting you down, down, down completely."

Erik grew panicked when the weightlessness of his body increased and he found it further difficult to open his eyes. He strained to hear as the doctor lowered his voice. "Don't make me do this," Erik whimpered. "Please…"

"The deeper you go, the deeper you are able to go and the deeper you go, the deeper you want to go and the more enjoyable the experience becomes," said the doctor in a very soft voice. "Now you are resting comfortably in a deep peaceful state, going deeper and faster and deeper and faster all the time, until I bring you back. You will only accept those suggestions which are for you benefit and that you are willing to accept."

"I can't...!"

"As a result of these suggestions, you will feel as if you are headed for a certain and predetermined success," the doctor continued. "You will be able to act, think, and feel as if it were impossible to fail. You will look back, back, back, deep down and see what it is that you want to remember."

"I'm not allowed to..."

"That object causes you so much sadness and pain, you must let it go. Bring it out. Explore these deeper dimensions of experience, discover these changes taking place in your life, and tell me. You can trust me; I will help you."

Erik grew silent and the doctor waited patiently. The recorder hissed softly as it wound through the tape and the clock continued ticking behind Erik.

"*If I tell him what I remember, I'll die,*" Erik mused. "*But if I don't remember what it is I need to remember, then Father Greenfield will die...*" Tears suddenly streamed down Erik's face.

"Why do you cry?" the doctor asked, growing concerned. "Did you remember something?"

"No matter what I do," Erik muttered, "I'm still dying."

"We all die at the end," assured the doctor. "Now, I'm going to count from one to five and at the count of five, you will tell me what you can recall."

"I can't tell you," Erik cautioned. "I'll die if I tell you."

"One. The memory you're suppressing is nothing to be feared."

"No."

"Two. By telling me, you will release the fear that surrounds that memory."

"No."

"Three. Once you tell me, you will no longer be hindered by guilt of that memory."

"No."

"Four. You will feel better overall once you tell me the memory."

"No."

"Five. You will tell me what you recall."

Erik struggled with his words as he fought for control against the compulsion to speak. "I... It's not a lot, but... So... here's what I can remember..."

Erik woke up thrashing and screaming. He swung at the first person who approached, knocking them down.

"Hold him down!" a voice shouted.

"You're not killing me here!" Erik roared and sat up. He looked up and around, finding himself in a white room surrounded by machines. Feeling fiery pain shooting through his arm, Erik yanked out the intravenous stuck in his skin and punched another orderly who came in, throwing him against the other who struggled to his feet. "I will destroy you all!"

A security officer rushed into the room moments later and Erik held up his hands in guard.

"Shoot him!" the orderly thundered and Erik dropped low for a tackle, rushing the guard before he unsheathed his gun and barreled him out into the hall.

"Feddy!" Brodie's voice wailed. "Calm down!"

Erik threw a hard punch into the officer's face and the two orderlies jumped on his back, wrestling him down.

"Let me go!" Erik screeched and shook them off.

"Ferdian," a familiar voice called as Erik kicked off the orderly on his right and hurled the other into him, sending them crashing to the floor. He stood and stomped on the officer before he could get up. "Erik!"

Erik whirled around, facing the elderly doctor standing in the middle of the corridor. Erik yelped once tackled and taken down to the floor. He screamed when more orderlies arrested his arms and legs, trying to pin him as he fought to get free.

"Let him go!" the doctor called. "Let him go!"

"He's a danger to everyone on this floor!" the security officer hollered and withdrew his gun.

"Give him six," one of the orderlies shouted. "No, eight!"

"Don't inject him with anything!" the doctor shouted. "That's an order!" Erik let out a wrenching scream when jabbed in the arm and hip with needles. He worked a hand free, socked one orderly in the face and grabbed another by the ear, ripping his skin. "Let him go!"

Erik screamed louder when stabbed in the chest and the fiery serum pumped into his body. Released from their hold, he scrambled and backed away, heaving for breath. Looking around, the walls began moving and melting and Erik shuddered when surrounded by large men in white, armed with guns and needles.

"Leave me alone!" Erik wailed. "Don't touch me!" He took off for the corridor and Brodie raced after him.

"Feddy, wait!" Brodie called after him. Picking up his speed, he jumped on Erik, hurling himself against the young man and they tumbled to the floor together.

"Let me go!" Erik screeched.

"I'm not letting you go!" Brodie growled and grabbed Erik by the arm, flipping him over onto his back. Erik wrestled with Brodie as the older man wrapped his arm around his throat.

"Let go!" Erik rasped and shouldered Brodie's chin then hurled him overhead, sending him crashing into the window above him. Brodie grunted as he struck the floor and Erik scrambled to his feet.

As he advanced, he halted when a shot rang out in the hall, sending fiery pain through his thigh. Erik stumbled and screamed in agony. Whirling around, Erik faced an officer on bended knee, holding her service pistol with both hands.

"Don't make me kill you!" she shouted.

"You're dead!" Erik bellowed and charged. The officer fired again before Erik threw a punch, hitting his side. Erik staggered back, stunned and held a hand to his guts as blood released through his fingers.

Brodie shook off his stun and sat up on his knees. He looked up in shock when Erik stumbled and his blood dripped on the floor.

"No, don't kill him!" Brodie cried and clambered to his feet. He ran to Erik and yanked the young man back by the sleeve, whirling him around. Erik threw a weak punch and

Brodie ducked, returning with a hard sock into the young man's chest with his left. Erik coughed and held up his arm, blocking the next body blow then ducked down, shouldering into Brodie and launched him on the ground.

Brodie held Erik back by the throat with his free hand as Erik straddled him and grasped the older man by his face, grinding his thumb into his eye. Brodie screamed and tightened his grip, digging his nails into Erik's neck.

Erik stiffened when fired in the back and loosened his grip. His breath thinned and he looked up from his place on the floor over Brodie, spotting the woman he always saw in old photographs coming across the lot holding her overcoat close to her body against the cold winds.

Erik slackened his grip when his limbs grew heavy, eventually letting go. Brodie pushed him aside and Erik crumpled against the wall, gasping hard for breath.

The doctor raced over, followed by the retinue of orderlies and three more guardsmen. The other warden trained her gun on Erik, waiting for sudden movements.

"Damn it," the doctor hissed as he approached and knelt at Erik's side.

"The hell?" one of the orderlies snapped. "What a monster!"

"He ripped out Narasu's ear," another orderly complained. "He'll need stitches!"

"Get out of here, everyone!" the doctor shouted. "Out!"

"But, he's dangerous and psychotic!" the officer argued as she sheathed her pistol. "I'm not going anywhere until his ass is doped up and hogtied in solitary!"

"I can handle this, now do as I say!"

"I'm not going anywhere."

Brodie rose to his feet and wiped at his face with his sleeve. "Thanks, but you did enough," he said to the officer. "Please leave... I trust Doc and he says he can handle him."

"I'm close," the guard grumbled. She backed away and the group left the corridor.

Brodie grabbed a nearby chair, slumping into it. "What's wrong with him?" he asked moments later as the doctor withdrew a silver pen and pressed a switch on its side, revealing a blue light.

"Please, leave me be," the doctor muttered, shining the light into Erik's blank eyes.

"Do you need any help?"

"Get yourself fixed up, please?"

"It's not that bad. He didn't put out my eye if that's what you're worried about - it's medical-grade acrylic."

"Then don't bother yourself."

"Why he react like that?" Brodie murmured. "I know he's a vet and all, but I didn't know he was that disturbed..."

"Can you hear me?" the doctor called to Erik. "Wake up..." He pat at Erik's cheek and Erik's eyes focused.

"Doctor!" Erik yelped and grabbed the doctor's collar with his bloodied hands. "Don't let them," he croaked.

"Don't let them do what?"

"Please..."

Tears streamed down Erik's face and he buried his head into the man's shoulder, sobbing.

"It's all right," the doctor murmured, gently petting Erik's head. "I won't let them."

Brodie left his chair and stood over the two, hands in his pockets. "What's wrong with him?" he asked.

Erik suddenly seized then fell slackened as his eyes rolled to the back of his head.

FORTY-SEVEN

Erik roused from deep sleep and groaned when his head throbbed in great pain. When he opened his eyes, he found himself on the parlor couch in the house he vaguely remembered, next to a much younger John Greenfield who reclined back with a strong drink.

"I was beginning to worry about you," John Greenfield said. "You were out for a really long time."

"How did I get back?" Erik asked, sitting up. He winced when the room spun around him.

"I sent some people to look for you..."

"Oh no!" Erik clutched his head as the dizziness worsened.

"And to think Genovera found you passed out drunk!"

"Please don't get upset...!" Erik wailed and slumped back into the couch.

"I'm not... that hangover you have is punishment enough." John Greenfield sighed heavily. "Please don't scare me like that again, Ace."

"I'm so sorry!" Erik moaned.

John Greenfield ran a hand through Erik's hair. "It's okay. You're here with me and you're safe."

"Dad," Erik said, leaning against him, "are those guys you work for really that bad?"

John Greenfield gulped down the liquor before answering. "You shouldn't rely on others to help you determine what's good and what's bad," he murmured. "In no time at all, you'll just simply be under someone else's control."

"I'm not sure I follow…"

"Yes, they're really stressful to work with, but I wouldn't call them bad."

"But you've been drinking more since you started working for them…"

"That's true but…"

"Wouldn't it affect your work?"

"Not too much. I hold off until evening and get cleaned up by morning." John Greenfield tousled Erik's hair and pushed against him gently, sitting him up. Erik watched John Greenfield peel off the couch and head for the mini bar.

"What are you working on that has you this stressed?" Erik asked softly.

"I'm working on a way to save Kevin," John Greenfield replied as he prepared another drink.

"Is that the sole reason…?"

"Not because Smiley asked me to," John Greenfield muttered.

"Then why?"

"I care about him too." John Greenfield put away the bottle. "It's as simple as that." Turning to Erik, he pointed at him, smiling crookedly. "Promise me one thing, Son."

"What is it?" Erik rose to his feet as John Greenfield staggered then hurried over, grabbing his father's arm to keep him steady.

The front door opened moments later and Erik's mother entered. "Gerald!" she cried, dropping her belongings. "Are you okay?"

"Sis, I'm just fine," slurred John Greenfield. He placed a heavy hand on Erik's shoulder. "Everything's just fine, aren't they, Son?"

"I..." Erik pulled away, flushing darkly. "I was just...!" He clenched his teeth as his mother entered the room and snatched the glass away from John Greenfield's hand.

"Gerald, you've had enough," she reprimanded. "You can barely stand up!"

"Whatever, Shana," John Greenfield grumbled and stomped away upstairs.

"What am I going to do with you?" Shana muttered, placing the glass aside.

Erik stared at Shana as she retrieved her bags and headed into the kitchen. He bit his fist as he stood in the doorway, trying to figure out who exactly she was.

"He's so cold to her and she's so resigned," Erik mused. *"They're not close like husband and wife should be, I think..."*

Shana looked up and gestured to the refrigerator. "Do you want a sandwich or anything, Justin?" she asked.

"I'm okay, Mom," Erik answered. Plopping into a chair, Shana sighed heavily and switched on the radio. Entering the kitchen, Erik took a seat across from her at the low table. "Mom," he began, "why are you and Dad so distant?"

"Because I remind him too much of his sister," Shana replied wryly. Hearing a bang, Shana looked up, startled. After another, she swiftly immediately stood. "Gerald?" she called and raced out the kitchen.

Erik left his seat and followed her, watching John Greenfield storming outdoors. Shana was at his heels, yelling after him as he entered the car in the driveway and she banged the roof with her fist.

The telephone rang, jarring Erik and he hurried to fetch it. "You got Schumacher," Erik greeted. "Name, number, message?"

"You don't have much time left, Gerald," said a mysterious voice over the line.

"Who is this?" Erik demanded.

"They're within your range. What is your answer?"

"What do you mean, 'your range'? What answer are you looking for?"

"We'd love to talk it over at leisure, but there are more pressing matters at hand..."

"What are you talking about?"

"We know you have access to restricted data in regards to the CENTRA Program. We also know you received orders from Schnell whose grudge against the Corporation knows no end. We know he is hiding somewhere nearby and without a doubt be coming for you. So we will come after you first."

"What do you mean by all this?" Erik shouted. "Who are you?"

"You must make a decision."

"I'm sorry, you have the wrong number," Erik said hastily and slammed the receiver into the cradle.

Shana later stormed back indoors, her face pale and wet with tears. John Greenfield came after her, face red in rage.

"I still won't have anything to do with him," John Greenfield thundered. "There's nothing we can do with the mess he made!"

"There might be something!" Shana protested.

"I knew nothing good was going to come out of it," John Greenfield growled, heading for the mini bar. "As soon as I looked at him..."

"Gerald!" Shana marched up to him and snatched the glass out of his hand. "I'm worried because I know better that you won't leave it alone, no matter what happens!"

"What are you talking about?" Erik asked.

"It's nothing to worry about," Shana said and left for the kitchen, pouring out the contents of the highball glass.

"It's too late!" Erik called after her. "I'm already involved!" He pointed to the phone with his thumb. "Someone left a message..."

"What kind?" John Greenfield demanded. Erik repeated what he heard and John Greenfield dropped his flask of whiskey, shattering the bottle on the carpet. "Surely they haven't...!" John Greenfield glanced at his wristwatch. "Justin, it's getting too dangerous for you to stay here."

"But...!"

John Greenfield headed for the front door and paused when a uniformed officer entered, pointing a pistol at his chest.

"*This isn't good!*" Erik thought as the officer motioned the pistol to the couch. "*Those look like the guys who had that roadblock...*"

"Forget it," John Greenfield snarled. "I don't take orders from you!"

"Full of piss and vinegar, eh?" the officer grumbled and

whacked the piece against John Greenfield's face, whipping back his head. He staggered back, holding his busted lip. "We've got checkmate in this battle, so hear me out, Schumacher..."

Hearing a scream, John Greenfield turned toward the kitchen where two more officers entered, with one holding Shana hostage and the other jamming a sleek black semi-automatic pistol against her head.

"What's this have got to do with my family?" John Greenfield yelled. "Whatever you're planning, I don't agree with it!"

"You've got no choice, Schumacher!" snapped the officer across from John Greenfield. "Either you work for us or we come after you and yours!"

"No dice!"

"I'll tell you one last time - what's it gonna be?"

"Justin, get outta here!" John Greenfield commanded. "Save yourself!"

"Wrong answer!"

Erik nearly fainted when the officer fired and Shana slumped forward, her blood and brains splattered on the walls and carpet.

"Shana!" John Greenfield screamed and the officer turned on him, bringing him down with a hard punch to the face.

"Be careful with what you say," snarled the officer, pulling back the safety and pointed the loaded pistol at Erik. "You're dangerously close to losing the next one."

"Dad!" Erik cried. "This is serious - just give them what they want!"

"No!" John Greenfield cried. "I'll always protect what's

important... You're important, Kevin's important..."

"Then be quiet," snarled the officer, "and watch closely as I break you..."

"I won't let you hurt him!" John Greenfield screeched. "I will destroy you, even if it costs me my life!"

"Then this next bullet is for you." The officer trained his gun at Greenfield. "Goodbye."

Erik rushed the officer and tackled the man, bringing him down to the floor. The officer rolled with the fall and fired at Erik, shooting his arm and shoulder. Erik grabbed the man's arm, wrestling for the pistol's control.

John Greenfield viciously attacked the other two officers, socking one across the face and kicked the other in the guts to the ground.

Erik cried out when struck across the face with the officer's free hand then growled when pushed against his face. Erik bent over and bit the officer's wrist, forcing him dropping the gun.

Picking up the weapon, Erik hurled a punch into the officer's face, dazing the man.

"Justin, go!" John Greenfield ordered while stomping on the fallen guard.

Erik shoved back the second officer grabbing at John Greenfield from behind and pointed the pistol at them. "Back off!" he shrieked, "or so help me, I'll blow you away!"

"You don't know how to use that thing, kid," he snapped.

"Any dummy can use a gun!" Erik pulled back the hammer and winced as he fired, with the force of the kick throwing him rearwards. The officer behind Greenfield staggered away and held his profusely bleeding shoulder.

"Damn it, you shit!" he howled and Erik broke into a run, racing outside as the other two officers chased after him.

Erik tripped over his steps and turned out of a grab by the officers. A shot rang out and one of the officers tumbled down, grabbing his ankle as he cursed in pain. The secondary officer turned to his partner and Erik glanced over his shoulder, spotting John Greenfield standing in his front yard, pistol in hand.

"Please draw what strength you have left...!" Erik prayed, running away. *"I don't want you to die!"*

Erik came to a halt as several people ran away in his direction, clearly frightened. He immediately tucked the stolen gun into his waistband and pulled out his T-shirt, hiding it.

"What's going on here?" Erik called.

"Get out of here, kid!" a man yelled, hustling down the street. "You're going to get killed!"

"What?" Erik ducked as an explosion rocked the street and the force threw him back, spraying him with glass and metal debris. Citizens in the area screamed in shock, terror and pain.

"The bus exploded!" someone cried.

"Do you think it's terrorists?" another called.

"Somebody call for Medical Assistance!"

The officers approached Erik, panting hard for breath. The one who held his bleeding shoulder stood over Erik while the other with the injured ankle stood several paces away, looking ahead with eyes wide in fear.

"Fall back!" he called. "Zeya's on the scene!"

"Shit!" the officer snapped and they took off in the opposite direction.

Erik struggled to stand, seething as his back and legs seared in pain from numerous cuts.

"Justin!" John Greenfield called from afar. "Are you all right? Hang on!"

Harried footsteps neared Erik and he looked up at John Greenfield kneeling toward him, bloodied and bruised.

"Dad," Erik called weakly, "are you okay?" He grasped John Greenfield's arm, holding firmly as the man pulled him to his feet.

"I'm fine," John Greenfield answered and ran a hand through Erik's hair. "Let's get you out of here."

"This is so crazy..."

"I'm just glad you're not seriously hurt!"

Erik brushed off the gravel and bits of metal and glass on his legs. He tensed when calm footsteps approached and looked up, spotting a young man in a navy double-breasted long overcoat and black jumpsuit exit through the smoke and flames from the downed bus.

Erik swallowed hard, noticing the young man had Kevin's appearance in addition to curly hair and blue eyes, with the exception of pale skin and blond hair instead of tanned skin and dark hair.

"So, are you really just that lucky," the young man asked once he approached, "or just completely stupid?"

"What?" Erik spat. "Who are you?"

"Are you speaking to us?" John Greenfield demanded.

"The name's Zeya," the young man replied. "And yes, I'm speaking to you."

"What do you want?" Erik snapped, standing before John Greenfield. "If you came here for my dad..."

"I came to warn you," Zeya pulled back his coat, showing off a golden pistol strapped to his thigh. "That you're on the verge of death."

"In reference to what?" John Greenfield snarled. "I'm not killing again!"

Erik gave his father the black pistol he had. "Dad, take this," he said and John Greenfield nodded, taking the weapon.

"Go before you make me do something I really don't want to," John Greenfield spat, pointing his handgun at Zeya.

"Not very bright, are you?" snapped Zeya and he unleashed the golden pistol from his holster.

John Greenfield withdrew his own small silver and blue automatic, directing it in Zeya's direction. "I've got two to your one, you jerk," he snapped. "Now leave my son out of this, or you're seriously going to hurt."

"I don't need to tell you again," Zeya growled.

John Greenfield fired and Zeya seethed as he staggered back, holding his blown hand.

"Dad, don't attack people!" Erik cried as John Greenfield pointed both pistols at the young man.

"What do you expect me to do?" John Greenfield yelled back. "He's here to kill us if you hadn't noticed!"

"But...!"

"Now try to point that thing at me again, you piece of shit!" John Greenfield shouted and kicked the young man down. "I'm tired of you people threatening me!"

"Dad, knock it off!" Erik grabbed for his sleeve and John

Greenfield pushed back.

"Shut up, Justin!" John Greenfield tucked the silver-blue pistol into his waistband and grabbed Zeya's collar, yanking him up. "I've got way too many questions for this guy.... I want answers, Zeya!" Zeya spat in his face and John Greenfield punched the young man across the jaw. Zeya sagged and his eyes rolled to the back of his head. "You're passing out?" screeched John Greenfield. "How can you be that weak?"

"You there!" a voice bellowed. Erik backed away as John Greenfield looked up, spotting an officer standing in the street. "What are you doing here? Did you cause all this damage?"

"Are you crazy?" Erik yelled. "We didn't do this!"

"I'm not letting you off easily!"

"Shut up, you fiend!" John Greenfield shouted. "I've got enough to worry about without you starting in!"

"Put down that weapon!"

"Dad, what are we going to do?" Erik cried. "Public Security are here!"

"Let me think," John Greenfield grumbled as he let Zeya go and tossed the gun aside on the ground.

"Maybe we can talk to them and try to explain everything," Erik said quickly. "Hopefully we can clear this mess up..."

Zeya began stirring. "Please, help," he said weakly. "Officer, this guy blew up that bus back there... I tried to catch him, but he beat me up and took me hostage."

"What?" John Greenfield shrieked.

"Hey, you liar!" Erik shouted, grabbing Zeya by the collar.

The officer withdrew his revolver and pointed it at John Greenfield. "Don't move!" the officer commanded. "You're under arrest for assault and battery first thing!"

"Heh, serves you right," Zeya sneered as two more officers approached and tackled John Greenfield then wrestled him down to the ground. "Now you will belong to us while you're in confinement."

"You jerk!" Erik yowled and punched Zeya upside the head.

"You're coming with me to have a talk at the station," the officer grumbled as John Greenfield was handcuffed and the weapons collected. "We'll go over the fine details later."

"Whoever you are," Erik snarled as he let the young man go, "I'd better not see you here again!"

"Oh, we will," answered Zeya while the officers led John Greenfield away. "Though I'd rather we didn't."

The mysterious young man rose to his feet and shoved Erik to the ground before running away down the street. Erik looked toward the accident, frowning at watching the twisted steel burn.

"*I wish I didn't have to go home,*" he thought, standing. "*This is too serious...*"

Erik turned away and returned to his house. Along the way, he heard a car drive up and idle behind him. Whirling around, Erik recognized Genovera in white short jacket, pale beige blouse and white slacks behind the wheel of a compact sedan. She leaned over and opened the passenger door.

"I'm not too late am I?" she called.

"Dad's already in police custody," Erik replied.

"Get in," Genovera ordered. Erik blew a heavy sigh and trooped for the car. "Tell me," she said once he got inside, "what happened?"

"I didn't know what to do," Erik murmured after explaining the situation. "I didn't want to leave him, but I couldn't go with him."

"So what are you going to do?"

"I need to fix this somehow." Erik broke down into tears. "They just killed her, just like that... right in front of us!"

"There was nothing you could have done to stop them..."

"You're probably right... it might be true, but I do want to help him; I just don't know who to trust right now to help..."

"I'm sorry, but I don't want you to get involved."

"I think I'm already in too deep to get away from it now." Erik gripped the edge of his seat, overwhelmed by his emotions. "This won't end simply by pretending to forget all that happened!"

"Well, the first thing to do is to get Gerald out of the detention center," Genovera said as she shifted gears, "and I have an idea on how to go about that."

FORTY-EIGHT

Riding on long stretches of back roads, Genovera later pulled up into the lot with a looming five-story building surrounded by a high gate with barbed wire across the top.

"Here we are," she announced, "building Forty-Seven." Genovera cut the engine and turned to Erik. "We will have to make it inside without getting seen."

"What do you mean?" Erik asked. "This doesn't look like the county jail…"

"Because it's really not," Genovera explained. "This is a storage facility owned by The Corporation in which both your father and I work for. Those officers you told me about seemed too crooked to be County Public Security." Genovera exited the car and motioned Erik to follow. "I don't think anything will happen, but we have to be very careful."

"Whatever."

Erik exited the car and stood nearby, glancing around. The area appeared desolate, devoid of trees and only populated by stark beige buildings, electricity and telephone poles, gravel roads and parking lots.

Genovera headed for the building's side with Erik at her heels. "Once we get in without you being seen," she went on, "that'll be the least of our troubles."

"I'll manage," Erik murmured.

"Missus Zachary," a voice called.

Genovera froze and Erik immediately stepped behind a post as an officer approached in his security vehicle, waving.

"Oh, good afternoon," Genovera nervously replied, quickly taking her stride and closed the gap between them.

"Why are you back at the offices so late?" the guard asked, giving a nervous smile when Genovera leaned against the car door. "Has the team requested your work on the CENTRA Program?"

"No, of course not," Genovera answered, "rather, I..."

The guard held up a hand when a dispatcher called a code over the radio. The officer picked up the microphone. "Copy," he responded.

"What's all the chatter about?"

"Did you hear about the Omicron project?" the guard said to Genovera. "It was deployed today and they're waiting for results..."

"Really, I didn't know!" Genovera replied, feinting surprise. "Let's hope no one gets arrested by County!"

The guard snorted. "Well, I have to get going and start my shift."

"I'll be working tonight, so if you see any strange people milling about, they're my colleges I requested from Gateway."

"Cool, I'll keep note of that." The guard waved her off and she turned around, breathing a heavy sigh of relief. Once the security officer drove away, Erik came out of hiding.

Genovera waved to Erik and he quickly caught up to her side. "Whew," she murmured, "we barely got lucky!" Genovera squeezed Erik's arm. "Stay with me and stay close."

"I'll try," Erik muttered.

"That was a little too close; I didn't expect to bump into him!" Genovera shuddered. "If he was in a bad mood, he'd be more confrontational and I don't work well under pressure!"

They later entered the building after the officer parked his car and went in ahead of them. Genovera led Erik down a series of corridors before coming onto a door marked 'G. Zachary'.

Entering the office, Erik looked around, noticing the many file cabinets in the room and a messy workstation covered by papers and files before a large desktop computer. His sight fell on a large bright electric blue spherical plush toy with notched edges and blank pale purple eyes near the monitor. Erik approached, picking it up and gave it a squeeze, hearing a squeak.

"What's this?" Erik asked as Genovera shut the door behind her and leaned against it.

"It's an enlarged microbe," Genovera explained. "You just caught the common cold."

Erik snorted. "What is it you do here?"

"It depends on the job," Genovera replied and left her place at the door. Approaching a set of cabinets behind her desk chair, she opened a drawer and pulled out a first aid kit. "I'm sure your back and legs are killing you, so let me clean it up before it gets infected."

"It's not that bad," Erik protested.

"Don't be so tough. I can see it on your face."

Erik sighed and Genovera pushed the wheeled chair toward him. Erik sat in it backwards, squeezing the stuffed microbe. "Can I keep this?" he requested.

"Sure."

Erik set the microbe aside on the desk's edge and winced as he pulled off his shirt. Genovera gasped. "What did those monsters do?" she said in dismay and opened the kit, pulling out a bottle of antiseptic, tweezers, and a package of square gauze patches.

"It only hurts when I think about it," Erik murmured.

"Why didn't you tell me you were shot?" Genovera demanded. "The bullet's still in your shoulder!"

"I didn't want you to worry."

"I worry enough about you."

"Please, don't."

Genovera blew a heavy sigh and started the task of pulling out glass and metal from his skin. Erik seethed in pain and grabbed the stuffed plush, squeezing with all his strength as he ground his teeth to keep from crying out.

Once finishing extracting the bullet and the embedded pieces of glass and metal, Genovera wiped down his cuts with antiseptic and taped his wounds. "I don't want you to wear that shirt again," she directed and pulled out of her short jacket.

"I'm not wearing that," Erik snapped.

"It's either this or letting it get infected again." Genovera held out the jacket. "Or would you rather wear my blouse?" Erik grunted and tossed the microbe at her. She caught it with her free hand and set it aside. "Take it." Erik snatched the jacket then reluctantly pulled into it. "Now stay in here and don't wander off," Genovera ordered. "I'm going to look for Gerald. Keep the lights off, okay?" Erik nodded and Genovera stepped out, shutting the lights on her way out.

Waiting until her footsteps were distant, Erik switched on the light and sifted through her desk and cabinets. Finding a file folder titled 'Program CENTRA' he pulled it out and gasped when he found his and Kevin's hospital records.

"*Why would they have this?*" he wondered and scanned Kevin's chart copy. He blew a sigh of relief when he read Kevin was stable and not in a vegetative state. "*He's in an induced coma because his injuries were really bad. So he's barely hanging on, almost close to death yet not, which means...*"

Hearing footsteps out in the hall, Erik placed the chart back in the folder and cursed himself when he accidentally bumped the drawer, locking it. Yanking against the stuck door, Erik broke out in cold sweat when footsteps neared and raced across the room, striking the switch. He held his breath as he hid behind the door once it opened.

"Place him here," Genovera directed and two men entered, placing John Greenfield's unconscious body in the nearby chair. "I have to fill out the rest of these forms..."

The door closed after the men left and Erik turned on the light. He dropped the papers he held and cried out in horror when he saw John Greenfield's unconscious body stripped down to his underwear and covered in dark bruises, cuts and burns.

"Those monsters!" Erik wailed. "They did this to you... over what? Why?" Erik fell to his knees as tears ran down his face full force. "It's over! My life is over...!" The door opened and he heard a gasp from behind.

"Justin...!" Genovera yelped.

"Leave me alone!" Erik screeched, glaring back at her. "Why

did you have to torture him?"

"Justin, please," Genovera protested, "he was fighting and they just knocked him out!"

"His clothes too?" Erik stood adamantly to his feet. "Why did you want him dead?"

"He's not dead!"

"Then tell me what's going on; I want an answer! Why?"

"Please, just let me explain!"

Genovera approached and Erik pushed her away when she tried to grab his hand. "I don't want to hear it!" Erik shrilled. "Just get away from me; you ruined my life!"

"I know you've been through a lot," Genovera murmured, "and I'm sorry if you were hurt, but if you'll just..."

"I don't want you near me anymore!" Erik pushed past Genovera for the door. "What does it matter if I hurt or not? I'm getting out of here!"

"Please, don't leave!" Genovera begged and Erik stormed out the office, barreling past surprised guardsmen. Genovera ran after Erik once he came to an electronically locked door.

"Leave me alone!" Erik screamed and threw a wild punch.

"Please," Genovera pleaded as she stepped out of his swift blows, "let me take you home. I'm sorry for bringing you here."

"That's all you can say!" Erik yelled. "Is 'sorry' the only word you know?" He threw a hard slap and Genovera gasped, holding her cheek in stunned silence. "Please, just go away!"

"Justin!" Genovera grasped Erik's arm. "You have every right to be angry."

Erik shoved her back and she staggered rearward before falling onto her back on the floor. He stood over Genovera, hands clenched at his sides and heaving for breath in incensed rage. "You're working for those monsters!" Erik thundered. "How can I trust you? I never want to see you again!"

"I understand." Genovera sat up and blew a defeated sigh. "However, if you don't calm down, they'll hurt me too." Erik said nothing as she stood and dusted herself off. "Now come with me before they punish you for seeing too much!"

Sighing in defeat, Erik went with her, following her lead on the way out.

Genovera pulled in front of Erik's house and he stepped out, slamming her door then stormed up the walk. Approaching the porch steps, Erik felt dread punch him in the guts as he tried the front door and it opened with ease.

"*This isn't how I left it,*" Erik mused upon entry. He paused in step, chilled when he found the room cleared and the carpet and walls cleaned of blood.

"What the--?" Erik yelped, surprised.

Passing the television, he switched it on and headed into the kitchen. He turned on the radio, tuning it to the local news station and sat at the table, listening intently. After the newscast, Erik grew perturbed. Checking the overhead kitchen clock, Erik returned to the parlor and sat on the couch, watching the evening news.

After the bulletin's broadcast ended, Erik drifted back into the kitchen, more disturbed than before. "*There's no information about the attack this afternoon,*" he thought in dismay. "*It's not on the telly or the radio!*" Erik fixed himself a sandwich then entered the parlor, setting his snack aside on the nearby end table. *"Why wouldn't the news report something so crazy? Is someone covering this up?"*

Flinching when the telephone rang, Erik let it ring for a long time, then finally reached for the receiver and cautiously picked up the line.

"Justin!" Mahjin's voice called from the other end. "I've been trying to reach you for over an hour!"

"I'm fine," answered Erik slowly. "I just…"

"Now listen to me, whatever it is you saw, you're just being paranoid. You're not in danger at all."

"But…!" Erik dropped the handset when he heard the rear door opening. Running into the kitchen, he gasped and shrank back when he spotted the mysterious young man sifting through the cabinets. "You're Zeya!" Erik yelped.

"So, you remembered me, eh?" Zeya snapped. "It doesn't matter." He withdrew a knife from one of the drawers. "I see you returned here… too bad the Cleaners didn't wipe you out too."

"Cleaners?"

"So where is the case?"

"What case?" Erik spat. "I don't know what you're talking about!"

"I should kill you and search at my leisure."

"What?" Erik let out a wail in pain when Zeya hurled the knife at him, pinning his shoulder to the wall. "You crazy--!" Erik shrieked.

"That's enough, Zeya!" a rough voice barked. "With Agents snooping around, it won't be as easy to conceal deaths since we can only call the Cleaners once." Erik swallowed hard as a middle-aged man with a wide-brimmed hat and dark overcoat entered the room, holding onto a silver attaché case. Smoky sunglasses covered his eyes and he grinned deviously. "We want him alive for right now... after we get what we need, it'll be best to kill him far away from here, don't you think so?"

"You're that creepy orderly from the hospital!" Erik cried.

"Of course, and you're the one I gave the business card to." The mysterious middle-aged man chuckled. "I'm surprised you have such a good memory." He grinned darkly. "You might prove useful later..."

"You can't come in here!" Erik yelled.

"Justin Schumacher... Weldon Springs High School, first year, parents live separately, lives with his father," said the mysterious middle-aged man. "You barely make ends meet with your aunt's clerical salary from the Security and Intelligence Division and your father working odd jobs building or restoring things of mechanical nature."

"What do you mean, my *aunt's* clerical salary!" Erik shouted. "My *mother* works at the Federal Records Center...!"

"Hadn't they told you?" The mysterious middle-aged man chortled. "Shana Schumacher is your *aunt*, Gerald Schumacher's *sister*. Now that she's out the way, he has no chance of avoiding us now."

"You liar!"

"Since we're now on the same page, I have a deal for you if you wish to hear it."

"No deal; now get out of my house!"

"I have here in this case a hundred million dollars and the cure for your brother barely hanging by a thread in the hospital now," the middle-aged man continued, ignoring Erik's protests. "Sell me those documents your father has hidden and we leave you alone."

"My *brother*...?" Erik shook his head. "You mean half-brother?"

"*Twin* brother."

"You're crazy!" Erik screeched. "I'm going to call the cops once I get down from here!"

"Is that a 'no'?" the middle-aged man snapped.

"Do you think I'm that stupid to fall for that?" Erik shouted. "If you're done, then get out of my house!"

"Fine, have it your way."

"Damn you!"

Zeya grinned devilishly and sauntered forward. "It's no use," he said. "He won't simply listen to reason."

"It's unavoidable then..." The middle-aged man waved at Zeya. "Tear him apart, right here, right now. Strike him down where he stands!"

"So you finally show your true colors!" Erik growled.

Zeya grabbed Erik's face in his hand. "I guess I do get my chance to play with you," he said brightly. "I'll let you beg only once..."

Erik spat in his face. "Don't you dare touch my family!" he screamed. "I will destroy you!"

"It's too late," sneered Zeya, "we already own them."

"What are you doing?" the middle-aged man bellowed. "Stop toying around and kill him now!"

"Complying with your order," Zeya said mechanically. Erik grunted when Zeya punched him across the head, knocking his world out of focus. "Resilient, eh?" The second blow knocked him out.

FORTY-NINE

Stirring, Erik opened his eyes, finding himself in a hard bed and staring up at a ceiling with peeling yellow paint. Glancing to his side, he noticed the bars also had the same-flecked paint.

"What am I doing here?" Erik muttered and sat up. He seethed, clenching his aching burned hands and the agony traveled up his arms and throughout his back.

Realizing he was dressed in dark navy pants with matching shirt, Erik looked around his surroundings and sucked in a thin breath when he noticed several other young men in blue jumpsuits milling around in a large pen surrounded by bars.

In the section he stayed in, Erik saw other metal bunk beds with a thin pallet, worn sheets and a single blanket. Ahead was a large area with plank tables where several torn magazines rest and on the side wall were several stalls without doors with stainless steel toilets.

An argument broke out between two men and a circle formed as a fight started. Erik climbed out his bunk and landed hard on his heels. He stiffened when a hand grasped him by the arm and Erik whirled around, spotting Clayton wearing the same outfit he had. He frowned when he noticed Clayton had a raised scar across his cheek.

"What's with that look?" Clayton asked, grinning and held

out a pair of dark blue slip-on shoes toward him. "You might need this," he said cheerfully.

Erik grunted and took the shoes, slipping them on his bare feet. He winced when his right toe was pricked. "Ouch!" he muttered and withdrew the shoe, shaking it out. A translucent blue pen with a golden nib clattered on the floor. "What's that doing there?"

"Don't ask me what hell I had to go through to hide it," Clayton complained.

Erik raised his eyebrow as he picked it up and put the shoe on his foot. "What are you doing here?" he asked instead. "What are we doing here?"

"We're on the last leg of getting erased," Clayton explained. "Their data's insufficient, so they no longer need us."

"How did you know we'd be in the same holding cell together?"

"We're both quite dangerous."

Erik leaned against the bars and tucked the pen behind his ear as Clayton took a seat on the bunk below and drew up his knees, looking out at the fighting circle.

"Are we getting gassed or something?" Erik questioned.

"No - firing squad. It's easier. Then it's off to the acid vats." Clayton snorted. "All it takes is a few keystrokes and we're gone. Not even ones and zeroes."

"But what about the others?" Erik complained. "Aren't people going to talk when a lot of folks come up missing?"

"Nobody cares about crazies and criminals, remember?"

Erik looked to Clayton, stunned. "I'm branded as a criminal?" he squawked.

"It's easy to break laws, remember?" Clayton shrugged. "These days, all you have to do is cuss out a public security officer and that's considered assault. For that, you instantly get two years in the slammer."

"I don't remember breaking any laws," Erik complained. "They're punishing my dad for something he did. They're going to send a robot with my face to kill him."

Clayton laughed and looked up at Erik. "You can't be serious!" he crowed.

"Yeah, they knock me around, get my blood and other samples and build this horrible machine remanufactured with my face and my memory. They're going to claim him - me - cured and send him home and that's the end."

"You're crazy," Clayton said, shaking his head. "All that's straight crazy!"

"Do you really think so?" Clayton bit his fist, trying to contain his laughter. "But I don't know if it'll really work. I know for sure my mind is terribly messed up and I can't tell if I'm hallucinating, or having weird dreams or recalling things."

"Well, all the drugs they give you can make you have weird trippy dreams," Clayton replied.

"Do you think I'm making it up?"

"I'm not really sure." Clayton calmed and grinned at Erik. "So, you ready?"

Erik raised an eyebrow. "Ready for what?"

"If now's a good time to see if you're real."

"What?"

Clayton unfurled from his position on the bed. "When the fight gets ugly and the guards come in, they'll be too distracted and leave the door open," he explained.

"That's... er, good to know?"

A loud whistle pierced the air and Erik looked at the group as a riot broke out, with the other young men joining the fray.

"Here's our chance," Clayton said as he rose to his feet. "I only have one shot."

"Tell me where you need me to be and I'll help," Erik promised.

"Keep yourself alive, Erik," Clayton said seriously. "We need to meet up again if we're going to destroy these bastards."

Erik winced when pain flashed behind his eyes and the voices he grew to hate echoed in his head.

Keep yourself alive...

Alive...

Meet again...

Again...

Erik let out a cry and held his hands to his head as the burning sensation worsened in his arms and hands.

"Snap to it!" Clayton yelled, punching Erik's arm. "Come on!"

"Sorry," Erik muttered and shook his head, then numbly followed Clayton beyond the crowd as several guardsmen came in with batons, beating the other prisoners.

"Stay close," Clayton said and took off his hat. He pulled apart the hatband and withdrew the key card, handing it to Erik. Erik palmed the card, gripping it tightly as Clayton placed his cap back on and his hands glowed dimly in frosted blue light.

The young men ganged up on the guards, overwhelming them and Erik raced for the door with Clayton at his heels. They entered the corridor as a loud buzzer screeched in the halls and emergency lights turned on, flashing red and orange.

"Left!" Clayton called when they reached a break and Erik hustled in that direction.

Coming to a door with three locks, Erik hastily swiped the card and pressed his left hand into the reader, then the card against the thumb verifier. The door buzzed open and Erik screamed when he met a group of guards on the other side.

"Damn it!" Clayton growled as Erik backed away and the officers entered, surrounding them.

"They're trying to escape!" one warden shouted as he withdrew his gun. Clayton formed the steel blue short sword and immediately lopped off guard's hand.

Let's do this! Show them how it's done!

Erik raced back down the hall, leaving Clayton with the group and cried out when another set of officers came through the corridor from the other side.

"You're done, kid," one guard snarled as he withdrew his service pistol.

"*I can't let them kill me,*" Erik thought, backing away. "*I can't let them copy me and kill Father Greenfield!*" He bumped into the wall and the pen in his ear clattered to the floor.

"Shit!" one guard yelped. "The bastard's armed!" The officer advanced and Erik bit the card between the teeth as he rushed the man, dropping down for a shoulder tackle.

Launching the officer into the group behind them, Erik let out a yelp when grabbed by the collar and whirled around, ducking from a pistol swung at his face. He grasped the guardsman's wrist, pulling his hand away before he fired, shooting his comrade instead who struggled to get up and hurled him down to the floor.

"Get reinforcements!" cried the officer as Erik worked the gun free and smashed the man's face with it.

"Don't make me use this," Erik snarled and pointed the pistol at the group. Backing away, he picked up the fallen key card and tucked it in his palm against the handgun. "I don't like killing people, but if you push me, I *will* push back!"

Grabbing for the instrument with his burned right hand, the pen cackled in yellow light and the agony in his arms and hands lessened when a golden rapier formed in its place.

"You're done!" the officer shouted and Erik stabbed the guard's chest before he fired his pistol, then slashed the second across his throat.

The third officer rushed Erik with his fist raised aimed for his head. Erik whirled out of the attack and kicked the man's back, throwing him into the opposite wall. The guard crashed to the floor and Erik stomped up to him, dispatching the man with a swift pierce between the eyes.

Hearing more men clamor the halls once the riot in the holding cell worsened, Erik hustled for the exit.

"Clayton," Erik cried, "where are you?" He entered another hallway, stepped over severed bodies and searched frantically for his friend, fearing his death.

"Erik," Clayton called once Erik turned the corner, "keep them busy!"

Erik watched the young man behead an officer and tossed Clayton the gun. "Here, take this!" he called. "Conserve what you can!" Clayton caught the weapon and tucked it in his waistband.

"There they are!" a voice shouted and Erik whirled around as the group charged after them. Erik swung back with ferocious speed, cutting into arms and hands, disarming them before they had a chance to retaliate.

A sudden shot rang out, shattering the wood and plaster above Erik's head, creating a large crater. Erik gasped and backed away from the wall. Another shot followed and an invading pain rammed into Erik's solar plexus. Erik doubled over easily like a folding chair and coughed up bile as he sank to his knees in agony when the searing affliction burned his side. He looked down at his bloodstained hand, bewildered at the sight.

"Shit!" Clayton screeched and Erik looked up, watching Clayton jump on the armed rifleman's back, impaling the back of his head. "Come on!" The guard slumped to the floor and Clayton grabbed the longarm, slinging it over his back.

"Don't worry about me," Erik moaned as he staggered to his knees. "I'll make it."

"Take the keys," Clayton ordered and Erik unhooked the ring of keys on the guard's belt as Clayton took off through another corridor. Erik ran after him, ridding survivors Clayton left behind when he cleared the path.

Approaching another set of doors, Erik handed Clayton the keys and swiped the card. The machine buzzed when read incorrectly. "Damn it," Erik grumbled and wiped off his blood with his sleeve, then tried again. "What's with the keys?" he asked when he pressed his hand into the reader.

"Shit, the hell's taking so long?" Clayton grumbled when the palm reader flickered.

"I'm sorry I'm a bloody mess!" Erik spat sourly.

"It's not your fault; I'm sorry," Clayton murmured. After several long moments of analysis, the computer pinged, allowing access. Clayton pushed open the door and Erik staggered ahead.

"How much further do we have?" Erik moaned.

"Through here!" Clayton called and darted for the trash chute as the blade he held vanished. Clayton bit the ring of keys and took off the rifle he wore over his shoulder then dove into the narrow space, slipping through easily.

Erik approached and froze when another shot blew part of the wall away near his head.

"Where you think you're goin', boy?" Behr's voice snarled. "You're not leaving that easily!" Erik whirled around, facing the head guardsman flanked by four junior officers armed with rifles. "You're outnumbered, both physically and with firepower!"

"Don't push me!" Erik shouted. "I *will* cut you all down!"

"That's just words of a desperate man!" Behr chortled. "Don't bother, boy. You're headed for the scrap heap."

"Am I really dangerous that you need help, old man?" Erik thundered. "You want me gone, come after me yourself!"

Behr snorted and waved the men back who lowered their weapons. "You got yourself a deal, boy. I told you you're gonna be sucking on my fist."

"Let me see you land a solid one," Erik growled and pointed the rapier in the man's direction. "Bring it!"

Let them feel our pain!

Behr withdrew his pistol and Erik made a swift clearing slash, clipping the gun's edge and Behr's finger.

"Shit!" the guard snarled and Erik charged forward, then suddenly turned on his heel, slashing at the man's back before Behr made a grab. Erik backed away when Behr collapsed to all fours and the others advanced, aiming their guns on Erik. "Let him go," Behr hissed from his place on the ground.

"Sir!" one officer protested.

"He's only making this fight short because he knows he's gonna die soon." Behr let out a short laugh and sat up on his knees. "Ain't shit he can do with a skinny piece of tin foil anyway and besides, he's bleeding to death!"

"I better not see you again," Erik spat.

"If you somehow survive," Behr snarled, glaring back at Erik, "I'll remember this!"

Erik pointed the blade at the guardsman's shoulder. "Give me the gate code," he demanded.

"Over my dead body," Behr retorted. "The way you're leaking, you won't even reach the damn gate!"

Erik turned toward the group of riflemen surrounding them and pointed the blade in their direction. "Do you know it?" he shouted.

"No, kid," one officer replied. "Only he does."

Erik growled and kicked Behr's side, then took off, charging through the group before they retaliated and raced for the side door. Trying the key combination, Erik let out a frustrated cry when the door refused to open.

"You might as well as forget it," Behr's voice called. Erik turned, watching the guardsman walk toward him. "That has a retina reader. I don't know how the hell you copied those keys, but you're at the end of the line, boy. Give up and accept your fate."

"Watch me walk away!" Erik shouted. He looked down at the bloodied card he held. *"It's imprinted on the card,"* he thought, turning it around and using the opposite end where the thumbprint was located. *"Hopefully it'll take, he said..."* Putting the card against the reader, the machine hummed as the laser went over the bloodied plastic.

"You might as well forget it," Behr snapped upon approach and folded his arms across his chest. "Hurry up and fail so I can beat your scrawny ass!"

The computer chirped and the door unlatched. Erik turned to Behr, giving a malicious grin as he tapped the edge of his nose. "Ah ha, I win," he wheedled.

"You're not getting out of here without that gate code," Behr snapped and turned toward the nearby fire alarm, flipping up its cover. "So either way, you're fucked!"

"Watch me walk away," Erik declared and took off into the main corridor. Behr hit the switch and alarms blared, ringing loudly throughout campus.

Erik rushed through the major artery and paused when several officers charged the hall from the front entranceway. Turning back, Erik sensed cool air blowing in and spotted a rear door propped open with a chair that had a pool of blood at its feet. He hustled for it, making his escape.

Bursting outdoors, Erik met cool fresh air and overcast skies with low-hanging dark clouds.

"Over here!" Clayton called from the gate's other side,

waving his arms.

Erik ran for the gate with barbed wire and cables along the top of the fence and stopped short when he saw Clayton wearing a pair of gun harnesses slung about his waist. "Where'd you get those?" he asked.

"I thought your ass died!" Clayton said instead.

"I'm tougher than that!" Erik retorted.

"Get down!"

"What?"

Clayton unleashed a pair of pistols from his belt and fired in Erik's direction. Erik hit the ground, cringing when Clayton shot down the guards who came after them. He then left the gate, running toward a red box near the gate's end. Using the keys, he opened the lock and struck a lever.

"Let's move it before they hit the override switch!" Clayton called once he returned to the gate.

Erik got up, noticing the group dead with shots to the head or chest. He tossed the rapier over the gate and it sailed easily before striking the ground, tip first. Erik then searched the dead bodies, taking the pistols and chucked them to Clayton who caught them.

Biting the card between his teeth, Erik pulled out of his shirt and tied it over his arm then climbed the gate. Placing the shirt over the top of the wires, he scaled it and dropped down onto the ground below. Reaching for his shirt, a loud buzz unexpectedly whined from the gate and a sharp charge threw Erik back, forcing him to the ground with a hard thud. He curled over on his side, moaning.

"Forget it," Clayton barked and ran up to Erik, picking up

the key card. "Did you get the main gate code?"

"Only Behr knows and he's not telling," Erik groaned, sitting up.

"Come on, there's got to be an alternate way."

"I don't know how much longer I can hold up," Erik complained.

Clayton grabbed Erik by the arm and yanked him to his feet. "We can make it," he urged. "Don't you want your dad to live?" Erik nodded. "It's death if we stay here." He handed Erik the key card and Erik took it, looking down at the flecked blood across its surface. "Forget the pain and let's go!"

"Alright, but if I slow down..."

"I'll pick you up," Clayton promised and took off for the gravel path leading toward the main gate. Erik grabbed the rapier and raced after him.

When guardsmen appeared in the yard with their guns drawn, Clayton used the rifle he had and fired back with swift deadly accuracy, dropping them down via only head shots. Erik crossed the green to the dead bodies, taking any arms he could find.

"How'd you learn to shoot like that?" Erik asked once he returned with the haul and they continued for the gate.

"I was a quinary," Clayton answered.

"Canary?"

"Quin, base five," Clayton responded. "I served five years in the Defense Forces."

Erik said nothing when Clayton cleared the remaining guards who aimed to stop them. Once dispatching the two protecting the gate, Clayton turned to Erik who dropped what he held and collapsed to his knees, clutching his profusely bleeding side.

"You're a pretty good shot," Erik gasped. "Do they teach that in the Defense Forces?"

"They don't teach sniping like that," Clayton replied.

"I thought they'd have more guys out here to stop us," Erik said instead. "When I came in, they were everywhere!"

"The reason we didn't have more on our ass was because I took care of it while you were taking your sweet time."

"That's good to know..."

Clayton looked toward the gate, studying it. "Do you think I can force the lock open?" he wondered aloud.

"It's by computer," Erik answered. "Shooting at it won't do a thing."

"I'm trying anyway."

Erik glanced down at the key card he dropped and noticed a reflection near the magnetic strip in the sunlight. "Wait!" he called as Clayton withdrew a pistol and aimed at the lockbox, holding with both hands. Erik picked up the card, bending it in the light. "He put the code on here!"

"What is it?"

"Five, One, Zero, Nine, Five..." Erik finished reading the remaining the numbers and Clayton approached the keypad, punching in the series. The heavy iron creaked, slowly swinging open.

"Will you be okay to make it?" Clayton asked and approached Erik's side.

"I think so," Erik replied faintly. "Until we cross that threshold..."

Clayton frowned when Erik suddenly fell forward on the ground. "You're not dying on me, damn it," he muttered and approached Erik's downed body.

Clayton dropped the pistol back into its holster, then slipped off the rifle from his back. He bent his knees and slipped his hands under Erik's arms, hoisting up his body. Flipping him around, he slung Erik's arm over his shoulders and hoisted him crosswise on his back.

Clayton then took up the rapier, sliding it into his gun harness and grabbed the rifle. After scooping up the fallen key card in his free hand, Clayton made his way through the open gate for the road.

FIFTY

Erik groaned when he roused to consciousness, smelling antiseptic and hearing beeps from vital-taking machines. Opening his eyes, Erik found himself in a dimly lit room, lying in bed covered by sheets.

Glancing to his side, he spotted Brodie sitting in a chair next to his bed, draped with his overcoat across his body, snoring softly. Sitting up, Erik hissed in pain when his injuries signaled agonizing aches in his shoulder, back, side and thigh.

"I can't stay here," Erik muttered, touching his bandaged side. "I've got work in the morning..."

Turning toward the machines, he reached over and followed the cables toward the outlet then yanked them out. Gently pulling away the intravenous lines in his arm, Erik clasped a hand to his wound and staggered to his feet.

Padding over to the door, Erik peered out, noticing a security guard posted outside his room, armed with her service pistol and reading a magazine. He clenched his teeth and glanced back to Brodie who continued sleeping.

Returning to his bed, Erik sat on the edge and looked at his nightstand, staring at the telephone. He wondered about potential contacts and mulled over various telephone numbers, only to have nothing come to mind.

Looking to Brodie, he reached over, tapping him gently on his knee. "Hey," Erik whispered and Brodie grunted when tapped harder. "Hey, Mister Avers?" Brodie grunted again. "Hey, wake up!" Erik glanced out the door, watching the security guard leaving her post when her male partner arrived with a cup of coffee.

"How's the new gig at the mines?" the female officer asked, taking the coffee.

"It's steady," replied her coworker. "Earlier there was some investigation where we had all those Security and Intelligence Division suits snooping around. It was nasty."

"Over a damn copper mine?" retorted the officer. "Seriously?"

"I'm not sure what's going on. I heard some chatter about the new bots not working right. Faulty chip or whatever."

"Okay, see you in an hour!"

"*That reminds me,*" Erik mused, recalling the database he worked on at the offices. He tapped Brodie on the thigh and the older man blew a soft sigh. "Mister Avers, come on, wake up!" Erik said softly. "Did you take a sleeping pill?" When Brodie said nothing else, Erik grabbed for the coat and took it away. "I need help getting out of here! Get up!" After pulling into the overcoat, Erik leaned forward and tapped Brodie on the chest. "Come on, old man, wake up!" Blowing a frustrated sigh, Erik reached down and grasped Brodie's crotch, giving a firm squeeze. Brodie stiffened, moaning. "Wake up," Erik hissed.

"Yeah, Feddy?" Brodie muttered sleepily.

"What's Clairese's number?"

"Exeter... eighty-five sixty-two..."

Erik let go and approached the phone then dialed the number, listening. He looked at Brodie who shifted in his seat and drifted back to sleep as snores escaped him.

"Hello?" Clairese's voice murmured after several rings.

"Will you come get me?" Erik asked.

"Who's this?"

"Your father's drunk horny friend."

"Oh!" Clairese blew a sigh. "Don't scare me like that." She then suddenly giggled. "Don't tell me you're drunk again!"

"Yeah, got my ass handed to me and now I'm drying out at The Clinic."

"Is my father there?"

Brodie moaned and shifted in his chair again. Erik leaned forward, putting a hand on his thigh to quell him. "He's taken a pill," Erik responded.

"I'll come and leave a note for him then," Clairese acquiesced.

"Before you go, I want to ask you something."

"Sure."

"You're a chemist, aren't you?"

"H-how did you know?" Clairese asked, surprised.

"Kanbal Industries is a chemical agency, so why else would you work for them?"

"True..."

"I have some questions. Please come get me."

"I will."

Erik glanced to Brodie who grasped his hand and noticed the gold band he wore on his left. "Oh, and tell them I'm your husband."

"Wait, what?"

Erik set the receiver back in the cradle and pulled out of Brodie's grip.

"Hey," Brodie murmured when Erik slipped off the ring, "what are you doing?"

"I'm just borrowing it," Erik answered.

"Give it back when you're done... I want Sweetheart to have it."

"Promise." Erik slipped the ring on his hand and looked at the door, watching and waiting.

Later, Erik heard a minute ring and searched his coat pockets, withdrawing his phone. He immediately pushed the button. "What is it?" Erik hissed.

"I've been trying to contact you for ages!" Gina's worried voice said over the line.

"I told you I was at the Clinic!" Erik protested.

"They wouldn't let me in," Gina retorted. "They had you in a restricted area."

"Couldn't you make up a lie or something?"

Erik's phone suddenly beeped and powered off before he heard Gina's answer. Erik growled under his breath and looked out the door, spotting Clairese coming down the hall with curlers in her hair. His face grow warm when he saw her dressed in an old T-shirt slipping off her shoulder, faded jeans molded to her curves and draped in a short padded coat.

"Hey," the guard snapped when Clairese approached. "Nobody's supposed to be on this floor!"

"Why not?" Clairese demanded.

"He's violent! We keep him doped up for everyone's safety."

"Well, that violent man is my husband!" Clairese thrust forward her hand, showing off a gold ring with a large glittering stone. "He's a veteran, and sometimes he sleepwalks and has nightmares."

"That's a hell of a rock on Defense Forces pay," the guard replied, leaning forward and inspecting her ring. "I did Fifteen and couldn't eat off that!"

"He did a lot of dangerous missions." Clairese put her hands on her hips. "You know with the more kills you make, the more pay you rake. Isn't that how the saying goes?"

"Yeah... But look lady, that was no sleepwalking nightmare!" The guard scoffed. "That bastard's vicious!"

"That vicious bastard just called me to come get him!" Clairese spat. "Now which do you prefer, *him* fighting you or *me* fighting you to get him home?"

"I'd prefer you tie his ass up at night then, lady!" the guard said. "Go on and get the hell outta here before my partner gets back. She wants to kill him for real!"

"I'll try my best." Clairese entered the room and grinned at Erik who gave her the thumbs up. "So, Tiger, how did you sleep?"

"Horrible," Erik replied and stood unsteadily to his feet.

"Wow, fighting at the bar again? What will I ever do with you?"

"I had to show those kids how to fight properly," replied Erik, smiling wryly. "They said I was too skinny to serve."

Clairese chortled and approached, holding out a hand to Erik. "Here, let me help."

"Thanks, Sweetheart."

Clairese draped his arm over her shoulders and held his

hand, pulling Erik along out the room.

"Hey, I never saw no ring on you when you came in," the guard groused when he noticed Erik with Clairese. "The old man had one!"

"He was holding it for me," Erik retorted. "I tend to drink too much."

The guard put a hand to his gun holster then glanced at the clock. "Fuck it, get the hell out," he muttered as they continued to the elevators. "I don't feel like taking your shit."

Clairese walked Erik down the corridor toward the elevators.

"Where'd you get a ring like that?" Erik murmured.

"That piece of no good shit who thinks money will buy my happiness," Clairese said bitterly.

"Did he want it back after you left?"

"Of course; I lied and said I pawned it."

"Why keep it?"

"To keep off horny men like you from jumping my bones."

Erik snorted. "But it's *you* who want to jump my bones!"

"Some men like screwing around with a married woman."

"You didn't wear it earlier."

"I keep it in a safe place until I need it."

Approaching the elevators, Clairese pushed the button and once the cars came up, the door opened, revealing the female officer.

"Shit!" she yelped and Erik's eyes widened. He froze when Clairese withdrew a canister of pepper spray from inside her coat and sprayed the woman. The officer screamed in pain and Clairese pulled Erik away once the doors closed.

"Come on!" Clairese cried, hustling for the stairs.

"Fuck my life," Erik moaned, hobbling after her.

Throwing open the door leading to the stairwell, Clairese let go and hurried down them. Erik ground his teeth, straining to keep up and hissed in pain when the stitches in his thigh broke, forcing his wound bleeding again.

Erik heard the door slam open and footsteps slowly coming down the stairs. "I ain't gotta chase ya," called the male security officer. "I know you're pretty torn up."

"What about your partner?" Erik called over his shoulder. "She wants to kill me."

"You got maybe a twenty-minute head start."

"Then what do you want with me?"

"I hear you're one bad motherfucker. You like to whack guys, like that politico Yagnersian and some other folks in high-up places."

"So what about it?" Erik huffed for breath as he made his way down the stairs, growing tense when he heard the officer take his time.

"Rumors say he was corrupt," said the guardsman. "He was killing people with those faulty machines he let loose on the market, especially for overseas mining projects."

"Oh? That's good then, I suppose."

"So what are ya? Some protest group? Terrorist gang? Federal gig?"

"I wish I knew."

Erik approached the lower stairwell door and pushed it open, stumbling out onto the parking lot. He put his hands on his knees, panting hard for breath. Moments later, Clairese screeched up to the curb in her compact car and Erik briskly approached, throwing open the door.

"Take me to Mercado Corp's offices," Erik ordered as he slipped inside.

"You're just in a hospital gown!" Clairese complained and shifted gears then sped out the garage.

"I got some clothes there... Laundry drops it off Friday morning."

"Why do you need to get to the office? What's going on?"

"I'll let you know when you get there."

FIFTY-ONE

Arriving in front of Mercado's building, Erik stumbled out the car and searched his pockets, withdrawing his wallet and phone. He pressed the power button and cursed when the phone's battery meter flashed, indicating it was dead.

Walking up the steps, Erik tried the front door and growled when the door refused to open.

"Why not try around back?" Clairese called.

Erik nodded and returned to the car. Clairese went around the building's side where they watched the laundry truck pull away. Standing at the rear steps was the white-haired maintenance worker in the gray jumpsuit and black cap, wheeling a large green bin of clothing folded into bags with yellow tags stapled on.

"Wait for me," Erik said and stepped out the car.

"What if Security pops around?"

"Go around the block then come back." Erik shut the door and hurried up the stairs. "Hey, Mister!" he called. "Hold the door!"

The maintenance man glimpsed over his shoulder and smiled. "Oh, Number Five!" he called and waved. "You're early!"

"Quarterlies are supposed to be turned in this morning,"

Erik said. "I want to make sure everything's right so we won't get audited."

Stepping inside after the man pulled in the cart; Erik turned and waved at Clairese. She waved back and the door shut behind him.

"Didn't you see Security around?" asked the maintenance worker as he pushed the cart down the corridor.

"He probably was asleep somewhere," Erik answered, keeping in step. "I just want my clothes and I'll be out of your hair."

"Sure. Which office?"

"I'm not sure of the number, but the name is Avers, Brodie."

"Oh, office Five-eighty-two." The worker dug through the stack of laundry pallets and withdrew a large stack of pressed shirts and slacks. "There you go."

"Thanks."

"Keep going straight and you'll reach the elevators."

"Great."

Erik raced ahead for the exit.

Erik entered the fifth floor and approached door 82. Trying the handle, he opened it and switched on the lights. Erik set the pile of laundry aside on the desk and slipped out of his coat then pulled off the hospital gown. Tearing the fabric in half, he rolled it and tied the cloth around his bleeding thigh.

Ripping open the laundry bag, Erik grabbed his lavender shirt and slipped it over his shoulder then sifted through the rest of the clothing, taking a pair of dark slacks. Once he dressed, Erik looked around the office, taking in his surroundings.

On the walls, he saw photographs of Brodie with his wife, a slender woman with bobbed brown hair who wore various outfits in beige, with matching flat-heeled shoes and pearls. He frowned when his head began to hurt, looking at more pictures of the woman in a variety of scenes, some by herself, while others with their daughter Clairese. Reading the diplomas from colleges Brodie attended and awards of service from Mercado, Erik grew unsettled.

"You've been working with these guys for a long time," Erik murmured, noting the perfect attendance award for twenty years at Mercado.

Approaching the desk, Erik saw smaller photographs of Brodie and Giuseppe and several other men and women from the Defense Force. He paused when he came across the photograph he took from Osphena clipped to a folder labeled 'G-745'.

Erik took the folder and left the room, heading to his office down the hall. Reaching into his desk drawer, he grabbed the logbook and hurried out the room.

"Yeah, he's up here," Erik heard the maintenance worker say.

Erik raced for the restrooms and hid in the shower stall behind the lockers. He leaned against the wall when his legs grew weak and opened the folder, finding a dossier on Osphena. Flipping through the other stacks of papers, Erik noticed they were also collected information on the rest of the company in the photograph.

Erik froze when the door to the restrooms creaked open.

"You all right?" called an unfamiliar voice. "You're bleeding, I've noticed..." Erik clenched his teeth when footsteps resonated through the room. "Did someone shoot you? Stab you?" Erik slipped the logbook into his coat pocket, listening to the stranger open the stall doors. "I'm sure you're wondering why I'm looking for you. You're not sure who to trust anymore, right?"

Erik swallowed hard and broke out in cold sweat. Looking at the folder he held, Erik thumbed through the information, assimilating the paperwork. "*Osphena Kyaserin, Geneticist, unmarried,*" he read. "*Worked in Medical Ambulatory Surgical Hospital during the War...*"

"Just tell me what you're looking for," continued the voice, "and I'll tell you if I have to kill you."

"I don't know what I'm looking for," Erik called back.

"Oh? It seems that you're sniffing around in places where you shouldn't."

Erik scanned the next sheet. "*Shana Schumacher, Records, unmarried,*" he read. "*Security and Intelligence Division personnel during and after the War, until her death...*" Erik dropped what he held when his headache worsened.

"What's the matter?" called the voice. "You sound like you're in a lot of pain."

"It's nothing," Erik snapped. "If you want to kill me, don't play around and get it over with."

"Until you tell me what you want."

"I'm telling you, I don't know." The echoing footfalls clopped along the tiles into the locker room. Erik peered around the stall, seeing a man's shadow grow larger in height. "How can I prove that you're hunting me for the wrong thing?" Erik demanded.

"By telling me what you know," answered the stranger.

"I'm telling you, I know nothing."

"Well then... It seems I can't get through to you."

"Don't push me," Erik spat and stepped out the stall as the shadow came closer. He sensed the presence of the other behind the locker and swallowed hard when he faced his opponent who had his features, with the exception of brown hair and green eyes. The young man wore a dark red suit, black overcoat and black boots.

"So push back," said Erik's counterpart.

"Only one of us is getting out of here," Erik said evenly and clenched his hands at his sides. "It won't be you."

"You're still too weak from those injuries and drugs in your system." His counterpart folded his arms across his chest. "Now, we can solve this dilemma in two ways - have a big nasty fight that will ruin your assignment and get more people killed than needed, or give up the information you already know."

"Here, it's all in the folder," Erik said, pointing to the floor. "I was to pick it up."

"What an idiot," the brown-haired stranger said and snorted. "Either that or you're an older model."

"What?" Erik shrugged. "I don't trust computers... They lose data over time."

"If you say so." Erik stepped aside as the young man approached. "Pick it up," he demanded. Erik crouched down and scooped up the fallen paperwork then froze when he sensed cold steel at the back of his head. "Give me your phone," growled his counterpart.

"What makes you think I have it?" Erik retorted.

"I *know* you have it. She's waiting outside for you, isn't she?" The brown-haired stranger tapped Erik's head with the pistol's muzzle. "She's waiting for you to call her because she can't come in unless you give her the code, otherwise she'll wait until a certain amount of time has passed."

"Is that so?" Erik said sarcastically.

"So call her, bring her in, and I can rid of you both."

"Sure." Erik reached in his coat pocket and withdrew the phone. "It's all yours."

The young man reached for the cellular and Erik grabbed his wrist, hurling him over his head. Slamming the brown-haired assassin over into the stall, Erik reached for his other hand, wrestling for control of the gun. It discharged, shattering the glass and Erik cried out when cut across the cheek and on his feet.

The brown-haired stranger shoved Erik back, sending him tumbling head over heels on the floor. Landing flat on his back, Erik yowled when he struck his head against a nearby locker.

"You're through!" bellowed the assassin and pointed his silenced pistol at Erik.

Erik watched in stunned silence when he heard a muffled shot ring out and his counterpart dropped to the floor with a bullet between the eyes. Blood began pooling beneath his body and Erik gasped weakly for breath as he scrambled to his feet.

The maintenance worker stepped in, armed with a silenced high-powered pistol and his beaten toolbox. "I still got it," he murmured and grinned.

"Thanks," Erik said gratefully.

"Anytime."

"Would you grab those papers for me?" Erik asked timidly. "I don't have shoes."

"I noticed that." The worker put aside his toolbox on the locker room bench. "You know, I'm surprised you're back to work again."

"You *know* me...?"

"We met a long, long time ago." The man took apart his gun and put it inside the toolbox then left for the shattered stall, collecting the paperwork. "You helped me get out of a bad situation and I helped you get back at the bad guys who put you there."

"You did?"

"Sometimes I wonder what would've happened if you stuck around..."

"I don't...?"

"Here." The man handed Erik the folder. "Be careful out there."

"How old are you?" Erik asked as he took the paperwork.

The maintenance worker grinned. "How old do you think I look?"

"White hair notwithstanding...?" Erik shrugged his shoulders. "Twenty-five? Thirty maybe?"

The worker chortled. "Then you wouldn't believe me if I told you."

"Okay."

"I'm Fifty." Erik's jaw dropped open and the maintenance

worker laughed out loud. "Hard to believe, huh?" he went on. "I still get carded when I want to buy a beer now and then."

"What about the mess?" Erik finally managed to say.

"By the time everyone else clocks in, it'll be nice and clean."

Erik nodded. "Again, thanks."

The maintenance worker nodded back. "Anytime."

Erik left the bathroom, heading back downstairs.

FIFTY-TWO

Exiting outdoors, Erik spotted Clairese's car pull up in front of Mercado Corp's building. He hastily approached and she leaned over, opening the door for him. Erik slipped into the passenger side then she sped away.

Setting the folder aside on the dashboard, Erik withdrew his logbook. "Turn on the light," he said and Clairese reached up, switching on the overhead light. "Tell me what these are used for." Erik read off the list of chemicals and minerals and Clairese nodded as he spoke.

Clairese repeated the list to herself and grew pallid as her eyes widened. "What the–?" she yelped and looked to Erik. "All you're missing is Chromium, Zinc, Manganese, Vanadium, Selenium, and Molybdenum!"

"What are you talking about?" Erik cried. "I haven't said anything about those!"

"Those were the latest purchase orders!"

"What exactly are you working on?"

Clairese shook her head and returned her sight to the road as she continued driving. Erik grunted, tossing the logbook on the dashboard then picked up the folder, opening it.

"*Joseph Stone, Database Management, unmarried,*" Erik read. "*Known as Giuseppe Petra before the War, worked in*

Communications Support, later Electronics Engineering..." He moaned when his headache worsened and furrowed his brow, pressing his fingers against his temple.

"Do you need something?" Clairese asked.

"A stiff drink when we get back," Erik muttered.

"Sure."

Erik read the next sheet, scanning the name. "*Melvin Zachary, Programmer, separated... F-35 Aeronaut First Class for Air Corps during the War, later Aviation Logistics...*" Shutting the folder, Erik rubbed at his eyes when his sight began to waver from the thudding pain behind them. He tossed the papers on the dashboard, instead looking out the window of the passing scenery in silence.

Arriving back at Brodie's apartment, Erik dropped the folder and logbook on the cocktail table then sank into the couch, groaning in pain. Clairese headed for the kitchen and returned with two lowball glasses of vodka in ice.

"What do you plan to do next?" Clairese asked, handing Erik a glass. "You'll have to clock in a few hours from now."

"I'm not thinking about that right now," Erik muttered and gulped down his drink. "Get me some tweezers and some alcohol, will you?"

Clairese set her drink aside and left for the bathroom, later returning with a first aid kit, a pair of tweezers and a large bath towel. She set the case aside on the table and handed Erik the tweezers then draped the towel over her shoulder.

Erik took the tweezers then put his feet on the table as she came around and knelt beside him. Reaching forward, Erik pulled out a small shard of glass still stuck in his skin from the top of his foot.

"How could you walk around with that still in you?" Clairese cried, horrified. "Are you in pain at all?"

"The drugs are still in my system," Erik replied and dropped the glass into the nearby ashtray. "I'm feeling pretty numb right now. But it'll eventually wear off and it's going to be Hell."

"Let me help."

"Whatever."

Clairese opened the kit and withdrew another pair of tweezers then took his left foot, helping him remove glass silvers embedded in his skin while Erik worked on the other. After ridding the glass, Clairese put the towel down on the floor and uncapped a bottle of hydrogen peroxide. Erik put his feet on the towel and she poured on the liquid, watching the chemical bubble and hiss over his cuts.

"Get the rubbing alcohol," Erik demanded.

"It'll burn like crazy!" Clairese yelped, alarmed.

"I don't want it infected. Just get it!"

Clairese blew a short sigh and set the peroxide aside on the table then hurried for the bathroom. Erik reached over, taking her drink and immediately swallowed its contents. Clairese returned with a bottle of green liquid. "All I have is menthol," she replied sadly. "He's got arthritic hands."

"It'll do." Erik set his glass aside and grabbed the nearby pillow. Clairese uncapped the bottle and knelt at Erik's feet. Pouring on the isopropyl alcohol, Erik hunched forward, screaming into the pillow he held. The pain released and he fell into darkness.

Erik moaned when he sensed movement as he slowly came to. He found himself in the back seat of a sedan and looked up and around, noticing Clayton in the passenger seat, pointing a pistol at the driver, an olive-skinned young woman with short brown hair.

"What are you doing?" Erik asked weakly.

"I'm getting help for you," Clayton replied. "You're too banged up to keep going."

"They'll call the cops on us if we go to the hospital."

"It's okay, I got a plan."

"What's the plan?"

"The nice lady is going to stop at the first gas station she sees and pull around back," Clayton replied. "Then she'll call a friend for us."

"Please don't hurt me," the woman pleaded.

"I won't hurt you as long as you do as I say."

"Please, lady, don't run away," Erik rasped and lay back. "He's deadly accurate - he served as a sniper for the Defense Forces!"

"Oh no..." the woman mewed.

"That's right," Clayton darkly affirmed. "I can kill a man at twenty-eight hundred yards."

"T-That's a mile and a half!" the woman sputtered.

"Right, so please, don't do anything stupid."

Later the sparse roads turned wider with more traffic as they entered the city. Passing a sign stating a gas station was ahead, she turned off on an exit ramp and entered a busy street.

"There's a station on the corner," Clayton noted. "Get to it." The woman swallowed hard and nodded, pulling around back. Putting the car in park, Clayton waved the pistol at the woman. "Get your phone," he ordered. "You're making a call for me."

"I thought your friend had to go to the hospital," the woman said softly as she reached for her purse.

"I'm pretty tough," Erik murmured.

The woman withdrew her cellular phone. "Do you want my phone?" she asked.

"No, you're dialing a number for me: Swinburne thirty-eight sixty-four."

The woman nodded and dialed the number as directed. "What should I say?" she asked.

"Tell me what you hear."

"The number you dialed is no longer in service," the woman murmured.

"Dial Bugle sixty-one ninety-five, then at the tone, dial Drexel." The woman did as told and flinched when a loud tone went through the line.

"What's going on?" Erik complained. "Did you get a facsimile machine?"

"It's processing," Clayton replied. "Just wait."

After several moments, a series of short and long tones beeped. Clayton nodded, listening intently. Erik also listened and took in a shallow breath when he realized it was Signal Code. After a moment, dial tone followed.

"Now, you're going to buy us a few things," Clayton said to the woman. "I suggest you don't try anything because you really don't want to see how good of a shot I am."

"W-what do you want?" the woman asked.

"First, your phone." Clayton held out his free hand and the woman handed it to him. "Secondly, a change of clothes and a razor. Also, I'm keeping your purse."

"But–!" the woman protested.

"All you need is money. Now get in there and do as I say."

The woman blew a dejected sigh and withdrew her wallet from her purse then stepped out the car. Clayton glared at her as she walked across the lot and entered the building.

"How do you know she won't say anything or run?" Erik asked. "Can you really see her from here?"

"She's going to say something of course," answered Clayton, "and it won't be long before someone shows up."

"What was the message about?"

"We'll get picked up before Agents get us. The computer's got our location. All phones emit tracking and positioning signals, you know."

Moments later, the woman returned with a shopping bag. Erik sat up, surprised.

"I thought for sure you'd run away," Erik commented once the woman entered the car.

"I'll take you to a motel or something if you want," she answered.

Clayton put the gun on the dashboard and took the bag the woman handed over. "Why the change of heart?" he asked.

"I heard over the radio about two escapees from Keystone Reformation Center and I remember my brother was sent there," she explained. "He worked for Metro Sanatorium and something happened. They claimed he broke down from stress and went to Keystone for three years, and after they claimed he was cured, he wasn't the same."

Erik moaned and clutched his painfully pounding head. "Keystone, you say?" he murmured.

"What did he do?" Clayton probed.

"He never told me."

Clayton handed her the keys and she started the car.

The woman pulled into the lot of a rundown motel and went inside to pay for a room. She later returned and opened the door, gathering her belongings. "Come on," she said and Clayton glanced to Erik.

"You okay to walk?" he asked.

"I think so..." Erik replied and opened his door, clutching his side. "How long do we have to wait here?"

"Until the heat dies down, then we'll move on."

Erik followed the woman into a room and saw a large bed in the center capable of holding three people at best. On both sides were a small nightstand and an overhead television rest on the left with a space heater on a shelf next to it, while a box air conditioner sat on the right of it. In front of the bed, rest a larger set of chests with a wall mirror and offside to the right a path led to a small bathroom. Near the front door where the woman stood, was a low walnut table with a small microwave on it, resting before a large overstuffed chair.

"I'll be back and get more things," assured the woman as Erik approached the bed and sat on the edge. "Do you need anything specific?"

"Aside from a doctor?" Erik moaned.

"I'll be back."

Clayton later entered the room with several bags and set one on the nearby table, then unlaced his gun belt and set it on the chair. He headed for the bathroom and Erik lay back in bed, staring at the ceiling. He later dozed off.

Erik moaned when he felt a cold compress to his face. His eyes fluttered open and he looked up at Clairese standing over him.

"Do you think you can still go to work?" Clairese asked. Erik groaned and sat up on his elbows, finding he lay on the couch and his coat removed. He looked down, noticing his feet bandaged.

"I need to go," Erik muttered. "My assignment isn't over yet."

"What are you looking for?"

"I'm not supposed to tell anyone, but I'm a dead man anyway." Erik lay back and put an arm over his eyes. "A man named Derrick Andrews was working on a project coded 'Divinity'. He got killed over it and I'm supposed to find out why."

Clairese paled and set the towel aside. "I'm working on that project," she said softly. "We've been ordering minerals from Midco/Sanato and shipping chemicals to Mercado. The results are sent to AMASTCOMS. I'm not sure what they want, as it's been heavily invested by Gen-Tech to ensure production."

"I need to know what he was killed for," Erik complained. "Now I'm a target."

"I'll look into your logs and see what the correlation is in the main database."

"Don't get caught. Someone's been snooping and it's already been flagged."

"Is it related to the folder you have?"

"What about it?" Erik sat up and noticed the folder open and the papers spread on the table. He gasped when he saw one labeled 'Genovera Zachary'.

Moments later, the door unlocked and Clairese and Erik turned, watching Brodie walk in with a bag of Erik's belongings.

"Oh, there you are, Feddy!" Brodie said brightly and set his clothes near the couch. "You gave me a scare, buddy. There was a big thing at the clinic when you came up missing."

"Are they going to send Public Security?" Clairese asked.

"No, I talked them out of it." Brodie pulled out of his coat and draped it across the couch's back. "Put on a pot of coffee will you, Sweetheart? I'm going to shower and change."

Erik sat up and glared at Brodie as he walked past for his bedroom.

"Why are you looking at him like that?" Clairese inquired.

"I'm thinking," Erik muttered.

"Oh, I don't want to hear it." Clairese stormed back for the kitchen and started banging pots. "I don't hear a thing!" she called.

Erik snorted and rose to his feet. "It's not that," he shot back, "but you might hear some noise."

Brodie exited the bedroom moments later in his bathrobe and with a lit cigarette dangling from his lip. Erik stalked over, following him into the bathroom.

"What do you think you're doing?" Erik snarled as Brodie opened the closets and withdrew several towels.

"I'm about to jump in the shower," Brodie answered and smirked. "Why, care to join me?"

"Don't even think about it," Erik retorted.

Brodie shrugged. "I can't help it."

"Why are you looking into Genovera?" Erik demanded. "What about the others?"

"You had that picture and I thought if I did some digging for you, it might jar your memory." Brodie smiled and pat Erik's head. "Hey, it seems to be working, eh?"

Erik narrowed his eyes and pressed firmly against Brodie's bare chest. "It better be simple info gathering," he hissed.

"Oh, it is."

Erik snatched Brodie's cigarette away and stalked out the room, returning to the parlor. He paced and smoked, fuming in silence. Later the telephone rang and Clairese called for Erik. "Are you sure they're looking for me?" he called back and put out his tapering cigarette in the ashtray.

"Positive," Clairese answered. "They asked for Ferdian and you're the only one with that name."

Erik blew a hard sigh and entered the kitchen, taking the receiver from Clairese. "What is it?" he spat into the line.

"I see you're up to your old tricks again, Mister Ferdian," Giuseppe's voice snarled.

"It couldn't be helped," Erik retorted. "You pushed and I pushed back."

"What are you after?"

"I should be asking you that."

"This isn't over."

"Savvy."

"Do you need anything?" Clairese inquired.

Erik hung up the line and took a seat at the kitchen table. Clairese approached with a mug of black coffee and Erik glanced up at her. "What is it you want?" he grumbled.

"You seem really distressed," Clairese murmured.

"No shit!" Erik spat, bristling. "You would be too if someone wants you dead over information you can't remember!" He ran his hands through his hair and blew a heavy sigh. "Someone tried to kill me over something they think I know. I need to call someone but it's dead."

"I might have a charger that fits," Clairese suggested. "Where's your phone?"

"In my coat pocket." Erik put his head on the table, moaning. "If I sleep, then I forget everything. The drugs they gave me at the hospital really screwed me over and that doctor..."

"Yeah, Feddy, about that doctor," Brodie's voice said over him. Erik looked up, facing the older man dressed in a pair of navy pinstriped slacks and pale gray dress shirt. "He had some pills filled for you. You should pick them up at the Pharmacy today."

"I don't know where it is," Erik snapped.

"Mercado has one. I sent it there on your employee account."

"Thanks."

"What kind of pills are you getting?" Clairese wondered aloud.

"Why do you want to know?" Erik grumbled and hid his head in his arms again. "Do you plan on selling them?"

"If they're happy pills, why not trip awhile?" Clairese murmured. "I don't want to see you hurt."

"Don't waste your breath."

"You should get ready, Feddy," Brodie reprimanded. "We need to clock in soon - got quarterlies today that we can't miss."

"What if we do?" Erik mumbled.

"We get axed instantly."

Erik sat up, raising an eyebrow at Brodie. "Termination?" he asked faintly.

Brodie nodded and appeared concerned. "You look like I just read your death sentence, buddy," he murmured. "It's hard to find work for vets like you. You don't want to slum it up."

"Thanks." Erik rose to his feet. "Fix me three creams, no sugar."

"Sure," Brodie replied.

Erik returned to the bathroom and shut the door behind him. He leaned against the door and the pain he suppressed suddenly overwhelmed him, dragging him down into a sea of red.

FIFTY-THREE

"Hey," Clayton's voice called to Erik. "Hey, wake up."

"What is it?" Erik muttered. He opened his eyes, staring up at Clayton wearing a white t-shirt and denim shorts. In his arms, he held a gray long sleeved t-shirt and loose olive pants. Erik's eyes widened when he noticed Clayton was bald and free of facial hair.

"You look like a matchstick," Erik remarked.

Clayton smirked. "I'm just another skinny sexy bald guy," he retorted and dropped the clothes on Erik. "Get up and change. We got some stuff for you to tape up with."

"What about your head?"

"They know I wear caps. I don't think my head's going to get anymore tan than what it is now."

Erik laughed weakly then clutched his side and winced as he sat up. "So I'm not seeing a doctor?" he groaned.

"Not anytime soon. We don't have time."

"All I'm going to do is slow you down."

"I promised to carry you," Clayton asserted. "Now let's go."

Erik nodded and scooped up the clothes in his arms then limped into the bathroom. He found several boxes of hair dye, rolls of gauze, elastic bandage and tape on the back of the toilet seat.

"I might as well," Erik grumbled and picked up a container of red hair coloring, reading the printed instructions on the back.

After showering and carefully wrapping and taping his side, his hands, and his knee, Erik dyed his hair. He yanked off the cheap plastic gloves then pulled into his pants and ran the towel through his hair before draping it around his shoulders.

Erik stared back at the reflection of a fiery-haired teenager with freckles across the cheeks and tired blue eyes. He swallowed hard, uneasy at what he saw in return and touched the mirror with a shaky hand.

You're getting too close...

Erik heard a knock at the door and stiffened.

"You decent?" Clayton called from the other side.

"I got pants on," Erik answered.

The door opened, revealing Clayton who grinned. "Hey, you look better as a redhead," he teased and poked Erik's chest. "That color brings out your cute freckles!"

Erik glowered back and pushed him away. "I'm not used to it," he groused. "I could stand a haircut too."

"You need to grow it out some."

Erik pushed past Clayton and returned to the bed, sitting on the edge. "Where did the lady go?" he inquired.

"She said she was going to pick up some miso soup and ramen," Clayton answered.

"I don't know if we can trust her."

"I'll get rid of anyone who tries to hurt us," Clayton vowed.

"I told you, you don't have to watch out for me."

Clayton frowned. "I do this because I want to."

"As far as they're concerned, we're still together," Erik protested. "We need to split up."

"How far do you think you'll go?" Clayton snapped. "You're hurt and you're not familiar with the area!"

"But—!"

"You don't have much of a plan, do you? You can't get by just winging it!"

"Well...!"

"We need to reach Cicero Park and just get out of here... keep going and don't stick around in the busy areas for too long."

Erik blew a heavy sigh and ran his hands through his hair. "Fine," he mumbled.

Suddenly the phone on the nightstand rang and Erik let out a yelp in surprise. Clayton put up a hand and picked up the receiver. He motioned to Erik and pointed ahead. Erik turned in the direction he indicated, noticing a pad of paper and pen resting atop the microwave. He left the bed and reached the pad and pen, tossing the items to Clayton. Clayton caught it and immediately scribbled a note before hanging up the receiver.

"What's that about?" Erik asked.

"Coordinates," Clayton replied.

"Are they on their way?" Erik demanded. "What's all this mean?"

"It means that we're going to need some rest for tonight," Clayton answered. "Pickup is postponed."

"Where are you sleeping?"

"Where you're not sleeping."

"You're driving me nuts!" Erik complained.

"You need some rest. We're both tired." Erik moaned and dropped on the bed's edge. Clayton stood over Erik, appearing concerned. "Look, I'll camp out near the door in the chair there and you can have the bed. Please, just get some sleep and leave the worrying to me, okay?"

"Sure, whatever..." Erik draped an arm over his eyes while Clayton took a seat in the chair and picked up the rifle leaning against the wall. "Say, Clayton," Erik said moments later.

"What is it?"

"Do you think they'll find us and really kill us so they can make robot assassins with our face and memory?"

"I wouldn't know," Clayton murmured. "I don't remember my family."

"What happened to them?"

"I wish I could say. They basically mind-fucked me and I can't remember anymore, just like you."

"Will they eventually erase me?"

"Most likely... But it doesn't have to be."

Erik yowled when slapped hard across the face and sat up with a start, swinging. Brodie grabbed his fist and pushed Erik's hand away.

"Hey, hey," Brodie said softly when Erik grabbed his collar. "You need to get ready, buddy."

Erik blinked and squinted at Brodie who smiled gently. "What happened to me?" he muttered.

"I guess your injuries got the best of you," Brodie answered. "Come on, get washed and tape up. We need to go in an hour."

Erik released Brodie's shirtfront and touched his face with

dark stubble on his jaw. "You look horrific," he noted.

"I'll shave once you get done in there. Now let's get going."

"Fine."

Brodie stood and held out a hand to Erik. "Need any help?" he asked.

Erik took his hand and let the older man pull him to his feet. "I should be fine," he grumbled.

"You don't look too hot, Feddy. I'll sit with you if you like."

Erik frowned and pointed to the door. "You're not watching me so you can get off," he spat. "Get out of here."

"Fine, but if you fall out and crack your skull open, remember I offered."

"Out. Now."

Brodie chortled and stepped out the bathroom, shutting the door behind him. Erik groaned and grabbed a towel from closet. Approaching the sink, he ran the water and washed his face, then looked at himself in the mirror.

Erik frowned at his sallow face with freckles across the cheeks and thinning shaggy red hair. He touched his scars across his eye and cheek, ran his fingers along his jaw and grew concerned when he noticed he had no facial hair, not even stubble. He left the mirror and opened the bathroom closet, finding a straight razor, shaving cup with brush and a small bar of shaving soap resting prominently over the towels and in front of bars of soap and bottles of shampoo and conditioner.

"How old am I?" Erik murmured. "Why can't I remember?"

"You okay in there?" Brodie's voice called outside the door. "I don't hear the water running."

"No," Erik called back.

Brodie opened the door and peered inside. "What's the matter?" he inquired.

"How old do you think I look?"

"I don't know, maybe twenty, twenty-five, thirty perhaps?" Brodie shrugged his shoulders. "It's hard to tell."

"I don't have any facial hair like you do."

"It's a genetic abnormality most likely - nothing to worry about. Some guys just can't grow any." Erik turned to Brodie who leaned against the door, arms folded across his chest. "I knew this one fella in my unit who's part-Chinese, part-Scottish, and some Portuguese and he was thirty years old. His face was smooth as a baby's bottom. Then later I met his old man, and I tell ya, he was a lion. Scary looking guy, if you ask me."

Erik smirked. "Thanks," he murmured.

"Sure, no problem. Is that all that's bothering you?"

"Why do you like me so much, Mister Avers?"

Brodie flushed slightly and waved Erik away. "Go on and get yourself together. We need to get those quarterlies turned in."

"Sure."

Brodie stepped out and Erik undressed then took off his old soiled bandages before stepping in the shower. He stiffened when he heard the door open and peeped out behind the curtain, noticing Brodie setting bandages and tape on the bathroom counter.

"I'm not trying to cop a look," Brodie announced, grinning. "Honest."

Erik narrowed his eyes. "Get out," he snapped. "You're really trying my patience!"

"Come on," Clairese called. "Stop being pervy and hurry up in there. I need to get to work too, you know!"

Brodie laughed and stepped out the room. Erik grunted and finished washing, then got out to dry off. Wrapping the towel about his waist, he approached the counter and pulled out the bandages. Putting down the toilet seat, he sat down and began taping up his side and thigh. Erik heard the door open and looked up at Clairese entering wearing her father's bathrobe tied loosely shut about her body. His cheeks warmed when Clairese put her hands on her hips.

"I'm just here to tape your shoulder and back," she declared, "then shoo you out of here so I can get ready."

"You don't have to do that," Erik murmured.

"Would you rather have that horny dog do it?" Clairese teased. "Just think —"

Erik put up his hands. "Please, don't," he said, alarmed. "I don't want to think and I don't want to hear it."

Clairese giggled and picked up a box of gauze pads. Erik turned around, facing the shower as Clairese approached and put on the pad on his shoulder. Erik held it down as she grabbed the tape and sealed it shut. Erik then grunted when Clairese used her elbow to hold down the gauze pad against his back, while tearing off the tape with her hands.

"There, you're all set to go," confirmed Clairese as she finished sealing the pad against his skin.

Erik stood and turned to face Clairese who smiled gently. He reached forward and Clairese shut her eyes as Erik adjusted a loosened curler. "You don't want to lose that," he murmured.

Clairese's cheeks flushed scarlet. "Thanks," she muttered.

Erik stepped past her and entered the parlor where Brodie sat on the couch with a dark blue tie hanging loosely about his neck, smoking a cigarette.

"Clothes are on the bed," Brodie directed.

"What are you thinking about?" Erik asked. "And don't tell me the obvious."

"What's your connection with those guys?"

"What do you mean?"

"Like Schumacher and Zachary?"

Erik clenched his teeth. "What about them?" he asked faintly.

"I heard they were mixed up in some big thing with that nasty scandal about AMASTCOMS regarding faulty equipment. It made the Defense Forces look real bad."

"I don't remember much about them."

"Well, I can tell you all sorts of stories about the War anytime you want."

"Did you work with them?"

"Yeah, helped them out."

Erik left for the bedroom and grabbed the pair of black slacks left for him on the bed. Dropping the towel, he pulled into them, and then sat on the edge, putting on a pair of athletic socks.

"Mell was a big shot pilot with the A-12 and the F-35, had the most kills anyone ever had during the War - 355!" Brodie said outside the door. "We had problems with the ComSat when the computers went down behind our lines and could only communicate via analog."

"I thought it was all digital," Erik said as he slipped into a navy dress shirt.

"Back then they were in the last stages of converting," Brodie explained. "Now we got lines open just in case that happens again."

"So what happened?" Erik prodded and exited the room as he buttoned his shirt. Brodie stepped aside, holding his lit cigarette in his hand.

"We couldn't get those boys over where Engineering Support was blowing up ports and bridges in enemy territory. They got there under heavy fire and Mell was able to punch through and clear them out, only using pods and his guns."

"That sounds difficult."

"Yeah, with no radar on top of that! And the crazy thing was that he never worked with missiles, said the payload wasn't enough. Anyways, he was going low in total suicide mode and the bastards got lucky - hit the one weak point in the plane and it shattered like glass!"

Erik approached the cocktail table and grabbed the pack of cigarettes and lighter left there, then made his way into the kitchen where a mug of coffee rest on the table. "Is that how he lost his leg?" he asked.

"Yeah, got mangled when he tried to punch out," Brodie said and entered the kitchen. "The damn thing jammed and he went down with it."

"How horrific." Erik sat at the table and picked up his cooling coffee.

"When our lines finally came back on, we heard chatter from medics on the ground that most of the Engineering Support boys got creamed. Schumacher and a handful of others survived. He was the only one that went out to the wreck and yanked Mell out. Got burned pretty bad doing it too."

Erik nodded and lit his cigarette. "Know anything about Genovera?" he murmured.

"Genovera...?" Erik glanced to Brodie who shrugged his shoulders. "I don't remember a gal by that name."

"Get the folder, will you?"

"Sure."

Brodie left and Erik smoked in silence, unsettled. Brodie returned with the folder and set it on the table. Erik opened it, sifting through the paperwork and pulled Genovera's file, scanning the paper.

"Genovera Zachary, Machinist, separated," Erik read. *"Cargo Transport during the War... Two children, male..."*

"What's the matter?" Brodie asked when Erik put the paper aside and held one hand to his head, grunting in pain.

"Just a headache," Erik muttered. "It says she was in Cargo Transport."

"Yeah, it took them awhile to get over there after the bridge was blown in the confusion. One of our pilots read his map wrong and took it out."

"I thought F-35's had integrated helmets with the main system?"

"Remember, ComSat was down, so that knocked out the ability to talk with the main computer. Delay was bad, like two minutes and you can't have that flying in real time."

Erik sat up and downed his coffee, then stared down at the cup. "I don't understand what they have to do with me," he complained. "My head hurts just thinking about it."

"You said you were a Duce," Brodie suggested. "Maybe you

met them during your time there?"

"How long did they serve?"

"I think Schumacher and Mell were Tenners. I don't know about that lady."

"Thanks."

"Yeah, no problem."

"You two are awfully quiet out there," Clairese called. "Come on, we need to go."

"On my way," Brodie called back.

Suddenly a digital ring pierced the air and Erik flinched, startled. "Hey, it's your phone," Clairese said from the next room. "I was charging it for you."

"Give it here, please," Erik said. Clairese entered the kitchen with the cellular and Erik took it from her, then pressed the button. "Hello?" he greeted.

"Good, you're okay," Gina said in relief. "I was worried after we suddenly got cut off."

"It ran down on me."

"I'll meet you after work. Please don't wander off."

"Is it important?"

"Very."

Gina hung up the line and Erik looked down at the phone, puzzled.

"Something wrong?" inquired Clairese.

"She's acting weird," Erik stated.

"I would be too if you gave me The Clap!" Brodie interjected. "I'm surprised she still wants to see you!"

Clairese let out a cry in horror. "Oh, eww, gross!" she squealed. "So those medicines you've got to pick up are antibiotics?" Clairese shuddered and promptly stormed out the room. "And to think I planned to seduce you tonight! Disgusting pig!"

Erik burst out laughing and Brodie chortled.

"Come on, Feddy," Brodie said. "Your shoes are at the door."

"Okay."

FIFTY-FOUR

Erik entered the offices with Brodie and they made their way upstairs. Erik yawned and Brodie gave a faint smile.

"I'll pick you up a coffee from the canteen," Brodie said. "Three creams, no sugar, right?" Erik nodded and they stepped off the elevator once on the fifth floor.

Erik waved at Brodie as he went down the opposite hall then headed for his office. Opening the door, Erik clenched his teeth when he found it ransacked with file cabinets open, papers and folders strewn about, and the computer running.

"The hell is this?" he growled and slammed shut his door. Coming out of his coat, Erik threw it on the back of the desk chair then started the task of picking up papers. He paused when he came across a sheet labeled: *Physical revelation - Case Study: Molecular Rearrangement of Subcutaneous Matter and Measures For Enhancement of Physical Capabilities Through Improved Regenerative Medicine.*

Erik sat on the desk's edge and thumbed through the thesis, frowning when the headache he had worsened.

"This is about the development of Armaments with the use of Core Irons," he muttered. "Somehow they're put into Autonomous Combat Units..."

Hearing a knock at the door, Erik looked up at Brodie who

opened the door. "Here ya go, Feddy," Brodie said brightly.

"What do you know about those combat androids?" Erik asked, taking the coffee Brodie handed him.

"Not that much, but my buddy Joey has a clue. He works on them for a living."

"I want to see him."

"Sure, no problem! I'll call him up. We'll see him after work." Brodie then frowned when he saw the state of the office and his face paled. "Hey, what happened in here?"

"Somebody was looking for something."

"Are you under audit or something?"

"Not sure."

"I'll ask Sinclair. He might know."

"Sure."

Brodie left the room and Erik sipped his coffee, glancing at the paper he held. "*Giuseppe has a clue I need*," he thought, setting his paper aside. "*He was an Electronics Engineer after all*." Erik put his coffee on his desk and started the task of cleaning his office.

Erik finished the last of the filing and returned to his computer, tapping the spacebar. He found his database open and checked the last saved version. Merging the two documents, Erik found no changes.

"Maybe they didn't find what they were looking for," Erik muttered and glanced at his clock, noting the time was a quarter to noon. He grunted and turned in his seat, unlatching his window then returned to his desk, taking out the ashtray.

The door opened moments later, revealing Sangita in a tan

blouse and beige skirt with brown knee socks.

"Aren't you coming down for lunch?" she asked.

"Why, what's going on?" Erik answered.

"It's the company meeting for the first-year quarterly with the higher-ups," Sangita explained. "We do this four times a year."

Erik stood and approached the other chair, taking his coat. "Why does everyone hate this sort of thing?"

"Because if we screwed up, we get the immediate axe," explained Sangita. "We can't make any errors because this is heavy stuff - Mercado's mainly contracted with AMASTCOMS and those hawks *will* petition to yank funding with anything dealing with their precious troops."

"I thought they didn't send live ones out there anymore."

"They don't. It's all Synthoids now."

"Shit." Erik sagged against his desk when his headache flared worse than before. He clutched a hand to his head and Sangita entered, concerned.

"Are you ill?" Sangita asked timidly.

"I think I'll get the axe around here," Erik mewed. "My database's been screwed with... The purchase orders were wrong."

"That's probably the same reason why Eisenheimer was let go," Sangita murmured.

Erik looked up, stunned. "What?" he squawked.

"He was let go last quarter because of the very same thing. We had a temp fill in until someone new got hired."

"Who was the temp?"

Sangita shrugged. "I don't know... Your position has the

highest turnover rate. Every quarter we get somebody new."

"Is there any other way someone could tamper with it?"

"Aside from hacking, but that's impossible as we're connected to the Agency of Advanced Defense Research Projects Network."

Erik's eyes widened. "The Agency?" he asked faintly.

Sangita nodded. "Who else?"

Erik moaned and his eyes rolled to the back of his head as he slipped to the floor.

Sangita screamed.

Erik woke up, feeling warmth next to him. He turned over and switched on the nearby lamp then sat up; finding the woman snoring softly on her side under the covers on the bed's other side. Erik looked to Clayton sitting in the overstuffed chair, rifle in his lap with his head down on his chest and eyes closed, asleep.

Leaving the bed, Erik approached the table with the microwave and found several packs of cup noodles, soup, and tea. He took one cup and opened it, then headed into the bathroom, running the tap.

Clayton suddenly snapped to attention, holding his rifle at ready. "Who's there?" he snapped.

"It's me," Erik replied. "Just heating up some food."

"Oh..."

Erik grabbed for his shirt left on the back of the toilet and returned to the room, putting the cup in the microwave, then pressed several buttons. Clayton sat back in his chair, blowing a heavy sigh.

Erik gingerly pulled into his shirt and took a seat on the floor, leaning his back against the bed. "How much longer do we have to hide here?" he asked.

"We're leaving in a bit," answered Clayton, "before the early risers."

"So while we wait, tell me something."

"What do you want to know?"

"How'd you learn to shoot like that?"

Clayton gave a wry grin. "Practice," he said cryptically. The microwave beeped before Erik could say more and Clayton set aside his gun. Clayton held up a hand at Erik who readied to rise from his position. "Let me get it," he said. "You just rest."

"I told you not to worry about me," Erik groused.

"Fork or chopsticks?" Clayton said instead as he left his chair and took out the cup noodles. He sifted through the nearby bag, withdrawing a pair of wooden eating sticks and a plastic fork.

"I wouldn't know whether to pick my teeth or my ear with those things," Erik cracked.

Clayton snorted and handed Erik the meal with a fork. "So, when do you get deployed?"

Erik raised an eyebrow. "What are you talking about?"

"Which branch did you sign for in the Defense Forces?"

"You're talking out your butt," Erik replied. "I'm only sixteen."

"Sixteen, huh?" Clayton chortled. "Tell me a new one!"

Erik set down his cup. "What are you talking about?" he retorted.

"You're twenty years old," Clayton insisted. "You know

signup is mandatory at age twenty. Even criminals like us. They put you in the expendable unit though."

"How old are you?"

Clayton grinned. "Thirty."

Erik's eyes widened. "You don't look a day over sixteen!" he yelped.

Clayton doubled over laughing. "I'll show you my VitaStat card once we get on with our lives," he said once he calmed down.

Erik ran a hand through his hair, stunned. "How can I be twenty years old?" he moaned. "I don't understand... I thought I was sixteen and besides, wouldn't it look weird if some adult was going to Wyndham High?"

"You're supposed to be out by the time you're twenty if you've flunked enough times," Clayton added. "Once Summer Session hits, you're gone."

"But why was I there again?"

"Did you fail a lot of classes?"

Erik shook his head. "No," he answered. "I had some kind of accident and it screwed with my memory. Apparently it has something to do with this girl Danae who hates me for something I've done."

Clayton nodded. "Makes sense," he murmured. "You did get pretty scrambled. I wouldn't be surprised if that part's been erased after getting in traction like you did."

"Wait... So you're saying those weird freaky dreams are *true*?"

The telephone began ringing before Clayton could answer. Erik immediately stood and hurried to the receiver, picking it up.

"Hello?" he said into the line.

"You need to get going," said a friendly male voice Erik recognized.

"Wait, Doctor...!" The line suddenly cut off and Erik looked to the receiver in stunned silence.

"What was the message?" Clayton asked.

"He said we needed to get going."

"Alright, eat up and we'll get going."

Erik put the receiver back on the cradle and sank to the floor, picking up his cup of noodles. He ate in silence, growing increasingly worried.

Later after breakfast and sharing a cup of tea with Clayton, Erik took the pen and paper, writing a note while Clayton armed himself with his gun belts.

"What the hell are you doing?" Clayton hissed, taking up his rifle. "Grab her purse and let's go!"

"At least let me leave a message that we're sorry for taking advantage of her hospitality!" Erik retorted.

"You're weird," Clayton spat.

Erik tossed the pad on the bed and sneaked over to the other nightstand, taking the woman's purse, and then raced out the door, following Clayton to the car. Erik dug around for the keys and unlocked the doors for him, then went around for the other side as Clayton put the rifle on the back seat.

Erik handed Clayton the keys and Clayton started the car with a roar, then peeled out the lot.

FIFTY-FIVE

Entering another gas station, Clayton pulled up to a pump and Erik dug into the purse, taking the wallet.

"Make it quick," Clayton ordered, "and get some gloves for your hands."

Erik nodded and stepped out the car, hurrying to the small mart. He looked around, took notice of the various security cameras inside and bumped into a rack of gloves. Erik quickly took a pair, slipping them into his pocket and he whirled around, laughing uneasily.

"Are you alright?" asked the attendant.

"I'm such a blond," Erik said, "like, this rack just totally jumped right in front of me!"

"You seem to be deep in thought..."

"There's a lot to think about, like the meaning of life."

"Yeah, the meaning of life..." The attendant gave Erik a concerned glance. "What happened to your hands?"

"Playing with fireworks," Erik answered immediately. "Finally got the stitches out. Had to get three of my fingers sewn back on!"

"Ooh, dangerous stuff."

Erik sucked in a thin breath as a security cruiser pulled up and an officer stepped out then entered the station.

"A cup of joe, Joe," said the officer as he withdrew his wallet.

"Gonna need some jack, Jack," the attendant quipped and they both chuckled.

Erik stood behind the officer, shifting nervously on his feet. "Come on, hurry up," he grumbled when the officer chatted to the cashier about the weather.

"Yeah, it's been raining off and on all day," said the cashier. "Weatherman said it was supposed to be sunny!"

"Heh, I'd love a job where I get paid to guess for a living!"

"My granddaddy's arthritic joints are more accurate than that fella!" The men laughed and Erik stiffened when he heard another door open.

Turning, Erik spotted an armed security guard exiting the restrooms moments later and browse the aisles, looking at snacks. Erik turned back to the officer and the cashier, growing increasingly annoyed as they continued their conversation. Opening the wallet, Erik withdrew a twenty and slammed it on the counter.

"Pump number two!" he said and hurried outside.

Erik returned to the car as Clayton pumped gas and got in, looking uneasily to the security cruiser parked near the station's front. Clayton entered the car moments later and started the engine.

"What are you so jittery for?" Clayton asked.

"Public Security," Erik murmured. He withdrew the gloves from his pocket and slipped them on his hands.

"They won't bother us; we're just nobodies."

Pulling away from the station, Clayton entered the road and Erik tapped his fingers against his knees, overcome with worry.

"I can't help it," Erik complained. "They already talked about us over the radio."

"They're looking for a skinny blond, not a redhead," Clayton pressed. "I'm telling you, stop worrying."

"But my hands...!"

"Just stop, okay?"

Erik blew a short sigh, growing frustrated. "What about you?" he muttered.

"They never mentioned a skinny bald guy." Clayton grinned and Erik gave a faint smile.

Pulling to a stop behind other cars, red lights flashed behind them and Erik glanced to the mirror, spotting the security cruiser at their rear bumper.

"Shit!" Clayton growled.

"She reported us!" Erik yelped as Clayton pulled through a gap in traffic and floored the accelerator. Shooting through a narrow opening on the busy intersection against a red light, the cruiser revved behind them in close pursuit. "We're dead in the water!"

"Not if I can help it!" Clayton snapped. "Hang tight..." He approached the entry on the freeway ahead and sped on the ramp, barreling down the highway.

Clayton swerved on the right shoulder, passing several vehicles and cut back into traffic. The police car revved close, sirens blaring.

"Pull over!" the officer commanded over the bullhorn.

Erik let out a yelp when the security vehicle bumped the rear of their car and Clayton immediately swerved to the left, then to the right, avoiding a spinout.

"He's expecting us to run out of gas," Clayton said as he pulled around cars and the speedometer reached seventy.

"What about crashing into somebody else?" Erik cried.

"I got this!"

Erik looked behind him, spotting two more dark sedans with flashing red lights tailing behind the one gunning after them.

Clayton turned the wheel hard to the right, cutting across two lanes of traffic and careened down the exit ramp. Erik heard squealing tires and crashing metal behind them as the security cruisers tried to follow. Looking into the side mirror, Erik saw one car on its side, another upside down and the third on fire.

Erik fell against Clayton when he zoomed down the ramp and ran another red light, banking a hard left on two wheels. Landing with a firm thud, Clayton burned through two more red lights then hastily jammed on the brakes, yielding to an approaching car backing out of a parking lot.

"Now what?" Erik mewed.

"We're catching a train," Clayton replied.

"Where to?"

"Cicero Park! How many times do I have to keep telling you that?" Clayton then sped forward once the car passed and darted around other vehicles in the road.

"Like we're able to buy tickets!" Erik spat.

"Just hop on and go North toward the mountains. You can't miss it."

Pulling up into the train station's lot, Erik clamored out the car and raced for the platform. Bypassing the station guard, he immediately jumped the stairs and over the turnstile, hustling for the light rail commuter train before its doors closed.

Slipping inside, Erik gasped for breath, watching the guard run up to him with his baton, shouting as the train pulled away. He saw Clayton run after the guard and unleash his pistol, shooting the man in the head.

Erik turned away and walked down the aisles, searching for an empty seat. He froze when he spotted a security officer checking for tickets and broke out in cold sweat when the dispatcher's voice over the guard's radio attached to her hip dictated details matching Erik's description.

Once the next stop approached, Erik quickly stepped off before the officer approached to ask for his pass. Leaving the platform, Erik kept going until he advanced onto another building in the distance. Erik came to a stop once he noticed many officers milling about campus and several in bomber jackets.

"I'm at the Air Corps base!" Erik thought in dismay, gripping his head when pain throbbed behind his eyes and his vision shifted in red tint. He staggered back, seething. *"Chicago said something about those pilots..."*

Shaking his head to clear the vermilion fog, Erik looked up and spotted a diner ahead. He walked casually for the entrance and came to a stop when several officers and pilots exited, talking jovially amongst themselves.

"Hey!" one officer said in shock.

"What's a civilian doing here?" grumbled another.

"Er," Erik said in apprehension, "I, um, have a message for Thompson."

"Which one?" one officer demanded, standing over Erik.

The others stood nearby, watching in interest.

"I was only told to ask for Airman Thompson," Erik continued. "He's the one with the security clearance..."

"Oh," the pilot brightened and stood up straighter. "That's me!"

Erik cleared his throat. "Er, Airman Thompson, your orders have changed... You fly out next week."

"I thought I had to fly out tomorrow," Thompson complained. "Oh, well... Here, how much?" He went through his slacks and withdrew his wallet.

"Erm, fifty dollars," Erik said quickly.

"Why would the higher-ups hire a civilian courier service?" one officer protested.

"Maybe the couriers they have are too busy," another answered.

Thompson handed Erik the money and Erik muttered his thanks.

"Hey," Thompson called after Erik as he turned away. "Send a message for me, will you?"

Erik turned around, shifting his weight on his feet. "Depends on the message," he replied.

"It's not too difficult. Tell Sergeant Mitchell that plans for the Crimson Project and the CENTRA Engine Interment are finally all systems go."

"CENTRA Engine Interment...?" Erik parroted. "Crimson Project...?"

"He'll know what I mean," Thomson said and handed Erik a twenty note. "I want him to have a head start before the guys at Gateway start begging for money."

"Sure thing," Erik hesitated. "Er, is there a restroom here?"

"Sure, go right in straight to the left."

"Right... Left... Gotcha."

Erik darted indoors and barreled for the restrooms. Entering a stall, he locked himself in and dropped to his knees, heaving for breath.

"*Then it's true!*" Erik thought, struggling to take in an even breath. "*They finally got that machine together and they're going with it to kill Father Greenfield!*" After calming down, he stepped out and approached the cashier.

"You can take a seat," said the cashier, "and I'll alert the servers."

"I'm not here to eat anything," Erik replied. "Does Airman Thompson who just left here come in often?"

"Sure he does," answered the cashier, "every afternoon for lunch."

"Give him this," Erik said, handing him the money.

"Lost a bet, eh?" The cashier took the bill and grabbed a gift card envelope, setting the money inside. She took a pen and scribbled the pilot's name on the front.

"He's a good player." Erik gave a faint smile. "Tell him to stop practicing so much and let us losers win sometime."

The cashier chortled. "Then it wouldn't be fair!"

Erik faked a laugh and waved at the woman. "See you!"

"You too!"

Erik left the diner and headed off base, entering onto a long stretch of road.

FIFTY-SIX

Evening came and the moon appeared from behind the clouds, shining a silver of light on the path. Coming up a steep hill, Erik reached the top, looking down at the city below twinkling in nighttime lighting. He heard a rustle and whirled around, searching for the sound's source.

Erik continued his way on the path and paused when he heard footsteps swiftly approaching. He stepped back against a nearby tree, catching sight of Clayton sprinting past. Erik called out to him and Clayton turned, surprised then tripped over his steps.

"Damn it," Clayton growled when he struck the ground. Erik hurried up to Clayton's side and stopped dead in his tracks when he faced a pistol in his direction.

"Please, don't shoot me," Erik pleaded and put up his hands. "It's me, Erik…"

"Don't scare me like that!" Clayton snapped and Erik held out a hand. Clayton took it and Erik pulled him to his feet. Clayton sheathed his pistol into his holster and continued onward with Erik matching his stride.

"They're doing it today," Erik murmured. "They're going to send out that monster to get rid of him and he's in Centerville, so it's easy to fake a visit and just…"

"We'll get there before that happens," Clayton promised, cutting Erik off.

"It was their plan all along to deploy those things for combat after using us as controls." Erik moaned. "Why do those horrible machines exist?"

"It's cheaper and easier to exploit a war by showing off your power," Clayton explained, "than to waste human lives and win by attrition."

"I wonder what war they're going for...?"

"Doesn't matter," grumbled Clayton. "It could be anywhere in the world."

"Either way," Erik muttered, "they'll be in for total annihilation since something's wrong with the machines."

"What?"

"The Dyna-Widgets and the E-Sys chips are incompatible, but that doesn't explain why they want us dead."

"There's something else at work."

Going downhill, they exited onto a small one-lane road, eventually walking along the shoulder. Later, a bright spotlight turned on in the distance and Erik and Clayton came to a pause as a security cruiser came up, idling alongside.

"What are you two doing out here?" the officer demanded. "This is a restricted area."

"Our car broke down ahead and we're looking for a gas station," Clayton replied. "I'm not familiar with the area..."

"How long were you walking?"

"We came out from back that way," Erik declared, pointing down the road behind them. "The moon was overhead that way." He pointed skyward.

"You two walked about three hours in the wrong direction," the officer replied. "Come on, I'll take you to the nearest gas station."

Calling in her intention over the radio, Clayton tossed his pistol to Erik who caught it and nodded to him. Erik came around the car as Clayton stepped up to the cruiser's driver's side. When Erik's information came up over her radio, Clayton yanked open the door, grabbing for the officer and wrestled her down to the ground.

"Don't even think about it!" Clayton thundered as the officer struggled beneath him. "Listen, lady, we don't want to kill you."

"Call off the CENTRA Engine Interment, the Crimson Project, and everything related to any of those programs," Erik shouted, "or so help me, I *will* put holes in you!"

"There's nothing I can do about it," the officer snapped. "You're just hacking at branches!"

"I don't believe you!" Erik snarled and pointed the pistol in her direction. "Be straight with me or I will destroy you!"

"You don't have the guts!"

The officer hurled Clayton back into Erik and withdrew her service pistol. Erik jumped out the way and squeezed the trigger, firing off a shot. The officer cried out when struck in the arm, dropping her gun.

"And that's just your arm!" Erik snapped.

Clayton scrambled to his feet, taking the pistol from Erik when the officer reached for her gun with her other hand.

"Don't think about it," Clayton snarled. "Tell me where's a good escape route and be straight or I'm getting rid of you."

"He's serious," Erik confirmed. "He can kill a man up to a

mile away!"

"Over the hill there," the officer said. "Even if you kill me, you won't get far!"

"Get going," Clayton commanded. "I'll catch up!"

Erik broke into a run for the hill, hearing a single shot. He let out a cry as the ground suddenly fell beneath him and flailed his arms as he plummeted into darkness.

Abruptly, a loud crack and sharp pain overwhelmed Erik's senses, clouded by dust once he hit solid earth. Numerous rocks slammed into his body, forcing his arm crooked and his ribs pierced his side as he rolled down into a jagged plateau.

Erik groaned once his rotating descent ended and he stared up at a starry sky surrounded by dim moonlit clouds. Moments later, a shadowy figure appeared above at the edge of the cliff, looking down at Erik.

Erik wheezed for breath as pain signaled in biting, stinging, burning, crushing agony. He gave up the fight once his vision dimmed then faded to dark mist.

Erik's eyes snapped open and he faced Brodie standing over him, appearing concerned.

"What happened?" Erik murmured and sat up. Looking around, he found himself in a plain white room with navy cots. "Where am I?"

"You passed out," Brodie explained. "You're in the infirmary."

"The meeting...!" Erik tried to get up and Brodie put a hand to Erik's chest, pushing him back down.

"Don't worry about it," Brodie said gently. "I covered you."

"No!" Erik wailed. "You can't!" He grabbed the older man's sleeve, horrified. "They'll get rid of you! They're setting me up to fail on purpose because they're hiding something!"

"What are you talking about?"

"The database… Someone's intentionally screwing with the purchase orders." Erik tightened his grip. "Get the logbook," he pleaded. "I gave it to Clairese."

"Sure, I'll do that. Right now, you need to rest, Feddy." Brodie gently pried off Erik's fingers. "I got your medicines from the Pharmacy. Wanna take it now or later?"

Erik blew a heavy sigh and lay back in the cot, draping an arm over his eyes. "Fine," he muttered. "I need something for this headache anyway…"

Brodie left Erik's side and Erik groaned when the pain in his head returned full force. Moments later he heard footsteps enter the room and moved his arm, facing a middle-aged man in a navy suit. Erik sat up, clenching his teeth when he saw Giuseppe smiling darkly at him.

"Is something the matter, Mister Ferdian?" Giuseppe said viscously.

"What are you doing here?" Erik snarled.

"I had a meeting with your coworkers and they told me you couldn't make it due to being ill."

"So what do you want with me?"

"You know what I'm here for."

"Tell me what those chemicals and minerals are for!" Erik demanded.

"You know very damn well what they're for!" Giuseppe snapped. "I can't have you talking about it either."

"So you're planning to get rid of me, like you did Eisenheimer! He found out and was going to report it, am I right?"

"I won't rid of you here - it'd be too obvious. But know that I'm watching you carefully."

"Watch me all you like," Erik hissed. "Because I will stop whatever it is you're planning and destroy it!"

"You won't live long enough to see that happen."

Erik rose upright and clenched his hands at his sides. "Get out of my face," he growled, "before I break it!"

Brodie returned moments later with a small white paper bag and brightened when he saw Giuseppe. "Hey, Joey!" he greeted cheerfully. Giuseppe turned and Erik tackled the man by the waist, hurling him down to the floor.

Giuseppe wrestled with Erik and Brodie dropped what he held, rushing over to Erik. He yanked Erik by the collar and pulled him off then pushed back, standing between him and Giuseppe. Giuseppe reached for his revolver beneath his blazer and Brodie pushed him away.

"Are you nuts?" Brodie snapped when Giuseppe pointed his gun at Erik.

"Who are you working for?" Erik shouted.

"It won't matter once you're dead!" Giuseppe thundered.

"Now hold on!" Brodie yelled. "Both of you, calm down!"

"He's up to something and is covering it up!" Erik insisted. "He's trying to use me as the fall guy!"

"You can't believe that madman!" Giuseppe retorted. "He's a dangerous criminal and he's trying to destroy this company!"

"Put that away!" Brodie reprimanded. "Do you want to get

arrested?"

"Don't tell me you're on his side!" Giuseppe spat.

"I'm on nobody's side!" Brodie protested. "Let's be civil and discuss whatever the problem is like sane human beings!"

"Civil?" Erik squawked. "He wants me dead over a damn database!"

"Shut up," Brodie interjected. "Now let's talk this out."

Giuseppe stood and put his handgun away back into his holster. "Name your place," he muttered.

"Let's stop by that coffee shop on the corner," Brodie suggested. "We'll all go after work. Good deal?"

Giuseppe glared at Erik and turned on his heel, storming out the room. Erik huffed and dropped into a nearby cot. Brodie picked up the fallen bag of medicines and tossed them to Erik who caught the bag and turned it over, dumping out two bottles of pills: one in a white bottle labeled 'Sinnesloschen' and the other in an amber bottle with a red skull and crossbones sticker on the side, labeled 'Laudanum'.

"Poison?" Brodie asked, raising an eyebrow.

"No, painkillers," Erik replied. "Twenty pills, take one every three or four hours."

"Is it highly addictive?"

"If I take more than I should, then I could accidentally kill myself."

"You only have enough for five days at best."

"It's controlled, so I have to go back and get more."

Brodie put his hands in his pockets. "I thought you had to take that every eight hours," he murmured. "Especially something as strong as that."

Erik smirked. "I have a high tolerance."

"I assume the other's antibiotics?"

Erik nodded and looked at the white bottle, scanning its label. "*Use your judgment if there is a need while awake,*" he read. "*Warning: may cause amnesia, nightmares, insomnia and night terrors.*"

"I'll get some water," Brodie muttered when Erik said nothing else then left the room.

Erik opened the white bottle and shook out two green tablets. Opening the amber bottle, he shook out one red capsule and Brodie returned with a cup of cold water. Erik took it, nodding toward him.

"Down the hatch," Erik announced and gulped down the medicines.

"Do you need anything else?" Brodie inquired.

"Did you call Clairese?"

"She said she'll see us later."

"I need to speak to her, now." Erik stood and Brodie frowned.

"What's the big hurry?" Brodie complained. "She's busy!"

"Call her again," Erik snarled. "This is important to me."

"Why can't it wait until later?"

Erik closed the gap between them and grabbed Brodie by his tie. "You're hiding something," he sneered. "Don't screw around with me!"

"I'm not," Brodie nervously replied. "I just don't want to get her in trouble."

"Don't you care whether or not *I* get in trouble?"

Brodie nodded. "I do," he faintly responded, "really I do!"

"Then do it!" Erik let go and shoved Brodie away.

Brodie blew a short sigh. "I'm sorry," he muttered and stalked out the room.

Erik scooped up the pill bottles and pocketed them then exited into the corridor where he spotted Giuseppe speaking to a security guard. He clenched his teeth and turned in the opposite direction, heading for the elevators. Erik tensed when he heard footsteps fast approaching and broke into a run.

"You're not eluding me!" Giuseppe shouted after him.

"Forget it!" Erik called back.

Erik turned the corner and raced for the stairs, taking two at a time. Rounding the stairwell, he waited for Giuseppe to approach and kicked him down the steps, watching him tumble head over heels then continued his ascent.

Erik pushed other coworkers out the way on the staircase when he ran into them, shoving others into Giuseppe as he neared and once he reached the fifth floor corridor, made a break for his office.

"Stop!" Giuseppe called and Erik froze when a gunshot resonated in the hall. He whirled around, facing Giuseppe who withdrew his revolver, pointing it in the air.

Erik turned, spotting Kass at her office door, startled. He grabbed her arm and pulled her to him when Giuseppe pointed his gun in their direction. Erik immediately covered Kass's mouth with his hand and she struggled against him.

"Don't scream, don't fight me," Erik hissed in her ear. Kass shook her head and Erik glared ahead at Giuseppe who stormed the hall. "You're not that good of a shot," Erik warned. "I know you got basic training in small arms, so if you try getting rid of me, you might hit her. You don't want that, do you?"

"It won't matter," Giuseppe responded once he approached. "All it'll take is a few keystrokes and you both won't exist!"

"What are you saying, that this girl is nothing more than a pawn?"

"Yes, one of many!"

"What is so important that you're trying to hide; why not bring it into the light, unless it's illegal?"

"You won't find out."

Erik backed away as Giuseppe closed in. "How can you be fine with killing an innocent person?" Erik jeered. "How can you not care about what happens?"

"You're the one to talk, Ferdian - you're a killer yourself!"

"If people die around me, it just happens. I've no part in it."

"Then you won't mind if she's nothing more than a casualty!"

Erik shoved Kass forward, knocking Giuseppe down and darted for his office. Slamming shut the door, Erik locked it and grabbed his chair, hooking it under the knob. He hurried to his computer and tapped at the spacebar, bringing up the database.

Erik grabbed his phone from his pocket and turned it on, dialing the number in his list, then set it aside as he placed it on speaker. He then started searching the modified changes in the database, cringing when he heard pounding on his door.

"What's going on?" Gina's voice said once the line picked

up. "What's that noise?"

"Never mind the noise," Erik retorted as he typed. "I need to find a correlation... the latest purchases were Zinc, Chromium, Manganese, Vanadium, Molybdenum, and Selenium."

"Those are part of eleven essential trace minerals in the Human Body," Gina answered. "Like Iodine and Boron."

"Human...?" Erik yelped, astounded.

"Why are you asking such weird questions?" Gina demanded.

"What's The Agency have to do with it?"

"I don't understand what you're going on about..."

"You know!" Erik shouted.

"Maybe your best bet is Osphena... She is a genetic engineer after all."

Erik gasped when he remembered the attaché case he took and his first encounter with Osphena. The door crashed open and Erik hastily stood, facing the security officer who stormed in with his service pistol drawn.

"Don't even think about it," Erik snarled when Giuseppe pushed past him and entered the office. "If you kill me, then you won't get what you're looking for."

Giuseppe grunted. "You finally remember," he grumbled.

"Don't push me," Erik warned and put a hand over the keyboard. "All I got to do is put in the final keystroke and wipe out everything."

"Liar." Giuseppe snorted. "The backups are automatically stored in the cloud, so even if you wipe out the data on your end, it still exists elsewhere." Erik clenched his teeth when

Giuseppe laughed at him. "Who are you trying to fool? I've worked with computers for years, and with databases especially. I know what you're using and can easily recover whatever you do. You don't have the tools to wreck your work."

Erik clenched his hands at his sides, growing dismayed. "You'll get what you want this evening," he growled. "Now get out of here!"

"No, you're getting it for me *now*. If I leave you be, then you'll only destroy everything."

Erik smirked. "What makes you think I have the capacity to destroy the backups from the cloud?"

"I know you know some dangerous people." Giuseppe waved his revolver at Erik. "You may not be that bright, but you tend to talk and people listen."

"What do you want from me?"

"I want you to rid the data you've collected thus far."

"Fine, the backups are at Osphena's apartment - most likely in her office."

"She never mentioned it to me."

"Because I put it in the most obvious place."

Erik's phone beeped and Giuseppe narrowed his eyes. "You–!" he snarled. Erik grinned and did nothing when Giuseppe approached, clocking him across the face with the pistol. Erik staggered back against the window, holding his busted lip.

"You'd better hurry," Erik teased, "if you really want it."

"You're coming with me," Giuseppe growled. "Take your phone."

Erik scooped up the cellular on the desk and made no

protest when Giuseppe grabbed his arm.

"Hey," Erik snapped at the security guard when Giuseppe dragged him toward the door. "Why aren't you doing your job?"

"My function is to make sure nobody gets killed," the guard retorted. "He didn't shoot at you and you didn't attack him." The guard shrugged his shoulders. "If Mercado wanted a cop, they should've gotten a cop."

Erik grabbed the guard's collar, baring his teeth. "I'm getting you when you're off the clock!" he hissed.

"That's enough," Giuseppe sneered and kneed Erik's back. Erik released his grip and the guard stepped aside, watching Giuseppe pull Erik out the room and down the hall.

"Hey, where are you going?" Brodie called when Giuseppe led Erik to the elevators, keeping his revolver pointed at his back.

"On a little trip," Erik replied. "I forgot something important."

"Don't follow," Giuseppe snapped back at Brodie. "Take care of things here."

Stepping on the elevators, Erik grinned at Brodie who approached and waved at him.

"Will I see you later?" Brodie asked.

"Only if you want to," Erik said and the doors hushed close.

Entering onto the ground level, Erik grunted when pushed forward and reluctantly made his way across the parking lot toward Giuseppe's car.

"What makes you think I'll willingly come along?" Erik

groused. "What makes you think she'll just let you go through her apartment? If I'm suspect, it'll look bad on her for harboring a criminal, now wouldn't it?"

"Shut up," Giuseppe hissed.

"You're acting totally shady. Wouldn't someone report you for treating me like this?"

"All I have to say is that you put me up to it - they'll believe me over you any day."

"An answer for everything, huh?"

"Don't force me to do something I'll regret," Giuseppe threatened.

"As if you can make my life any more difficult than what it is now!" Erik yowled when his captor kicked him forward at the back of his legs.

"Now get in the car!" Giuseppe growled.

"Wait!" Brodie's voice called.

Erik staggered against the sedan and turned around, watching the man wearing a short leather driving coat over his navy suit hurry across the lot. Giuseppe frowned when Brodie approached and sheathed his revolver then stormed over to the driver's side.

Brodie opened the rear passenger side door and Erik stepped in, scooting over as Brodie followed while Giuseppe entered the car.

No one said anything as Giuseppe drove to Osphena's apartment.

FIFTY-SEVEN

Giuseppe pulled into the alley behind Osphena's apartment where another dark sedan idled near the refuse bin. Erik clenched his teeth as he stepped out and Brodie followed, withdrawing his pack of cigarettes with lighter.

The doors to the other car also opened, revealing Gina wearing a dark overcoat and smoky sunglasses. Her driver also stepped out, adjusting the gloves on his hands and the silver reflective glasses on his face.

"I never thought I'd run into you again," Gina said coldly when Giuseppe exited.

"I should've known it was you," Giuseppe snarled.

"We both want the same thing," Gina said calmly. "Either you call her or I do."

"And then what?" Giuseppe snapped. "Do you think she'll show you favor?"

"It's a part of the job. Whether or not she favors me is not a concern."

"Will you two hurry this up?" Brodie complained, lighting his cigarette. "I'm freezing my balls off out here."

Erik took the cigarette from Brodie and took a deep drag. "Freezing balls?" Erik interjected and blew smoke over his head. "I don't see how they'd freeze given they're already blue."

Brodie chortled, lighting another cigarette and Gina frowned at them, appearing disgusted.

"Call her," Giuseppe ordered. "Tell her to come here right away."

"What makes you think she'll leave her job?" Gina spat.

Giuseppe withdrew his revolver, pointing it at her and the driver unleashed his pistol from at his back, pointing it at him. "If you have me call her," Giuseppe warned, "I'll let her know of a death in the family."

"She won't believe either one of you," Erik piped up. "Why not have *me* call her?"

"What makes you think she'll listen to you?" Gina squawked.

"She's got something I want and I got something she wants," Erik replied, smiling wryly. "It's the same as he wants, so..." Brodie flushed brightly and Gina furrowed her brow, also turning scarlet. The driver smirked in response. "Well?"

"Give Mister Smith your phone," the driver ordered.

"He'll have to get it himself," Giuseppe countered. Erik bit the cigarette between his lips and left the car's side, approaching Giuseppe. He held out his hand and Giuseppe shook his head. "In my pocket," Giuseppe grumbled.

"You just want me to cop a feel, huh?" Erik retorted and reached in, sifting through the man's blazer pockets.

"I still hate you," Giuseppe sneered, glaring ahead at Gina. "Ever since you came along, you've caused nothing but problems for me."

"Oh?" Gina snapped back. "I should tell you the same!"

"You like that, eh?" Erik muttered as he searched Giuseppe's slacks pockets. Giuseppe's face paled as Erik pulled against the man's waistband and reached around, extending a hand in Giuseppe's back pocket. "How bad you want me?"

"I think you're enjoying this a little too much, Feddy," Brodie remarked when Erik leaned forward and withdrew the phone.

"I will destroy you," Giuseppe growled.

"Savvy," Erik hissed in Giuseppe's ear.

"Stop teasing him, Feddy," Brodie reprimanded.

"It seems you're enjoying it a little too much, Mister Avers," Erik quipped and pulled away, leaning against the car's hood. Withdrawing his cigarette with his free hand, Erik tapped the ashes and flipped the phone open with his thumb, turning it on.

"You're the weird one," Brodie shot back.

"What kind of numbers you have in here?" Erik asked casually after waiting for its bootup sequence. Scrolling through the contacts list, Erik wagged a finger at Giuseppe. "Ooh, naughty boy. I see you've been calling your boyfriend lately."

"Hey," Brodie protested, "don't put anything on me!"

"Do you dream about me when you do him, Mister Avers?" Erik teased and Brodie's flushed face turned chalk white. Gina's driver guffawed.

"Please, stop it," Brodie complained.

"Here we go, our favorite lady." Erik looked to Giuseppe, smiling maliciously. "Isn't she your best friend?" He pushed the button and put the phone to his ear.

"Hello?" Osphena answered after the first ring.

"Hey, beautiful," Erik said, grinning. "I need to see you real bad."

"Oh, is that so?" Osphena paused. "What are you doing with his phone?"

"He came over to play and you know he likes to play rough. Will you have time for a quick one?"

"What's brought this on?" Osphena asked guardedly.

Brodie snorted as he stifled a giggle and the driver snickered when Erik nudged Giuseppe with his foot, running up his calf.

"Ah, you see through my ruse," Erik continued. "I need something for my headache and you're the only one I could remember who took it away easily."

"What about that other one you sleep with?"

"Oh, him? It's just to sleep, nothing more." Erik glanced to Brodie who bit his hand, trying not to laugh aloud. "He's always the one giving me the headache."

"I'll be over soon."

"Please, come over. I'm on your stoop and I'm tired. Your friend here really knows how to hit all the right spots." Erik stomped on Giuseppe's groin and Giuseppe grunted in pain, staggering back. Brodie hurried over, grabbing Giuseppe's other arm and twisted it behind his back.

"I'm leaving now," Osphena said. "Don't wander off."

"See you soon." Erik flipped the phone closed and set the device on the hood then stalked off, heading for the apartment's front steps.

Erik sat on the stoop, looking skyward at the cold winter morning. He heard footsteps approach and stood, facing Gina and her driver coming up the stairs.

"Where's Mister Avers?" Erik asked as Gina walked past

him and entered the complex.

"He's busy," answered Gina vaguely.

Erik looked to the driver who only grinned, saying nothing else. He fell in stride behind them, following them upstairs to Osphena's apartment.

Upon entry, Erik made a direct path toward Osphena's home office and started searching for the case, going through bookshelves. The driver entered moments later, searching through file cabinets.

"What is it we're looking for?" the driver muttered.

"I had it and I left it here, but I wouldn't know what to tell you what it is."

"Basically you're saying you'll know it when you see it."

"Right."

Erik approached the desk and sifted through the papers scattered on the face.

"Did you find something?" the driver asked as Erik paused and picked up a single sheet.

"*Sixty-five Elements of the Human Body*," Erik read. Scanning the list, he grew uneasy when he recognized half the items on the list. "*These were involved in the purchase orders*," he mused. "*Mercado, Gen-Tech, and Kanbal were all involved, even getting Andrews and possibly Eisenheimer killed in the process.*"

"You find something, Mister Smith?" asked Gina's driver.

"Nothing important," Erik muttered and folded the paper. He tucked it in his coat pocket with the other sheets and they continued searching the office.

Later the front door opened and Erik heard Osphena's

voice. "Gina!" she cried in surprise. "I didn't expect you here!"

"Ossie," Gina said sadly, "I wish it was just a friendly visit."

Erik left the room and exited the hall into the parlor, finding Osphena dressed in a dark blazer with matching skirt and light green blouse under a black tweed coat wearing green-tinted glasses. She stood at the door in stunned silence, holding a small white plastic bag while Gina sat on the blue lumpy couch's arm.

"You got the usual for me?" Erik asked nonchalantly and approached, taking the bag. "Nice, you got me two packs and a fifth. You were planning to seduce me, weren't you?" He made his way for the painted table in the rear behind the kitchenette.

"What...?" Osphena started, at a loss for words.

Erik opened the bottle of vodka and took a long drink from it then set it on the table. Withdrawing a pack of cigarettes, he pocketed the second pack and found a butane lighter in the bag's bottom.

"We're looking for something, obviously," Gina said when Erik stayed silent. "Related to the Divinity Project."

"What does he have anything to do with it?" Osphena protested.

Erik casually lit his cigarette and dropped into the chair, leaning back as he blew smoke over his head. "It's that case you took from me," he said, dropping his lighter in his pocket. "Also, the key card and transmitter. I want it back."

Osphena's voice quavered. "I don't know what you're talking about!"

"I remember having it when I left and got into your car," Erik spat. "The card and the transmitter were in my coat pockets!"

"I didn't go through your stuff," Osphena pressed. "Honest!"

Erik let down his chair, glaring at Osphena. "Who dropped me off then?" he demanded.

When Osphena said nothing else, Erik jammed his burning cigarette into the chipped paint-stained cup and rose from the table. "Then what *else* is he looking for?" he shouted. "If he already got what he wanted!"

"I don't know," Osphena wailed. "I'm just as clueless as you are!"

Erik stormed over to Osphena, withdrawing the papers in his coat pocket and thrust them at her. "What's the meaning of all this?" he thundered. "Tell me, or I'll start breaking some necks!"

"They're related to the Divinity Project," Osphena said softly after glancing at the paperwork. "They're the new version of the old CENTRA Project..."

"What are you saying?" Gina cried in horror. "They can't be bringing it back online! After the last time–!"

Erik clutched his head and doubled over when a loud screech resounded in his ears. Gina and Osphena looked to him, concerned and he screamed when the noise grew louder. The voice he grew to hate spoke to him amidst the static.

Destroy them, Ferdian!

They're all traitors...

They no longer deserve life!

Dispose of them; erase them before they erase you!

"Ferdian...?" Gina murmured.

Erik suddenly stood upright and marched into the kitchen. Opening the drawers, he rummaged through them, withdrawing a cleaver. Turning to the two women, he gave a sadistic grin.

"Why are you looking at us like that?" Osphena asked apprehensively.

"You're really not going to hurt us, are you?" Gina questioned evenly.

"I have to," Erik answered mechanically. "The voices are telling me to."

"You know you can resist; you don't have to listen to it."

"But they cause me so much pain..." Erik stalked across the floor. "The only way to make them stop is to give them what they want."

"What is it they want?" Osphena mewed.

"They want you both dead."

Erik approached Osphena and she backed away until she met the door. She gasped once Erik closed the gap between them and he grabbed her by the chin, holding firmly as he pressed the blade's edge to the side of her neck.

"You're going to punish me first," whispered Osphena, "aren't you?"

"I'd like to," Erik replied, still smiling, "but let's leave it to Fate or Karma or whatever." He glanced to Gina. "Get a coin and see who goes first." Erik turned to Osphena and let go of her face as he pressed against her, then ran his free hand through her curly reddish-brown hair. "How would you like it?" he stated. "From the tips down?"

"W-what do you mean?" Osphena squeaked and cleared her throat. Erik grasped her hand and ran the blade's edge atop her fingertips. She shut her eyes and shuddered. "Please, don't..."

"What about joint by joint?" Erik lightly bit the first joint of her pinky finger and Osphena moaned, wavering. Erik pushed her back against the door, thrusting his knee between her thighs as he kept her standing and tapped the cleaver's edge on the tip of her nose. "Or should I skin you layer by layer?"

"I don't have a coin with me," Gina said softly moments later. "I mainly carry bills or plastic."

"Then what do you do with the change?" Erik snapped.

"I try my best to break even."

Erik turned and paused when he heard a high whine, facing Gina pointing an oversized pistol in his direction. Before he could react, a dull shot filled the air when she fired, releasing a blast of electricity. Erik screamed, overwhelmed with the discharged shock once hit with a pair of barbs and dropped what he held, collapsing to his knees.

"I didn't mean to overwhelm him," said the driver's voice from behind as Erik heaved for breath. "I wanted to use him to fight those other guys... I didn't realize he would turn on you two."

"It's okay," Gina replied. "It was a risk..."

"What are you saying?" Erik groaned from his place on the ground.

"What I'm saying is that I can take over you any time I want." The driver stomped over and kicked Erik's back, forcing him on all fours.

Erik let out a hacking laugh, glaring back at him. "What are you saying?" he spat. "You can possess my body or something?" He scoffed. "That's not possible!"

The young man gave a devious smile and pressed his foot

against Erik's back, keeping him down. "In a way," he answered, "I can." He reached inside his slacks pocket and withdrew a small machine with digital readings and several buttons and dials. "This is a controller and with it, I can control anyone with a receiver and make them do whatever I want within a mile radius."

"A receiver...?"

"You have a tracking chip embedded in you," the coachman explained as he reached behind his ear and withdrew a small screwdriver tucked there. "It sends a signal and can receive a signal. That's how we've always found you when you thought you were somewhere safe."

"But what about that controller you have?"

"With this, it sends a signal that can change the impulses in your brain. Depending on the frequency, it can make you fight, defend, or pretty much anything." The young man unscrewed the machine's backing and began tinkering with the circuits.

"Who are you?"

"I'm nobody important, Mister Smith. All you need to know is that I can pick up your signal that lets me know which direction you're coming from."

"What about Gina?"

"I've only a scrambler," Gina responded.

"I'm confused."

"And so are we."

Erik narrowed his eyes. "At least give me a name!" he shouted.

"Call me anything but late for dinner." The young man grinned and let Erik go. Erik scrambled to his feet, clenching his hands at his sides.

"Everyone broadcasts a signal," Gina explained. "Everyone who works for The Agency and in all their divisions are all microchipped as part of the contractual process. Therefore their energy is unique." She gestured broadly to the room. "I can tell where anyone is at any given moment once I tune in."

"Why aren't you affected?" Erik complained.

"Because hers is turned off and mine is scrambled, sending something back to throw them off," answered the driver as he screwed the case back in. Turning the dial, the machine came to life, its small LED lights blinking on and off.

"Apparently he used the wrong signal and you reacted badly," Gina clarified.

"How much longer do I have to endure your meddling?" Erik snapped.

"Not too much longer."

The young man pressed several buttons and Erik grunted when he heard a low tone. He clutched a hand to his head, moaning when he heard a sequence of digital beeps and looked to Gina's driver who quickly tapped a series of key presses.

Osphena grabbed for Erik when he staggered backwards into her. "You need to be more careful!" she spat at them.

"I should tell you the same," Gina said flatly. "He's dangerous."

"Then stop playing with fire!"

"Who are you to say?"

Erik shook his head and yanked out of Osphena's grip once the noise stopped, then pushed her aside. "Both of you need to stop!" he spat. "I'll make this easy on you both." Throwing open the door, Erik stomped downstairs.

FIFTY-EIGHT

Erik stepped outside and stormed the alley. Frowning when he spotted Giuseppe's car with fogged windows and rocking, he approached and knocked on the glass, then casually lit a cigarette while he waited once he heard a startled cry and the car stilled.

"Get your pants on and pack your junk in," Erik said in annoyance when the door cracked open.

"What do you want?" Brodie asked nervously.

"Two questions. One - what was in that case and two - what did he do with it?"

"Schematics and he kept them for his personal project," Brodie answered weakly.

"Did you get a 'where' or 'why' out of it or did I interrupt?"

"Look, Feddy, hear me out..."

"My life is on the line, about to go up in smoke and all you're worried about is getting off!" Erik kicked the door, flinging it open. He grabbed Brodie by the collar and yanked him out, throwing him down to the ground. Brodie groaned, clutching his side as he turned away and Erik clenched his teeth, noticing the dark bloodstain on the older man's shirt and scratches and bruises on his neck and face.

"He thought he was using me," Brodie said weakly, "but I

listened out for things because I wanted to help you..."

"Have you been following me?" Erik shouted.

"Not quite..."

Erik growled under his breath. "I don't like your story!" he sneered.

"Sweetheart asked me to... She was curious and so was I." Brodie took in a ragged breath. "Joey was the only one I knew who had access to a lot of things, top level things."

"What about the database?"

"I admit - I tinkered the files to hide the orders. I had to... We had to hide the Divinity Project because it was never officially sanctioned!"

"Whose idea was it to update and bring it back online?" Erik peered inside the car, finding Giuseppe lying back on the backseat with his coat draped over his body. "Are you dead in there?" he spat.

"No," Giuseppe rasped.

"Then tell me."

Giuseppe let out a hacking laugh. "You'll eventually find out," he hissed. "You'll see..."

Erik stepped away from Giuseppe's car and slammed shut the door then turned to Brodie, lending a hand. Brodie took it, groaning when pulled to his feet.

"How much time do you think I have left?" Erik demanded.

Brodie shook his head. "I wouldn't know," he murmured.

Erik draped Brodie's arm around his shoulder and helped him inside the apartment. "So what was this," Erik commented as he approached the elevator, "some kind of suicide pact or sick game you two liked to play?" Brodie shook his head, refusing to answer.

Later upon return to Osphena's apartment, Erik left Brodie on the couch and Osphena hurried for her bathroom, returning with a first aid kit. Erik approached the table in the rear and unscrewed the cap on the vodka bottle, taking a long drink. Setting down the liquor with a firm bang, he clutched the table's sides, taking in a deep breath.

"It won't be long," Erik said moments later. "If the chips you said are true, then he's got one coming for me, for us, like he did Eisenheimer."

"What are you thinking?" Gina asked.

"The CENTRA Project..." Erik let out a distressed laugh. "It's too late for me, isn't it?"

"What are you going on about?"

"Aren't I an older model? Won't the new one just trash me with a flick of his wrist?"

"You're not a machine," said the driver sternly. "You're a man, and very much Human."

"I doubt it," Erik said softly. "They've really messed with my head and even tried to make me a zombie if I can trust my memory..."

"Please don't speak anymore," Gina pleaded. "I need to think of how to get you out of this mess."

"I put myself in it, right? So only I can get myself out."

"Don't leave!" Gina protested when Erik took the vodka bottle and stormed across the floor. Gina left her place on the couch and grasped his arm before he walked past. Erik shook off her grip and whirled around, throwing a punch. Gina stiffened when he stopped mid-swing and flicked out his finger, poking the wing of her nose.

Erik gave a crooked grin. "Ah, ha, I tease," he slurred. Gina's face paled and Erik took off her dark sunglasses, placing them atop his head. "Your eyes..."

"What about my eyes?" Gina asked, raising an eyebrow.

Erik took her chin in his hand and peered close, admiring the indigo color. "Now what's with that look?" he complained and took another swig from the bottle.

Gina appeared pained and pushed Erik away. "I don't like it when you tease me like that," Gina said softly. "Please don't be mean."

Erik narrowed his eyes and prodded Gina hard in the chest with his finger. "I'm through with this!" he spat. "I'm through with you too!" He stomped for the door and swung the panel open wide then stepped out into the hall.

"If you get yourself killed," Gina shouted at his back, "I'll never forgive you!"

The door slammed shut behind him and Erik leaned against the wall, drinking from the bottle as tears streamed down his face full force.

Erik stumbled down the stairs and made his way outdoors, pulling down his sunglasses when his eyes smarted from the late afternoon sun. He hurled the empty glass at Gina's car, shattering it against the hood. Erik then started walking around the city streets, pushing past other civilians along the way and muttering apologies when he did.

He pulled up his coat collar as evening came and the cold

winds increased its intensity. Erik went through alleyways and behind abandoned buildings, crisscrossing various streets, bypassing stores, refilling stations, libraries, and others, walking down the sidewalk or on the road when no walk existed to step upon.

The faint rays of dusk with its pale violets, blues, pinks and reds came to paint the skies when the sun set and the traffic became heavier as the populace returned from their day jobs, entering the roadways back to their homes.

Erik eventually left the city's boundaries, walking the highway's shoulder leading out into various territories. He happened upon a side road and continued down it, approaching a large factory with its smokestacks billowing dark clouds in the air.

Erik spotted a large mound of coal in the distance and two bright yellow bulldozers pushing the mineral aside as another truck came up to dump more into the ever-growing pile. Crossing the factory's parking lot, his loafers crunched the gravel and the sun set lower in the sky, casting shadows around him. He kicked one glittering iridescent stone aside and looked up at the main office below the factory where workers milled inside.

Erik spotted other young men in navy uniforms with silver buttons file inside from the rear and let himself in the front door, happening upon a group of miners in heavy dark green uniforms and steel-toed black or tan boots, wearing various colored hard hats with head lanterns, sitting variously assembled at the white plank tables. They ignored him, drinking coffee and eating assorted pastries, watching the overhead television as diverse evening news reports played.

"Hey, what's on the telly?" one miner asked.

"Why bother?" another complained. "There's nothing worth watching."

Erik leaned against the door and folded his arms, watching the group in silence.

"Hey, there's that special report," someone piped and the volume turned up in response. Some in the room hooted at the television as a reporter droned on.

"... the leader of clean energy, Rayshine Incorporated after the ribbon cutting ceremony today of the new Corite mine in Dunabe County. For those who are not sure what Corite is, it is a clean-burning coal-like substance..."

"That's us, guys," a young man near Erik said, leaning back in his chair. "We're finally getting recognized for the good we're doing in this world!"

"I doubt it," said another miner.

"Once they get tired of us mining this crap Corite for this stupid energy company," complained a third, "they'll tell us that they ran out of people to send and we'll be the next ones to fight over there, wherever that is!"

The supervisor guffawed. "You can't be serious," he said, rolling his eyes. "They got those Expedients now, and shitty ones at that. We gotta keep them on line to do the heavier shit we used to do. Be happy about it."

"Right, if those Seattle and Texas punks can prove this so-called clean-burning coal joke!"

"Obviously, otherwise Downtown wouldn't be running the shit!"

Several men laughed and Erik stood straighter, slightly puzzled. "Is there such a thing as clean-burning coal?" he wondered aloud. When Erik got no answer, he changed his question. "Then what are you mining?"

"Some weird diamond-like rock that heats hella slow in the pyre," answered a miner close to Erik. "The shit makes money so I'm not worried about it."

"Don't be such a pain," snapped the foreman as he withdrew a cigarette pack from his pocket. Erik took out his lighter and leaned over, lighting his cigarette. "Oh, thanks."

"No problem," Erik said.

"You're one of the suits checking on us?" he asked, blowing smoke through his nose.

"Yeah," Erik replied. "I'm one of the slaves to the machine sent to sniff around."

"Lemme show ya around," the overseer said as the other miners stiffened, growing nervous.

"Hey, I'm not with the Security and Intelligence crew," Erik said calmly. "I heard they were making noise at the copper operations a few days ago."

"Yeah, it was pretty messed up, Mister...?"

"Smith."

"Wallace." Erik nodded and followed Wallace as he left the lounge area. "Yeah, Mister Smith," said Wallace. "We were having problems with the latest outfit. They were acting real screwy... Something wrong with the chips I heard."

"What was going on?"

"There was some talk about shutting it down because the changes they wanted caused some safety violation."

"What kind of change?"

"Upgrades, you know?" Wallace led Erik through a corridor toward the rear offices. "Here's our tech department who keeps tracks of those damn buckets." Knocking on the door, Erik heard a voice on the other side and Wallace opened it. "Hey, Gallagher, here's Inspector Smith. Get cracking."

"Shit," Gallagher grumbled.

Erik opened the door wider and stepped in, facing a young woman with short sandy brown hair wearing faded jeans, yellow sweatshirt, and short brown boots who sat before a computer terminal. On her wrists, she wore silver and turquoise bracelets.

"Don't tell me you're the tech department," Erik teased.

"Budget cuts will do that," Gallagher said wryly without turning around from her terminal.

"I'm not making citations or anything," Erik said gently. "Just taking a look around."

"I don't know whether to be relieved or scared," answered Gallagher. "Those SID clowns have been out for blood and they nearly shut it down over some hacking scare."

"Really now?"

Gallagher nodded. "The machines had some unofficial code inserted that made them hardly function correctly. They thought it was the work of commies or terrorists or something."

"Was it?"

"I couldn't find the source - it was layered in deep."

"Anyone you know who could be close to the project?"

"Some fella named Ronan, but they sacked his ass last year."

"What about before that?"

"Nothing else comes to mind. As for the source, Schumacher I think it was came up with the design and Zachary keyed the code. Smart guys, but they got put out for rabble-rousing is how the rumors go."

Erik frowned. "Did they get Terminated?" he murmured.

Before Gallagher could answer, a whistle blew and the woman shooed Erik out of her office. He backed away and turned around, finding Wallace gone.

Erik stiffened when he heard a familiar voice address the miners and ran down the hall, peering around the corner. He clenched his teeth at the sight of a tall middle-aged man in wide-brimmed hat, wearing black aviator sunglasses and bomber jacket with jeans and jackboots ascend the steps.

"Hey," a voice said to Erik from behind, "what are you doing here?" Erik whirled around, facing an older man with graying nape-length dark reddish-brown hair and narrow brown eyes. He wore a dark blazer and matching slacks with a stark-white dress shirt, skinny black tie and oxfords.

"Checking out the scene," Erik answered.

"Were you sent in from Keely?"

"Sure."

The man in the dark blazer gave Erik a critical look and turned away. Erik followed him, entering an office at the corridor's end with a large oak desk, folders stacked on one side, a computer on the other and a desk phone in the center. Erik clenched his teeth when he noticed the name plate on the desk's edge, reading 'Brien Zeadeas'.

"Zeadeas isn't a common name," Erik murmured.

"No, it's not," said Brien as he took a seat behind the desk in a plain office chair.

"So...?" Erik shrugged his shoulders.

"We passed the safety inspections the other day," Brien filled in.

"Just needed some more info about the machines used," Erik replied, leaning against the door frame. "Digging around for the creator of the program and trying to pinpoint the problem, you know - usual inspections stuff."

"I see." Brien picked up the phone's receiver and dialed a number. "I need to verify this."

"So are you calling me in?" Erik challenged.

"Why, is that a problem?"

Erik gave a faint smile. "Go ahead."

Brien pressed a button. "Yes," he said into the line. "We've got a rogue G-seven-forty-five on the grounds of the Number Twenty-Six plant."

"Hey!" Erik snapped and clenched his hands. "What do you think you're doing?"

"No," Brien continued, ignoring Erik. "He's not overly hostile."

Erik entered and picked up the phone, ripping it out the wall. Brien dropped the receiver, stepping away when Erik threw the phone to the floor, breaking it into pieces.

"I'm not a monster!" Erik thundered as Brien reached in his blazer and withdrew a small revolver.

"I have orders to terminate if you try to harm me!" Brien spat.

"I'm not here to hurt anyone," Erik growled. "I just want

answers to some questions."

"I don't trust you." Brien pointed the revolver at Erik as he reached under the desk, depressing a button hidden there. "You need to return where you belong."

"And where is that?"

"In the scrap heap where you should've been years ago!"

"What are you going on about?" Erik shouted.

"Technically, you do not exist. You were created from a lab, to live out only one purpose: fight and die." Erik paled and Brien smirked. "Think of it as a great cause for this country! You're saving millions of our fighting men and women in the armed forces from dying a senseless death."

"What kind of nonsense is that?" Erik demanded. "I'm Human! I live, I breathe, I get drunk, I get sick... How dare you call me a machine!"

"Because you are." Two heavily armed guards entered the office and approached the desk, standing ill at ease as they waited for additional orders. "We've come a long way since then. Nevertheless, your use has long ended and you have to be tossed out. You're not fit for reprogramming."

"You were supposed to be decommissioned," said the guard on Erik's left, "and moved to mining projects."

"It was supposed to be simple," interjected the guard on Erik's right. "Erase, reassign, move on. But for some reason, you didn't take and fought back."

"The punishment for going against Policy is Termination," Brien said coldly and sheathed his gun away. "We can't have you cutting up and getting in the way of the latest Defense Works project."

Erik said nothing and gave no resistance when taken by the arms at gunpoint, then hauled down the corridor. He heard Gallagher shouting from her office.

"Who would think Federal Special Services would be interested in our output?" she thundered. "I have the data right here—!"

Erik grunted once tossed outside onto the parking lot in front of a black van with darkly tinted windows. His glasses fell off and he clamored to his feet when four armed guards exited from the rear, equipped with high-powered long-ranged rifles.

"Come along now," said the rifleman before Erik, "and all will be fixed."

"You have no choice," the guard behind Erik warned. "You can't fight us at your level."

Erik put up his hands on the defensive. "I'll give it my best," he warned. "Liquid courage and all!"

"Apprehend him!" the squad leader called.

Erik turned and grabbed the guard behind him on his right, grasping his sleeve and hurled him overhead into the group at the steps bottom, sending them slamming to the ground.

Whirling around, he charged the remaining guard and tackled the man by the waist. They crashed through the office building's window, shattering glass and debris as Erik threw a sucker punch into the guard's face once on the floor.

The downed armed guards scrambled to their feet as Erik got up and backed away when two riflemen approached. One fired a shot, grazing the arm of Erik's coat.

"The next one won't be a warning!" the rifleman shouted.

"Suck it!" Erik spat and took off down the corridor. He immediately entered Gallagher's office and slammed shut the door.

"The fuck-?" Gallagher yelped when Erik grabbed her by the arm, yanking her out of her chair and whirled her around. Erik gasped when he looked into her widened hazel eyes.

"Franny?" Erik cried.

Gallagher kneed Erik in the groin, forcing him forward and slammed her elbow down on the back of his neck, felling him instantly. "Stupid Doofus!" she shouted.

"Shit..." Erik moaned when her office door slammed open, revealing a pair of guards. "I need to work on my charming personality some more..."

"Did he hurt you?" one sentry asked as two others grabbed Erik by the arms and dragged him out the room.

"No," Gallagher said, looking down at Erik. Erik struggled against the two guards when pulled up and grunted once struck in the side and again upside the head with their gunstocks. "Wait!" Gallagher called after the wardens dragging Erik down the hall by the collar and back outdoors.

The other four remaining were back in the van with its rear cab open, with one attending to his injured comrade while the other two waited for Erik.

"In ya go," the guard over Erik grumbled and picked him up by the arm then tossed him in. Erik yowled when he struck the metal and crumpled in the corner.

"Drug him," ordered the leader.

Erik wrestled with the three guards when the one who sat

in the rear cab came forward with a blue-serum filled syringe. He let out a cry as the needle cut against his skin.

"Hold him!" the warden snapped and Erik grunted once his head slammed into the floor, held in place by a heavy arm.

Erik seethed as the guard jammed his elbow in his face and let out a wail once the needle abruptly rammed into the side of his neck. Erik stiffened as the plunger pushed down and his skin burned at the injection site. He wheezed for breath, choking on air when the sensation of suffocation took over.

"Don't take him away just yet!" Gallagher's voice called from outside the van.

"He's getting hauled out, lady," the warden over Erik snapped. "Orders are orders."

"You don't want SID on your ass, do you?"

"Shit! You mean he was one of their workers?"

Erik grunted when kicked out and he rolled over on the ground, hitting the dirt.

"Fuck, we're gonna get cited big time," one sentry complained. "I didn't know they had any G-seven forty-five's under contract!"

"Look, lady, we ain't gonna say shit," said the leader, "if you don't say shit!"

"Say what?" Gallagher called back. She noticed a pair of brown sunglasses on the ground and picked them up, placing them atop her head.

The doors slammed shut and the van took off, throwing gravel as it returned to the road. Gallagher knelt at Erik's side, running a hand through his hair. Erik struggled for breath and squinted up at the young woman with hard narrow hazel eyes who looked down at him, concerned.

"Hey," Erik murmured and reached up with a weak hand, taking the sunglasses. "Why did you save me?"

Gallagher smiled faintly. "I made a promise, remember?" she answered.

Erik put the glasses on his face. "What did you promise?"

"We were going to run away together."

"Yeah?" Erik reached forward, brushing his hand through her short hair.

"Yeah."

"Your hair..."

Gallagher shut her eyes, blowing a shallow sigh. "When I thought–" she started in a wavering voice.

Erik let out a weak laugh, cutting her off. "Does that offer still stand?"

"I promised you that, like, ages ago!" Gallagher said and took his hand. "Did you get married?"

"No... Why?"

"You have a ring on."

"Oh?" Erik squeezed her hand. "So, let's run off together."

"Sure..."

Erik shut his eyes when his world came crashing down.

FIFTY-NINE

Erik groaned once he came to, swamped in pain. He found his eyes too heavy to open and his arms refused to follow commands issued by his brain. Erik struggled to speak and when he couldn't form words, he gave up, listening to the sounds around him.

A constant drip echoed in the room and a low breath of wind sighed outside. When the drugged tiredness faded, Erik's eyes slowly opened, finding himself in a darkened space with a small silver of light shining through from a crack in the wall.

He sat up, finding his arm tied in a sling and his chest taped by bandages with gloves still on his hands and his left knee still wrapped. Scrambling for the light, Erik felt for the space, peering out and saw nothing but brightness on the other side temporarily blinding him.

Pulling away, Erik felt around in the pitch, trying to figure where he was. Later he happened upon dimly-lit lanterns hanging on the walls and his eyes adjusted to the low light, finding himself in an abandoned mine.

Erik followed the path, coming across a small gas-powered generator and a folding table rest against the smoothed walls. He heard voices speaking softly and stiffened when he heard his name mentioned.

"He's going to need a doctor after all this," answered a familiar male voice. "Clayton said he was hurt quite badly."

"Let me go check on him," said another man's voice and footsteps neared him.

Erik let out a yelp in shock when he recognized the middle-aged man with narrow violet eyes wearing a black jacket with silver chains accenting the sleeves of his jacket, dark jeans and leather motorcycle boots entering the cavern.

"Mahjin!" Erik cried and reached out with his free hand, touching his straightened brown hair. "Why'd you change it?"

"Something different," Mahjin answered and grinned. "How you're feeling?"

Erik ran a hand through his own hair, overwhelmed. "I'm not sure... A bit out of it."

"Possibly the painkillers." Mahjin gestured to Erik. "Let's go. We need to get going."

"Go where?" Erik demanded. "I need to see Father Greenfield."

"You can't see him right now." Mahjin started walking away.

"He'd better not be dead!" Erik shouted. "You're taking me to Centerville so I can see him!"

Mahjin stiffened and whirled around, stunned. "How did you know?" he demanded.

"Doctor Schnell told me," Erik spat. "I need to get there before they kill him!"

"You can't do anything about it!" Mahjin protested.

"If you won't take me, I'll find a way."

"You won't make it."

"Then you're telling me he's alive, right?" Mahjin said

nothing when Erik pushed past him.

Erik shaded his eyes when he neared the mine's exit, stepping out into chilly air from earlier rains and facing the late morning overcast sky. He passed two men dressed in jeans and heavy jackets, posted near the entrance sitting at a small folding table playing a game of cards. One was an older man with short curly graying sandy hair and bright blue eyes and the other was a tanned young man with long dark brown hair and narrow gray eyes.

"Mister Schneider?" Erik said in shock.

The curly-haired man glanced up from his hand and smiled brightly at Erik. "You remember me," he said cheerfully. "It's been a long time."

"And you?" Erik asked the other man at the table.

"That's Doctor Cardenas," Schneider answered.

Cardenas gave a slight wave. "*Buenos días*," he murmured.

Erik nodded back in acknowledgement and left their side, looking around the desolate area. He noticed a pair of tire tracks on the muddy grounds, finding parked nearby a beaten white pickup truck and an older black motorcycle. He heard Mahjin approach from behind and glanced at the older man as he walked past, fuming.

"Where's Clayton?" Erik asked.

"He's out and about," responded Mahjin, approaching the motorcycle.

"Did he ever get to Cicero Park?"

"You're standing in it."

Erik gave Mahjin a blank stare and Mahjin rolled his eyes.

"Cicero Park was one of the former mining operations. They

shut that plant down years ago over safety violations." Mahjin straddled the vehicle, kicked the stand and started the ignition. "Come on, I'll take you over to Centerville."

"I don't think I'll be able to," Erik muttered.

"I'm the only one who can get you there," Mahjin snapped. "Now get on."

Erik blew a short sigh and sat behind Mahjin, wrapping his uninjured arm about his slender waist to hang on. Mahjin withdrew a pair of dark glasses from his jacket pocket and put them on, then revved the engine. Erik pressed his face against Mahjin's back and grasped tightly as the man sped out of the plain.

Mahjin pulled off onto a side road, going toward a looming large tan brick building with many glass pane windows. The sun broke from behind the clouds, reflecting off the glass and brick making the building appear white and the windows crystal plates glowing in sand.

Mahjin passed a large sign in white marble set in a slate-gray granite base, chiseled and painted in black block gothic letters labeled 'Centerville'. He then idled at the blackened wrought-iron gate.

Moments later, an armed guard dressed in a charcoal-gray uniform with silver buttons stepped from her post, slinging her rifle over her shoulder. She approached Mahjin, appearing perplexed.

"What are you doing here, Zachary?" she asked. "You're not on call here."

"Greenfield's got a visitor," Mahjin replied.

"Oh?"

"He wouldn't believe me, so I need to quell the kid, you know?"

"What happened to him?"

"I did some time at the Reformation Center," Erik replied. "They had to beat me into compliance."

The guard chortled and returned to her post. The gate groaned when it slowly opened, the chain whirring as it pulled back. Mahjin inched forward and eased through the gate, parking on the lot's far side.

Erik stepped off the motorcycle and made his way for the double doors. He entered the building, finding its interior white, from walls to ceiling to floor, and had solid black desks with other stainless steel furniture.

Erik looked around, noticing the employees carried about their duties also wore white, with the only break in the near monochrome were the different shades of skin and hair color. Erik passed other nurses in their uniforms, orderlies in their white scrub shirts and slacks, and doctors in their dark drab suits underneath starched consulting jackets, approaching the front security desk.

"Excuse me," Erik said toward the guard who thumbed through a gaming magazine. "I'm here to see John Greenfield."

"Down the hall," the guard muttered, "Sector Fourteen, Room Eight."

Erik glanced down the corridor, then walked in that direction, following the painted numbers in red block letters. He grew nervous as he entered through many hallways until coming onto another corridor eerily silent and seemingly devoid of life.

Erik tensed when he heard only his footsteps across the floor. Spotting the number plates, Erik raced down to Number Eight then paused when he spotted it partially open and heard voices inside.

Opening the door, Erik stepped in and stopped in stunned silence when he faced John Greenfield in a blue scrub suit sitting in an orange plastic chair with matching table. Across from him sat a young man with Erik's appearance wearing a red and yellow tracksuit. Erik noticed John Greenfield's long brown hair hung about his shoulders and his glasses were missing.

"Father!" Erik yelped and John Greenfield looked up, startled.

"What's going on?" John Greenfield cried as Erik's counterpart stiffened, immediately breaking out in cold sweat. "What happened to you?"

"Don't talk to him anymore," Erik commanded. "He's sent to kill you."

"You can't believe that!" said the young man. "He's obviously sick!"

"You can forget it," Erik spat. "I'm taking you down."

Erik's counterpart laughed. "With what?" he vaunted and turned to Erik, smiling maliciously. "You're injured and all I have to do is blow on you and you'll crumple!"

"Don't push me!" Erik shouted, clenching his hands. "I've had enough!"

"Just watch." The young man pushed away from the table and Erik stood on the defensive, anticipating his attack. "Are you serious?" he crowed. "Despite your condition, you're still willing to fight me?"

"You're not hurting my dad," Erik spat. "If I die over it, then I'm at peace with it."

"Listen to this guy!" Erik's counterpart said and laughed. "He's just a raging maniac!" He turned to John Greenfield, pointing a thumb at Erik. "The poor guy's lost it!"

John Greenfield looked to Erik, then back at the other blond. "Prove it," he said softly.

The young man clenched his teeth, frowning when John Greenfield folded his arms across his chest, appearing serious. "You can't...!" he started.

"As far as I'm concerned, the treatments they're giving me to correct my thinking are making me see things," John Greenfield answered. "Prove you're real."

"Before you do that," Erik interjected, "I just want to know one thing - why?"

"Why?" Erik's counterpart let out a short bitter laugh. "I'm not wasting my energy. Besides, you know you can't be saved, so resign yourself to your fate. Breaking out of here will never happen, because no one cares about you."

"I realize now I've got to remember at all costs," Erik said firmly. "I've got to never forget..."

"You can't even remember what you're supposed to forget," the young man teased. "Let me help speed it along." He withdrew a translucent blue pen with a crimson nib from his pocket and formed a violet saber.

"I don't have time for this!" Erik growled when the young man pointed the blade in his direction.

"Come on!"

Erik dodged and twisted out the young man's furious swipes when he advanced then turned from a slash, getting his sling cut away. Clattering to the floor at his feet was the blue pen with golden nib. Erik stiffened when the young man with his face pointed the saber at his chest.

"Don't bother," Erik's counterpart snarled. "Reach for it and you're through!"

"I don't know how that got there," Erik protested.

"Liar!"

"I can't use it anyway. Besides, you're right, I'm too banged up to combat you."

"Then just die."

"Not happening!"

Erik stepped out of another stab and grabbed the young man's sleeve, ducking down as he shouldered his counterpart, then hurled him over to the floor with a crash. Erik wrenched the assassin's wrist, struggling for the blade.

The assassin grabbed Erik's face, pushing back and batted him across the head. Erik dropped down, straddling him and bent over, biting hard on his arm. The young man screamed and let go, forcing his weapon clattering on the floor.

"That's enough!" a voice shouted. Erik looked up, facing Mahjin at the door armed with a high-powered seven-shot revolver. Mahjin pointed his firearm in their direction and thumbed back the hammer. "Against the wall, both of you," Mahjin ordered.

Erik rose to his feet, clenching his teeth and his counterpart sat up, clutching his wrist.

"Are you going to kill me?" Erik asked weakly. "Why not get rid of us both?"

"I need to know something first." Mahjin stormed into the room and kicked the other young man in the side. "Get up and against the wall, damn it!"

"What's the meaning of this?" the young man snarled. Mahjin fired, shooting the floor near him and blasted a borehole into the tiles. Erik paled and the young man immediately scrambled to his feet, frightened.

"Good," Mahjin said brightly and shut the door behind him. "Now one of you is leaving here alive. The other will be off to the chipper."

"H-how are you going to do that?" Erik stammered.

"Like I said, you need to tell me something. Once I get it, the other one is dead."

"Wait, what?" Erik's double squawked. "You're saying if I don't have this information, you'll kill me? I thought it would be the reverse!"

"Unfortunately, I *need* this information. Having you *dead* won't help."

"What is it you want to know?" Erik asked faintly.

Mahjin grinned. "You'll have to *tell* me."

"What if we get it wrong?" asked the other.

"I'll shoot you." Mahjin chortled and waved his gun. "I've got six more in here."

"You're not serious!" the young man spat.

Mahjin fired and the young man screamed, grasping his thigh as he staggered against the wall. Erik recoiled, watching blood quickly spread, staining his pants. "You know the body's quite resilient," Mahjin said brightly. "There's eighty percent where I can hit you and you'll keep standing - that is if you don't bleed to death first."

"What do you want to know?" Erik pleaded. "How much time do you have?"

"I wish I had all day, but I don't."

Erik looked to John Greenfield who sat rigidly at the table, his face pallid. "Are you going to let him do this?" Erik complained.

"Stop wasting my time!" Mahjin shouted and struck Erik across the face with the handgun. Erik cried out, staggering back as he clutched his jaw.

"What do you want to know?" Erik muttered and spat blood on the floor. "How do you want us to tell you and how can you figure if we're lying or not?"

"Only one of us can be sure if you're lying." Mahjin glanced to John Greenfield who appeared uneasy. "If you're right, he'll say so. If you're wrong, you'll get another bullet." Mahjin turned back to Erik and grinned cruelly. "You'll only have three chances between the both of you. The last one *will* be fatal." Erik frowned, unable to come up with a response. "I suggest you start talking," Mahjin threatened. "I don't care who goes first."

Erik took in a deep breath. "I don't remember," he muttered, looking down toward the floor. "No matter how hard I try, it won't come to me."

"Then you're dead." Mahjin pointed the gun at Erik.

John Greenfield jumped to his feet. "Wait!" he cried.

Mahjin fired anyway and Erik screamed when struck in the arm. Erik slipped to his knees, clutching his injury as blood ran through his hand. "Everyone's told me I have schematics about a weapon," he moaned.

"He's right," answered John Greenfield nervously.

"Keep going," Mahjin snapped. "You have two more chances."

"Corite powers the weapon," Erik's counterpart answered dully.

"That's true," John Greenfield confirmed.

"Armaments are developed to use Corite," the young man continued. "They're masked as pens for portability and pass detection."

"True," John Greenfield agreed.

"Contrabands affect Core Irons," Erik said. "So from what I understand, since they're injected in the body, there's got to be something in the body to use it." Tears suddenly streamed down his face. "So that means...!" He looked to his counterpart who struggled to breathe through the pain. "I can't be like you!" he cried. "I'm real! I think, I feel pain... It just can't be a damn Emotion System chip! No matter the calculations, a machine can't feel!"

Mahjin turned to John Greenfield. John Greenfield nodded and Mahjin turned toward the young man, shooting him in his other leg. Erik's counterpart slumped to the floor, moaning in pain.

"Anything else?" Mahjin jeered.

"*Was I wrong?*" Erik wondered, growing confused. When Mahjin turned the gun on him, he immediately spoke. "They're used with Dyna-Widgets," Erik explained. "I was told they have DNA for the creation of combat androids."

"He's correct," John Greenfield said softly.

"Soldiers give a sample when they enlist and train so that it can copy the body they're replacing," the young man said weakly. John Greenfield nodded when Mahjin glanced to him for confirmation. "They have to serve a minimum of two years."

"I don't understand," Erik mewed. "Why were they cutting into me? Twice they tinkered in my head. What are they looking for? I'm not a machine, so why do they keep treating me like one?"

John Greenfield cringed when Erik cried out once shot in the leg. Erik fell forward, gagging from the pain.

"*I'm wrong again!*" Erik thought, horrified. "*Which is it?*"

"You're both down to one," Mahjin snarled. "Make it count."

"Ace, please," begged John Greenfield. "Please, remember for me."

"What's your name?" Erik demanded.

"What?" the young man groaned.

"You heard me!" Erik shouted, glaring back. "Tell me your name!"

"What a stupid question!"

Mahjin pointed his revolver at the assassin's head. "Tell him your name," he hissed. "Otherwise, this last one's for you."

"Erik Hart."

Erik recoiled when Mahjin fired and the assassin's body crumpled on the ground, watching blood pool beneath the blasted open skull and spread toward his feet. Erik grew numb, unable to speak when John Greenfield left his place from the table. John Greenfield rushed up to Erik, dropping to his knees beside him and embraced him firmly.

"*I was so close to death,*" Erik mused, unable to focus. "*Father Greenfield asked me before about my name. I'm not Erik Hart... He's dead, he doesn't exist, and Ferdian doesn't either...*" He started laughing at the sheer absurdity of it all then broke down sobbing once everything hit him at once.

"I'm sorry," John Greenfield murmured in Erik's hair. "I'm so very sorry, Ace..."

"Please don't let them kill me," Erik bawled. "I want out of this nightmare..."

"You'll live," John Greenfield promised.

"I want to wake up!"

"You will."

"What if I don't?"

"Crying won't help. Keep it together a little longer."

Erik nodded. "I'll try," he murmured and took a deep breath in an attempt to check his emotions.

"Stop lying to him," Mahjin griped. "You can never escape; believe me, I know!" He grunted. "I've tried a thousand times and a dozen more..."

John Greenfield pulled away, glaring up at Mahjin standing over them. "We can try again!" he protested.

"It's no use," Mahjin growled. "We belong to them forever!"

"No," John Greenfield exploded, "we've got to keep trying - don't be so quick to give up!"

"They will keep coming after us."

"We won't take 'no' as an answer!"

"They already denied us everything... we might as well be executed to get out of this misery!" Mahjin let out a short laugh. "But they will deny us that too!"

John Greenfield rose upright, glaring at his friend. "Don't be so cold!" he snapped.

"I can't help it." Mahjin tapped at his chest. "I've got no heart, remember?"

John Greenfield clenched his hands and threw a sucker punch, launching Mahjin to the floor then turned to Erik and held out his hand. "Get up," he ordered. "We're leaving while we still have a chance."

Mahjin groaned, clutching his profusely bleeding broken nose. "Good," he muttered, sitting up, "they didn't screw with your head too much."

"What makes you think they'll let you waltz out of here?" Erik spat, slapping away John Greenfield's hand. "We're going to lose. I'm busted up and you're pumped full of drugs!"

"Who said I was drugged?" John Greenfield replied, dropping his hand at his side. "They can't use my mind if it's full of Contraband."

"Then how...?"

John Greenfield left his side, taking up the fallen saber and the other pen. "Stay behind me," he directed, "and stay close. I don't want to slow down... I've only one shot at this."

"I trust you."

Erik rose to his feet and glanced to Mahjin who stood unsteadily, sheathing the emptied revolver. John Greenfield tossed him the other pen and Mahjin caught it, forming a silver staff.

John Greenfield hurried for the door and slipped out, racing down the corridor. Erik looked to Mahjin who wiped at his nose with his sleeve.

"What are you looking at me like that for?" Mahjin grumbled.

"Were you really going to kill me?" Erik asked.

Mahjin grinned and tapped the edge of his nose, then stalked out the room.

Erik reached the door and shut it, leaning against it as he blew a heavy sigh. "If what they were saying was true," he murmured to himself, "then there's no real need for me to go with them." Erik slid to the floor and shut his eyes when the numbing agony penetrated his senses.

SIXTY

Erik groggily awakened and tried to get up, only to get a violent shock to the system. He let out an agonized hoarse scream, fighting to break free of his binds. A stronger jolt zapped through him, forcing Erik still.

He panted hard for breath and looked about his surroundings, finding himself in a cold metal room with titanium walls and floors with riveted panels. Facing the ceiling, Erik noticed it had the same treatment with the exception of blue plate lights installed, shining down harsh white light.

Erik then looked to his left and right, noticing he was strapped to a steel table with iron harnesses, hearing the buzzing of energy coming from a source beneath him, warming the harnesses strapped to his wrists, ankles and about his neck. He lifted his head slightly, finding he wore simple shorts crafted from a cotton-like material, coated in a thin insulated gel to absorb the electric shocks.

"Eleven," called a hollow ominous voice from above and Erik howled when another jolt zapped through him.

"Why are you doing this to me?" he wailed, and then cried out when hit with more electricity.

"Twelve," said the same cold unaffected voice and Erik received another shock, sending his brain reeling within his skull. He lost focus of the buzzing blue-plate lights and his vision grew dim and fuzzy.

"You have been proven defective," announced the mechanical voice. "It's a wonder you were left to live this long." Another jolt darkened his hazy vision and he struggled to stay awake.

"Now I see why you're so intent on having me take these stupid tests," Erik yelled, "and having that doctor ask me those stupid questions... You're using me because you want my memory, right? To use as raw data to destroy me, right?"

"We've got what we needed from you."

"*It's not enough,*" Erik thought as the last jolt separated him from his body. He saw himself floating over his bruised and scarred form, looking down at a young man who happened to share his appearance. "*I still can't remember what she wants from me...*"

"That's enough," interjected another voice. "Start the restructuring process." Darkness came quickly.

Free falling in the wide-open darkness, Erik hovered in front of a large three-storey house with blue shingles and white trim. He watched a tow-headed young man in gray sweatshirt and jeans open the front door. Pulling away, they became one once ran into. Erik hurried down the steps; meeting with John Greenfield dressed in a dark brown suit under a white lab coat.

John Greenfield pushed up a pair of large gray plastic wide-framed glasses threatening to slip off his nose and set down the briefcase he carried before embracing Erik.

"Listen, Son," John Greenfield said softly and held Erik by

the shoulders. "There's going to be some changes."

"What is it?" Erik asked.

"Do you remember meeting Doctor Zachary that day in the rain when you were chased?"

Erik shook his head. "I don't remember anything like that."

"I answered the door and you gave me a piece of Corite you found," John Greenfield explained. "You were taken from me a long time ago and you eventually found your way back to me... So I had to take measures to make sure you didn't get hurt again."

Erik appeared briefly puzzled then smiled. "But I'm okay now, aren't I?"

"That's why I need to take you to the doctor's office. We're moving soon and if you're going to school, your shots need to be up-to-date."

"I don't see a real reason to go." Erik shrugged his shoulders. "I just went with Doctor Fleisher and the doctors there said I'm healthy!"

"Her name's no longer Doctor Fleisher, understand?" John Greenfield huffed. "Around here, she's just Miss Jane."

"But...!"

"You have to come with me."

Erik grew increasingly worried when John Greenfield left Erik's side and stalked toward a small compact sedan with tinted windows. Erik picked up the case and followed reluctantly after him.

"What's this for?" Erik demanded as he opened the side passenger door.

"What do you mean?" John Greenfield muttered and

stepped into the driver's side.

Erik grew uneasy when he entered the car with John Greenfield and the older man started the car. Erik opened the briefcase he held, finding folders and papers inside. John Greenfield said nothing as he drove through the quiet suburban streets lined with rows of large maple trees and weeping willows while Erik read the papers, learning about applied technology and genetic engineering.

"Are you taking up a college course?" Erik asked moments later.

"It's research," John Greenfield answered.

"How long were you into this sort of thing?"

"Thirteen years now."

"Thirteen years... That's as old as I am!"

"You're older than what you look."

Erik laughed and wagged a finger at John Greenfield. "Don't kid me, Doctor Schumacher."

"Don't call me that anymore," John Greenfield snapped. "I'm not a doctor and I'm not Schumacher. I'm simply..." He let out a heavy sigh and tightened his grip on the steering wheel. "Son, listen carefully. What I'm about to do may not make any sense to you, but I'm doing this to protect you."

"What are you protecting me from?"

"Look at yourself, your arms, legs, hands... You've been mutilated, drugged, burned, all in the name of science."

Erik pushed up his sleeves, finding nothing but flawless skin. "What are you talking about?" he protested. "I don't have any scars!" Erik rolled up the cuffs of his jeans, looking down at his legs. "You're sleep deprived, Doctor Schumacher!"

"Please," John Greenfield spat tersely.

Erik swallowed hard. "Where are you taking me then?" he asked timidly.

"We're seeing some friends."

"Can you be any more vague?"

"Remember that you have a soul, just like we do. You should be allowed to make your own decisions and find your own destiny."

Erik snorted and glanced out the window. "I thought my fate was already predetermined."

"It shouldn't have to be."

Erik watched the suburban streets give way to small town, then eventually to a long stretch of two-lane road. Finally, they came to a stop atop a hill where many redwood cabins dotted the landscape.

"What's going to happen to me?" Erik asked quietly.

John Greenfield stayed silent and shut off the engine then stepped out, gesturing at Erik to follow.

Erik returned the papers inside the case as John Greenfield shut the door and headed up the hill. Erik unwillingly stepped out the car, taking the briefcase with him and hurried after John Greenfield who ascended the track.

They reached the trailhead an hour later after walking in silence and turned on a switchback, going down a little-used path. Eventually the two happened upon an abandoned-appearing cabin with a plank deck and glass pane windows shrouded in shifting shadows.

John Greenfield came to the door and put his hand on the knob, then turned and waved at Erik to follow who stood at the path's end, apprehensive.

"I don't like it," Erik complained.

"Why are you suddenly nervous now?" John Greenfield gently asked.

"I've been here before..."

"Yes, you have."

"But..." Erik shook his head. "I don't have any scars," he said helplessly.

"I know and for good reason." John Greenfield held out his hand. "Now come."

Erik blew a distressed sigh and trudged up the walkway, entering inside with John Greenfield. He came to a pause once indoors at the sight of Genovera who had her long raven hair pulled up in a loose chignon, wearing a white blouse, navy slacks and boat shoes working on a machine in the main room with small hand tools.

Nearby, a young man with long shaggy flaming red hair typed at a keyboard in front of a monitor. Erik noticed Arizeh strapped down nude to a table in the room's center, struggling within his binds while the doctor Schnell paced nearby, writing down whatever Genovera would state aloud.

"Why isn't he covered?" John Greenfield exploded and stormed in, grabbing a sheet crumpled on the floor near the table's foot. "Let him keep some dignity!" He threw the sheet over Arizeh's scarred form.

"Please, Gerald!" Schnell snapped and stopped his pacing, then withdrew his pocket watch from his vest pocket, glancing at it. "We only have a few more minutes until the generator shuts down. So we need to hurry this along."

Arizeh screamed, jerking harder against his restraints. Genovera put a small wrench between her teeth and pulled a small pen-sized screwdriver from behind her ear, tightening a bolt. A low buzzing reverberated into the room and she pointed to the red-haired young man at the monitor.

"Now!" Schnell commanded.

"Five-hundred and counting," called the mysterious red-haired man and John Greenfield backed away as a mechanical whine started in the room. Moments later, a strong jolt shocked Arizeh, forcing him still.

"What are you doing to him?" Erik cried. "You're not going to do that to me, are you?" He dropped the case he held and burst outdoors.

"Son, wait!" John Greenfield called.

"Twelve-hundred," the red-haired stranger called and another zap came through, followed by a scream.

Erik tore through the woods, only to trip on a rock and fall face first into the dirt. John Greenfield tackled him and held him down tightly to keep him from escaping.

"Son," John Greenfield murmured in Erik's ear. Erik squirmed, struggling beneath the man's grip, trying to escape. "Listen to me; this is for your benefit. I'm trying to give you a few more years!"

"By cooking my brains?" Erik wailed.

"No, come back and see for yourself." John Greenfield let him go and rose to his feet, holding out a hand. "I won't force you to come. You can request to leave any time you wish. Just please, tell me so."

"This isn't a trick, is it?"

"I've no reason to do so. We're doing this outside the Agency's influence. If we're caught, we'll be put to death."

"Death?" Erik appeared uneasy. "I don't want you in trouble."

"Then come with me."

Erik sighed and took the John Greenfield's outstretched hand, getting pulled to his feet. They both returned to the cabin and Erik paused at the door, watching Arizeh clutching the red-haired stranger by the throat, throttling him. He choked and gasped for air, clawing at his wrists. Schnell sat at the computer, calmly typing data.

"Please!" the young man wheezed. "We're not trying to kill you here!"

"Kevin," Genovera called calmly from her place near the table. "Kevin, please let him go."

"Why are you trying to get rid of me?" Arizeh demanded.

"You can go any time you like."

"Why am I here?"

"Let him go and we'll tell you."

Arizeh turned to Erik, glaring at him. "Who are you?" he sneered. Erik shook his head, afraid to answer.

"Kevin," John Greenfield answered slowly. "Kevin, please listen to your mother."

Arizeh's face flushed red and he let the young man go. The red-haired stranger sank to his knees, gasping for breath as the color returned to his face. John Greenfield left Erik's side to tend to him while Genovera smiled brightly at Arizeh, holding out her hands to him.

"Please come," she said gently. Arizeh walked over, numbly

waiting while she reached under the table in a box and withdrew a change of clothing. "We're going to get you changed into something more comfortable, and then we're going to take you home for debriefing."

Genovera placed the articles in his arms and Arizeh looked down at what he held, puzzled. Taking Arizeh by the shoulder, Genovera gently led him towards the cabin's rear, walking into another room and the door clicked shut behind them.

"Are we ready for the next deprogramming?" John Greenfield asked.

"In a moment," Schnell called from behind the terminal. "I'm resetting the parameters."

"There should be no changes," John Greenfield spat and stood behind Schnell, looking over his shoulder.

"Number Three C-O-one-ninety-two-A Unit Galkan has some difficult arrays to erase due to his unique programming," Schnell replied.

"What do you think caused it?" grumbled the stranger on the floor.

"It seems something to do with his genetic makeup," Schnell replied. "His records and his DNA don't quite match up... We're only getting partials that we can't trace."

"Will the deprogramming be successful then?"

Erik cleared his throat, finding the courage to speak. "What's this deprogramming you're talking about?" he asked timidly. "You're talking about me, aren't you?"

Hearing no answer while John Greenfield continued conversing with Schnell, Erik approached the young man on the floor and held out a hand. The redhead looked up, startled.

"Why are you giving me that look?" Erik protested.

"I can never get over it," said the young man. "It's too uncanny…"

"What is?"

"That you look like me."

"We're different," Erik protested and looked down at his hands then to the stranger's. "We're both pale," he said. "But I have a pinker undertone and you're more yellow." He knelt at the redhead's side and peered closely at his face. "We both have freckles on our faces but not anywhere else." He traced a scar across the young man's nose. "How'd you break it?"

"In a fight," the redhead answered, clearly disturbed.

"You shouldn't fight."

"But I have to."

Erik grabbed the young man's face in his hands, looking deep into his eyes. "Your eyes are purple, mine are blue." He let go then gently pulled at his hair. "You have red hair, mine's blond. Is your hair naturally that way?"

"It is."

"Why do you look weird?"

"What do you mean?"

"That's enough," John Greenfield said upon approach. "Come on, get up."

Erik stood and John Greenfield led him to the table. Schnell left the terminal and picked up a ledger book, writing information in its pages. The red-haired young man left his place on the floor and returned to the computer, blowing a hard sigh.

"What are you going to do to me?" Erik demanded.

"I want you to believe me when I tell you this," John Greenfield replied. "I care about your well-being and I want to keep you safe as long as I'm physically able."

"Are you saying that to him or you mean that to me?" asked the young man behind the computer. John Greenfield tensed but didn't acknowledge.

"Why did you call him Kevin?" Erik asked. "That's not his name."

"That's his new name for now," John Greenfield answered. "It will keep him safe."

"Will you give me a new name too?"

John Greenfield nodded. "You'll also be getting a new life." He hugged Erik tightly. "You will be mine and you will be safe."

"Again, him or me?" the young man spat.

John Greenfield let go and glared back at the redhead. The young man smirked and reached into his shirt pocket, taking out a cigarette tin.

Schnell walked around, glancing at the machine's dials. "We only have one chance to do this right," he warned as the young man withdrew a filtered cigarette and put it to his lips, then continued typing at the keyboard.

"Son, undress and lie down for me." John Greenfield said gently.

Erik raised an eyebrow. "You won't tie me down, will you?" he challenged.

"You'll only be restrained for a moment to keep your limbs from breaking," John Greenfield explained.

Erik nodded and pulled out of his shirt. "Will it hurt?" he queried.

"It'll be over quickly; you won't remember."

"What are you trying to make me forget?"

John Greenfield gave a wry smile. "I want you to forget the ugliness in the world, that's all."

"Please forgive me," Schnell murmured, biting the end of his pen. "I should have realized my mistake long ago..."

"Then now's the time for redemption," John Greenfield assured. "You've already admitted to making terrible mistakes, so we can forge ahead and correct them."

"It's ready at five-hundred," the red-haired stranger announced.

Erik finished undressing and kicked his clothing to the floor then lay back on the table. John Greenfield kept quiet as he strapped down his arms and legs, and finally his head. John Greenfield placed the sheet over Erik's body and touched his cheek, smiling sadly.

"Am I a mistake?" Erik asked.

"No, Son," John Greenfield answered, "you're not."

"Now!" Schnell called and John Greenfield stepped away as the high whine generated in the room. Schnell approached behind the young man at the monitor and blanched, dropping the book he held. "That can't be right..."

"What's wrong?" John Greenfield asked.

Schnell pushed the young man aside and jammed at the keyboard, typing furiously. "It's stuck!" he shouted. "Get him out of there!"

"What?"

"You're going to kill him!"

Everything flashed in red as a strong volt of white-hot

electricity coursed through Erik's head, then faded to noiseless white.

CONTINUED IN BOOK THREE:

BORDERLINE

Erik Hart gets in over his head when he accidentally breaks an important company computer while on reassignment. Unwilling to lose his job, he agrees to pay for it by working for the cruel taskmaster Zachary, an enigmatic man who seemingly knows more than he lets on...

When Erik becomes a target for breakneck enforcers, he finds rogue scientists willing to help him disappear if he can finish one final job in return. His search for answers leads him to a powerful origination bent on stopping him by every ruthless method at their disposal!